Obama Jones
and
The Logic Bomb

by Rod Kierkegaard, Jr.

 dogma press

ⓓ dogma press

First dogma press trade paperback edition 2012.

ISBN-13: 9780615637723
ISBN-10: 0615637728

Also Available by Rod Kierkegaard, Jr.

Mirrorland

The Department of Magic

The God Particle

Family Cursemas

for Lou Stathis

LOGIC BOMB [loj-ik bom]

— *Noun.* A hidden piece of code intentionally inserted into a software system that will set off a malicious function or an unusual change in program behavior inside any virtual application such as a Sim (Simulated Immersive Media), onGrid game, flattie (flat-screen DVD), legacy computer program, group journal (glog), or the nano-processor language of a common appliance such as an iRist. The bomb can be activated by an undocumented set of conditions or voice commands, iRist swipes, input device signals or waves, or other stimuli. To be considered a logic bomb, the payload should be unwanted and unknown to the user of the software.

— *Wiktionary of Enriched Standard Language*

(WESL), 2049 Edition

1.

On July 11, 2024, at 8:02 AM, the city center of Washington D.C. was destroyed by a nuclear explosion. The Burmese device was roughly in the 10-kiloton range, slightly less powerful than the atomic bomb that leveled Hiroshima, delivered by a modified Taepodong-4 ICBM purchased from North Korea. Missing its intended target by a mile or so to the northeast, the warhead exploded several hundred feet in the air above Gallaudet College, whose buildings were instantly vaporized.

They—along with their contents and the people inside them—were transformed into a radioactive column of dust rising miles into the air. The initial blast, meanwhile, spread in every direction, destroying most of the structures all the way down to Union Station. The Senate Office buildings, just to the north of the US Capitol, collapsed, along with the United States Supreme Court Building. To the west, the shock wave roared down the National Mall, severely damaging the Capitol Building, the National Gallery and the Smithsonian Castle and burning to death thousands of tourists and unemployment protesters occupying the huge tent city on the Mall in front of them. The Washington Monument was transformed into a tottering, needle-like steel skeleton; to its north, the White House, with its reinforced concrete walls, barely withstood the blast, but its windows shattered inward, killing anyone standing near them. The dead included the President of the then-United States of America. On Capitol Hill, about a quarter of the members of Congress were also killed immediately; government casualties overall, however, were generally low because of the hour of day and the fact that members of Congress rarely remained in the city during the summer.

The force of the bomb was being dissipated as its energy was absorbed by the mass of the destroyed buildings and neighborhoods, but windows were still being punched out during those first seconds in buildings as far away as the Potomac and Anacostia Rivers. The first wave of destruction was followed immediately by a second, as debris, mostly tiny shards of glass from destroyed office buildings, formed a lethal horizontal rain killing any pedestrians in the downtown area still left alive after the initial burst of radiation. Now the streets were filled with smoking rubble and dust, twisted metal, burned-out hulks of vehicles, and huddled victims with their skin and clothing on fire.

By 8:03, over 30,000 people had died in less than a minute.

Twenty five years later to the day, Obama Jones and his wife, Kim, met each other for lunch just after noon on "Seven-Eleven", as the anniversary of the bombing was popularly known, in the rebuilt downtown area of the city. It wasn't that people celebrated the day; in fact, it had never been made a Federal holiday specifically so that they wouldn't. Few could even remember the events surrounding the negotiating standoff that had led to a failed rogue nation attacking the United States in the first place. But for most North Americans Seven-Eleven still remained a day to take things slow and gravely reflect on the things that really mattered most in life.

Like your marriage.

On his way to meet his wife outside the mag-lev Retro Center subway station, Obama found his path blocked by a HELP, or "Habitation-Eliminated Locationless Person". What made the incident even more disturbing was that Obama had a haunting feeling he'd seen this person somewhere before. Had the myn once been a coworker? A Teaching Assistant from his college years? Nothing rang a bell. Whatever, the guy was exhibiting obvious symptoms of schizophrenia and psychotropic Tourettism – but at least his clothes were clean and he looked well-fed. He was about 50, came up to Obama's shoulder, had a mane of wiry pepper-and-salt hair overgrowing his skullcap tonsure, a scraggly beard, and was sunburned to the color and texture of polished rosewood. Obama guessed he was of Indonesian or Polynesian heritage. Or Japanese, maybe. At first Obama had just assumed the HELP was a hologram—Jonessa Qali's "Egg-Parenting Rights for Gay Penguins" crusade had used a similar "in-your-face" ad campaign shock-tactic a year ago—but then Obama caught a strong whiff of rancid curry from him. So the guy was real.

"Wiiboot," the homeless person said loudly, placing a hand on Obama's chest. "Wiiboot, amen!" Other pedestrians segged or walked quickly past, ignoring the two of them, grateful to have escaped. There was something oddly ominous, even threatening, about the HELP. For a moment, Obama thought he was saying "Reboot" or "Robot"— the myn's thick Asian accent made it hard to tell. Obama just backed away smiling, trying to avoid any physical contact. You were taught in the Department to fully engage and report the incident to HHS so the case-file could be accessed, but of course that was a joke in real life. There were no Federal social workers to be found in their cubes in Manacera City, not on a weekday lunch hour on Seven-Eleven. Which, this year, fell on a rare sunny day. But now the guy was shouting at him.

"Detach! Detach, amen. Wiiboot, amen!"

In desperation, Obama reached in his pocket and handed him the only piece of negotiable currency he had on him, an old promotional Retro token, which his tormentor angrily waved off. "Wicked little smile," he hissed accusingly, pointing a finger in Obama's face. "Oh, wicked little smile. Remember, every word counts, man! Every word counts!" Then, as if forcing himself to disengage—probably echoing the training of some past court-mandated therapist—he mumbled, "Detach, amen, detach, amen, detach, detach" over and over again. Once Obama was down the sidewalk and clear of the arcade the myn stood screaming "Wiiboot! Wiiboot! Amen!" after him. It was annoying. It was disturbing. And it almost spoiled his anticipation of a stolen lunch date with Kim.

He and Kim had only been married for a year but had lived together for about two. Obama still couldn't believe his luck. Marriage was totally old-skool, and it was mainly only traditional immigrants, polyamorist groups, and lesbians who bothered with it these days, but Obama had decided he was maybe an old-skool kind of guy, after all. In a totally 'linked way, of course.

Obama and Kim lived in one of the new Riverside Harborplex towers, part of a huge exurban development that stretched from the Anacostia River south into Maryland. Obama worked for the

Minority Assistance Department, in the New Minorities Accreditation Division, and Kim worked for a law mega-firm downtown. He'd met her on WiiLive just after she'd moved to the North American Federal Administration Area. He'd already been there for almost three years and had become increasingly bored and lonely. It was always the same pattern: you moved to a new place at the same time as a bunch of other noobie interns, you hung out together at work and gamed together onGrid afterwards, met up for face-time at clubs, got wasted together on weekends. Then slowly your posse drifted apart or hooked up into couples or polys, moved on to new jobs in new cities, and so finally at some point you had to restart your social life all over again. To reboot it. Or "Wiiboot" — now he couldn't get the word out of his head.

But everything had changed when he'd met Kim. She made real life amazing, way better than gaming. He felt like he learned something fresh about her every day. It was as if her Chinese genes had programmed her to just sort of morph into a modern version of a "traditional wife" — in private, at least — the moment they'd gotten married.

All Obama's remaining male friends were whipped by their womyn or myn or poly-amorous-partners ("paps") and did nothing but complain to him about them behind their partners' backs — complain, that is, when they weren't escaping all weekend onto the Grid. But Obama could never bring himself to join in. He didn't have a single actual complaint about Kim. She was perfect. He tried to formulate an imaginary criticism or two on the way to meet her but couldn't. He didn't even mind her faults, the way she was too-patient with her mother's long lugubrious iTooth calls, letting them interrupt their precious weekends for hours; or the times she forgot to flush the toilet or to turn the lights off, which helped contribute to global cooling. So what? She was more important to him than saving any stupid planet.

Which reminded him. He stopped and bought her some edible flowers, roses and violets, from the Uighur vendor outside the Micky's at the corner, visually monitoring the credit swipe with his iRist. 10 Unos. You couldn't be too careful these days. He banished the treasonous thought — part of his job involved promoting the legal rights of immigrants — and cradled the spray of buds protectively in their stiff plastic wrap. He hoped Kim would like them.

And then suddenly there she was on the sidewalk in front of him, hair severely tied back, dressed in a black business suit with heels. She'd walked the two blocks down the street from the New-Day Ziggurat where she worked, one of the many block-sized ultra-modern office buildings built downtown since the holocaust of '24. He presented her with the flowers, and they kissed. He hoped the Gene-Modified flowers really were edible.

Kim was originally from Texas and had the same kind of mixed-up genetic heritage Obama did, but in her it had come out making her look mainly Han Chinese and classical Greek. She had a wide face, huge brown eyes, and soft pale skin covered with big dark freckles like flecks of cinnamon. When you first saw her you were struck by her grace and dignity. Everybody said so, though in different words. These alone were such rare qualities that they surprised people, but it was the manner they lent her that really set her apart from everyone else. It made you almost forget her beauty and her brains. Or at least take them for granted. In a world full of so-called "unique" individuals, Kim actually was.

They had reservations at the Ol' Debit Grill on 15th Street, which sat atop the gleaming new glass UNESCO Obelisk. The window beside their table had a magnificent pano view of the vast expanse of scorched, blackened ruins and fused debris known locally as the Fallout Zone after the Fallout Grid game series, which was so popular that Grid-linked "bumpers" could be seen blindly wandering through the Zone at all hours of the day or night, utilizing its physical features as a gaming shell.

In point of fact, very little — if any — radioactive fallout had actually fallen in the Zone; most of the mushroom-shaped dust cloud that had formed over the city on Seven-Eleven had been blown off by the prevailing south-easterly winds over northeast Washington, Prince George's County, and Annapolis, before dispersing in the Chesapeake Bay. Fortunately, there had only been a few thousand more casualties due to this exposure. Most people in its path had been saved later by mass injections of Novamune, a radiation-reversing steroidal protein injection developed by an Israeli-American research lab in the early 'teens.

While most of the city had been rebuilt, the Mall area — along with the shattered hulks of the monuments and museums, the Capitol, and the White House buildings — had all been deliberately left to rot by the UN in order to discourage nationalism. From high above, it was a fascinating and eerie sight, like gazing down into ruins on the ocean floor.

For lunch, Kim ordered in-vitro organic-farmed salmon wrapped in green nori and swimming in agrodulce sauce, while Obama chose a rice-wine-broiled seitan steak with caramelized spiced hemp and purple-potato rings. Neither of them was used to alcohol during the work-day, but they drank a half-bottle of Chardonnay with their meal. Afterwards, Kim got a bit tipsy, and they decided to go home instead of back to their offices.

They lived six blocks from the Manacera City Harborplex Retro-rail station. Their plex had been built over the derelict remains of the old Bolling Air Force Base, directly across from the confluence of the Anacostia and Potomac Rivers. Their building was called the Marbela. Kim swiped them into the lobby, which was already looking a little run-down and neglected. The building's AI no longer even bothered to greet them by name, which was a bad sign.

Condos were like WiiGames, people said: obsolete the minute you bought them. They'd been in this one for nearly two years; it was already time to flip it and move closer in. Or farther out. Obama sighed. Only two of the three ascensors were working, and they had to swipe again to get into one. But he didn't mind the extra security, for Kim's sake. She often worked late hours.

Obama caught sight of his own face in the ascensor's Active-Matrix Organic Light-Emitting Diode mirror screen, cringing a little as always at the long horsey face and big bump in the middle of his nose. His skin was jet-black, and his eyes had the gentle, quizzical look of a Talmudic scholar behind the polymer aerogel-rimmed spectacles he affected to make himself look more serious at work. His vision was actually perfect. His wooly hair was cropped very short around the gaming skull-cap tonsure that gleamed with galvanic conduction emollient. He could have worn a hair-extension over it as Kim did, but most guys his age didn't bother. What did Kim even see in him? he wondered. She could have had her pick of anybody she wanted.

"Let's go to bed," she decided, as the ascensor doors opened onto their floor. They only barely made it.

Sex in the year 2049 was both random in gender and ultra-pornographic in practice — at least OnGrid — but not nearly as common in real life as it had once been. Except among the poorer immigrants and religious nuts. Kim's parents had been both, and Obama was, like his revered namesake, the child of a hippie mother in Hawaii. He and Kim were also "womb-rats" — born naturally, rather than in tanks — and usually preferred penetrative "whole-sex" to "holo-sex", the more normal neural-assisted Gridlinked holographic variety.

But even primitives like themselves usually took prescription arousal pills like Orecta and Clitalis and used AI directors, remote dildonics, holographic multiple partners — even Sony sex robots (if they were very wealthy), which were so realistic they breathed and secreted fluids. And of course, spider-cams that captured the action from every conceivable single angle for future upload onto the Grid's YouVee (the colloquial abbreviation for Ultra-Wiifi HoloVision) service.

In their innocence, or maybe just frugality and lack of imagination, Obama and Kim had always preferred simply to blunder and fumble around in bed together until they got it right. This made them feel as though they'd invented sex themselves. And after the first few couplings — which they'd mainly engaged in publicly just to make their friends stop nagging — they hadn't even bothered to upload their personal YouVee-captures any more. Sex had somehow turned private.

What Obama loved best about sex was basically every single second of it. With Kim, anyway. Crude and unsophisticated as their love-making now was, he loved the pulse in her eyelids, the feeling of her pulse against his skin, her hot breath against his open mouth, the tumble of her clothes onto the floor, the wild glistening of her body. Something ticked near the bed: a digital emulation of the noise of a clock. Her skin was pale against the black of the bedcover; her long hair a deeper, more lustrous sable as it spilled across it. They pulled apart for a moment, both gasping for air. "What did you put in that wine?" she asked him. She was smiling.

"Chocolate?"

"Oooo, you know how I love chocolate, even if it is against the law. But I'm not sure I can trust you," she said, teasingly. "How do I know you're not giving any to other girls?"

"Because I only want you." It was true.

"You want me more than … ?" She named a few popular sim stars, including Jonessa Qali. This was a long-time favorite game of hers. He told her yes to each one. He meant it.

"And I can prove it," he said. She was still wearing her panties; not for long. He nudged the pink, silky triangle off her hips and down her thighs with his nose while she squirmed and giggled. Then he took her in his arms, and she stopped laughing. Now it was a race to the subliminal ticking of the synthetic clock, punctuated by her soft cries and their ragged, gasping breath. Her shoulders, her belly beneath him, were shining, damp with sweat. So were her arms clinging to him, pulling him hard into her. At last, she bit him, her signal that she was coming, and he climaxed wildly inside her. "Whose slave is whose?" he asked her, while they were kissing again, their hearts still pounding.

"Oh, I'm definitely yours," Kim replied, meaning that it was her turn to get up and pad naked into the kitchen in search of snacks to bring back to bed. When she came back carrying several flexi-bags filled with chips and nut mixes, she stared down at his midsection pointedly and said, "Again? Already?"

"Almost." That was the effect she had on him, just the sight of her wandering around the condo naked. Personal gods, he was lucky.

They took longer the second time and made it last all the way till dark. When they were both finally worn out, she said, "Promise me you'll never do that with anyone else? Just me?" On their first "date" OnGrid, she'd told him she was the most jealous person alive. He liked it. It was very flattering.

"I promise."

There was a sudden loud, annoying chime; the front doorbell. "UnEx delivery," said the building AI helpfully in their iTeeth. It wasn't uncommon, though by no means frequent, for Kim to get home-delivered snail-mail which, for legal reasons, she had to manually sign for. She put on a pair of pajamas and a bathrobe and went out into the front foyer.

After a few minutes, when she didn't return, he put on his pants and shirt and followed her. He found her standing rigidly in the foyer in front of the open front door, looking as if she'd been attacked by the delivery-bot. In fact, he almost didn't recognize her — it was if he'd found a stranger in the room impersonating her. He'd never seen his wife looking so hopeless and forlorn; in their two years together, he'd never even seen her cry. But now her eyes were reddened and dilated, her cheeks as colorless as wax, the muscles in them working like snakes under the skin. She was holding an opened UnEx pack clenched in one hand with a printed-out sheet of paper on top of it. You didn't see those often.

"MPG, Kim," he said finally. My Personal God(s). "What's wrong?"

"Jury duty." She sounded like she was trying to keep her teeth from chattering. He felt an inane desire to laugh at her, but managed not to. Her reaction was comical. He could remember his dad complaining about jury duty when he was a kid. It had been a minor annoyance, like going to a dentist.

"Jury duty? Seriously? Is that all?" From the way she was acting, he had imagined all kinds of really scary things. Like that her job had been terminated. Or she'd just received a positive test result from a medical clinic. Or received some kind of official notification that her mom had suddenly died. "I mean, I thought it was something really important. Just, I dunno, blow it off if you're so upset. Or attend it onGrid — aren't you supposed to do it that way anyhow? I've never heard of anyone actually having to physically report for jury duty."

She turned to look at him, and he could clearly see her eyes brimming over with tears. "This isn't regular jury duty, Bam," she told him. "You don't get it; I'm a lawyer, so I do. This is a United Nations Federal Grand Jury summons. It just came by registered UnEx. UnEx! I've heard of this happening to people, but I never thought ..."

He closed the front door, put an arm around her, and tried to lead her back into the living room. She had lovingly decorated the area of the foyer around their personal altar with mirrors and expensive vases, and they had both lived in superstitious terror of breaking something near it. He brushed against the spray of flowers he'd bought her earlier; she'd put them in one of the vases, and now they got crushed up against her. The candied petals started falling onto the carpet. "Come on, honey, chill. Why don't you just fight this in court? Or talk to a judge. I mean, they'd be crazy to want a lawyer on a jury anyway, right?"

"*Bam!*" She was practically screaming at him now in frustration. "You just aren't getting it! At most we have a few minutes before they get here. Federal grand juries are sequestered — sometimes they spend years in hiding offshore. They're given new identities to prevent tampering. We learned about it in law skool. If we don't get the fuck out of here in the next few minutes and find someplace to stay with no bots or WiiFi, they'll take me away from you forever! No!" she yelled, frantically pushing him away as he tried to calm her down. "My old life is over. Once the marshals swear me in, you'll never see me again. I'll never see you or Mom again!"

There was a loud thump overhead, and they both looked up. "They're landing on the roof," she said in a strangled voice. *We live too close to the Federal court buildings by air,* Obama thought. *We should have moved sooner.* And just like that, all at once and for the first time, he believed her, and his heart froze.

Normally Kim was great in emergencies; it was Obama who panicked. Now he was the one who had the common sense to want to get out of the apartment right away, and Kim who went all limp and passive. He opened their front door manually and dragged her out into the hall as the building AI began to chatter in their iTeeth. "Warning! Warning!" it said over and over, so loudly that it made his cheek-bones vibrate. "You are currently in violation of UN Federal law! Do not attempt to leave the premises. I repeat —" He stuck a finger in his ear and switched off the iTooth while he called the ascensor. Kim's face looked completely blank now, but he could see dried tear-tracks running down to her chin.

It could have been worse. The SWAT team that burst out of the ascensor was made up of locals who spoke Enriched instead of robots or sullen foreigners. The Chief Marshal was a weary-looking womyn with short blonde hair and a Virginia accent. She swore in Kim right there in the hall while three other marshals dressed in gleaming black body armor, looking like huge insects tagged with smart-badges, held their HAKMOR assault rifles trained on Obama. When he tried to interfere, one of them said, "Please step away, sir. Everything you say is being recorded and can be held against you in a court of law."

"I don't care!" Obama found himself shouting. "Arrest me, too, so I can go with her!" One of the black insects seemed to bow his head slightly, as if in mute sympathy.

"I must repeat, please step away, sir. Grief counseling is being provided." A small middle-aged Middle Eastern womyn in a head-scarf and plump bullet-proof body vest stepped out of the ascensor and swiped Obama's iTooth several times unsuccessfully.

"You should keep communication channels open," she said reproachfully in a high piping voice with an accent.

Kim was trembling all over. "Can I at least pack a bag?" she asked the Chief Marshal.

"I'm sorry, no, ma'am. Everything you need for your new life will be provided for you. I promise it's not as terrible as it seems right now." The Chief Marshal looked at both of them briefly but not unsympathetically. "This isn't a job any of us enjoy, but we have to do it by the book, guys. Honest. I can't tell you where you're going or what case you'll be hearing, but I can tell you that some jurors end up preferring their new lives. Sometimes they get to live in really amazing places like Paris or New York or villas of their own on the Gold Coast. Believe me, a lot of Unos get thrown at this program."

Behind her, one of the menacing insects snorted. The top of his black helmet was painted blue, the color of peace. "We never see any of it," he said hollowly.

"Right, now you two really need to say goodbye," the blonde womyn went on as if by rote. "You may kiss, but I must ask that your hands remain at your side. I am also required to inform you that all of your personal digital appliances and credit accounts have now been deactivated by court order, ma'am, and you will receive new ones to replace them in due course.

"Any attempt by either of you to re-establish contact by digital or any other means, until such time as such contact is cleared by the court, is a violation of the UN Charter and will be punishable by law. Understood?"

Obama blurted, "You mean the judge might actually let us be together again someday?" He caught a brief pitying glance from Kim after they kissed. She closed her eyes and pressed up against him as hard as she could.

"I'm supposed to lie to you and say yes," the Chief Marshal answered slowly. "But to be truthful, I've never heard of it happening. I shouldn't be telling you this, but my advice is, make a new life for yourself. Act like the other person is dead, and just start over."

"I am dead," Kim whispered.

"That is the grief speaking," said the counselor, as Kim was steered into the ascensor. The doors hissed closed.

"No!" Obama screamed. The little womyn made no attempt to stop Obama from following the marshals up onto the roof in the second ascensor, but instead followed him into it.

"Your emotions are very normal, you know, Mr. Jones," she informed him on the way up. "But I cannot release you tonight until you have signed a digital consent form stating that you have completely read and understood our bereavement checklist." By the time the doors opened again, Obama could see that the group of marshals was halfway across the car-pad, escorting Kim toward the idling black Federal airvan that stood on its three landing pods with a rear sliding door left open.

It was sharply cold outside. There was a dark deserted roof-deck behind the ascensor lobby that the residents used for sun-bathing and watching the distant 24th of October fireworks and holographic displays over the UN Peace Park every year. The aircar pad was right in front of him, its landing area outlined by a glowing green hexagon; several parking spaces beside it were illuminated by fiber-optics. A ring of blinking red lights lit the radius of the building whenever a car was on approach or standby status. Obama had only read about rooftop parking in the condo rules; he and Kim hadn't been able to afford an aircar, of course. Now they never would.

He broke away from the womyn and ran toward the group. One of the gleaming black figures, almost invisible in the night, turned and blocked his path silently with a patient, practiced air. Over his shoulder he caught a glimpse of Kim's white face straining back toward him for one last look as she was bundled into the van.

"Please take care of yourself, Bam!" Her voice broke. "Remember to eat!" The door slammed shut, and Obama started crying.

"She's barefoot!" he called after them. "Can't I at least bring her some socks?"

The wind seemed to pick up as the last of the marshals, the one who had been restraining him, silently disengaged and slid into the van's passenger seat. The gull-wing door closed. The liftoff thrusters roared, and a cloud of dust and engine exhaust rose up around the machine. Then the Hyundair van smoothly lifted off from the roof, climbing quickly and vertically in a tight spin, its under-chassis covered in tiny blinking lights like an antique theater marquee. It turned, gained speed, and slowly flew off to finally disappear into the darkness high over the glittering city.

"When we have gone over the checklist together, then I can go home," said the womyn at his side. She touched his arm. "I will tell you something personal — this has happened to me too, once." Obama stared at her. Her face was a blur. "They took away my son some years ago. He was only 18, you know. That's why I joined this department, in order to find him."

"And — and did you?" It came out in a hoarse croak.

"No, not yet," she said reluctantly, fingering her badge. "But I am a Federal employee. Anything is still possible."

2.

Obama Jones was a Federal employee, too. When he got to his office building the next morning, the Minority Assistance Department on 6th Street SW, he had to fight his way through the usual ring of chanting demonstrators outside the front entrance, which was studded with bollards and concrete barricades against terrorist attacks. CAC — the Coalition of the Appearance-Challenged — had been protesting the UN's denial of their application for minority status for the past month. Such a designation was intensely politically desirable, as well as potentially very lucrative. It guaranteed proportional representation in the United Nations Congress in Geneva; coveted "victim-status" in hate-crime prosecutions; and access to special tax deductions and social services entitlements such as supplemental disability payments.

There were actually few real CAC members left among the demonstrators this morning, however — the organization was so well-funded that it had hired a professional protesting service, which recruited local HELP to march around chanting and banging on plastic trash-can lids all day. Wearing Halloween masks or plastic pig-snouts and carrying printed placards that read "Facial Justice Now!" and "Are We Not Humyn?," the protesters were orchestrated by a kind of galley-slave overseer who sat loudly beating a row of oil drums beneath a huge cartoon hologram of a malevolent pig. The racket had been giving Obama headaches for weeks.

The MAD building was a vast cylinder that from a distance exactly resembled an old-fashioned HEPA filter. It had been built back in the days when the UN had mandated strict "green" measures against global warming. The internal heating and air-conditioning systems had been designed accordingly; the entire structure had been smart-wired to "breathe" according to the average outdoor temperature and seasonal azimuth of the sunlight. None of the temperature settings could be altered or the windows opened. The aircar pads inside the ring of glass sky-lighting on the roof had been carpeted with grass, and a hedged maze had been carved out by the World Psychological Association in the employees' leisure area symbolizing the Conflict of Order and

Chaos. This, it was thought, would help them relax. Such techniques created individual "tranquility islands" and "pocket-climes" inside the building, while vastly reducing its carbon footprint.

But because the global mini-ice age, which was refreezing the polar ice caps and lowering ocean levels, had begun since the building's blueprints had been created, the structure was now impossible to keep warm or dry. Consequently, portable liquid-ceramic heaters had to be run inside every office at prohibitive cost for most of the year, battling the automagic air-conditioning during portions of the fall and spring. The greenery on the roof and top floors leaked down into the sky-light panels, infecting them with an ineradicable fungus, and moisture collected permanently inside the double-glazing. Metal meshed nets had been rigged high above the vast central foyers to contain falling debris from these, and condensation inside the emergency stairwells was so heavy that it sometimes took the form of an artificial rainfall that had to be collected and diverted by plastic sheeting.

Just inside the main front entrance, visitors and employees alike were greeted by a looped holographic mission infomercial towering nearly three stories high. An animated three-dimensional Number One asked a series of questions to a smiling cartoon Mother Earth about his rights as a world citizen, against a background of upbeat inspirational muzak. "Remember," she boomed lovingly at the end of each loop, "Every *One* is a minority!," as all the little numbers held hands to form a humyn chain across the planet.

This morning, it took Obama nearly 15 minutes to get through security. Normally he was swiped and scanned routinely, but the antique CT machines were all broken, so he had to submit to a manual strip-search beneath the giant "The Future Is Brown" banner that permanently overhung the great round interior lobby. He'd forgotten to remove the remains of the previous day's box-lunch from his manbag, so they tripped a hard-plastics detector alarm, and his favorite fork and spoon were confiscated. By the time he finally got upstairs to his cube, his neighbor in the next one over, Scott Vega-Choi said, "Carmen wants to see you." Then he added, "Amigo, *que pasa*? You look like a piece of dried-up dog shit."

"I had a bad night. Scott, what do you know about inter-departmental access? I mean, about how it's mapped?" Obama had forgotten to eat or shower or even change clothes. He'd spent the night feverishly Goggling any information he could retrieve on the United Nations Federal Grand Jury Protection Program. Not surprisingly, he'd found little. Even if information was available, he finally decided, he'd probably have had a block put on him on Wii by the Department of Health and Human Services. He'd swiped into each of the other Big Four domains but with exactly the same results.

He felt frantic with the urge to just do something. Anything. No matter how futile or pointless, doing something seemed better than doing nothing. He felt suppressed rage and violence boiling inside him like a volcano, and was constantly tormented by waking dreams replaying the events of the evening before. Things he should have said, should have done. And now, he thought, it was too late for any of them.

"Um ... not a whole lot? It's pretty seamless. I've never had any problem retrieving data even from HHS." Scott was a Chinese-Filipino Californian, a "nuffing," as salaried employees were universally called, because they worked "good 'nuff" to just get by. He was cradling a cup of Black Khat; Obama smelled it and suddenly felt weak with hunger. He put down his bag and sat heavily at his station.

"But we access everything on the Grid through the Big Four, right? I mean, there aren't any backdoors."

"Well, theoretically we all have to have the right clearance for each department level," said Scott slowly. "But that's strictly need-to-know, keyed into our personal accounts. Duh, you know all this shit better than I do."

"Right, right. It's just — well, you know each UN department tries to keep its own records to itself. We have our own data here that we don't let anyone else touch — some of it's not even scanned into the Grid. I mean, even Sony or the president couldn't access them without a court order and an army of interns. But I need to get into files in other departments that I'm blocked from seeing." He slumped forward in his ergo-pod and held his face in his big hands. "Truthfully, I was never much of a hacker in skool. I mean, I modded games just like everybody else, but my skills aren't great, and now I need to learn fast. I'm willing to pay for it bigtime." Scott nodded knowingly, then glanced around the office over the tops of the cubes to see if anyone was listening.

"Yeah, I sorta get where you're coming from. Maybe I can hook you up with a friend later. But 'migo, first you gotta go see Carmen. She already knows you're here. Hey, maybe she can help you out with your access issues," he called after him when Obama got up and left his cube on his way to the ascensor. "You never know!" For the first time since Kim had been taken from him, Obama felt the distant echo of a distracting emotion, a tiny, very faint urge to laugh. Carmen, his boss? Help him out?

Carmen's nickname in the building was "Shelob." Scott swore she had weighed over 250 kilos some years before Obama had come to work there; now, after multiple stomach-staples, she still weighed nearly 170. Carmen Crowfoot was the Director of New Minorities Accreditation; she liked to say she was a member of every minority there was. A full-blooded Native-American from the Huron Nation of western Ontario (former reservations were granted precisely as much autonomy as former sovereign nations under the UN Charter), she certainly, Obama thought on his way up to her office, must have been a charter member of the CAC, whose interests she tirelessly advocated. Not that she seemed aware of any challenges to her own appearance. She was the most conceited womyn he'd ever met, as well as being loudly, cheerfully, and obscenely abusive to everyone in her division. Or outside it. In fact, she routinely sexually harassed all her staff, regardless of gender.

Luckily for the more sensitive employees like Obama, she was confined to a motorized custom "L'il Rascal" wheelchair because of an aversion to walking under her own excessive weight. It dully registered somewhere in the back of his mind that there could be no happy reason that his boss wanted a meeting this morning, but he didn't care. He fully intended to resign as soon as he'd hacked the Justice Department's records. It even briefly occurred to him to try to somehow force Carmen into using her access level on them — but he would never get away with it. Every square centimeter of the MAD building was covered by security cams and crawling bugs, though he'd heard that only half were actually operable at any given moment. And if what Kim had said was true about the Juror Protection program, its data was probably only cleared for the highest-level officials and the Justice Department employees who actually handled it.

Although not all of them, he decided, remembering the grief counselor from the night before. She had left her iFace address on his iRist: yasmina_housmanzadeh@doj.hhs.gov.un. He found himself cynically wondering if the story she'd told him about herself was true or just part of her training. *Kim,* he thought again. *Kim.* An image of her face in his mind, the sound of her name. Over and over like a heartbeat.

He exited the ascensor on the top floor, barely noticing the dim organic shadows cast by the algae on the skylight panels. Normally the walk from this lobby down the hallway to Carmen's offices caused him a lot of tension — it had even sent him bolting to the restrooms once or twice — but now exhaustion and misery had made him indifferent.

He was stopped in the outer office by Carmen's Administrative Associate, the only AA who had ever, somehow, mysteriously managed to last more than a few weeks in the position. Her name was Camille Lyonesse, and she was the department siren. She was tall and voluptuous, with skin the color of latte and round thrusting breasts that caught Obama's eye even in his current miserable condition. She had long wavy copper-colored hair and a look of the Italian Renaissance in her face, as if Botticelli's "Venus" had been repainted by a Mogul court artist. Her pale blue eyes were almond-shaped. She liked him — was always finding obvious excuses to run into him at lunch or query his iTooth on pointless topics. It was, quite frankly, weird, and it made him uncomfortable. Even now she was rising from her pod to say hi, something she rarely bothered to do for anyone else.

"Oh, you look terrible, poor 'migo," she said smiling sweetly. "Bad night?" She must know something. Maybe Scott had already ratted him out. Or was what happened to Kim last night already on file here? He mumbled something in reply. She put her hand on his arm sympathetically. They had politely Goggled each other's iFaces when they'd first been introduced, but he could never remember whether she had a partner or not. He really didn't care.

"Is she in?" he asked.

"In and impatiently waiting." She held onto his arm a moment longer than necessary, then pointed him at Carmen's office door, which hissed open after it briefly scanned his biometrics.

Carmen's office was the size of a small gym, its walls claustrophobically covered with out-of-date flat visualization screens, and she liked to keep it as overheated as possible. She was wearing a black suit-jacket over her mammoth sausage-like arms and shoulders, but because she always sweated heavily, had unkissed her formal white blouse nearly down to her navel, revealing moist mounds of glistening flesh. She seemed in a cheerful mood; a wide grin split her broad face, giving her the appearance of a genial toad in bifocals.

"Obama!" she bellowed happily the moment he was in range. "I'm grounding you! No, no," she waved off his next words, "I just got the meme from HHS — you're suspended a week for bereavement. You don't get the full package because your little wifey didn't actually croak, technically speaking, but I'm canceling all your clearances as a precaution so you won't waste your time off trying to chase around after her. You're busted down to intern status." She drove her Rascal out from behind her desk, wobbling precariously over its arm-rests.

"That's not fair, Carmen," protested Obama. "I don't want a week off!"

"Don't thank me, thank Camille — it was her idea. Besides, the grief counseling and all the rest of that bereavement bullshit is mandated. I don't believe in it myself. When my mom passed I went out and partied for a week. Best blind sex of my life. Look, I know you're probably gonna be majorly horny pretty soon with wifey out of the picture, so you should come out to McLean sometime and hang. Get nasty with an Earth goddess — everybody says my vagina juice rules."

"Thanks for the thought," he said politely.

"*De nada*, you know I'm hot for you, 'migo. And you can lose that hang-dog pouty expression of yours — I'm just playing with you. This is a promotion, dumb-ass!"

"Huh? What do you mean?"

"When you come back you'll be sitting on the CAC jury. You'll be one of the all-important committee members deciding the ultimate fate of their application. It's a really huge deal — you have no idea of the strings I had to pull to get you get this gig. You'll be hanging with a bunch of high-flying politicos. You'll have all kinds of clearances, 'migo, like total access to the updated Humyn Genome files! It could lead anywhere for you. You could even end up as a rival Division head in a year or two. Then I'd have to call you 'sir' instead of 'shit-for-brains!'" She cackled.

First the stick, then the carrot, thought Obama on his way back out the door. It was as if somebody wanted to bribe him not to go after Kim. He didn't even notice the soulful look Camille sent after him.

Whenever you were suspended from a UN governmental position, no matter how temporarily, you had 15 minutes to leave the building and by law had to be escorted outside by Security. Obama packed a few personal possessions, including a framed iPhoto show of Kim, the screen of which had now gone dark, into an orange plastic octohedron, and was led back down through the main lobby into the street. "I'll be in touch, 'migo," Scott told him over his iTooth; Obama ignored the other messages from coworkers, including two from Camille. He stood for a moment, surrounded and deafened by the CAC protesters, then crossed the street and went down into the Federal Center Retro station. The segualator was out of order, so he had to take the stairs.

Almost without volition, he took the old Blue Line to Retro Center, suddenly finding himself in exactly the same spot where he'd been accosted by the Indonesian-looking HELP. For a crazy moment he stood still there, looking around in every direction for him, feeling like if he were able to somehow re-enact that moment, he could turn the clock back to it — could meet Kim for lunch armed with this terrible new knowledge, and convince her to run away with him to South America or someplace. "Wiiboot" their life together. Someone screamed at him to get out of the way, and the illusion was broken.

Manacera City, because it had always been the hub of North American government, had never been on the cutting edge of fashion. Commuters tended to dress conservatively and, ever since the advent of global cooling, warmly. Most people were bundled up, even at midsummer, in dark coats and jackets of quilted Nitinelle with microfilament heating coils, embedded microchips, and built-in exhaust fans. Because Nitinelle was a conductive fabric, many jackets functioned as living billboards, with the animated logos of favorite games or YouVee or sim stars splashed across them.

People usually wore Lyocell smart-shoes or boots made of Ultrasuede, a micropore rubber crafted to retain shapes and resist dirt and stains. A hip minority sported natural, or "Greenspun," fabrics micro-woven from cotton, hemp, bamboo, flax, or soy fibers chemically impregnated with corn polymer polylactic acid. Under their coats, the wealthier and more fashionable would be wearing spray-on Syntex shirts and dresses and even underwear.

In addition to the commuters — most of them Federal employee nuffings — the streets were also full of bumpers and exarchists. Bumpers were younger people who remained booted up into the Grid while they functioned more or less normally in the real world. They wore neural-lace game-caps, often with armored headgear such as helmets over them, as well as dark wraparound monitor glasses that displayed both their actual environment and the corresponding virtual version of the city onGrid. Because of inadequate collision detection, they wore protective pads on their knees and elbows, as well as rigid, codpiece-like groin-protectors.

Exarchists, who were so-called after the anarchistic youth enclave in Athens which had spawned the violent anti-globalist, anti-capitalist riots across Europe during the Great Panic of 2012, rejected the Grid entirely. They viewed it as a corporatist plot to enslave the poor. They routinely committed random actions of violence, such as slapping commuters, vandalizing expensive aircars or smashing shop windows, occasionally erupting in iTooth-coordinated communal riots whenever their welfare payments were threatened. They also sprayed epithelial animated graffiti all over the city, often hiring themselves out to agencies representing corporate advertisers or politicians. President Manacera himself was said to be a fan of the exarchists and had even attended one of their "squattapaloozas," or meticulously choreographed spontaneous festivals featuring live muzak, random sex with strangers, and illegal drugs, such as cheap chocolate. "I think we're all just a little bit exarchistic at heart," he'd said. "I know I am!" Even if you secretly hated hooligans, it was still cool to have a president who was open in his thinking like that.

Obama walked the four blocks up from Retro Center to the New-Day Ziggurat where Kim had worked. A huge Nitinelle banner hung from it that read "LAWYER UP!" He stood outside it on the sidewalk and stared up at the aircars lazily wheeling over it like sea-gulls. He'd checked last night and then compulsively re-checked; both her iTooth accounts had already been cancelled. He'd tried several of her colleagues at New-Day, Hogan Hartson, but none had returned his messages. He wanted to get inside the gleaming building, to at least go up and retrieve her personal stuff from her office to see if it offered any kind of clue to where she'd been taken. Without an appointment, though, or Kim's account to swipe, he stood zero chance of getting through security.

While he was standing there, someone almost walked into him. The myn first turned away as if to escape, then slowly turned back again to face him. It was Nathan Herrera, Kim's immediate superior, the junior partner who'd first recruited her into the firm. He and Obama weren't close but they'd met socially several times. "Obama," Herrera said with obvious reluctance. "Look, we can't talk here. Disconnect whatever coms you run, and walk a few blocks with me. I'm on my way to an early lunch."

Herrera was a pot-bellied yellow little myn, goatishly bearded, who was famed for his bad taste in clothes. The black pinstripe smart-suit he was wearing now was creased and rumpled as if he'd slept in it, and there were food stains on his shirt. He was also a public crusader for NAMBLA and spoke at Myn-Boy conventions all over the continent. "My suit is blocking most of the bugs, but a few always stick. This office is surrounded by them like swarms of flies. Most fly over from there." He pointed across the Convention City Center in the direction of the mammoth Venerable Arnold Porter Pyramid on the other side, New Day's principal legal business rivals in the city.

They crossed 13th Street against the traffic-bots, which started sending them nagging messages. "But some of the eavesdropping is from the DOJ," he said quietly when they were in the middle of the street. A light drizzle was falling. "When someone gets summonsed like that, we're not supposed to ever mention their name again. Technically, I'm in violation of a court order just talking to you. She was instantly erased from our files. Every case she worked on got her credits wiped; we can't even give out references like we would for a former employee. It's spooky. They just disappeared her. It's never happened to anyone at our office before. But I've heard of other cases — just nobody that young. Most Federal Jurors are senior citizens nobody cares about."

"I was hoping to at least pick up her things," Obama said when they reached the other side. Tiny droplets were beading up on Herrera's smart-suit.

"What things? No, seriously, it's like she never existed. That's how you have to view it, amigo. You gotta try to accept it — it sucks, but that's life."

"But isn't there anything we can do to fight it?" Obama asked. The lawyer had an abstracted look on his face, like he was handling a half-dozen iTooth calls at once. "Can't we file an appeal or something? I mean somebody must have already taken it to SCROTUN." SCROTUN was the Supreme Court Review of the United Nations.

"It's not my area of specialty," Herrera said at last, still focused on his iRist. "I mostly deal in sexual contract law, as you know. But I read up on it after I got the news, because, well, K — she — was so special, and I was actually pretty attached to her — and I gotta tell you there is absolutely no chance of our beating this thing in court. Accept it and move on. I have." He briefly clapped Obama on the shoulder. "Got a date, gotta run. It was good of me to take the time to see you. Even if I never did."

Obama spent the rest of the day at the Federal Courthouse buildings, being shunted around from department to department and getting nowhere. Herrera might have been personally unpleasant, but he was apparently right: it was as if Kim had vanished into thin air. During one of his many waits for an AM-OLED screen to free up so that he could physically apply for information and interviews (technically, so that he could apply to apply for them), Obama Goggled glogs on the subject of jury duty.

Grand juries, he read, could be traced back to the Assize of Clarendon, an 1166 act of Henry II of England, though there was some evidence that the ancient Athenians had used a similar system. It had been used as way of bringing indictments before a criminal court and had all but disappeared outside the former United States by the year 2000. But after CommUnion, the United Nations had unaccountably adopted the practice. Bit by bit, the rules of sequestration had been expanded to prevent tampering, and even made permanent to avoid constant appeals based on mistrials, until the current version had evolved. Less than .001% of the world's population would ever be selected for a Federal Grand Jury. That, and the fact that nobody ever returned from serving on one with tales to tell, accounted for why even a Federal employee like Obama was totally ignorant of the system.

Not that it would have made any difference if he'd known about it, he told himself, as he ascended the Harborplex segualator, exiting the station past the holographic ads for Amazone, iShop, and WiiBuy. There was nothing he could have done, anyway. But he still stubbornly refused to believe there was nothing he could do about it now. It was getting late. He'd been reluctant to go home at all, with no Kim, but there was always the faint hope that somehow she'd managed to get herself released with some lawyer's trick or threat and was waiting for him there now. And of course, with all her accounts canceled there would be no way for her even to ring his iTooth to tell him.

Usually he tried to be home before dark, though the streets were always brightly lit, and security cam-bots crawled along the ledges of the apartment towers. Unfortunately, there were still disadvantaged minority youths about, many of them immigrants who had been driven by poverty and educational discrimination to antisocial acts of violence or destruction. They preyed on the nuffings, often stealing their iRists or smart-clothes. Most of the "meenies," as minority kids were popularly called, were too young to be sentenced to anger management — even if HHS could afford to respond to emergency policing calls — and it was increasingly rare that non-hate crimes were ever prosecuted anyway. But at least their biometric visual data and DNA were collected by the bots and filed away for future reference.

A few meenies were begging now from the indifferent drivers of the hybrid "greenie" groundcars stalled in rush-hour traffic, most of whom were too wary to lower their windows. Overhead, Flopeds, Vespairs, and the heavier and louder air-hogs skimmed the streets and sidewalks, often just above the level of ground-traffic. Occasionally, these flew so low that they posed a hazard to pedestrians. There were no traffic lights, but bots hovered above each intersection, enforcing the computerized traffic laws and expediting traffic flow. High above, a few gas-guzzling aircars drifted by. Manacera City was the last jurisdiction in North America to strictly enforce air traffic lanes, so ironically, it was the only urban area left where you could actually see the night sky free from blinking lights. Though, of course, the tops of buildings were covered with them, along with aircraft collision poles, as a safety precaution. Shifting holographic billboards advertising spray-on clothing and lunar emigration enshrouded a few of the taller towers in the distance.

The Safe-T-lights built every few meters into the sidewalks sent his shadow racing ahead of him, long and lanky but oddly fat-headed, like the ghostly rider of "Ichabod Crane." Obama was tall and rangy and deceptively strong — Kim always told him that his size had appealed to her from the start. His father was an African-American Air Force master-sergeant from Knoxville, his mother half-"haole" (*her* father had been an Israeli acupuncturist) and half-Samoan. They'd met in Hawaii, where they now were living again after retirement.

Obama had been an affectionate and gregarious child, and had always wanted a brother or sister; his parents had tried for more children but hadn't been able to get the license. They were the only parents of anyone Obama knew who were still married; when Kim was in her teens, her father had run off with a real estate agent who was selling their Houston home, so at least she'd had the chance to know him. Most children didn't know both their parents. A lot of tank kids never met either of them.

Directly across the Potomac River from the Harborplex lay Reagan International Aerospaceport. Now Obama could see its millions of lights brilliantly illuminating the far shore like a crystal palace, above which a huge holographic representation of the ancient president looped soundlessly in front of a transparent United Nations flag. Reagan was famous for something, just like the president Obama was named for, but Obama could never remember what.

A cold wet breeze came from off the water, and Obama shivered. He turned left off Arnold Avenue onto March Place to his dark and empty apartment. When he turned on the lights, he discovered that almost all traces of Kim had been removed from it.

3.

In 2004 The Sony Corporation patented the first neural-lace input device that conducted galvanic electrical impulses directly into the skull; the following year Nintendo introduced motion-sensing game controllers for its Wii platform. Within a decade both companies were attempting to combine the two technologies, and by the early '30s gaming helmets incorporating interlaced skullcaps, blackout goggles and noise-blocking earphones had become the industry standard.

The old games and virtual online environments had featured crude 2D, and later 3D, graphical information; once it was possible to saturate synaptic receptors directly with a stream of bio-encoded electrical signals, the gaming experience became utterly realistic and immersive. Digitized information was experienced by the user as reality; instantly the old-skool forms of visual-based entertainment became obsolete, like the text- and graphics-based "Internet." Each gaming platform carved out a networked domain of its own.

A wave of mergers and acquisitions had followed over the next few years, as the "Big Four" engaged in a competition that nearly bankrupted them all, at one time giving away their hardware almost for free and charging nominal flat fees for monthly use. Legacy Internet giants like Amazon and Google had been swallowed up by Apple's iShops and MS 'SoftWorld, while Sony's SeventhLife and Nintendo's WiiLive focused on social networking.

In the end, all four had been forced to create a common global gaming Grid, absorbing the world's antiquated corporate and government servers at about the same time. You still booted up into one of the Big Four, and paid them — individually — but the shared Grid environment itself was now universal. Only some of the older data, buried in abandonware and legacy code morgues, varied substantially. And it was inside these that Obama Jones hoped to find some kind of current record-keeping for the United Nations Federal Grand Jury Protection Program.

How you booted on — what you looked like to others, what your initial environment looked and felt like and how it was set up to function for you — was up to you. And it varied pretty wildly from individual to individual. Some onGrid companies even sold pre-designed boot-up packages for the inexperienced or unimaginative. These were called "skins." When you changed your skin it was called "rebooting," a term that had once meant restarting the computer back in the days when individual personal computers had still existed. Obama had outgrown the need for creating exotic skins when he was a teenager; now he just booted up as himself, without any other sort of avatar, and used his own living room as the boot-up environment.

Kim had loved ancient media and had insisted on covering one wall with a flat-screen panel; her favorite old "flattie" film DVDs were still stacked beside it, like the Japanese children's musical classic *Alakazam the Great* and the even older black and white *Harvey*.

Obama used a mock-up of the Fujisonic OLED flat-screen while he was onGrid as a metaphor for a visual control panel, subdividing it into several dozen translucent rectangles containing favorite navigation paths and social rooms, shortcut icons to gaming worlds or personal daemons, news feeds, iTooth inputs, cycled security visuals from the condo's security cams, work-projects, and allocated space for mandatory advertising. He could access or enter any of these rectangles merely by touching it, keeping ghostly miniature versions of the rest while porting, flying, driving, walking, or otherwise navigating through them. Data search and retrieval, however, was boring, and he preferred to do that sitting on the couch.

In real life, Obama had noticed the couch was starting to smell of old feet. He needed to take a shower before he pulled another all-nighter on it. There was a crumpled blanket on the floor beside him, because he often got cold while gaming — he'd never figured out why.

He picked up the blanket to put it in the laundry, but he still found it hard to face going into the bedroom. He'd received an iTooth message from Mrs. Housmanzadeh on his way home saying that a Federal forensics team had swept the apartment while he was at work and had removed the rest of Kim's possessions. Even so, they'd missed a few things, like the dent of her head on the pillow. And the smell of her in the sheets. And the personal altar on the table in the foyer, where a looped hologram of Kim and Obama taken at their wedding normally played in front of the offering bowls. Last night he'd even prayed at it.

Finally he mustered the courage to step into the ultrasonic shower, glimpsed one of Kim's shampoo combs with one or two of her long dark hairs still wrapped around it, and almost instantly ended up on the sculpted floor of the stall sobbing uncontrollably. It took him nearly half an hour to drag himself out and dry off.

Now he'd finally cracked up, doing anything at all was a problem for Obama: eating, sleeping, even mandatory waste recycling. He tried to do things blind, groping his way around the place so he wouldn't be ambushed by any more of Kim's overlooked stuff. He found a shopping list she'd written in a kitchen drawer and, weeping, pressed it to his face. He felt as though he'd gone crazy. *Who wouldn't?* he thought. What he really needed to do was to go completely crazy, to come out the other side. In other words, to lose his mind so totally that nothing would ever hurt any more.

Grow a pair, amigo, Obama told himself at some point. *You're acting like Kim's dead. She isn't. She's sitting somewhere in a hotel room or Federal holding cube right now thinking the same kind of thoughts you are. You owe it to her to stop acting like a crybaby and be a man. As long as she's still alive somewhere, it's your job to keep looking for her until you find her.* He could almost hear his dad's voice barking those words to him. If Obama could only message him right now, they were probably pretty much exactly what he would say.

Unfortunately he couldn't. His dad was currently institutionalized at a Kaui Wellness Center for Seasonal Associative Disorder, a syndrome somehow related to global cooling. They wanted to send him to the Moon to cure it.

Suddenly Obama felt ravenous. He took a Hol-foods cryorganic meal octagon out of the Liquid Cooler's freezer and put it in the hydrowave, then carried it over to the couch along with a bottle of Green Chi-Cola. When he was finished, he covered himself with a clean blanket, hooked a liquids tube into one corner of his mouth and put on his game-cap. Helmets had come a long way since the days of the old plastic monsters; Obama's Sony MD2052 was made of a soft black micro-pore aerogel-foam fabric and looked like a baby's snow-hat. Flaps came down over his ears and eyes and froze into place. He kissed the chin-strap together and booted up.

Once onGrid, he waved and finger-clicked and turned the vidscreen into a mosaic of still photos of Kim swiped from his iRist — someone at the HHS, he had discovered in a fury the night before, had already wiped all his stored videos of her. In fact, he didn't have any home security cam files more recent than from the previous midnight. He scrolled back through them and saw that a large block was missing from this morning, presumably from when the forensics team had been in. They'd done a clumsy job of wiping their traces clean, though. There were still stray shadows at the frames of missing segments, and a few shots from the ascensor of the group leaving. Weirdly, there was also a 40-minute segment missing from nearly an hour after that.

He scrolled back and forth over it just to make sure, accessing views from various cams. Something caught his eye and he checked it out again. It was Kim's comb, the one inside the shower stall. Immediately after the team had left, it had lain to one side of the blistered soap-ledge — but after the second security wipe, it was centered. He zoomed in as far as pixel resolution allowed and froze both images. There seemed to be more hairs on it before it had been moved than after, but maybe that was just his imagination. Why would they want to steal her hair? For the DNA? But they already had her — they could get all the DNA samples they needed.

Wondering about her DNA made him think about Kim again, where she was at this very minute, what she was doing. *Don't stop eating, honey,* he thought. *Get some sleep.* The loving thoughts acted on him like a narcotic, and he fell asleep himself.

But sleeping onGrid was an unpleasant experience. It was hard to get any deep REMming done with a steady stream of electrical signals bombarding your brain. Plus, it was a waste of money when you were metered by the minute.

He was awakened suddenly by an ad that dumped him onto a lo-grav L'il Rascal inside an opulent restaurant at the Hanging Gardens of Babylon Casino on the Moon. The sensation was very relaxing. Smiling Seniors cheered and waved at him as he whisked past. "Low gravity, low financing," the speakerine whispered to him in a thrilling tone. "Now you too can live like a king or queen at the fabulous Fuji Gold Coast Retirement Resort on the Sea of Tranquility. Enjoy golf, tennis, gambling, and water sports at the weight you've always dreamed of. Choose from a variety of over 500 individual living space models — or design your own! Relax in the comfort of year-round climate control with our patented air filtration and radiation shielding systems. Meet old friends or make new ones! Enjoy world class cuisine. You'll be over the Moon at Fuji Gold Coast. All UN Federal Assistance and Social Security credit packages apply."

The speakerine was interrupted by a bot from Make-a-Will Dot Com, a male model who sympathetically informed Obama that Kim's company life insurance and health plans had been cancelled, but even though she officially didn't exist anymore, under UN law he was entitled to collect Kim's juror's compensation, which was not to exceed 10 Unos per diem. The exact sum, Obama thought, when he managed to force himself fully awake, that he'd paid for her flowers only yesterday. Or was that the day before yesterday? It seemed a lifetime ago.

There were three messages from Kim's mom, which he didn't have the heart to reply to right now. And one from Scott Vega-Choi, whose avatar, a giant armored panda wearing a death mask, approached him furtively from the gloom of Grid limbo ("Grimbo," the kids called it these days). "Hey," Scott said. "I fixed it up with a 'migo of mine to meet you tomorrow at noon. Remember the place we all met up before the Lonely Boys Reunion Concert? Meet him there — he'll know you."

Obama booted down and curled up on the couch under the blanket, where he fell into a deep sleep. Most of his dreams involved Kim being taken from him over and over, but there were several where he had an urgent message from the homeless "Wiiboot" guy, who kept coming out of the Grimbo to wake him up. He found himself being shaken awake, his heart pounding, by Mrs. Housmanzadeh. She was still wearing her vest and was carrying a large bag with a gold UN logo on it.

"What are you doing here?" he asked after he'd sat up. When he'd first woken up he'd felt a wild stab of hope that it was Kim, then a crushing sense of disappointment. The little grief counselor gazed down at him with a faint distaste.

"I was on my way to work. You must check in with me each day, it is the law."

He shook his head dazedly. "But how did you get in?"

"The Program has key access to this flat until you complete your counseling. This is very important for you, you know. If you keep 'blowing off' our meetings, it will go on your permanent record. You seem like a nice boy to me, and I don't want that." She moved off toward the kitchen, as if finding him asleep and wrapped up in a blanket had made her uncomfortable. "I cannot stay for long this morning, but we can hold yesterday's session now. What would you like now for breakfast?"

After he ate, he took the Green Line to the Columbia Heights Retro Station, then the long underground segualated people-mover to the Ontario Place Station on the Brown Line, where most of the lo-res holos were in Spanish or Gwangdong. This segged him up past the security scanners into the Ontario Mega-Plex; the Black Khat where he'd met Scott's posse all those years ago was inside the decaying Madam's Organ Open Market, which had once been a vast, ornate theater of some kind. First Mrs Housmanzadeh had made him memorize the stages of "acceptance." Then they'd done some role-playing. Now he was experiencing an emotion he'd rarely felt before — the urge to kill somebody. Preferably an HHS employee.

In 2008, it had been widely anticipated by city planners that Manacera City — or, as it was then called, Washington DC — would become a "sustainable green" oasis. Streets would be paved with grass. Rooftops would become gardens. Buildings would be engulfed in ivy and hanging plants. Vast elevated farmlands would be constructed above urban ghettoes. The Mall, converted to a water park, would stretch from the Potomac, filled with "ecotopian hub" islands, and Anacostia Rivers. These projects had had to be abandoned, however, during the governmental financial collapse of 2012, and the Mall became a sea of mud covered with squatter camps during the "Manic Depression" that followed. Then, in 2024, the city was nuked.

After Common Union 10 years later, it had been renamed. The Pentagon, spared the devastation on the other side of the river, had been converted into a Peace Museum. Most of the other famous government landmarks had been allowed to remain as they were: crumbling ruins, inhabited only by rats and outsized mutated insects.

Twenty-nine Eco-towers had been built ringing the Capital Beltway. This had been named the FORTway (Future Oriented Renewable Technologies) system. The towers had been envisioned as multi-functional structures, emphasizing public spaces for the community to gather, and incorporating new public transit hubs. Rainwater would be collected for water, power would be generated by wind and sunlight, and multitier hydroponic farms would grow food for the city. Lasers, anchored to each tower, would serve the city's defenses when needed.

In practice, however, the new mini-ice age had coincided with a dimming of sunlight across the northern hemisphere, and winds had rarely exceeded the constant 30-mph mark needed to achieve energy sustainability. The curving solar-paneled carapaces of the soaring structures had soon become covered in rust and mold and had begun falling off, and the exterior carbon-filament glasspex had become repeatedly buried in graffiti, despite generous ongoing UN programs to remove it.

The Market, in a neighborhood largely spared both the nuclear destruction of Seven-Eleven and the modernization spree that followed it, sprawled haphazardly among the ornate rococo pillars and into the opera boxes of the old Ontario Theater, a commercial maze overhung with crude holos and grimy old flat-screens. There were bakeries, seafood and butcher's stalls, jewelers and smart-suit stands, antique clothing and book shops, chocolatiers, a long Amish ice cream and pancake counter, two open-air restaurants, and a central meeting place where about a hundred Asian womyn were playing Quingo. There was also a constant muted roar, damped by the darkened domed ceiling high above. Stains from the air conditioning and fire-sprinkler systems trailed down the mildewing walls. The Black Khat was tucked away near the main entrance, the only international chain represented in the building.

The Black Khat had gradually become the planet's largest franchised coffee-house by catering to individual tastes. You could file a blood sample confidentially at any branch and have the nutrient, sugar, and caffeine levels of any drink you bought from them anywhere in the world custom-blended for your optimal absorption. It was Italian Caffe Month, and Ennio Morricone Hip-Hop remixes were being played over a wide holographic newsfeed over the bar.

It was another of the ubiquitous Election Specials on the Cartoon News Network: after 16 years in office, UN President Jose Manacero had declined to run for a third term but was angling to become Prime Minister in Geneva — assuming, of course, that his Green Planet Democratic Party, or "Greens," maintained their narrow majority over the old New Party, or "Blues." There were also several minor parties that might be included in a coalition government, like the Peoples' Party International (the "Reds"), the Pan-Islamist Party (AQI), and a smattering of legalized nationalist opposition parties.

Right now, the planet's most trusted news-reader, a three-dimensional representation of Disney's Snow White cartoon character, was analyzing the latest polling trends. The sound was muted, but subliminal text crawled through the air across the top and bottom. A tiny Goofy signed for the electively aurally-challenged in the lower right-hand corner, with five 'toon fingers on each paw instead of his usual four.

Obama glanced around the crowded coffee bar but could find no obvious candidate for the job of Scott's amigo. Or maybe too many candidates. Everybody there looked twitchy — looked like crap, in fact. *Maybe it's the greenish lighting,* he thought — then caught sight of his own reflection against the wall. He looked like crap, too. Obviously this place just attracted that type of client. A pale guy at the bar in a game-cap and dark monitor-glasses turned to stare at the floor like a visually-deprived person, then nervously motioned Obama over to perch on the pod next to him.

He was a bumper. "Man, you're giving off signature com noise in every direction," he said with a slight accent. *Iranian,* Obama guessed. They were the hardest-core "black-hat" hackers in the world. "Bring any bugs in with you?"

"I don't know," said Obama.

"Yeah, well, just keep your voice down and let the chatter drown it out. You can call me Freedom." Freedom continued to stare several centimeters to the left of Obama's face; in order to perceive Obama at all, he was virtually 'jacked in somewhere, either to an iCam embedded in his cap or into the Black Khat's own internal security cams. When they attempted to bump fists, he missed. "*Ciao, ciao,*" he said. "Go on, order something — make it look real." His beard stubble, Obama, noticed, was so black it was almost blue, like tiny cobalt filaments.

Obama ordered a frozen vanilla soy-black carob frap blended with 200 mg of khat, caff, B12, and anabolic green steroids. Freedom reordered whatever he was drinking, which smelled vaguely like badly cured leather. After the barista brought their drinks over, Freedom hunched forward protectively over his and started talking very rapidly and indistinctly. "Basically, you want me to help you hack into HHS, am I right?"

"Right."

"How are you planning to pay me, 'migo?"

"Well, like normal...with a credit swipe?" asked Obama, confused.

"No good." Freedom drained most of his drink through a straw in two noisy inhalations. "You got any cut-out accounts off-shore? Can you spoof one? No, I thought not, you look like a total regular Jose. But you gotta have something to barter with, man. Got any PAPTASE?" Prostatic acid phosphatase was the most powerful pain-killer on the planet, 10 times stronger than morphine. It had been banned by the UN because terminally ill patients became addicted to it so easily, but it remained a popular favorite with teenagers. "OK, I guess it'll have to be 'Stim," the Iranian said with a sigh. "Gimme 500 Unos worth of 'Stim — Gamestim, not Brainstim, it's like twice as fast — and we have a deal, 'migo."

"Deal," said Obama, punching the proffered fist. 'Stim was a drug that enhanced the gaming experience, so that an hour onGrid could feel like a whole day. It was also a common way to cram for tests or get through office text-work after hours. 'Stims were a family of selective synaptic re-uptake exhibitors wedded to dodexedrine and technically illegal, but as with PAPTASE, most drug vendors were under 21, so HHS declined to prosecute them. Some off-brand coffee bars, supposedly, would even add it to your caff if you paid extra. It wouldn't look good on his credit record, thought Obama, but he didn't care. His days at MAD were numbered anyway — trying to hack the Program records was a felony, and technically he'd already committed conspiracy to do so. He was a criminal now, outside the law. Not such a regular Jose after all.

"Myself, I use a brother. Name of Osama X." Osama was still the second most popular name in the world given to male babies. Jose was first. Obama was third. "He hangs in front of the Halston Cart outside the Shaw Station. Mostly sells chocolate. Check with you again tomorrow, same time, same place. And try to kill some of that personal noise of yours, amigo — you stink!"

Chocolate was the most widely abused illegal substance in the world. Linked irrefutably by medical evidence to childhood obesity and theobromine toxicity (leading over time to epileptic seizures, heart attacks, internal bleeding, and eventually death), it had finally been banned by the UN in 2038, but its prohibition, like that of tobacco products, had not been an unqualified success.

Twitching noticeably, Freedom edged from his pod and limped out through the automagic glasspex doors with a halting, high-stepping gait. Obama realized all at once that the poor guy suffered from muscular dystrophy. At least his handicapability meant that Freedom was immune from arrest, so that, hopefully, HHS surveillance on him would be slight; however, it might not prevent him from ratting Obama out afterwards. Something to worry about when the time came.

Obama craned his neck up to watch Snow White, who had switched from international to local news. An unlicensed ring of brothels had been busted operating out of Federal Administration Area middle skools. This was considered a serious violation of WHO guidelines, and the parents of the children involved were being sued for the lost tax revenues, since the prostitution itself was not a crime, merely the tax evasion. However, a major network was interested in turning the Gridcam uploads into a scripted reality series.

He finished his frap and got up to go. He had almost reached the door sensors when the entire glasspex front wall of the Black Khat violently exploded inwards at him. A half-second later he heard a deafening crack like a peal of thunder. Even as the shower of glasspex shatter-beads drilled into him, he was falling backwards, along with every other patron in the place; he slid across the floor yelping in pain as the lights went out and Snow White blinked and froze. Now he felt a blast of heat. Next came a sound like hail, as debris rained down all over the Market, and a chorus of security sirens whooped and blip-beeped and trilled. Then the screaming started.

4.

" — the Madam's Organ bombing marks the third such terrorist attack in the Greater North American Federal Admin Area in the past few weeks, coming as it does in the wake of the Long Island Mag-Lev rail bombings and the Engineered Ebola outbreak in Los Angeles. Now this. So far, neither the rejectionist Warriors of God wing of CIENA or the White Terror Commando has claimed responsibility for the attack, which bears the signature trademark signs of both. But could it be the work of a lone sociopath?" A half-meter high Snow White rotated slowly in midair to stare into the corner of Mrs. Housmanzadeh's cube and solemnly announce, "Here to give their thoughts on today's outrage in Manacera City are our own Shrek and Jiminy Cricket."

"Snow, the presence inside the Market of both a pork butcher's and live lobsters could suggest the work of PETA, who as you will recall were involved in last year's — "

"Ow!" said Obama.

Mrs. Housmanzadeh was leaning over him with a pair of tweezers, plucking out embedded glasspex pitted in his cheeks and forehead. The bomb-proof material, universally used in cars, was supposed to bead harmlessly when exploded, but in practice sometimes had the same effect as birdshot. His spectacle lenses were cracked and the vision through them fractured. They were only an affectation — his vision, unlike that of most other North Americans, had never needed correcting — but it was a lucky thing he'd been wearing them anyway.

"There," she said finally, dabbing at the tiny cut with an Io-wipe. "Perhaps this is the last one." Inside the office she had discarded her boots and body-vest in favor of an ornately printed dark blue silk robe and a pair of old sandals. Up close, her patchouli body oil was overpowering and more than a little stale. Her cube shared an outside window, and over her shoulder he could see a constant line of aircars streaming from the direction of the Ontario to land on adjacent roof-pads. "So much processing and counseling to do now," said Mrs

Housmanzadeh, clucking loudly. "No time even for lunch. Such a tragedy today, you know. Was it very bad there?"

"Yes, it was," said Obama. After the explosion, he had staggered stunned out into the entrance hall, his clothes steaming from the drizzle erupting from the ceiling sprinklers, and had stood for a few moments staring into the darkened, smoky shambles of the Market before being hurtled into by hysterical shoppers emerging from it in twos and threes. The bomb blast seemed to have been centered somewhere between the Black Khat and the Quingo Booth, where an Allura Sensex robot had been calling out the 5-dimensional letters for the Seniors. Sony had originally marketed the Allura line as a sex toy for the wealthy, but the global economy had kept teenage humyn labor so much cheaper that in the end most of the bots had been bought up by gambling casinos and luxury hotels, where their hyper-dexterity and scrupulous honesty made them worth their high price. They were also used as stewardesses on Moon shuttle flights.

Obama noticed that a twisted piece of the Allura's arm had landed in the wreckage of the chocolate shop. Kim, he had always thought, had borne an uncanny resemblance to the Allura. *And still does,* he reminded himself. *She isn't dead.* Unlike at least half of the Quingo players.

The center of the marketplace had instantly become a shambles of burning debris, scattered food and half-recognizable pieces of smoldering machinery, through which shocked survivors lurched around trying to save each other. A group of Asian womyn Seniors squatted or sat in the middle of the floor, praying and rocking back and forth.

Every pane of glasspex in the place had been smashed. Obama had seen blood spattered all over the stainless steel ice-cream equipment of the Amish, bodies lying around it like crumpled rag-dolls, part of a torso buried in a stack of blackened, burning books. A running shoe had smoldered directly in front of him with a piece of splintered bone sticking out of it. A dead iRist was lying right beside it; without thinking, he'd picked it up and slipped it into a pocket. As he'd done so, a group of Laotian bakers carrying an old womyn had crashed into him, and he had allowed their momentum to push him out through the main front doors and into the street.

It had taken him a moment or two to adjust his eyes to the glare; then he'd noticed flakes of white ash slowly falling everywhere. One had melted on his face, stinging his lip with cold, and he started. It hadn't been ash, but snow. Snow in the month of Thermia! Or, as his parents still referred to it, July. As he stared up into the grey sky, the first of the shrilling Emergency Rescue vehicles had started spinning down to land in the middle of Columbia Road.

A team of black-clad HHS SWAT troopers was first to reach the scene and now was cordoning off the street and sidewalks with sticky-net. The sight of them had filled Obama with a rebellious sense of anger and loathing, and he'd edged away toward the Retro Station steps. "Civil emergency! Do not leave the area!" the traffic bots sternly warned him. "I repeat, do not leave the area!" But he'd escaped anyway, ducking down into the station. As he did so, it had occurred to him to wonder why Freedom had exited the Market quite so abruptly.

"I think we can say you have already had your session for today," the grief counselor was telling him now. "You have learned some perspective for your own personal emotions, I think, seeing the pain of others. This was a good life lesson." Behind her Shrek was amiably toting up the body count on a transparent white-board. Reception inside the heavily shielded Federal Courthouse office building was poor, and the beloved cartoon figures sometimes pixilated or even disappeared in a cloud of what appeared to be fairy-dust.

That night, after he'd spent a miserable couple of hours trying to calm Yvonne, Kim's mother, by iTooth, he found another message from Scott Vega-Choi. "Tried to check what went down with my dude Freedom today," the skull-masked panda told him, "but he's blowing off my messages, 'migo. Sorry about that." Whatever. Obama doubted he'd ever see Freedom again, even if that Black Khat reopened anytime soon. He'd have to look for help elsewhere. He felt totally empty and defeated. Everything he tried was a dead end.

Then he remembered the iRist he'd rescued from the Market floor. It had probably been nuked by the blast, but you never knew. He plugged it into his recharger, then went back onGrid to access it. After a few swipes it chimed, and he was able to hack into it. It appeared to belong to someone named "Joyful Kalinga." He first checked the casualty lists, then Goggled the local "Lost & Found" and ran a global search, but found no mention of the name anywhere. The iRist itself was initialized but had been wiped completely clean.

It took him a few minutes to realize what it actually was. They'd been getting complaints for months at MAD about Zimbabwean vendors who'd been selling stolen iRists to undocumented workers with the IDs and biometrics of dead political prisoners burned into them. Obviously, there'd been a dealer or a stand selling these inside the Market. Slowly the implications of it sank in. He could use this to forge a false identity. Maybe Obama Jones couldn't hack into the DOJ records, but "Joyful Kalinga" might...

But he'd have to go about it just the right way.

First he needed to get back to Scott. He found him deep inside the collapsed core of a WarHammer death star battling an army of mutants with shoulder-firing antimatter mini-nukes. "Hold on a sec," Scott said. After an exchange of nuke-fire he froze the action around them outside an invisible time-out bubble.

"Sorry," Obama said. "I need a couple of favors." It felt weird to stand unarmored inside the molten core of a star. It was hot and he existed at three times his normal body weight. "I've decided to give up on this data-hacking thing. I was sort of, well you know, upset and angry. But I see now it was all just crazy talk."

Even under his space armor, Scott — or the panda version of him anyway — appeared relieved. "Yeah, Carmen told me about Kim. I'm really sorry, my brother. But you know you can't get her back that way."

"Right. Well, I've been pretty confused about things, but I see now that what I really need is to get back to work," Obama said with a total lack of sincerity. "Thought I'd clean up some of my back office projects while I'm stuck here at home."

"Good thinking, 'migo," said Scott.

"Problem is, I'm completely locked out of my work files. I need all the personal data for a bunch of asylum-seekers." He swiped Scott with the list. The name of Joyful Kalinga was buried deep inside it. "Mind snagging it for me tomorrow?"

"No problemo."

"And I could use some 'Stim to help me get through all this boring shit."

"Awesome," said Scott, obviously impatient to get back to his gaming. "OK, meet me at the Micky's across the street tomorrow at lunch and I'll hook you up. Just don't get me blown up too, amigo, ha ha."

As he ported away, one of the mutants, a huge blue-green bio-mechanoid monster with a number of extra weapons and external organs, waved at Obama fondly. "It's Camille from the office," a message followed him. "Hi, Obama; what's up?" He ignored it. The message balloon hung around optimistically for a while, started to sulk, and then disappeared back into Grimbo.

Porting through the Grid was like flying through a million flickering photo-show frames at hyperspeed. In theory Grimbo was infinite. In practice, only as much of the Grid as had been constructed by programmers and modders actually existed. At first, it had been believed that all of the Gaming and Social Networking Worlds could exist on a single digitized simulacrum of the Earth and Moon, each overlaid on top of the others like parallel universes. It had soon become evident that this model simply hadn't included enough real estate, and additional planetary systems and even galaxies began to spring up around hundreds of alternate Earths. To make matters worse, the original planetary coding had been done using legacy languages, and it was already crumbling under the weight of all the sophisticated data demands of the newer games in much the same way that the physical infrastructure of the real planet had deteriorated under heavy use. So the trick was to stay portable once you were onGrid and not get stuck in data traffic.

Back doors and worm-holes existed everywhere in order to speed this process up, so that in time most of the gaming population was more or less clustered on the Grid inside the same types of virtual urban centers that they inhabited in real life. Part of the reason for this was simple lack of imagination — people were most comfortable inside environments they were familiar with — and part of it was the realism of the gaming experience. In the early days, gaming worlds were just visual representations on a screen, but now that gaming had become completely subjective, it was easy to become psychotically disoriented by exotic environments.

Most people played it safe. The older he got, the more Obama did, too, he found. So he tended to stick to the generic "City Center" model as a central portal whenever he was exploring unknown social neighborhoods. The default skin for his was Manacera City, and he'd never bothered to change it.

Of course, the virtual version of Manacera City didn't correspond precisely to the real one. Only the versions of the really rich big cities like Tokyo, New York, or Milan did, because they paid big Unos to private companies to scan and model them down to near-molecular level. The arcade in front of the fake Retro Center, for example, more closely resembled that of the Rue de Rivoli in Paris, and was filled with shops like Mikki Moto's and Nonpareil that didn't exist in North America.

Some didn't exist in reality at all. The Capitol Building, whose crumbling ruins the UN had refused to restore in real life, was based on the original version onGrid. A few fantastically corkscrewed skyscrapers graced the horizon, along with the spires and turrets of a "Ten Flags," and about 70% of the pedestrians and seggers on the sidewalks, or floating or flying above them, were vividly costumed "daemons," artificial gaming AI constructs. Still, it shouldn't have come as a total surprise to Obama when, once he came out of the portal, he spotted the Indonesian-looking "Wiiboot" HELP guy from a virtual block away. Obama was so shocked that he came to a dead stop. By the time he had ported forward through the crowd, the guy had disappeared.

What was a homeless — Habitation-Eliminated — person doing onGrid? Obama couldn't shake the feeling for the rest of the night that it had been a sign or portent of some kind, just as it had turned out to be on the day Kim had been "disappeared."

Because all Federal office buildings contained mandated elementary skools and daycare centers, the Micky D across the street from MAD was always half full of screaming kids. Lunch was a moveable — sometimes even a forgettable — feast for Scott, so Obama arrived too early and soon got bored and restless. His messages piled up on Scott's iTooth unanswered. Where was he? Finally, Obama started getting hungry and decided to go ahead and order.

The failed merger between the McDonald's and Walt Disney corporations, broken up by the UN's Antitrust Division, meant that Micky's had been forced in desperation to staff its counters with replacement cartoon figures owned by other companies. The squat three-dimensional avatar who took Obama's order was both unrecognizable and incomprehensible. "Don't you know who I am, son?" it demanded truculently when Obama refused to order extra sea-fries.

"Um, no."

"Yosemite Sam, thassoo!"

"Well, I recognized Yuri the Bear, anyway," Obama said defensively. He wished he was at a Bro' King instead. They still had Eenie and Meenie from the "Three Stupid Wombrats" cartoons working behind the counter.

He was in the middle of his second OrgasMeal (unavailable for pre-skoolers) when Camille Lyonesse hurried in through the front doors, looking flushed and slightly out of breath. She peered around until she spotted Obama, then came over and sat in the green sanitary pedestal across from him. Every single sexual minority in the place — gay, dom, sub, bi, tranza, and 'buser — had turned to stare at her hungrily.

Obama had forgotten just how attractive the womyn was. He felt like he could almost scent some powerful musk she gave off like a wild animal. Her too-perfect, normally slightly spoiled features looked radiant today, as if the mere sight of him was suffusing them with happiness. "What happened to you?" she asked in astonishment. "What's wrong with your face?"

"I got caught in the bombing yesterday," he told her.

"Wow, how awful! But you're OK now?"

"I guess."

"Scott couldn't make it," she went on in a conspiratorial tone. "Carmen's got him slammed in her office right now, so I snuck off and came to see you instead. Hope you don't mind."

He mumbled something with his mouth full. Who was she anyway? Where had she even come from? He'd never been able to figure her out. Overlaying the soft Botticelli lines, her face had a sharp, clever Hindu cast to it, as did her dark, honey-colored complexion. But where had the Titian hair, which he'd bet was completely natural, come from? Or the blue eyes? Or the flat Mid-American accent? Why wasn't she in Holowood? Why was she an Admin instead of a major sim star on the Grid? She was way too good to be true. And she wasn't dumb, either — she seemed far smarter than Carmen. And Carmen was eerily shrewd. What did Camille really want from him? It was all a big mystery — and he was hardly the only person in the office who felt that way. But they weren't at the office now.

"I brought the data you wanted," she told him sweetly, almost humbly. They swiped iRists to transfer it. "Oh, and this." She slipped him a baggie which he assumed contained the 'Stim. "Just let me know if there's anything else you need. I mean, anything at all I can do for you, Bammy. Scott told me what happened — I can't stand to think of you all alone at home." She reached across the remains of the Happy Meals and touched his hand.

"Thanks," he said, unable to meet her eyes.

"No, I really mean it." She sounded sincere. "I'd be happy to come over and cook for you. Or clean the place up. I know it must be super tough for you right now." "Cook" for him? Nobody did that anymore; it was dialogue straight out of an old flat-screen movie. But he found, to his shamed amazement, that he had half an erection just from all this attention from her. People said you could get them from the real pork in the OrgasMeal, but that was just advertising hype; it had definitely been Camille.

On the way home Obama tried to figure out exactly why he hadn't invited her over. *I mean, aside from the fact that Kim's only been gone three days,* he thought. Yet it was also true that he was beginning to feel physically lonely — and that some part of him knew he was probably going to end up having to start his life all over again sooner or later. Reboot it. Why not sooner? Why not with Camille? It was obvious she really, really liked him. Most guys would kill just for a chance just to have sex with her. Much less have her cook for them. What was wrong with him?

It was, he decided, that a rebound relationship with her sort of felt like it was the last item on Mrs. Housmanzadeh's twelve-stages-of-grief checklist. In fact, it was almost as if the Federal Grand Jury Protection Program had hired Camille Lyonesse to play the part.

A hologram pixilated into life just in front of him on the Retro car. It was an ad for the new UN initiative to replace all hexagonal recyclable containers with octahedrons by the end of the decade. "Remember, Eight is Great!" a scantily clad Slavic girl smirked seductively at him.

Something else was bothering him now, too. He didn't feel like himself. He literally didn't feel like he was Obama Jones any more. Or maybe it was just that he didn't want to be Obama Jones any more, for the foreseeable future, anyway; the gentle, sweet-faced, uncomplaining guy who got grief (and grief counseling) from everybody. *Obama Jones,* he thought. *The bright and dependable, if unambitious and, let's face it, unimaginative public servant. Obama Jones the good citizen, who never complained, never protested, never even cheated on his taxes. Obama Jones, the regular Jose.*

Tonight he wanted to be somebody else. Somebody dark and vengeful and dangerous, moving silently on a desperate solitary mission through the streets of the city at night. An evil genius, a desperado, a shambling primal force for destruction who could walk through walls, who would blackmail and intimidate and steal — and even kill — in order to get Kim back. An avenger. A lone wolf. Not a myn, but a man. A man called Joyful Kalinga.

Obama was sick of being lonely and weak and miserable. He was going to be Joyful, he decided. Even if it killed him...

5.

Joyful Kalinga would be the opposite of Obama Jones. Whatever Obama was, Joyful wasn't. Obama used the stodgy, reliable Nortelia; Joyful opened a dodgy Qwerizon account. Obama accessed WiiLive; Joyful spoofed a feed over the seedy and disreputable 'Softworld. Obama only used a little 'Stim now and then; Joyful chronically chewed khat, drank alcohol, and smoked ganja. Obama was polite and shy; Joyful happily leered at every womyn he met.

By UN law all world citizens had the inalienable right to travel, live, and work anywhere on the planet. In practice, however, most of the world's former nations still enforced fairly strict immigration policies, reflecting the harsh realities of a globally managed economy. Generally speaking, only the most genetically endangered, politically repressed, or physically handicapable minority members were granted fast-track Green status. Obviously this would have to be the case for Joyful Kalinga. There was absolutely no data on him inside the Green Resident file that Obama had opened and then got back officially from MAD — only blank entry fields. Obama was free to make up whatever he liked.

He decided that Kalinga would be about 5 years older and 10 kg or so heavier than he — he had been losing weight over Kim — so eating enough to hover somewhere between the two weights, his own and the imaginary Kalinga's, would provide him with a worthy goal. Obviously, they were the same height and had the same eye and skin coloring. Occupation? "Political Prisoner." Education? Kalinga was a gangster, a toughened guerilla fighter forged in the ethnic ghettoes of Harare; Obama typed in "Hi Skool" (currently the official designation for K-12 equivalency at the Department of Education).

Marital status? Three concurrent wives, locations unknown. Probably perished under torture at the hands of the ZLA. He chose three first names for them at random out of a Soweto iTooth Directory. Children? Also three, he decided, one dead from disease, the other two believed missing (here he listed a vanished UNARM case worker as a contact). Special skills? Kalinga was a killer, trained in the use of the knife, the garrote, and a variety of weapons including assault rifles and hand-held missiles. For good measure Obama added a lengthy prison record and "HIV-Positive" under Personal Health. The last thing he wanted was for Joyful Kalinga to be offered a job. Although, he reflected cynically, he'd seen senior staff openings at MAD, as well as faculty positions at universities, filled from resumes much like this one.

"Enriched Standard Language skills: Poor" should help. He would have to remember to speak with a heavy African accent while in character as Kalinga — and ignore anyone who attempted to speak Nshona to him. He would pretend he could speak only Ndebele. What he would do if anyone insisted on speaking Ndebele at him, he didn't know. Drool, maybe. Obama opened a credit account for Kalinga at Citibanc and laundered several thousand Unos into it via Sony SeventhLife's "Gaming Dollars." He forwarded Kalinga's iTooth calls to a dummy Gridmail account, created his iFace, and activated his iRist. The man was almost ready to walk out on his own.

Obama next spent a day or two playing with Kalinga's appearance, then had himself scanned at a local parlor for the official onGrid biometrics. At a charity stall he'd bought a shiny dark blue suit that appeared to have once been a rented wedding tuxedo. It still had a huge greasy hand-print on one shoulder that had never been laundered out. Transparent socks, pointed alligator shoes. He shaved his head and bought some costume dentures with fake gold fillings onGrid. Then he used glue to simulate facial scarring and covered himself with temporary epithelial dye tattoos. Fingerprints were easy to fake; he'd bought a kit for fun as a teenager. Retinal scans and DNA remained a problem, however — all he could do for Kalinga's profile was to use his own and hope the duplication was never properly checked. These could at least be kept offGrid. He hoped.

Kalinga's gaming avatar became a variation of his real life appearance but with added height and weight, gold teeth filed to sharp points, red eyes, lurid facial scars and tats, a wide-brimmed black hat, a shoulder-holstered Smith & Wesson, and body armor worn under a long black duster coat. He kept the orange alligator shoes. The last time Obama Jones had designed a gaming "skin" from scratch was back in his hi skool days. He found himself enjoying it. For an hour or two, he even stopped thinking about Kim. Then he crashed from the 'Stim and lost interest in everything else.

The problem was he'd also lost track of time, and it was now the weekend. Freedom from religion — except for Muslims, of course — had long been considered a basic humyn right, enshrined in law. Consequently, attempts to "dereligulate" the Christian calendar had been attempted by some UN agencies as early as 2017. At first the old Esperanto names had been used — "Lundo," "Mardo," etc. — but these had proved wildly unpopular. Besides, they were still based on the names of pagan gods. Eventually, the names of the week had been renamed "Oneday," "Twosday," "Threesday," "Foursday," "Fiveday," "Slackerday," and "Gameday." Kim had been taken away on a Twosday and Obama had been suspended from his job on a Threesday. It was now Slackerday, and Obama found himself too demoralized and listless even to get out of bed. Mrs. Housmanzadeh's nagging, it seemed, had at least served some purpose — without it, he had no compelling reason to get up. Or to open his eyes at all.

When, finally goaded by hunger, he'd staggered out of bed and into the living room around sunset to the electronic racket of the local muezzin, he booted up and discovered he'd stranded Joyful Kalinga idling on AI-mode the night before inside a room of some social role-playing game. Half a dozen womyn had left their iTooth numbers in his drop-box and two were still trying to score with him automagically. It was unlikely all of them really were womyn, of course, but the fact was that even when he wasn't even actually there, Joyful was already doing better at parties than he, Obama, ever had. It was depressing. Even scary. No way was he ever going to let Camille meet the 'migo. She'd never be off his back.

"Oh my goodness, yes!" the AI Joyful was saying to them now. "Joyful soon be loving you inside that sweet ass of yours! And your fine sistah too." Yikes! What else had he been saying? Obama had used a generic South African Xhosa inflection agent dialed up to its least coherent Enriched ,and had let the AI respond autonomously to external conversation overnight. Of course, it was more than possible that every avatar in the room was either a daemon or else on AI mode, too. And hopefully, no one there had the resources to trace Joyful back to him. Still, it was embarrassing.

But why should it be? he thought, as he slipped back into Joyful's skin. Six years ago, at Obama's first job for the state-owned Unibanc, he'd shared a cube with a South African guy named Eugene. Eugene had been a full-blooded Zulu and easily the politest and most studious person Obama had ever met, quieter even than Obama was himself. But once, on a corporate retreat, some of the junior staffers had conspired to get Eugene drunk on real old-time Russian vodka. Suddenly he had unleashed at the giggling womyn around him a string of the most amazingly sexist obscenities Obama had ever heard. Most of it Obama had mercifully forgotten, but now he strained to remember exactly what Eugene had said to them.

Eugene had had another quirk, too. Whenever someone first greeted him, he'd reply, "Yaybo," which he'd said was Zulu for "hello." Then, if a second person said hello, he'd repeat "Yaybo" in exactly the same pleasant tone. But if one *more* person did after that, he'd erupt in a blood-curdling multi-syllabic tribal whoop during the third "Yaybo" so that it came out as "YeeeayyyeeaayyeayBO!"

Now he was suddenly Joyful, Obama decided to try to channel the drunken Eugene, even as he found himself saying, "First we go some play some sexy games, OK, pussy-pie?" The two womyn continued to ogle him. One was wearing a demure black cocktail dress and looked like a film noir siren, with half her wavy blonde hair hanging over one heavily mascaraed eye; the other resembled an 18th-century court vampiress from a sim. She was wearing a powdered wig, and they were both smoking cigarettes laced with ganja. The party was being held inside a room that appeared to be a virtual version of the Space Station lounge from the *2051: A Space Odyssey* sim/game series. Of course the mirror image of the vampiress was missing from the reflections in the panoramic vista portholes, but Obama was momentarily startled to notice in them how totally unlike himself he looked. *Nobody would recognize me now,* he thought.

"Hot," the vampiress coolly observed, blowing smoke. "Want to go back to our place?" Evidently they were a team. They were most likely either daemons, he thought, or else a middle-aged married couple from Europe or the American Midwest. The illusion of reality was so great he could smell the make-up and sweat on their bodies, mixed with perfume, and hear the rustle of their gowns. He knew it wasn't real, but he felt himself becoming aroused.

"Not yet, oh my, no! Joyful love that high life, oh my yes! He want to go play games with dice and a big wheel. I feel some big money coming to me tonight, mamma jugs! Joyful very lucky man, maybe you get good luck rubbing on you. And your sistah, too."

The two "womyn" stared at each other. "We could go to the casino," said the blonde. Obama got the feeling she was in charge.

Casino Royale was the most famous gambling spot in the world — even more famous than Harrah's Oceans 24/7 — and the hardest to get into. But tonight they ported right into the opulent front lobby past the credit sensors. Not on Joyful's account, he thought — obviously his two new friends were extremely rich. Or well-connected. Or were pieces of code belonging to someone who was. Why he'd demanded to go gambling at all he couldn't say; maybe he'd played too many *James Bond Agent 007* sims as a kid. It had just seemed like the kind of place where he might be able to buy some information. Or overhear it.

The problem was, most of the bugs and sensors he'd threaded into Joyful's skin wouldn't work in here. They'd be jammed by the casino-hotel's security. He wouldn't even be able to run a search-and-decryption agent later through their data to find out who'd been pinging him all evening, though there was an upside to that — no one could run a thorough trace-route on him, either.

"Let's see just how lucky you are," said the blonde one, who — according to the scrap of conversation he'd had the chance to scroll back through — had introduced herself at the party as "Simonetta." She took his arm and possessively led him between the arched lobby doorway into the main casino. The other womyn, "Gracia," took Simonetta's free hand, scooping up a pile of white chips along the way and dumping them into Joyful's massive palm. They were cold and hard to the touch, like Go stones. "You don't even like gambling," the blonde told the vampiress dismissively.

"True. I'm only here for the sex ... sistah." The two womyn glared at each other, and Gracia bared her teeth; it all seemed like part of a rehearsed act. At this point he was supposed to bare his own and roar at them both to shut up. How did he know this? It was as though Joyful were really taking him over. Obama found he had absolutely no idea what Joyful was going to say or do next. Well, that was the whole idea, wasn't it? To let Joyful be Joyful and shake things up? An elderly steward in a powdered wig and knee-stockings smoothly intercepted the three of them as they approached the crowded huge main roulette table.

"What will you be playing tonight, young mistresses?" he inquired disapprovingly.

"Big wheels, daddy," said Simonetta. As the steward gently cleared a place for them to stand beside the table, she leaned over to bite Obama's ear. Over the noise of clacking machines, clinking ice, and the buzz of conversation she whispered into it, "Can you guess what Gracia really is?"

Obama shrugged. "A demon? You husband?"

"My pet," she said. "I own her."

"Hey, I can hear you!" protested Gracia loudly.

"You can be replaced, darling. Maybe I'll replace you with Joyful."

"Joyful will decide that," he said coldly. He was a man, Obama remembered, used to juggling three wives. He caught sight of their reflections suddenly on the tabletop and realized he might be in trouble tonight. The security coding here was far more powerful than he'd first realized. Normally a user's skin was flexible, adapting to different roles inside different games. Some people changed theirs as often as they changed their clothes. But you were always in control of your own skin.

Not here, though — it was like being inside a sim, where you lived the same assigned parts as everybody else. The programming language that built and protected this place had altered all three of them without their consent, restoring Gracia's reflection and fixing her teeth. Fixing his own teeth, as well, and removing his hat, coat, and armament. For all he knew, it had removed his scars and tattoos, too, and now he was Obama again.

No. He peered at the back of his hand and saw a curl of tattooing still there. He was back to wearing his blue tuxedo, though — with the oily handprint. Only Simonetta was unaltered. He glanced around, meeting the curious stares of other people at the gaming table; they were, he saw, all dressed extremely formally and sported few of the monstrous mutations, bright colors, and ornamental excesses they might have elsewhere in the Grid. And no weapons, of course, including pointy teeth. Several of the others nodded at him or said hello. He raised his voice. "Yaybo, I am Joyful Kalinga. 'Kalinga' — that mean 'Tears of the Gods!'" Did it? He had no idea. A few of the men laughed appreciatively, at any rate, and a womyn clapped. He leered politely at her.

"Gentlemen. Ladies. Please place your bets," announced the Allura Sensex croupier. For a moment he was reminded of Kim again, then quickly shook away the thought. He didn't want any of Kim inside Joyful's head. But why a robot, here of all places? Obviously the croupier would be a daemon, but that could be coded to look like anyone. Why in this case would art so slavishly imitate life — particularly when the roles were reversed in reality? Maybe it was an expression of contempt by the management. Or irony.

But few other concessions had been made to real life. Once, back in his college days, Obama had visited the virtual Caesar's Palace Casino;

it had aped the retro look of the real Las Vegas, with thousands of ceiling lights everywhere and different gaming tables crowded together. This room was the size of a sports arena, with a high domed ceiling covered by a Canaletto fresco emitting its own discreet illumination, ringed by storeys of baroque arched porphyry and marble columns, beyond which the Venetian night was clearly visible, distant flickering globular lights and dark gondolas bobbing on the canal waters.

Gracia's was the only costume that seemed quite at home here. Everything inside the casino seemed to float, too. The gaming tables hovered above a sea-green marble floor, gleaming translucent ovals carved from jade and purplish quartz, their numbered token grids etched in gold and silver. Yacht-sized chandeliers of radiant white crystal drifted above them. Transparent holo guides to the rest of the complex spun silently in front of you wherever you walked. To the side, small courts had been set up for card games and dining, discreetly bounded by potted palms; there were lounges for smokers and drinkers and even diners. If not for the holographic election debates and football games visible above a few of these, the place might have been mistaken for an Italian cathedral.

Kim would have loved it. Aside from old flat-screen movies, her other passion in life had been art history. But here he was thinking about Kim again.

The Kim look-alike Allura robot spun the wheel; the glittering ball rattled loudly around inside it, then rolled and guttered to settle on black. Without Obama noticing, Joyful had placed the entire pile of chips in his hand on a black square. The robot glanced up at him.

"Mmmm ... you *are* lucky," murmured Gracia, kissing his other ear.

His luck held for an hour. Then two. Red, black, odd, even; it didn't seem to matter. He would go on brief losing streaks, but mostly he won. The pile of chips grew and grew on the table in front of him. He chortled with delight. He roared. He kissed the womyn whenever he won another big pile. By now half the table was imitating his bets, and a small crowd had gathered to watch. Finally the robot stopped and just stared at him. The steward materialized and said something to Simonetta in a foreign language.

"He says that's all for you tonight. The house has a limit with new customers."

"And I break it? Ha!" There was a mutinous muttering among his followers at the table. He raised his voice back to a roar: "Joyful big man tonight! Drinks for everybody, Kalinga pay! You want nice drinks, khat, bhang, kif, or ganja, whatever, Joyful Kalinga pay for all! Who this big man? What his name?" He wagged a big forefinger at them.

"Joyful Kalinga!" the crowd shouted back.

"YeeeayyyeeaayyeayBO!" Bellowing with merry laughter, he stuffed his pockets with chips and, accepting a cigar, paused while Gracia lit it for him. *Thank god for Eugene,* he thought. Suddenly, he felt hot, itchy, slightly drunk. Something was wrong; he didn't know what. And he was tired of these two "womyn." He managed to ditch them for a moment and snuck out through one of the outside porticoes to stare out over the canal. He finished his drink, a rum Collins, then tossed the cigar into the dark waters that lapped realistically at the mossy stone beneath his feet. He hated the taste.

He became aware of a dark figure standing near him. It was a myn: short, solidly built, in late middle age, wearing a black tuxedo and white tie. Looking closer, Obama suddenly realized it was the bum from Retro Center, the "Wiiboot" guy. The guy he'd spent part of an afternoon looking for. The long frizzy hair was slightly greyer, and he seemed maybe a decade older. But it was definitely the same person. He started to speak to him, then choked. He had "met" the myn in real life as Obama Jones, not Joyful Kalinga.

"Good evening," he said finally.

"Excuse preez, no Enguh-reesh," the man said, his eyes crinkling up. "You wait preez?" He poked his left ear in the universal 'Babelfish' gesture, then waited for the translation agent to load. Obama decided to do the same, so that he might be able to deal with the man comprehensibly. He loaded "American to British Enriched," then added the Xhosa filter dialed all the way down for good measure. Hopefully no one would notice he wasn't accessing Ndebele. "Ah, that's better," said the man, smiling thinly and bowing. "I am Sato Shiseki. Welcome to my hotel."

"Your hotel?" said Obama, surprised.

"Yes. You have won a great deal of my money tonight, Mr. Kalinga."

Obama couldn't think of anything to say to this. "Sorry about that," he replied at last. "Would you like it back?"

Mr. Sato — or was it Mr. Shiseki? — stared at him with hard eyes for a moment, then suddenly smiled again with real warmth. "You are a funny man. No, no, you keep it. I have more. Come, I'll give you a tour of the building while we talk." He grasped Obama's — Joyful's — arm almost painfully and ported them both onto the roof. A radiant glow rose up all around them into the night from the vast dome. Their footsteps echoed on the stone terrace around it like rifle shots. Looking down, Obama found he could see straight into the casino. Looking up, he could see stars. But his host steered him over to the balcony of a loggia covered in plants and vines climbing up trellises. Below, all the city lay sprawling beneath them, its canals pin-pricked out by light. The watery horizon extended several kilometers in every direction, then seemed to boil away in mist.

"Beautiful, isn't it?" said Sato. "This environment is unconnected with the rest of the Grid. It can only be accessed by porting. In other words, no one can come or go here without my permission." The Babelfish now gave his English an accent like one of the "Restored Posh" royal family.

"That's very impressive, mate. And ... unusual. Isn't it?" Obama, on the other hand, sounded like a soccer player.

"Unique, in fact. This is the only virtual island onGrid. It's a little luxury I allow myself. You see, Mr. Kalinga, I invented this." He waved at the glittering city around them. "I created all the code you see around you on the Grid. Of course, most of it already existed before I came along, but it was I who invented a common platform for it all. At that time I was Vice President of Engineering for Sony. But I screwed them contractually. Now every time someone boots up, I make another Uno." He smiled ruefully. "So as you might imagine, I really don't care about money anymore. I live very simply and traditionally anyway. I am much older than I look."

A moth flew around Obama's head, smacking against him, and was framed for a moment against the full Moon when he batted it away. "A nice touch," he told Sato. The cool breeze brought with it all the heavy smells of the city: the stinking warm ferment of the canal water, sewage, cooking spices, old stones, fennel, and wood-smoke.

"Yes, I'm afraid I included mosquitoes, as well — even maggots and bacterial parasites. I have always had an obsession for recreating nature precisely. For playing god. Now, tell me, Mr. Kalinga, why are you here tonight? What do you really want? I cannot believe you are here merely because you want to sleep with my daughter."

There was a sudden clicking of high heels, and Simonetta and Gracia came sleepily trailing out of the shadows into the Moonlight. Simonetta had changed her hair color from blonde to black, and Obama suddenly imagined he could see a resemblance between her and the man standing beside him. *Ridiculous!* he thought. *These people wouldn't be using their real appearances onGrid.* If they were even actual people. If he were constructing a daemon to host a place like this, this is exactly the script he would run. Sato was probably just a Sony "Easter Egg" or "Logic Bomb," as hidden code was still commonly called.

"No," he said, shrugging, stung back into being Joyful by the presence of the womyn. "One vagina is just like another."

Sato laughed uproariously at this, rocking back and forth on his heels, his eyes creased like a peasant's. "All right, what can I do for you then?" Simonetta came and took Obama's hand, as if what he'd just said had been an enormous compliment, and both "father" and "daughter" stared at him without blinking.

"I'm so bored," complained Gracia behind them. These types of inappropriate, deflected, or even random responses were typical of daemon AIs. But somewhere, someone would be listening.

"You should think of me as a spy or secret agent, Mr. Sato," said Obama. "I want information. Information that's kept someplace secret by our government."

"I see," said Sato. "And what do you have to pay for this information?"

Obama rattled the gambling chips in one of his pockets. "Money?" he said. Sato shook his head pityingly.

"I can get you any information you want, Mr. Kalinga," he said. "Come back and see me when you have something valuable to trade for it in return." He held up the palm of his hand, exactly as the vagrant outside the Retro station had done, to forestall comment. It even looked like exactly the same hand, but this one had a manicure. "You'll know what that is when you have it. Now I must say goodnight." He bowed again, then leaned forward to kiss Simonetta. "Wiiboot," he said. Then he vanished.

"We play sex now?" asked Gracia loudly.

6.

On Oneday morning, Obama Jones was scheduled to report to Mrs. Housmanzadeh in the Federal Courthouse Complex for the next-to-last installment of his grief counseling. It took him a while to find her office, because it had been moved down to a lower floor near the main lobby. He decided not to mention to her the advent of Joyful Kalinga in his life. It was up to Mrs. Housmanzadeh whether he could now be probationally released from his grief, or whether he might have to complete another week — or even another month —of it. He felt instinctively that she wouldn't understand about Joyful. However, she seemed surprised, perhaps even taken aback, by his answer when she asked him how his weekend had gone.

"'Good'?" she repeated, frowning.

"Well, I feel I made some excellent progress with closure," he said.

"How did you spend this time?" she asked suspiciously. He did not say "whoring and gaming." Nor did he mention that he'd come home with nearly a quarter of a million Unos worth of Gaming Dollars, which he'd instantly converted to real money.

"Oh, you know. Role-playing on the Grid. Thinking about my work. I guess I realized that a lot of people in the world are worse off than me." For a moment or two he wasn't sure she was buying this, but at last she nodded grudgingly and assigned him a support group sim to experience, all about the survivors of the Diablo Canyon nuclear reactor disaster. It was at that moment the building exploded.

This time the blast was far closer and more powerful than the market bombing had been. Obama was aware for an instant of a disturbance in the air around him, as if powerful fan jets were whipping it around in every direction. Then there was a deafening roar, and the floor buckled up and rose around them. Simultaneously, he felt a searing blast of heat and flame that came surging through the cube walls like a huge hot wave, tearing most of his clothes off.

The ferro-concrete floor collapsed. Obama fell through it to lie on a mound of rubble on the ground floor, groaning and half-naked. Debris rained down all around him, some of it tiny and needle-sharp, and instinctively he flung a protective arm over his eyes to ward it off. When he felt the rain slacken, he opened his eyes again and saw Mrs. Housmanzadeh lying a few dozen centimeters away. She was spasming uncontrollably and covered in sparks that flickered up and down her clothing like tiny fireflies. He tried to speak her name and reached an arm out to her; she gazed at him sightlessly. Her mouth opened and closed as if she were trying to tell him something, but he couldn't hear it. He realized he'd become completely deaf.

He took her twitching hand and saw that she'd been torn nearly in half by the force of the blast. There was blood everywhere. Suddenly, he decided that some of it must surely be his, too. The thought made him faint.

For the next few minutes he passed in and out of consciousness. He was aware of being very hot — his face and hands felt scorched and singed — and of pain in his legs and lower back. At one point someone's face arrived in his field of vision and mouthed questions at him which he couldn't comprehend. It was annoying. He closed his eyes and dozed off. Later he half-woke again with a splitting headache. He was being moved. He became vaguely embarrassed that he might urinate involuntarily. He felt as though he were floating. He was outside now, and the bright sunlight hurt his eyes. He saw faces staring at him, sidewalk paving-stones, sticky-nets everywhere, the moving arms and backs of SWATCops' gleaming black body armor. Siren lights were blinking and spinning, casting moving psychedelic stripes of light and color over everything in dead silence. The metal doors of an airbulance were opened in front of him, and he floated noiselessly into the vehicle between them. Something was jabbed into his arm, and he fell asleep.

He woke up groaning and dehydrated, strapped to a medical gurney in a deserted hospital corridor. The hall was painted a faded green. A fly lazily circled, then began to bat itself against the light panels overhead. His head hurt and he felt very cold. His neck was restrained by some kind of strap. So, he discovered when he tried to move them, were his wrists and ankles. He managed to peer down at himself, and saw that his body was covered in peeling burns, like the body of a nuclear blast victim.

He started trembling with terror. Where were the nurses and orderlies? A security cam crawled slowly up the wall beside him on its spider-legs, then stopped and swiveled both of its lenses in his direction. He heard the sound of footsteps echoing from down the hallway. *At least I'm not deaf,* he thought, uselessly trying to cock his head to look around. The footsteps came closer. The faces of two heavy middle-aged men, one Asian, the other Middle Eastern, suddenly intruded into his field of vision, to gaze down at him indifferently. One stood to his side, the other at his feet. They were both dressed in street clothes and wore rumpled ivory-colored overcoats.

"My name is Park Cha," said the Asian man. "And this is Al Malek. We are Detective Inspectors with the Department of Health and Humyn Services. We'd like to ask you a few questions, Mr. Kalinga. About bombs."

"My name isn't Kalinga!" Obama said guiltily. "It's Jones. Obama Jones." He couldn't feel his iRist, and when he tried to access his iTooth, he discovered it had either been removed or disconnected. He felt lost and even more naked without them.

Inspector Park stared at him impassively. "We know who you are. Your name is Joyful Kalinga. On Slackerday night somebody paid you UN 250,000. Then this morning you leave a manbag filled with Lastex in the north lobby of the Dorhn Federal Courthouse Building. In addition, your iRist was detected at the Madam's Organ bombing, and we have security cam files placing you at the scene."

"No! I'm Obama Jones! I can prove it — just call my supervisor, Carmen Crowfoot at MAD. Or check my biometrics." Where was his iRist? He'd left Kalinga's at home. The last thing he needed was for them to search his apartment again. Maybe he was better off saying nothing. But obviously they already knew plenty — about Joyful's gambling winnings, for one thing.

The other policeman, Malek, was shaking his head. "What we want to know is just how much Lastex was in that bag, how you detonated it, where you processed it, and who you bought it from. We want to know who hired or recruited you for the job. We want names and contacts. What we don't want is to waste our time listening to bullshit about how you're really somebody else."

"Do you have any idea of how many innocent people you killed today, Mr. Kalinga?" Park asked him in a conversational tone. He sounded almost pleasant. "HHS employees just like us? At least a hundred, maybe more. You can be very, very proud — it was the deadliest suicide bombing here in almost a decade. It should have killed you, too. And yet you managed to survive it."

"Yeah, so you're gonna be famous now," said Malek.

"You'll get interviews on YouVee news, maybe your own sim and game deals," continued Park. "You'll do a few years of anger management at a Federal facility, then maybe community service. You'll be able to retire after that and live a life of luxury in a protection program. All at UN expense. So why not just tell us what we want to know, so we can go home — and you can get some proper medical attention."

"Where — where are all the doctors and nurses?" Obama asked.

"There aren't any," said Park. "We're the only ones here. And you. We'll be looking after you." Both men took off their coats. Park handed his to Malek, who sighed and then disappeared out of Obama's sight. "We were both really hoping to go home on time tonight, Mr. Kalinga. I guess we should have known better."

"I swear to you I'm not named Kalinga! My name is Obama Jones — check my records! I haven't bombed anybody! I swear!" He sounded lame even to himself. Malek reappeared wearing a butcher's apron and pushing a cart carrying what appeared to be surgical instruments. He tossed a second apron to Park, who tied it on. Both men snapped their hands into yellowish medical gloves. "What are you doing?" Obama asked.

Park leaned over to look into Obama's face, closely, so that Obama could see the dark grey hairs on his mustache. "We're going to interrogate you. Under duress. Until you tell us what we want to know."

"But torture's illegal! It's against the UN Covenant!" Obama said. His face was suddenly bathed in sweat. If this were just an act they were putting on in order to scare him, it was working.

The two policemen sighed again and looked at each other. Park said, "I don't think it will take much, do you? Honestly? Considering the condition you're already in?" Park reached down and poked the burns on Obama's thigh. Obama screamed. "Our biggest challenge," continued Park, "will be to keep you from dying while we're working on you.

"Let me explain to you how torture works, Mr. Kalinga — though my guess is you've seen plenty of it already. From both sides of the glass. See, on YouVee or the sims people are always holding out against it. That's a Holowood myth. They can't. Nobody can. You'll tell us exactly what we want to hear, trust me — everybody does in the end.

There is a trick to withstanding it for a while, though. They taught it to us as kids in the work camps in North Korea. You just say to yourself, 'I won't tell them anything until I count to 100.' Then, if you manage to get up to 90 or so, you say to yourself, 'OK, I got this far — let's see if I can make it to 90 again.' It's the only way to keep going, believe me. But I'm thinking you're too stupid to know how to count that high."

"I think we should start with the burns," Malek interrupted. "Come on, I'm still hoping to make it home in time for supper and my game."

"Teeth and nails first, Malek," said Park. "You know the drill."

The problem with Park and Malek, it occurred to Obama after he'd managed to survive his first few minutes — or maybe hours — of interrogation by them, was that basically that they'd both been doing this job too long. Neither man was imaginative enough to ask him the right questions. If they had, by now he'd have told them everything he knew — the whole truth, and nothing but the truth. He would have told them about Kim's jury duty, and about his attempts to trace her. He would have told them how he'd invented Joyful Kalinga, and every detail of the man's imaginary existence, including the code to open his credit accounts. But they didn't ask. They had a mental checklist of questions, just as the grief counselors did, and the answers to those questions were all they were interested in. They didn't want to know anything else.

So: he'd already confessed to being Joyful Kalinga, born in Zimbabwe to a lifetime of violent crime, trained as a terrorist and thug. He'd also confessed to both bombings and basically to anything else they'd asked him. He'd grassed out Freedom and Osama X as his contacts, and accused poor Mrs. Housmanzadeh of having recruited him for the Warriors of God terrorist group. He'd babbled anything that had come into his head. Every false detail or absurd piece of embroidery he has been able to think of had meant forestalling the return of the pain just that much longer. Because the pain was way beyond anything he'd ever imagined. Time seemed to contract, to stand still, to lose all objective meaning. Had they given him 'Stim?

Sometimes he seemed to hear a sound echoing against the hospital walls. Obama couldn't tell what the sound was exactly, but he didn't want to think it was that of a humyn voice — because a humyn shouldn't sound like that. He especially didn't want to think it was his own.

Somewhere an iRist chimed. After a moment Obama heard Malek's voice, as if from a great distance, saying, "Fucking hell! The ID check finally came back. The retinal scans and the DNA didn't match. This asshole really is Obama fucking Jones." Park said nothing. Obama thought, *My retinal scans and DNA don't match Kalinga's? How did that happen? I duplicated them myself.* "So what the hell do we do with him now?" Malek asked.

Suddenly Obama figured it out. He only wished he'd thought of it sooner. How could he have been so dumb? How would you go about torturing somebody without torturing them? How would you extract information from somebody illegally while technically obeying the United Nations Convention Against Torture, Articles 1-33? "Detach," he mumbled weakly. "Detach. Reboot." When half your teeth are missing and your mouth is full of blood, that last word comes out "Wiiboot." He'd been onGrid, or at least on some kind of Grid, the whole time. As the corridor vanished, he found himself wondering, *Was this how Sato came up with the term in the first place? After being tortured?*

He found himself in Grimbo. It was a weird experience to be there with no skin and no navigational tools or reference points. Obviously some kind of skin had been used on him to hurry him onGrid before he'd woken from the sedation, probably a generic skin, which was why he'd been immobilized in the fake hospital corridor — so he hadn't been able to see any reflections of himself. But now he'd booted down from it.

Unaccountably, he found himself thinking of Sato Shiseke again. If the old man had been telling him the truth and really was the designer or inventor or whatever of the Grid, exactly how did he visualize his creation? How would he navigate it?

"List," Obama said. Nothing happened. Obviously, verbalizing old computer commands wasn't going to get him anywhere. He tried to will himself into a central portal. Again, nothing. "Federal Grand Jury Protection Program," he said. And found himself inside an empty aerospaceport terminal. It looked like Reagan International. He glanced down at his legs but saw nothing. He was invisible. Apparently he existed on this version or side-street of the Grid only as some kind of ghost without a skin. A ghost with plenty of phantom pains, though — he could still feel his burns and oozing, crudely-pulled tooth sockets with agonizing realism.

"Security File Storage," he said. Now he found himself moving down a long hallway of anonymous doors. Each door had a holographic symbol in front of it, and he stopped to examine each in turn in order to puzzle out its meaning. He touched one, and its door opened. He caught a glimpse of rows of holographic file icons.

And suddenly found himself lying in a hospital bed. This time he knew it was real, because everything ached, most of all the insides of his ears. And his legs. And back. The two policemen must have yanked the game-cap off him and left before he'd woken up for real. That was what had wrenched him away from the Grand Jury files. He'd have to find a way to get back there. In the meantime, he was having lots of trouble waking up. He was hung over from the 'Stim and probably still sedated with something else. He felt empty, miserable, lethargic — just as he had on Slackerday. He reflexively checked his iTooth. He had 67 messages, most of them from Yvonne and his own mom. Six were from Camille.

The room he was in was a large single one. Above him, a soothing blue sky at dusk was being projected in place of a ceiling. Three walls were covered by a hologram depicting a forest glade with oak and birch trees. From time to time, generic bunnies and chipmunks gamboled and frolicked around their trunks, to the accompaniment of muted birdsong. He was obviously at the older, poorer Manacera City Hospital Center; the Two Georges HealthPlex would have had licensed scenes from Disney and Pixar sims. At least he wasn't in a WHO public ward — no holos at all in those. He chimed his mother back. "Hey Mom, it's me," he said, when she answered. "I'm OK. I'm in the hospital." His voice was feeble and rasping and his ears were ringing so loudly he could barely hear her reply.

"I know, thank the gods!" she said. His mother was a Pagan. "I saw it on CNN. They said it was a miracle you weren't dead. But you were always a tough little guy. Other children got sick or hurt themselves playing all the time — you never did. It's the Samoan in you. You never even broke a bone." She sounded almost disappointed.

"Just lucky, I guess." He told her about Kim, but it barely seemed to register.

"They want to send your father to the Moon," she said when he'd finished. "I don't want him to go. I don't want to move there either."

"Aw, the Moon's not so bad. My boss, Carmen's mom lives there — she visits her up there twice a year. Carmen says the low gravity is great for her weight. What does Dad think of the idea?"

"Oh, he doesn't care about anything anymore, just says 'fine' to whatever they tell him at that clinic. None of them are even real doctors there. But I don't want to move — we can't afford the Gold Coast on his pension anyway. I know Hawaii's a dump these days, but it's my home." She pronounced it the old-skool way: "Ha-VAH-ee." Several IV patches had been attached to him, and his thighs were swaddled in nutrient gel-paks. His scalp and chest were sticky with conducting emollient; the electrodes attached to them must have alerted someone that he was now fully awake, because a doctor and nurse suddenly came in through the hissing double doors. "Mom, I gotta go — the doctor's here now. Do me a big favor and tell Yvonne I'm OK?"

"Hello, hello, I am Dr Bannerji. How is our 'miracle man?'" asked the doctor cheerfully. He was a short, dark-skinned Bengali with long, very white hair. Without waiting for an answer, he bustled around to perch on a corner of Obama's bed, and swiped all the machines beside it one by one. "Amazing," he said.

The nurse took his blood pressure by wrapping her fingers around his arm and then squeezing, and Obama realized she was a Sana, from one of the older Sony robot lines. Sanas were far cheaper than Alluras, and had originally been manufactured for use as kinetic store mannequins. Upgraded, they'd become popular in hospitals as emergency nurses and surgical assistants. They had Sony's earlier, cruder version of the Alluras' expressive micro-filament musculature and humyn body-temperature, but only on the face and hands. This one only looked humyn from a distance. "What's amazing?" Obama asked.

"Amazing that you survived at all, Mr. Jones, much less survived relatively uninjured. You might have a couple of cracked ribs — you'd experience that as back pain mostly — and a few second-degree burns. Possibly a concussion. But we didn't find any other organic damage. You do remember the explosion, don't you?" the doctor asked. He shone a bright penlight into each of Obama's eyes in turn.

"Yes."

"Good, good!" said Dr Bannerji. "That's a relief. Maybe no concussion then. I'll give you nano-prescriptions for the rib pain and burns when you're discharged. You're a very lucky fellow, you know. The carnage today was very bad. Terrible. Would you like the YouVee news on?"

"No, what I'd like, actually, is to go home now," said Obama. He reached up to feel his scalp. No game-cap on it now. Or neural lace. Dr Bannerjee was making a comical face of horror and disapproval at him.

"Oh, no indeed, I couldn't allow that to happen, Mr. Jones. Not at all. We'll need to keep you under observation here overnight, I'm very much afraid. We've checked you out as thoroughly as possible, but there's always the chance of internal bleeding, you know. Or if you have a hidden spinal injury, you could wake up tomorrow and not be able to move at all. Oh yes, it has been known to happen. Besides, the moment you step outside this room, you will be recorded by mobile cameras and hounded by spy-bots for the news networks. No more peace and privacy for you! Also you will need to make a statement to the HHS investigators. So you see, it's just not on. At least 24 hours, Mr. Jones, that's our rule at this hospital."

"What about the HHS investigators who were already here? The two policemen who strapped a game-cap on me and filled me with 'Stim.'"

Dr Bannerji glanced nervously around, then said something in rapid Bengali to the nurse. To Obama he said in a very low tone, "Ah, those two men. I wasn't on duty here for that, I would not have allowed it if I had been. But they weren't from HHS, you know — they came directly from New York. They were the President's men."

"President Manacera?"

"Yes, they were with his Security Service, according to what I am being told now. A UNSS colonel and a major. They have top-level security, you know, and go anywhere they want. One doesn't like to argue with fellows like that."

Obama sat up in the bed and then winced. "Well, I didn't like what they did to me," he said. "I'm not staying here tonight as long as there's any chance of them coming back."

Suddenly the robot nurse turned and blinked at him. "Don't worry," she said firmly. "I won't let them in again. I didn't like them, either." Her voice sounded like Snow White's. Machines had always liked him. Behind her a little deer came shyly out from behind a tree. Obama tried to move his legs, and then wished he hadn't.

But later, after Dr Bannerji had gone, and he'd eaten a rice pudding under the watchful eye of the Sana nurse, he found himself unable to rest or sleep. He was plagued by unanswered questions. Why had two terrorist bombings taken place in the space of a week, both at the same places he was? Two was one too many for coincidence; it was getting to be a habit. Had the bombings been aimed at him? He didn't think so — it would have been so much easier just to blow up his apartment.

Or break into it and kill him, for that matter. No, it was obvious the bombs had been aimed at him only in the sense that he was being set up to be blamed for them. But why? Who would go to that much trouble? Or kill that many people in order to do it? Someone, he knew, had leaked his identity as Joyful Kalinga to the security services — and at such a high level that Jose Mancera's own agents, those of the chief executive of the United Nations, had known about it.

But Obama had taken nothing along with him to see Mrs. Housmanzedah that could have connected him in any way to Joyful. Not his iRist nor any article of his clothing. Nothing. He'd pulled off the false scars days before, and the tattoos had faded. None of it made any sense. None at all. And then someone else — someone who wanted to save him, not to frame him — had altered Kalinga's biometrics and DNA data inside his faked personal file. But who?

Major Malek's last words still seemed to hang ominously in the air somewhere: "So what the hell do we do with him now?"

Whenever Obama closed his eyes, terrifying images from the day rose up to meet them. The searing white heat and roar of the bomb blast, bodies torn apart and covered in blood, Mrs. Housmanzadeh trying to speak to him. The hard brown faces of Park and Malek staring down impassively as he lay screaming, his teeth torn out one by one with pliers, buckets of cold ice poured over his raw, oozing burns. Doors that opened to reveal a momentary glimpse of Kim standing behind them, only to slam shut in his face as he was dragged back to the green hospital corridor over and over and over again.

And so passed the night. Once he opened his eyes to find the robot sitting beside his door in a pool of pale light. She was knitting. The needles moved almost as fast as the eye could see, but silently, never once clacking together, as the sweater she was making seemed to assemble itself out of thin air.

7.

The first person Obama Jones met when he went back to work on Foursday morning was Camille, who'd apparently been waiting patiently for him downstairs in the main lobby. She emitted a happy little squeal when she saw him, and threw her arms around him. "I was so worried!" she said. "Are you OK, Bammy?" He hated for anyone, even Kim, to call him "Bammy."

"Careful — ribs," he gasped. "I'm fine, honestly. I'm just having a little trouble walking." Actually, his ribs had healed up almost overnight. He doubted they'd even been cracked at all.

"Yeah, you are sort of creeping along like a geezer. What happened to your hair?"

"The bomb burned it all off," he said. Well, it was only partly a lie — the blast had singed away his eyebrows and eyelashes, so that he now had the odd appearance of a hairless cat or dog. He was wearing new glasses, though, in an attempt to resemble Joyful Kalinga as little as possible. Because Colonel Park had been right: Joyful Kalinga was now an overnight celebrity. This morning it felt like he was the most famous man in America. Kalinga had now been officially identified as the alleged bombing suspect for both the Federal Center and Madam's Organ. Most of the news networks were running "Most Wanted" holos of him in one corner, culled from his gaming skin. The "Yo'Day" show had featured Grid holo-caps of his evening at Casino Royale, and somebody had created a Trip-Hop rap video of him from it entitled "Big Man," showing him screaming "Yaybo!" and demanding "Who this big man?" over and over again from a screaming crowd. "Joyful Kalinga!" they would roar back. The track was already topping the Billboard Music Chart. "Pop Idol or Violent Religious Cultist? Why is He Sacrificing the Innocent?" read the headline.

As was usual after any terrorist scare in the city, security had been doubled everywhere, and it had taken Obama forever to get past the scanners at the HarborPlex Station. The trains had been running late and had been hot and crowded. On the ride to work, a news holo had appeared on his Retro car showing Gracia advertising "My Joyful Night of Sex." Obama had swiped it to pay to access the full story.

In real life, it turned out that Gracia Dal Costa was a 14-year-old girl from a beach suburb of Rio de Janeiro. Obama had no memory of the events she described — he had booted down and left Joyful on AI when the three of them had left the casino — but listening made him squirm anyway. Although nothing he'd done with her was illegal, since the global age of sexual consent was 12. In fact, if Nathan Herrera's legal efforts were rewarded by the UN Supreme Court Review board in Geneva, that age would someday be lowered to 8. And, of course, it had happened onGrid — so it hadn't really happened at all, just as his being tortured hadn't happened. It just made him feel funny. As the torture had.

Gracia's real-life Enriched was very poor and had to be Babel-enhanced, but the gist of it was that sex with Joyful Kalinga had been a terrifying, if almost religiously ecstatic experience, that had gone on and on all night. She was convinced that Kalinga was a powerful African voodoo *houngan* or magician. "He told me he was a '*muti*' and ate powdered humyn testicles for sex magic," she said. She was selling the sim experience to a major network. There was no mention in the story of Simonetta.

"I tried to come see you at the hospital," Camille was saying now, "but that stupid robot nurse wouldn't let me in. Oh, and Carmen wants to talk to you right away — she's on the war-path. That's why I've been hanging here in the lobby, to warn you. And to do this — " She stood on tiptoe suddenly and kissed him. She was acting like a girlfriend now. On the way up the ascensor she held his hand. He was no longer sure just how much he hated it.

"I have just two fucking words to say to you," said Carmen, when he was helped into her office to perch on a pod. "'Joyful' and 'Kalinga'." Her walls were iridescent with flickering flat news-feeds. She claimed to suffer from some weird optic nerve disorder that made it impossible for her to perceive holograms without a neural-net. "Just what the hell is your connection with this guy? I found him in your files."

"Yeah, his name was on a list of political refugees I processed." Obama shifted his weight uneasily on his pod.

"So, what's the story? I've fielded nothing but media calls about him for the last 24 hours — my teeth are chiming like Notre Dame. I cannot tell you the kind of fucking pressure I'm getting from the board about this. Have you actually met the guy? You're listed here as his case worker." Carmen never bothered to wait for answers to her questions.

"No. I just processed the MAD validation of his minority status. There were lots of names on the list along with his, but I've never met any of them." Carmen rotated her electric cart around her desk and drove it up so close to him that her feet whacked against his. She appeared to be wearing exactly the same suit of clothes she'd been wearing the week before when he'd last seen her. But all her clothes looked the same every day anyway: black suits, white blouses.

"Well, I want you to meet him now," she said, scowling and puffing out her cheeks out like a bullfrog. "Now meaning yesterday. Or preferably even sooner."

Obama was confused. "You want me to find him so we can turn him over to the security services?"

Now she looked shifty. She smiled and glanced nervously around the room as if searching for bugs. "I want you to find him, yes. But I don't want you to turn him in to anybody, Bam." Her tone was greedy. She paused and almost smacked her enormous lips. "I want you to recruit him."

"'Recruit him?'" Obama felt almost too stunned to respond. His ears still rang and everything felt pretty unreal anyway from the pain-killers. "Recruit him for what? You mean you want him to work here at MAD?" He had a sudden vision of himself coming to work every day dressed as Joyful Kalinga, with his alligator shoes and fake scars and tattoos. The strain of trying to stay in character — any character, but that character in particular — would kill him. *Typical of Carmen to come up with such a crazy idea,* he thought. And it was crazy for so many reasons. Half the cops in the world were looking for Joyful Kalinga. His face was everywhere; he, Obama, would never even make it to the front door of the building, much less past security.

"Not exactly here at MAD, no ..." Her brow furrowed, and her expression became even slyer. "You know there's a whole crap-load of politics that goes with this job, Bam — shit I can't tell you about. Shit they don't even tell me, because I'm not at a high enough level." She stopped to slurp at a drinking nozzle attached to a day-glo pink Diet Peptase tube embedded in the tray of her Rascal.

"Long story short, we're at war. Not like in the old days with another country, but with other government departments. Specifically, the one biggest one, the one that's been bingeing like an Orca, eating everything in its path. Part of it's just about money. With the GGP going down every year and government growing, it means more departments and agencies are fighting over a shrinking pie. But some of it's just plain nasty, because we don't like each other. You know which department I'm talking about, Bammy; view this as a chance to get even with the bastards who took your Kimmy from you." She patted his knee. "The fucking HHS."

"At war?" What was she talking about? War was banned by the UN — surely she was just being full of it, as usual. Though it was true that the HHS was obviously running its own secret Grid. Still, Obama just couldn't seriously see rival UN agencies bombing and killing each other and running amok in the streets. Maybe Carmen had finally gone completely crazy at last.

"That's why we need a psycho like Kalinga on our team," she was saying. "Because he's dangerous. He's already hurt them bad once — maybe he'll hurt them even worse once he's on board with us, sucking at our tit. This guy is a real player, Bammy, a guy who walks through walls. He's a stone cold killer. Look at those dead eyes. He's a firestarter. A soul-eater. I find him fascinating. Frankly, we need his skill set — nobody else here's got any *cojones*."

Behind her, a huge 2D bumper for Shrek's popular night-time "16 Minutes" news show appeared, asking "Who Is This Man Called Kalinga — Really?" So far, at least, no one seemed to have actually connected Obama to Kalinga. The only mention of Obama Jones had been a brief local story at breakfast-time entitled, "Double Dose of Bad Bombing Luck Dogs District Dude." Obviously, the statement he'd given to the HHS team yesterday had been leaked. And obviously, they knew he wanted Kim back. But neither was a good enough reason for him to want to blow up HHS offices and kill its employees.

"There's no way I can get in touch with him now," said Obama. "I mean, seriously, not in real life with everybody looking for him like this. Besides, I'm no detective." He didn't relish the thought of Park and Malek paying him another visit, either.

"Agreed," said Carmen promptly, and he saw her trap close a little too late. "No way he's still in town right now. He's probably off shore in Havana or Caracas or someplace. He's too smart to get caught like that. No, you need to go looking for him on the Grid. If I know anything about that bad boy — and I feel like I already kinda do — he'll moon his ass at the world just to keep his public stoked up. Go onGrid and get Cammie to help you find him." She spun her Rascal around its rotational ball and retreated behind her desk-slab.

"'Cammie?' You mean Camille?"

"Sure. She can find anyone any time on the Grid. I don't really have a clue how she does it, but she knows all this cloak and dagger bullshit. She's the one who got rid of the bugs here in my office when security couldn't do dick." Carmen paused to chime her admin by iTooth. "I'll bring her in on this right now. You know Cammie came to us from the UNSS in New York, right? She even took a cut in pay to work down here. Boyfriend trouble."

"Look," Obama said in a panic-stricken tone. "Honestly, I don't believe this Kalinga guy even did those bombings. In my opinion, they're after the wrong person. I know he's being portrayed by YouVee as a bad hombre right now, but he was a political prisoner in his own country. I mean, he was repressed! There's nothing in his file to suggest he's even been trained to detonate a bomb."

Carmen's little black eyes glittered like a snake's. "Exactly. There's nothing in his file at all, thanks to somebody's slacking. Or maybe somebody's wiping it clean. There you are, Cammie." Noiselessly, Camille had come up behind Obama and gently put a hand on his back where Carmen couldn't see it. "I'm not asking you to have sex with the guy, Bam — not in real life, anyway," Carmen went on. "It's just that in love and war, none of us can always choose who we have to go down on. Sure, I agree with you the guy is probably just some kind of cuddly Nelson Mandela when you get to know him. But what if the cops are right and we're wrong? What if he really is a cold-blooded psychopath? Although, I gotta say that I personally find that sort of sexy and exciting. Be sure to tell him I said so when you see him. Tell him, oh I dunno, that I'd like to have him out to stay with me in McLean sometime."

She looked at Camille. "Promise him anything. You two have my authorization to do whatever you have to do — but get it done! All three of our asses are on the line. This came down from the very top. So you better hope you're wrong about Kalinga; they don't want him unless he's what everybody says he is." She stared hard for a moment at Obama. "This is your real assignment, Bammy. But now you need to get down to the conference hall and attend to your other one. It's almost as important."

"My other assignment?" he asked stupidly.

"The CAC Accreditation Jury," she said. He'd totally forgotten about it. "Luckily, this one is all yours. I stuck my neck out getting you onto the panel, but it will only be your job on the line if you screw up. Camille, get him on his feet and brief him on his way down. Give me five minutes, though — I need to have a word with Norberto first. And give this 'migo a khat or something, hon. He looks like crap."

Norberto Efrain Zollto was the Director-General of MAD. He was a half-Incan, half-Hungarian Chilean who often boasted that his great-grandfather had been a wanted Nazi war criminal. He was also, despite his hooked nose and weak chin, generally regarded in senior United Nations circles as the vainest man in the Americas. He was about 50, had skin like teak, was proud of his puffy waistline, and affected an enormous grey mustache that swept back across his pitted cheeks to meet his thinning hair, which he brushed back into a dramatic coif. No one had ever seen him wearing anything but brightly printed pajamas; he wore these to the office whenever he bothered to actually come in, along with thong sandals and silk Japanese bathrobes. Occasionally, usually on important occasions, he remembered to limp; he claimed to have been a victim of spina bifida at birth.

Carmen worshipped him. Norberto Zollto was the only person Obama had ever seen her speak to respectfully, and she was docile, even meek, whenever she was around him. For once, Obama greeted both of them with relief when he saw them together inside the conference hall. He was scared to be alone with Camille for long, now that he'd found she'd worked for the President's Security Services in New York. Was she an agent? Had she worked for Park and Malek? Had she been the one who'd turned him in to them? Did she already suspect he was really Joyful Kalinga? Obama's flesh crawled every time she touched him. Which she was doing a lot now.

And yet, the more she did it, the more he had come to expect it. And even look forward to it, in a conflicted kind of way. *Is that perverted of me?* Obama wondered.

The conference hall was a perfectly round three-storey room in the center of the cylindrical MAD building. It was modeled on the old UN General Assembly Hall in New York City, though of course on a much smaller scale. Stair-stepped levels with desks and pods sculpted into them descended toward a central dais; behind this was a huge, curved, mixed-use holographic and flat-projection screen. Right now it was simply displaying a "The Future is Brown" logo.

The walls were lightly stained with damp. A gallery for observers, which no one had ever been known to use, ran the circumference of three-quarters of the second storey. Camille and Carmen left the hall, and closed the double doors behind them. The other six jurors sat down, so after a few seconds, Obama did too. Zollto made his way up to the dais and took the rostrum. Today he was limping heavily. The ceiling lights dimmed.

Zollto addressed them formally in his rich, mellifluous voice. "Welcome to the Minority Assistance Department's juried review of the application for full United Nations Minorities Status by the Coalition of the Appearance-Challenged," he said. "The findings and final recommendation of this panel are, by law, merely advisory" — he paused dramatically — "but, as you know, are traditionally accorded the mandatory status of a public referendum by both Congress and the president. It gives me great pleasure to announce these proceedings officially open."

Zollto went on to outline, in very broad terms, what the panel was expected to do, and then gave a brief overview of the history of CAC. "What drove these good citizens, sensitive humyn beings just like you and me, to band together and proudly proclaim their handicapable status? In a word: repression. Millennia of discrimination both in life and in literature. The constant, unconscious — yet nonetheless hurtful — slurs and slanders of the more fortunate in our society.

"It is the contention of these brave CAC folks that physical ugliness, for such they are honest enough to baldly call it amongst themselves, is in fact genetic. This is indisputable. It is your brief to decide for the rest of us whether it is an actual evolutionary step, or merely pop culture and social convention, that sets the ugly culturally, ethnically, practically, and even racially apart from the rest of society. My views on the subject are well known." He paused for their polite laughter, and one womyn clapped. "But on you alone rests the weight of this momentous decision."

Zollto then introduced, one by one, each member of the jury. Most of them appeared to already know one another, though Obama was acquainted only with LaDonna Slaughter-Townley, who was the Director of the Social Welfare Agency at HHS. All the jurors seemed either to be at directorial level or else distinguished academics. The other two males on the panel were Dr Ayub Munir Khan, Chairman of the Sexual Politics Department of the University of East Anglia, and Professor Jalan Kunti Aso, of the University of Tokyo, one of the world's leading geneticists. The rest of the womyn consisted of Dr Angel Plassnik, Director of the Zurich Museum of Aesthetic Philosophy; Rainbow Secakuku, President of the Council of Native American Nations; and People's Tribune Cao Ding, Chairperson of the House Subcommittee on Emerging Minorities, an aurally challenged proportionally-elected member of Congress so radical that she refused to respond to any communication not written to her or made in sign language. She made no acknowledgment of her introduction.

Two of the womyn were in carts similar to Carmen's. Cao Ding had a guide dog, as well. Dr Plasnik was high-end autisal, and both Ms Slaughter-Townley and Professor Aso had Asperger's Syndrome. Internal debate promised to be a lively challenge.

"And last" — Norberto was kind enough not to add "and least" — "is our own Obama Jones, Deputy Director of the Accreditation Division here at MAD." Several of the panel nodded at Obama briefly while he tried not to show his stupefaction. Since when had he been promoted to Deputy Director? Surely this meant a big raise. Would it also mean his own office? He half-stood, then fell awkwardly back down onto his pod.

After the introductions, the official MAD "mission holo" was played. Obama closed his eyes. He'd seen this so many times that listening to it now made him feel sort of sick. *But maybe that's the pain-killers wearing off,* he thought.

"In 2008, the first year of the Great Panic," the overvoice was saying, "Professor Steve Jones, a brilliant young geneticist at University College, London, boldly predicted humynkind's future path over the next half-century. Pointing out that we were no longer divided into small isolated communities where genetic mutations might take root, Professor Jones foresaw nothing less than the End of Evolution itself."

Now came the familiar tones of Professor Jones: "World-wide, all populations are becoming connected, and the opportunity for random change is dwindling. History is made in bed, but nowadays the beds are getting closer together. We are mixing into a global mass, and the future is brown!"

The overvoice continued. "Swiftly, the Great Panic was followed by the Manic — or as some have termed it, the Bi-Polar — Depression, which engulfed the world throughout the 'teens and twenties, causing wild swings in the global economy and leading to a dozen brief wars. At the same time, the global warming foreseen by such visionaries as the American Vice President Al Gore was superseded by the unforeseeable and brutal reality of the current mini-ice age. Yet UN scientists swiftly determined that the very same environment-friendly 'Green' programs designed to combat earlier climate change were now even more relevant than ever!

"As with humyn biological evolution, so the 2030's witnessed, too, the death of the planet's outdated economic models, both democratic socialism and unfettered global capitalism. In their places arose an entirely new system of international political and social economic order, the benefits of which every world citizen enjoys today: that of 'co-operatism'. No longer is arbitrary decision-making, either in government or the marketplace, entrusted to a privileged few. Life is far too precious to be risked by reckless or unsafe practices, whether they be climactic, medical, political, social, or sexual. Every citizen of the world has the inalienable legal right to stability and security from birth. Thus, all important decisions at every level of life are now undertaken by committee. As our beloved UN President Jose Manacera explains …"

Here followed a number of brief moving images of the beaming, benignly avuncular figure of the president, leading into the old campaign trail clip where he famously was capped folksily saying, "There's an old joke that a horse designed by a committee is a camel. Well, seems to me that if you're lost in the desert and your horse has died, then you'd be mighty damn glad to meet up with a camel!" The overvoice explained, "The camel, of course, was to become the unofficial campaign symbol for Manacera's Green Planet Democratic Party ("Greens" or "Jeepeedeepies") for the next 16 years." This yielded to holos of the World Common Union celebration ceremonies of 2034.

"Now that the humyn race stands at the halfway point to a new century, we have already learned the truth and wisdom of Professor Jones' prophecy. We have witnessed, as a planet, the end of all 'apartness.' Consequently, the future can only hold even more 'togetherness,' as all creeds and colors, all ethnicities and minorities and even genders increasingly come together as one. And in that hate-free and undiscriminating future every *one* will increasingly be a minority. Yet taken together, every single *one* will add up to a unanimous majority, combining the best in all of us. Not blue or purple or orange" — this metaphor was illustrated by a parade of goofy, cavorting brightly painted cartoon characters — "but a perfect melding of every color on our precious green planet. Remember — the future is brown!"

The cartoon figures then burst into the International Anthem, "One World." They sang, "One world ... one world ... let's get together and feel all right ..."

A bored rustling succeeded this presentation. Several jurors cleared their throats or sipped from their liquids-tubes while taking iTooth calls, and Norberto Zollto hastily reclaimed the podium to lecture the jurors on panel procedures and scheduling before recessing them until the next day. When Obama finally returned to his cube, he was ambushed by Scott Vega-Choi.

"Wow, 'migo — I just heard. Congratulations on your promotion."

"Thanks," said Obama. "I think."

"Getting a new office?" Scott asked him enviously.

"I don't have a clue. To be honest, I only just heard about it. Nobody's really told me anything."

"I guess that's how to get ahead here," said Scott, with surprising bitterness. "Just keep getting yourself blown up. And make friends with a few known terrorists, huh — wish I'd thought of that first. Well, anything I can do to help. As usual. Oh, and by the way, Camille wants you."

"I know." Obama stuffed the introductory CAC briefing kit into his manbag and it kissed closed. "Tell her I had to leave early, OK?"

"Are you crazy? Where are you going?" Scott called after him.

"To a funeral," Obama called back.

According to the information he'd goggled that morning, Mrs. Housmanzadeh's funeral was being held at the NOVA Mosqueplex that had been built near the site of the old United States Pentagon building in Northern Virginia, which was now the UN Peace Museum. Obama took the Blue Line out there, fearful that he would be too late for the event. But when he arrived for the *Masjid*, which was being held in a sort of satellite hall of the main mosque, he discovered that the real funeral had already been held at a local cemetery the day before. However, since womyn had been excluded from it, the family had decided to open to all today the funeral prayers, or *Salat-ul-Janazah*.

The stocky, darkly bearded, balding myn who greeted Obama in the front lobby asked him, "You are not a Believer?"

"No," said Obama. The myn frowned.

"Were you a coworker of my aunt's?" he said.

"I was with her when she died." It was, Obama thought, an answer worthy of Zollto. The myn's features cleared at once, and he looked almost friendly.

"Please wait," he said. The man walked quickly over to a group of middle-aged womyn wearing different shades of blue head-scarves and spoke to one of them. No one here, noticed Obama, seemed to be wearing black. After a moment the balding myn came back with one of the womyn, who bore a distinct resemblance to Mrs. Housmanzadeh, though she was taller, thinner, and younger looking. "My mother," said the balding myn. His mother elbowed him aside, and shook hands with Obama in the modern manner.

"I'm Ghaniyeh Azzam," she said. "Hussein tells me that you were with my sister when she died. Tell me — did she have any last words?"

"Yes," lied Obama. "I couldn't hear her very well, because of the bomb blast, but I'm sure she said, 'God's will.'" Mrs. Azzam's eyes filled up with tears.

"Oh, thank you!" she said, grasping his hand again. "Thank you so much. You know, it is very important in our religion to die at peace with Allah. Come with us — you are very welcome here." He suddenly felt guilty. He wanted to pay his respects to his dead grief counselor, but he also had an ulterior motive in being there: to see if anyone else from her department showed up. Someone — anyone — who might provide him a link back to Kim, or even a clue to how she'd been processed. Or where she'd been taken.

The *Salat-ul-Janazah* involved Obama's standing with the others in several lines facing *Qibla*, or Mecca, and keeping his head bowed while the imam recited the prayers in Arabic. Obama appeared to be the only non-Muslim there. He decided that it was possible that Mrs. Housmanzadeh's immediate supervisor, or the coworkers who'd been closest to her, were all dead, although so far at least (if you could trust YouVee news, something he was increasingly unsure that he could) the body count from the building had been about half that of the Madam's Organ attack.

After the prayers were concluded, there was a gathering of family and friends inside the Mosque at an Omar's Garden restaurant, one of several franchises represented inside the Plex Halal Food Court. "Our tradition is for womyn to bring food for the family," Hussein told him as they walked across the mosaiced central quadrangle, which was lined with plane trees. "Of course, these days everyone is too busy. So we decided just to eat here instead. We were lucky that it's summer."

"Oh? Why is that?" They were still in the grip of a cold front; it felt more like late autumn.

"Because the days are longer. It's forbidden to hold these prayers at sunset."

Once inside Omar's Garden, everyone in their party ordered, then found places at tables, just as they would have at any other restaurant. After Mrs. Azzam had introduced Obama to several members of her friends and family, he found himself sitting all alone eating his Vegan falafel wrap at a table overlooking the quadrangle through a glasspex window. He could see the main minaret and dome. The mosque was made of rust-red brick, ornamented with patterned tiles of gold, turquoise, and aquamarine. The dome looked like a huge blue china bowl turned upside-down. He found himself idly wondering if anywhere he now went was safe from a bombing attack. He certainly seemed to be a target, for whatever reason. But maybe it was just coincidence, as the news story had said. Maybe he was just some kind of jinx. Still, he didn't want to see the mosque blown up on his account. It was strange, but this hadn't even occurred to him today at the office. *Maybe if MAD blew up,* he thought, *it wouldn't be such a tragedy —* then he felt instantly ashamed of himself.

There was a collective whisper near the door, and he turned his head to see what was causing it. A tall, extraordinarily beautiful Caucasian womyn, a bulky bag slung over one shoulder, was walking toward him with an exquisite lanky grace weirdly mixed with a gawky awkwardness. She was carrying a UnEx box and wearing a severe-looking long grey coat with a lighter-grey business pantsuit under it. Her clothes were disheveled and clumsily arranged, as if she were just learning how to wear them. There couldn't be much doubt, Obama thought, that she probably looked a lot better out of them anyway.

Her hair was so blonde it was almost white, and as she approached, he saw her eyes were nearly the same color: a blue so pale they looked the color of ice. The only splash of real color about her was the bright red of her lip gloss. She was the whitest person he'd ever seen — in fact, she looked like the generic villainess model for a CAC discrimination ad on YouVee. A ripple of interest followed her through the room, and the womyn at Mrs. Housmanzadeh's family's tables stared at her with naked dislike. The womyn stopped right in front of Obama and stared at him arrogantly. Her lipstick, he saw, was slightly misapplied.

"Mr. Jones?" she said. She pronounced it funny, like "Meesta Juntz?" As she went on talking, he realized she had a South African accent.

"Yes?"

"My name is Siren Gunnarsdottir. I'm with Rizdee." As they shook hands, she swiped his iRist, and he automagically goggled her iFace card. "Rizdee" evidently was short for "United Nations Research Institute for Social Development." He'd never heard of it.

"May I sit down?" she asked, then did so anyway without his permission, directly across the table from him. A plaintive whine of complaint seemed to come from inside the UnEx box she placed on the floor beside her. The box continued to mutter in a muffled, high-pitched little voice. Then the womyn reached inside her bag and produced a life-sized gleaming plastic bust with long blond hair which she carefully stood on the table on her other side, beside the condiment tray. It was, Obama read on the product name-plate at the base of its swelling plastic breasts, a Mattel's "Hair-Salon Barbie." It weirdly resembled its owner. The stares from all around them grew even more intense and outraged.

"This," she said, indicating it, "is just a machine. It jams those noisy coms of yours and will keep our conversation private. I know it looks really weird, but it's a new technology." She gazed deep into his eyes and gave him a dazzling smile. "Don't worry, Mr. Jones. I'm not with any security service. And I'm not here to kill you. Or torture you. The reason I'm here is because I need your help."

For a second, something about her reminded Obama of Camille. Maybe it was those ice-cold eyes. Was she a Boer? Or some kind of Afrikaaner-Scandinavian Nazi? He had the overpowering feeling that if he gave Ms Gunnarsdottir whatever help it was she "needed," he was going to be very, very sorry.

8.

Ms Gunnarsdottir said, "I think I'd better begin by telling you that you are under constant surveillance by a person who works in your office at MAD. That's the major reason I've brought the Princess here along" — she indicated the Hair Salon Barbie — "to neutralize that person's bugs. Your coworker has hacked your iRist. You've had bugs put in your teeth, and stickies injected into your bloodstream. Surprised, eh?" She smiled at him again, this time cruelly. "Sorry if I'm busting up a little office romance or something. I honestly haven't a clue why she's after you. Her real name isn't 'Camille Lyonesse,' by the way. Trust me, she's a nasty piece of work — my advice is to steer as far clear of her as you possibly can."

"Um, OK," said Obama. He was struggling to comprehend what the womyn was telling him. It would have been too weird to deal with, except that he'd been thinking some of the same things himself lately, and what she'd just said seemed to confirm them. "What's a 'stickie', exactly?" He didn't like the thought of anything injected into his bloodstream.

"A tracking beacon. It's an old spy term; it means a 'stick-tight' or a 'tick.' In this case, stickies are genetically engineered iridium molecules that broadcast your position to tracking sats wherever you are on the planet. The two UNSS agents, Park and Malek, injected the stickies into you when you were in the hospital. They also put bugs in your teeth. Before that, 'Camille' followed you around everywhere by hacking into conventional HHS security systems. All your noise made that easy."

"If her real name isn't Camille, then what is it?"

"Good question. Let's just say the name she was born with was Simonetta Sato."

Obama felt his heart suddenly constrict. He felt chilled all over. *Camille* had been Simonetta onGrid Slackerday night? And she really *was* the daughter of Sato, the Japanese geezer who'd invented the

Grid? Now that he thought about it, there was a faint suggestion of a resemblance between them in real life. Something about the eyes, the set of the features. Then that would make 'Camille' an heiress to one of the biggest fortunes on the planet — maybe the biggest. Why on earth would she have chosen to spend the last few months as Carmen's AA? It was a shitty job in every imaginable way. And why was Simonetta after him? It totally made no sense. Ms Gunnarsdottir was staring at him again, half-smiling, as if she could read every thought in his head. Behind her, he could see out the window that it had begun to rain.

"She's been tracking your every move onGrid, too. And, by the way, I know you're really Joyful Kalinga. No — don't freak. I realize he's just a figment of your imagination. I'm not going to tell anyone about him."

Obama swallowed hard. "Why not? I mean, no offense, but why wouldn't you tell anyone? Everybody in the world is looking for him right now because of the bombings."

Her smile grew mocking. "Well, we both know he didn't have anything to do with those, don't we? Figments of imagination can't build bombs. Or have joyful nights of sex with teenage girls named Gracia."

"I left him on AI!" protested Obama indignantly, his eyes blinking with embarrassment. "I wasn't even there! Besides, how — how do you know all this?"

Ms Gunnarsdottir began stroking Hair-Salon Barbie's hair affectionately. "Because I've been tapping into Simonetta's bugs for the past week or so, onGrid and off. The Princess here goes both ways. Right! Now that we have those two points clarified, I'll tell you what I want from you. Today was your first day as a juror on the CAC Accreditation Committee, correct?" *Is that what she wants?* thought Obama. *For me to vote against CAC?* It seemed too absurd to contemplate. Why would anyone bother to tamper with a panel like this? Or had the cartoon been a reality? Was there some kind of shadowy organization of anti-minoritarian "beautiful people" working behind the scenes to keep the ugly "losers" of CAC permanently stigmatized as outcasts and pariahs in humyn society?

He nodded reluctantly. She went on, "Over the next few weeks you'll be hearing all kinds of evidence from them, most of it so moronic that it would send anyone sane into an instant coma. 'Appearance-challenged,' indeed! Most of these people have already turned their noses up at fully UN-funded cosmetic nano-surgical makeovers."

"That's a cruel thing to say," Obama objected. "Everybody wants to be loved and wanted for who they really are." She looked at him with a sudden seriousness, even compassion.

"Yes, you're totally right to correct me, Obama. What you just said is very wise and true." Now she sounded as though she were humoring some not-very-bright child. "But I'm not really interested in that side of the issue at all, actually. For all I care, MAD can mandate a single average IQ and the same nose for everyone in the world. What I'm interested in is the genetic testimony you'll be examining.

"The panel will have unlimited access to the Humyn Genome Project data that's kept in storage at MAD. As you know, this data began to be collected as early as 1990, but most of the early stuff exists only in data storage in legacy code — no single government agency has ever had the time or personpower to catalog and transfer it. DNA profiles only were put onto modern databases routinely in the mid-to-late 'teens and were finally ported onGrid over the last decade. The problem, Mr. Jones, is that my agency needs access to some of those profiles right now. Especially some of the really old data."

This was a lot to ask, and Obama needed to think it over. Trying to buy time, he said, "I'd be more comfortable if you just called me 'Obama,' Ms Gunnarsdottir. And would you like something to eat?" She wrinkled her perfect little nose and glanced around the room with distaste. The funeral party had retreated to a far corner of the restaurant, as if the very sight of the two of them — or perhaps the Barbie — was somehow offensive.

"No thanks, I'm allergic to garlic. Now, quit stalling. I don't expect you to actually convert all those old files; that would take a lifetime. I just need you to get inside and track down the records of a few genetic strains. Just a few families, really. I'll swipe a complete list onto your iRist in a minute. I could do this research myself, of course — I can access any data held at any Federal facility — but I have good reasons for not wanting my interest known. So I'm not blackmailing you or coercing you into doing anything, Obama; what I've just told you gives you power over me, too. We'll have to be willing partners."

"But not quite equal partners, right?" said Obama. She laughed. Her teeth were like a string of lustrous white pearls.

"Maybe not quite equal, no," she replied. "But I'll need your brains engaged while you're doing this. I don't want you hating or resenting me. And perhaps you'd better call me 'Siren', as well." She pronounced it "See-run."

"To be honest," he said, "it could be a lot of work. And it could cost me my job — not that I actually care about that anymore," he added. "It's just that — well, you said you could get access to any federal facility. Could you get into the records of the Federal Grand Jury Protection Program at HHS? If you have been bugging me, then you know what happened to my wife."

Siren's expression turned deadly serious. After a moment she said with a sigh, "OK, fair enough. I'll find out everything I can for you. I promise."

"How will I stay in touch with you?" Obama asked. Suddenly he felt terrified he might never see this strange womyn ever again, now that she'd promised him the key to possibly finding Kim. Gunnarsdottir reached down beneath the tabletop and handed him the UnEx box, which was still muttering angrily.

"I brought this along for you," she said. "It's a machine similar to mine. Consider it a getting-to-know-you present — 'partner.' Take good care of it, and take it everywhere you go. If you need me, tell it."

"What's all that noise it's making?" Obama asked.

"Coms chatter," said Siren. She cracked open a corner of the box, put her ruby-red lips close to it, and snarled, "Shut up!" Every face around them turned to stare at her again. She ignored them, and packed her Barbie bust back into its own bag.

"But won't Cami — I mean, Simonetta — notice that all her bugs are being jammed now?"

Siren got up to leave. "These machines are actually smarter than humyn beings in some ways, Obama," she said. "No offense. Your machine will feed her plenty of really boring data and reassure her that you're just following all your usual routines. That's partly what it was programmed for." He didn't ask what else it was programmed for.

Siren really was a breathtaking womyn, he thought, looking at her full frame. She provoked the same raw animal attraction in him that Simonetta had that day at Micky D's a week before. And not just in him, either. Both womyn affected everyone around them like wild animals unleashed inside a fast food eatery. Both seemed totally untamed by life, somehow outside its normal rules. Maybe that quality in Siren was what had reminded him of Camille.

No, not Camille — Simonetta, as he needed to think of her now. *At least now,* he thought, *after having met the stunning Siren*

Gunnarsdottir, it will be impossible for me to be attracted to Simonetta anymore. Even if I didn't already know that Camille — Simonetta — was spying on me for the Security Services.

Obama found himself standing up, too. "Why does she use that stupid name?" he asked. "Oh, I get it. Duh. Camille Lyonesse — 'Chameleoness'."

"Right." Siren strapped her bag back over her shoulder and turned to go. "Don't worry. My name isn't a pun. Or a palindrome, or anything. It just means 'mermaid.' Goodbye for now." She excited exactly the same degree of interest walking out of Omar's Garden as she had walking in.

After Siren was gone, Obama bussed the remains of his meal, then picked up the UnEx box and followed her out. As he walked past Mrs. Azzam's table, the womyn hissed at him, "You are only a spy!" All the way to the Mosqueplex Retro station, he fretted that she might be right. Hadn't he been spying out colleagues who might show up at the funeral? And wasn't Siren a spy, already snooping on Camille and pressing him to steal data from MAD? Even so, how had Mrs. Azzam recognized this? From just watching them? Or did she assume everybody with a Fed ID was a spy?

Maybe that was what the rest of the world thought his job really amounted to. Spying on them. He found himself thinking about Siren again. Didn't mermaids lure sailors to their deaths? In waters way over their heads?

When he got home he opened the box she'd given him. He'd been expecting another Barbie; instead Siren had given him a "Pooka" doll. Pooka, his iRist informed him, was a cartoon character from around the turn of the century, popular in Korea. His Pooka was a shiny rotund figure about 30 cm high, with an enormous head like a melon, surmounted by a helmet of black plastic hair and two round top-knots, one on each side of her head. She was wearing a sort of blobby red tunic, out of which protruded two little black plastic feet. Her eyes were diagonal slashes, her mouth a merry 'U' between two red circles. She had no nose. The figure gleamed like porcelain. "Take it everywhere with you," Siren had said. He kept the doll tucked under his arm while he hydrowaved his supper that night, then slept with it beside him on the night-table. The doll reminded him of the way Kim would look whenever she tied up her hair to clean house. *Dude,* he thought, *everything reminds you of Kim — including plastic toys.*

The next morning, Foursday, the panel was given the opening presentation by the law firm representing CAC. This consisted of an interminable succession of "expert witness" holograms, all of them of CAC members recounting their personal experiences as the victims of prejudice. Several witnesses cried; one had to be sedated off-cam. The proceedings were constantly interrupted by questions from the jurors, two of whom, Dr Khan and Ms Sekacucu, began to feud bitterly.

"Yes, but do we really need another minority?" Ms Sekacucu yelled at one point. "With the budget cuts we're already having to suffer through this fiscal year, is there really the money for another?"

The next witness was an Asian girl whose several back-street cosmetic surgeries had caused her facial bones to collapse, like the features of the 20th century pop star Michael Jackson. She was all but unintelligible. Obama found his attention wandering. Maybe Siren had been right: maybe the CAC suit was, well, not moronic, exactly, but just a little ... elective? He was no beauty himself, it was true, and he'd been sort of shy back in his hi skool days, but he couldn't recall having been traumatized by the scorn of any of the more popular kids. Was he appearance-challenged? He didn't think so. And nobody looked more hideous than Joyful Kalinga with his scars and tattoos and bad teeth, yet look how much everybody had seemed to love him (except for his alleged bombing victims, of course). Just that morning across the street at Mickey D's he'd heard two elementary skool-kids yelling "Yaybo" at each other.

Maybe it really is simply a gender-orientated issue, Obama thought, *as Dr Khan is insisting.* But lumped together, gays and womyn weren't really even minorities any more, were they? Most Senators and Tribunes in Congress were either womyn or gay myn, so statistically they were now a majority. Of course the truly "ughly," as CAC members referred to themselves, were still a minority. Hopefully, at any rate. Obama couldn't decide. It was such a complex issue.

He sighed and checked his iTooth messages. There were several from Simonetta. "Hiding from me?" one was captioned. Involuntarily, he glanced down at the top of the Pooka's black head peeking up out of the top of his manbag. Maybe the coms disruption really was working! But he wasn't going to be able to hide from Simonetta much longer. Not with Carmen breathing down his neck about Joyful Kalinga. What was he going to do about that situation?

Suddenly, he realized exactly what to do about it. The solution was so simple he couldn't believe he hadn't thought of it sooner. First, however, he would have to fulfill his bargain with Siren Gunnarsdottir.

At lunchtime — the other jurors had insisted on a two-hour recess every day, since they were all wealthy enough to eat at luxury restaurants downtown — Obama slipped down to one of the data morgues in the basement, where he hoped to find some of the HGP files Siren wanted. How, he wondered, would the Pooka handle the security cams on the way down? Would she somehow be able to wipe each one clean as he passed in front of it? Well, he'd find out soon enough if Simonetta was waiting for him there.

She wasn't. The little plastic statue had probably had nothing to do with that, of course; the sudden feeling of security he derived from its presence was probably just a placebo effect. He shrugged. So what? Any delusion was good enough for him at the moment.

There were two basement levels at MAD, above the six levels of the groundcar parking garage and immediately beneath the first-floor daycare center and elementary skool. The upper of these two levels was called Legacy Data Curation; the lower, Internal Security & Building Curation. Physical plant curators had once been called "custodians." Before that, they had been known as "janitors." They shared their floor not only with building security, but also with the water pipes and electrical cables, which snaked along the ceilings of the hallways. All the internal compressors, which used a forced-air/heated-and-cooled water system, were contained on this level, as well. The floor above it, as a consequence, suffered from wild swings of temperature, and in some cases, legacy data had been discovered to be degraded or even destroyed by the heat from the floor below.

The Humyn Genome Project databases had once been stored on old-skool computer servers all over the world, primarily at institutions and universities. The original project had merely involved sequential mapping of a single instance of DNA, and had been completed in 2016. Within the decade, the records of the NHGRI and Genbank had been consolidated at NIH; after World Common Union in 2034, they had been transferred to the newly-built but already rapidly aging MAD building.

Concurrently with the completion of the original project, the UN Humyn Genetics Commission had instituted several new and supplementary projects, including international police DNA databases; a more comprehensive medical and genetic research database; and the Historic Preservation Genome Project, which had collected and collated DNA from corpses, mummies, police files, and scraps of archaeological evidence worldwide and attempted to match them to diaries and records for positive identification. Together, all this collected DNA had added up to a myriad of tiny pieces in a giant genetic jigsaw puzzle, with the number of those pieces declining dramatically dating backward from the year 2000.

The biggest problem was that the data had outlasted the useful lifetimes of a number of storage devices, including that of the personal computer itself. Originally the information had been stored on tapes and data drives, then on floppy disks, CDs, DVDs, FlashDrives, Smartcards, SmartSwipes, and Crystal Chip Array Units. All these media had been accessed variously over SCSI, USB, FireWire, WiFi, MiFi, YouFi, and finally, WiiFi data ports, all of which required software converters and, in some cases, rare antique cabling and hardware. Even then, when the data had at last been uploaded onto the Grid, it had still required translation.

Some records, of course, had never been scanned at all, but remained as physical artifacts or so-called "hard copies," like books or journals. Unfortunately only a relative few of these had weathered the turbulent decades before CommUnion. Budgetary constraints and lack of political interest were two of the reasons progress in scanning had been so slow, but the third and unspoken reason was, of course, the UN PRIE (Proportional Representation In Employment) statutes. It was part of MAD's mandate to police this directive, so naturally the agency was expected to provide a model example.

Long before CommUnion, political pressure had been building for government agencies both in the former United States and Europe to hire the handicapable, particularly those with developmental disadvantages. These disadvantages included a wide range of categories. Aside from persons with mere muscular dystrophy or cerebral palsy, HEAPs (High-End Autisal Persons), NNIDs (Near-Normal Intellectually Disadvantaged), and HEDS (High-End Down Syndrome) were considered the most desirable handicapable employees; the terms "autistic," "retarded," and "mongol" or "mongoloid" had been banned (of course) by law, their use subject to hate crime prosecution. LEAPs, SIDs, and LEDS were less acceptable employees, particularly because many of these latter could not be relied upon to use the toilet or in some cases, to speak or move.

The least desirable employees of all, however, were the higher primates. As early as 2007, the higher primates had been accepted as citizens with full voting and humyn rights by the country once known as Spain. This had led to adoption of the measure a few years later by the former EU, and had been enshrined by UN law in 2018. Whales and dolphins had been granted similar status over subsequent decades, and there was now a powerful lobby for the same rights to be extended to dogs, cats, and robots. MAD, however, was not equipped with salt-water tanks, nor was the North American Federal Administration Area considered a warm-weather site, so the only appropriate employees for the Affirmative Primate Employment program at MAD were gorillas and chimpanzees. Of these, only one had physically survived: Priska, a lowland gorilla who was the lowest-ranking data-curator in the section which housed the HGP files.

When Obama arrived, Priska was the sole employee to be found in Legacy Data Curation. She had personalized her nearby office space, which featured a textured plastic flooring resembling natural grass, with scores of dolls and soft toys, including a huge yellow rabbit which waved at him as he walked through the door. There were also several large baskets containing rotting fruits and the shoots and leaves of plants.

Priska was about 140 cm tall, which meant that she came to just below Obama's shoulder whenever she stood fully erect, and she was wearing a rather dirty cotton frock with a pink flowery print on it over an adult diaper. She weighed just over 100 kg. Her black hair was shaved around the top of her scalp for the neural-net on which she depended to communicate, though in emergencies she could use a large plastic Fisher-Price "My First Symbols Keyboard" covered with duct-taped, customized keys with little colored icons on them.

Priska was thought to have a vocabulary of four or five thousand words, which she "signed" neurally onto the Grid and which then emerged from a holo with a sultry female voice, that of Aria on the hit sim series *Zombi Zoo*. Real zoos, of course, had been outlawed since the '20s, but whimsical recreations with cartoon characters remained popular with small children.

"Hi, Obama," said the Aria holo, after he'd allowed Priska to fondle and squeeze his chest in greeting. She often did this, it was believed, in order to distinguish humyn males from females. Her eyesight was very poor. "Obama bring Priska present?" she asked, pointing with a long ebony finger as hard as horn toward the bulge inside his manbag formed by the top of the Pooka's head.

required for YouVee and Grid-quality content. However, most of the older cameras in the data storage rooms were old-fashioned cyclops spider-cams, capable only of generating flat grainy moving images. While Pollack continued to recite, a flat-screen flickered to life on the wall above his head and began displaying the footage Obama had just requested. The lighting was poor, but he recognized Colonel Park and Major Malek immediately. After what they'd done to him, he'd never forget either myn, even when he saw them in shadow or silhouette. Involuntarily, he began trembling now at the very sight of them, and it was all he could do to keep his eyes on the screen. But he needed to know what had happened to the HGP files.

The two "bad myn" were shown walking down a hall in the data morgue, ignoring a plaintive-sounding Priska. One of them turned on her at one point and threatened her with a Razer — a flexible Tazer-rod — and she shrank away and started to scream, a loud keening noise from the screen that failed to interrupt Little Mahendra Pollack's speech or even engage his attention. Suddenly the cam-view shifted. Park swiped the storage-room door and it hissed open. The lights went on, and Obama saw that, just as it had been for him, the room was completely empty. The two myn went inside and looked around the room, argued with each other for a minute or two, and made iTooth calls. Then they left hurriedly. According to the file's time-stamp, this had taken place about two months ago, in late Floria — at about the same time that Simonetta had first started working for the company.

Obama turned to Pollack, who was still in mid-recitation, said, "Thanks, I'll try again some other time," and walked out of the big security room. Behind him, he heard the Rain Myn yell in a plaintive tone, "Wait, I'm not finished!"

So the files were all already missing even back then, thought Obama. *But where are they now?* Had they ever really been transferred to MAD? Were all the storage areas secretly empty? Or just the ones with the older legacy material that Siren Gunnarsdottir had requested? Thinking of Siren caused something else to occur to him. Why had the security-cam file displayed itself the moment he had requested it, without even waiting for Pollack's VeriSign? Obama glanced down at the Pooka in his bag. Was that one of the things the Pooka had been programmed to do?

As Obama walked off down the corridor, Raffi suddenly popped out of nowhere and said, in his startling bass voice, "Come on, I'll show you where they went." Before Obama could ask him what he meant by that, the little HEDS had scampered off and begun rapidly trotting back the way they'd originally come, pausing every now and then to turn like some kind of elf or leprechaun and beckon Obama to follow.

The hallway curved around the inside radius of the building, so that whenever Raffi trotted too far ahead, he became lost to sight. Increasingly, pools of water covered the corrugated metal floor, and the cinder-block walls were covered with rusty lime deposits from leakage. The air down here seemed distinctly colder to Obama, and he wished he'd worn a heavier coat. He suddenly slipped and slid forward on his soles a few centimeters; the puddles of water were turning to ice. Glittering icicles hung from the olive-green-painted water pipes overhead, and the walls ahead of him were covered with a coating of frozen condensation. He could see his breath.

"Come on, Obama!" Raffi called out impatiently. "We need to hurry now! I'm cold!" He disappeared down an intersecting hallway, which bristled with white rime-frost so thick that it looked like the inside of an antique ice-cream freezer. One of the curators was standing just inside this hallway wearing goggles and a parka and chipping off sheets of ice with a pick. He tossed these into the trailer container of a motorized utility cart.

Obama asked the curator, "Where did he go? And is it always this cold down here?" The curator stopped and pointed further down the hallway in the direction of an open door that cast a lemon-yellow rectangle of light out into the hall. Then he said, "It must be cold all the time here for the building heat to work." He spoke with a slight Slavic accent, Russian perhaps. "You see, this building was made for global warming, so the heat will not come on unless the central thermal register is very cold. That is the central thermal register," he added, pointing to a large sensor panel buried under several centimeters of clear ice. It was glowing with bluish icons and numbers. "We have to move in heavy refrigeration equipment into these rooms here and here to make this happen, you see. They are very expensive to run. But that is why is all this ice. Your little friend likes the cold, so he and the other Iddies come to play down here. Over there you can see them." He pointed again.

"What did you call them?" Obama asked, startled.

"ID's — Intellectual Disadvantaged. What do you think I said?" The Russian smirked to himself and started hammering away at the ice again.

Obama found Raffi inside the doorway with the yellow lighting. The little HEDS had put on a coat and gloves. He immediately grabbed the bottom edge of Obama's jacket and led him over to a large rack on the wall from which hung a variety of coats and hats. Obama chose the least dirty of these and slipped them on. There were liquid-ceramic space heaters everywhere. "We don't let it freeze in here," Raffi announced. "Come on in." He led Obama into a big, dimly lit room with unfinished cement walls like those of the parking garage in the levels just below. This room, however, was filled with data storage containers of every shape and size, stacked in neat rows. Some of these stacks nearly reached the ceiling.

"It's too hot in Priska's room," explained Raffi. "We didn't like it there, so Nancy said all these containers wouldn't like it, either. That's why we moved them all to this place — it took months. They need to be where it's cool, but Nancy said not to ever let them freeze. So we keep the temperature here at 6 degrees all the time." Nancy was Raffi's office "girlfriend," an ID-Savant, who worked in another Data Morgue next to his. "See," added Raffi. "There are the machines you need to read them with. Did we do good?"

Obama looked around at the haphazard piles of legacy reader equipment, then at the rows of stored data. It would take hours down here, maybe even several days, to discover and dig out the files he needed. But at least they hadn't been destroyed by the heat. Or by Park and Malek. "Yes, Raffi," he said with a big smile. "You did very, very good." But lunch hour was over.

He found both Carmen and "Camille" waiting for him when he returned to the conference hall upstairs. Both appeared to be extremely unhappy with him, but he found he no longer cared what they thought. "Where have you been?" snapped Carmen the moment she fastened her eyes on him. *If Simonetta's bugs were still working,* Obama thought, *she wouldn't have had to ask. They wouldn't even be having to ambush me here right now.*

"At Mickey D's, across the street," he said. "You didn't give me a meal expense allowance, so I couldn't go to lunch with the others." The two womyn glared at him.

"And you haven't been returning our messages. Why?" demanded Carmen.

"Sorry, I've been cramming for the CAC presentation. There's so much to catch up on, and these people you've fed me to are really heavy hitters. They're going to take me to pieces if I don't know my stuff." Obama thought he was being clever, but Carmen rudely waved this argument aside.

"I don't give a hot stinking heap of crap about this crip parade," she said, "and neither should you. It's Kalinga you need to focus on. Finding Kalinga. I thought I'd made myself totally clear." "Crip parade" was top-floor slang for a Minority Accreditation Review.

"Oh, him," said Obama. "That's easy." Did Simonetta give him a knowing look when he said this, or was he just imagining it? Surely she knew that he really was Kalinga. Well, vice-versa, technically.

"Easy?" Carmen turned beet-red and drew in so much air she seemed ready to explode.

"Sure. Think about what kind of amigo Joyful Kalinga really is. Psychologically speaking, I mean. Deep down, he probably really thinks he's some kind of 'big man.' Which means he's not going to let the geek who made that hit video of him make all that money without him. He'll be in touch to ask for his cut. He'll probably even want the poor guy to make a sequel. So all you have to do," Obama turned to Simonetta, "is use your contacts at the UNSS to hack into the geek's com accounts, and they'll lead us back to Kalinga sooner or later."

"That's the biggest crock I've ever heard in my life!" shouted Carmen.

"No, Carmen, I agree with Bammy," Simonetta said. "I think he's really got a line on this guy. We'll find him. I have a feeling it will be sooner than later."

"It had better be soonest!" Carmen retorted, and angrily drove off in her Rascal. Simonetta loitered behind, blocking Obama's path back into the conference hall.

"Is that what this is all about, Bammy?" she asked him in a low, almost imploring tone. "That you found out I used to work for the Security Services? I can explain all that."

"It doesn't matter."

"Well, obviously it does!" She put her hand on his arm and grasped his sleeve. "Look, Carmen's right about one thing: nothing we're doing here actually matters. Please just leave here with me now. Right this minute. Let me get you away from all this. I've got money — enough money for both of us. We can start a new life together. I can make you happy, I promise." Her eyes were wet and utterly sincere, like a begging dog's. *What an amazing actress,* thought Obama. *If I didn't know better, I might actually believe her.*

He shook off her hand. "Look, I'm really flattered — no, that's not right. I'm totally amazed that a womyn like you would have any interest in me at all. It's just that, well, this is all happening way too fast. Kim hasn't even been gone two weeks," he added, suddenly feeling real anguish. "I'm not ready for anything like this. It's just too soon for me to be thinking about starting a new life."

"Except as Joyful Kalinga," she said.

"That was a mistake. Just a dumb impulse. I don't even care anymore — you can tell whoever you like. Let them arrest me."

"I'm not telling anyone," said Simonetta, her blue eyes gazing at him limpidly. Today, they looked greener. "I thought it was cute. Anyway, it can be our secret. Just, well, have him get in touch soon, before things get any worse for you."

"You mean with Carmen?"

"Carmen is the least of your worries. If you let this all go too far, Bammy, then even *I* won't be able to do anything to save you." Now she was speaking almost in a whisper.

"You mean like you did with Park and Malek?" he asked her bitterly. She looked suddenly stricken.

"That wasn't my fault. I'd never do anything to hurt you — you of all people. You have to believe me!"

"OK, I believe you," he said insincerely. "But I really have to go — they're all back and sitting down now." Her mouth was opening to tell him something else when he slipped past her into the wide doorway.

As he took his place with the rest of the panel for the afternoon session of the crip parade (as he now most unfortunately thought of it), he wondered what exactly Simonetta had meant by "do anything to save you." "Save" him from what? And what had she meant by him "of all people?" He found he was barely able to pay attention to what Norberto was saying. Obama had the distinct feeling he wasn't going to be around for the final verdict anyway.

It wasn't, Obama thought, that he'd ever really loved his job all that much. Right now it just represented stability, something to distract him and make him get up every morning and go through the motions of life with Kim gone. And of course, he still needed the money; without Kim's salary, he wasn't sure he could meet the mortgage payments and condo fees without robbing their savings. He didn't count Joyful Kalinga's winnings as real money, since there was no way he could access them now without being tracked, even if the Feds hadn't already seized the account.

Nor did he suffer any longer from the illusion that he could use his position here to find Kim. He could go on Federal Assistance, presumably, if he got fired, so he didn't have to actually worry about starving, the way people had during the Manic Depression. *It might be smart to face this,* he thought, since it felt as though his job were turning to shit now, too, just like everything else in his life. Maybe he'd never really loved it, but at least he'd always respected it, felt like he was at least helping people. And unlike with some careers, he was doing no harm. *If you'd asked me two weeks ago,* he thought, *I might have described my life as pretty boring.* But now he'd give anything to be able to turn the clock back to that. Plain old everyday boring.

That evening, dressed in his own coat and gloves and carrying a large thermos of Black Khat and a hot supper, Obama slipped back down to Raffi's secret storage room. He found the door locked, but it opened at a swipe, thanks to the Pooka. He took her out of her bag and set her down to keep watch while he clambered around through the container stacks searching for Siren Gunnarsdottir's files by hand. By dawn he'd found all but one. He'd have to come back to keep looking for it later; now all he had time to do before he was due back at the CAC hearing was to port as much of the rest of the data as he could onto his iRist.

Bleary with fatigue, he returned to the storage room later that day at lunchtime, but still couldn't find the missing file. It was from the years 1952-2022 and seemed to cover several strands of records, mostly those of the Sweet family of Seattle, Washington. Maybe the file had been lost. Or stolen. Or erased. He set Raffi to looking for it, and when Nancy and their friend Bronwyn appeared he set them to looking for it, too, but with no luck. At last, out of sheer desperation, he asked them all, "Do you know where this collection might have been mirrored?" The three Disadvantaged persons studiously avoided looking at him.

"What?" Bronwyn said finally.

"Is there anywhere else where there might be more copies of this data kept in storage? This same data? Somewhere else than the MAD building, I mean?"

Raffi and Nancy exchanged glances. Nancy was taller than the other two, had mousy shoulder-length hair, and a mother who carefully dressed her every morning. She looked almost like an Advantaged person from a distance. But she normally had a slack, vacant expression and a tendency to slur her words. Not now, however. "The Moon," she said with great precision and firmness.

"Nancy is always correct about such things, I must say," boomed Raffi proudly.

That night, Fiveday night, Obama sat down at home to collate the data he'd found. The other jurors had begun defecting early in the afternoon, and the hearing had been recessed prematurely by Zollto, so Obama had been able to sneak off home early and nap for an hour two. When he had woken up, he had made round-trip shuttle reservations to go to the Moon the next morning.

The HGP data, he'd discovered, had a Japanese Genbank mirror on the Moon at the Willow Precinct Liberry near the main Gold Coast Aerospaceport in Clarkesville — though, oddly, this information was available nowhere in MAD's own records or even onGrid, unless goggled directly on a file-by-file basis at the site itself. Obama figured that Park and Malek had probably gotten there before him, but it still seemed worth a try anyway. The liberry's onGrid catalog had shown the material as still being there (for what little that was worth).

Obama had never been to the Moon. He wasn't sure he knew anybody who had, except for Carmen. Of course, wealthy people like Simonetta and Norberto probably had been there often enough that they didn't even bother to mention it. Nobody ever talked about visiting the former Canada, either. It wasn't like there was much to see in either place. But this was exciting — Obama had never gone up into space before, unless you counted aerospace trajectories on long-distance flights. The Moon tickets were incredibly expensive, too: 2700 Unos.

But maybe, just maybe, the trip would bring him closer to Kim. "Some of them even end up living on the Gold Coast," the Marshal had said the night they'd taken her away. Or something like that, Obama was pretty sure.

While he was making the reservation with Selene Japan, the Pooka started making muttering noises inside her bag again. It sounded like someone having a bad dream. "No, no, no" and "I won't let you do it" were the only phrases he imagined he could hear clearly. Coms chatter, Siren had said. He leaned over and shouted, "Shut up!" The Pooka lapsed into an outraged silence, and he felt instantly guilty. *Welcome to the world of Obama Jones,* he thought, *the man who can't even be rude to machinery.*

The data Siren Gunnarsdottir had requested from him seemed to consist mostly of family histories. The first name that caught Obama's eye was that of the Japanese Sato family, dating from the 1700s. This file seemed to end in 1975. He decided to read it first; obviously it had something to do with Sato Shiseki and his daughter, Simonetta. Which would explain why they'd sent Park and Malek to find it.

There were files on at least 20 other families, including the Ukrainian Zuckermans, dating from 1887; Obama had heard this name somewhere before, and tried to remember where. There was also an earlier file on the Sweets, from the American Midwest, beginning in 1864 and ending where the second, missing file on their history began, in 2020.

Zuckerman ... hadn't that been Obama's own grandfather's original last name? Before he'd legally changed it to "Ethan Peace" and become an acupuncturist? Before that he'd been a real doctor in the former Israel. Had there been some kind of scandal? Obama couldn't remember.

"Mom?" he said, when she answered her iTooth, "What was Grandpa Ethan's real name? Before he changed it, I mean. Wasn't it 'Zuckerman'?"

"Uh huh. His family was from Tel Aviv. But I think most of them died in the Second Holocaust."

"Why did he stop being a real doctor?"

"I'm not really sure," his mother said. "He never liked to talk about it much. But I think it had something to do with the cloning clinic he was working at. Back then cloning wasn't always easy or legal like it is these days." Lela, his mother, had grown up in a vegan household and so had elected to have him naturally, which was becoming increasingly rare. Most babies nowadays were gene-modified "Aquarians," brought to term inside a gestation or cloning tank. Only hippies and the poorest immigrants and minorities still continued to bear their own children the old-skool way, which was why these demographic groups had such higher rates for birth defects and ID kids. "Why are you so curious all of a sudden?"

"Oh, I dunno. Just something I'm working on reminded me of him." Yes, there he was: Eitan Zuckerman, born Tel Aviv, 1952. His maternal grandfather. But what were Obama's genetic records doing here? What did Siren Gunnarsdottir — or Simonetta, for that matter — want with them? "Oh, guess what, Mom — I'm flying to the Moon tomorrow!"

"Oh? Why are you doing that?" she asked suspiciously.

"For my work," he replied. "But while I was there I thought I'd check it out there for you and Dad, too. If I don't like the look of things, I'll tell you."

"I really wish you wouldn't go," Lela said. "I don't want anything to do with the place — it scares me. And I don't want you encouraging Homer to go up there, either." Homer was his dad.

"I won't say a word unless it's heaven up there," Obama told her before he disconnected. "I promise." He sighed. His mom was starting to act old. She was still only in her 50s. But his dad was 20 years older. *Maybe being around someone much older than you all the time rubs off,* Obama thought.

There was nothing more on the Zuckermans after 1968, so he switched back to the Sato file, which was huge. It had occupied most of an antique disk drive and had taken the better part of an hour to transfer. Most of it was in Japanese, so he went onGrid and switched to Babelfish. The name "Sato," it told him, meant "sweet." Or "sugar." Hmmmm. The Sato family had begun recorded life as a family of fishermen and fish merchants in Satsuma in the 1720s. Some had become wealthy, others had become soldiers — *ronin* — and even samurai. A few family notables had moved to Edo, including a famous priest and a wealthy arms merchant who had married into the minor nobility. The children of the latter had become government officials.

Meanwhile, another branch of the family had ended up in Tabuse, in the Yamaguchi Prefecture, where in Venteo of 1901 the most famous Sato had been born: Sato Eisaku, who had gone on to become the former Japan's longest-serving Prime Minister during the 60s and early 70s. He had won a Nobel Peace Prize in 1974. During his tenure as head of the Japanese Science and Technology Agency, the first formal genetics research program in that country had been launched. This Sato had died in 1975.

Sato Eisaku's memoirs and biographies were extensive but completely unrevealing, at least when Obama skimmed through them quickly. He saw no connection to Shiseki or Simonetta there, either, unless one of Eisaku's two sons had changed his name. But what really counted wasn't the documentation anyway, which was sketchy and incomplete — only the gene maps.

Why, Obama suddenly wondered, did all the families in these files have "Sweet" or "Sugar" in various forms in their names, like the Jewish "Zuckermans," the Russian "Sakarovs", the Italian "Della Zuccheri" or the Mexican "Dulceros"? There seemed to be absolutely no other connection between any of them, except that, every now and then, one seemed to be involved in genetic research of some kind. It was weird. It was as if all these families were part of a secret society or something. Had they all originally been candy makers? Sugar manufacturers?

The documentation of the American Sweets included several long journals, written by various family members, from which DNA samples had been successfully extracted. The first journal was from the 1860s and had been kept by one of the daughters of Thomas Sweet, who had emigrated to America from Manchester in 1849 and bought a farm in Iowa. Her name was Dora. The first entry ran, "Papa is much changed now that he has come back from the war," so changed that the mother of his three children had immediately run off with another man, a fiddle player. However, Papa soon showed a genius for animal husbandry, and the farm had become prosperous.

A decade later, however, when the two oldest children, Dora and Katherine, had grown old enough to get married, Papa had attempted to explain his biological theories to them. "He has made a great natural discovery based on the work of a German scientist named Mendel," read the entry, "that sound human stock must always be created by following the same conditions that obtain for the husbanding of our livestock. He has explained this very patiently to both Katherine and myself, though I fear she has little aptitude for intellectual understanding and has cried for days inside our room."

At some point in the early 1880s, the family farm had been sold, and the two girls had been uprooted to San Francisco with their father. Of the son, Edward, there was no mention. Dora had become a skool-teacher and Katherine had stayed home, seemingly in order to rear "poor Papa's other children." One of these, Thomas Millard Covey, had grown up to become a professor at CalTech and a leading eugenicist. He later had become a Director of Public Health for the state of California, during which tenure he had become best known for his attempts to sterilize "mental defectives." He had believed that mental defectives occurred unnaturally through inbreeding and incest. Thomas Covey, too, had published a lengthy memoir, but it made heavy going, and Obama fell asleep partway through.

He woke up early and packed for his flight to the Moon. The entire trip would take about 60 hours or so, most of which would be spent in transit. For the original Apollo astronauts, he'd read, it had taken three whole days to get to the Moon. Now it took a little over eight hours each way. Obama hoped he'd be able to nap on the shuttles and go straight to work on Oneday morning, when he was due back. There was a drug you took for the nausea induced by weightlessness, but they still recommended that you not eat or drink anything except water for 12 hours before each flight, so he was taking along plenty of Vitalife dermal meal patches. And antacids. And, of course, the Pooka.

Obama felt a thrill, half of terror, half of anticipation, in the pit of his stomach. He was going up in a shuttle! Up into space! Space even had its own special smell, he'd heard, that of burning metal and charred meat. Up there people bought little aerosol spray-bottles of space smell and brought them back as souvenirs, along with Moon rocks. If he had time, he'd have to remember to do that, too. He checked his iTooth while he waited on the roof for the aircab: 122 messages, 38 new. He scrolled through looking for any from Siren, but there were none.

There was a new one from Simonetta, though. It was captioned, "Forget me not …" *If only I could,* he thought. He didn't bother to play it.

The *Suki Moon* shuttle from Reagan International didn't go straight from the Earth to the Moon. It docked at Eunice Station, midway between them. Then you switched shuttles and flew on to Tranquility Base or Clarkesville or one of the other three main spaceports on the Moon. The stopover was included in the estimated travel time. "Eunice Station" was an affectionate nickname dating from the '20s, back when the United Nations International Space Station, or UNISS, was first being constructed. Eunice orbited at a point midway between the two planetary bodies, constrained by their mutual gravitational pull. This position was called the Earth-Moon system's Lagrangian, or L1, point.

Nowadays Eunice was manned almost entirely by Sony Endura robots, which were specially designed to withstand the periodic radiation storms that swept over the station. Security on the ground was even more intense than for a domestic Earth flight, because of fears of a terrorist attack on the space station. Each passenger and every article taken through the gates had to be completely scanned, so boarding took over two hours. Luckily, this morning's flight was only half-full. Many of the passengers were businessmen or tourists like Obama, but most were retirees on their way to new lives, or relatives on their way to visit others like them.

The Ground to Orbit aerospaceplane held 235 passengers and carried a crew of 12. From the observation window of the departure lounge it had the look of a shining metal pterodactyl — its design had changed very little since the first of the *Space Odyssey* films and sims had been created. "I've made a dozen of these trips already," the middle-aged man in the seat next to Obama's told him. "I do it several times a year to see me mum. There's absolutely nothing to worry about, just as long as you don't overeat. To be honest, the whole thing is rather a bore. It's so much like a being in a sim that I really might as well save the money and do all my visiting over the Grid."

The spacecraft gave a preliminary shudder, then slowly, creakingly began to move along the tarmac. The Allura stewardesses sat down and strapped themselves into their harnesses. The man offered his hand for Obama to clasp. "Hector Kirmani," he said. "I'm in diamonds." The shuttle gathered momentum, then began to hurtle unevenly down the pitted runway toward the Potomac River.

"Obama Jones. MAD."

"Ah, liftoff at last," Hector Kirmani said. They were airborne. Kirmani brought his mouth very close to Obama's ear and said, "You see the Sony robot stewardesses over there?"

"Yes?"

"Frankly, I think they are amazing-looking. And such sensitive features. In my opinion, they are far more beautiful than real womyn. Tell me, have you ever had sexual intercourse with one?"

"With a robot?" replied Obama in surprise. "No, I haven't."

"I have heard," said Kirmani in a confidential tone, "that it's the experience of a lifetime for the male organ. Perhaps we will both get lucky on the Moon."

10.

A hologram pixilated into life just in front of him. It was another scantily-clad Slavic girl, a redhead this time instead of a blonde. "Just two more weeks to go until we restart the clock!" she cooed seductively."That's right, time is finally going decimal! Starting on the first of Humida, each minute will have 100 seconds, and each hour will have 100 minutes. And best of all, we'll be switching over to the new 20-hour decimal day! You'll love your new times so much, you'll feel like there just aren't enough hours left in the day to enjoy them! Which means you'll be feeling years younger. So remember, Ten is In — and 100 is the new 60!"

The redhead was replaced by the somber yet genial features of UN President Jose Manacera. "Howdy," he said, smiling gravely. Obama always got the feeling the world president was speaking directly to him. "And welcome to Selene Japan Aerospacelines' regularly scheduled shuttle flight service to the Moon. For many of you, this trip is routine by now. For many others, it will be your very first visit into space, the thrill of a lifetime. I can well remember my first bout of weightlessness — whoops! I'd just come from a big state banquet in Tashkent, and I thought I was too much of a tough guy to wear my anti-weightless-sickness Gravanil derma-patch. Amigo, was I ever sorry! And so was the guy sitting in front of me, haha. So don't be a dope. Be sure to roll up your sleeve, and let the pretty stewardess do her job.

"Now, a serious chat, if I may, on the future of the Moon Colonies. I guess a lot of you know or are related to someone living on the Moon for medical or retirement reasons. But what you may not know is that only we, the Green Party, remain committed to improving the Moon colonists' lifestyles and expanding the Colonies' size and amenities. That's right, should they by some crazy accident seize power, our honorable opponents plan to cut back — or even curtail — both Moon Colony benefits and future construction.

"Now, I'm not running for president this time round. You know me, and I'll be grateful for just a humble post as Prime Minister of the People's Tribunes in the UN Congress. But you can count on my designated successor for president, current Vice President Coco Terrawati, to continue the pro-Selenic policies that have been a cornerstone of our proud UN record for the past 16 years.

"So remember: in Nyumbro, Go Green! Mother Earth will thank you — and so will her Sister Moon!"

"Pah!" said Kirmani. "It's all a hoax, these elections. Just bread and circuses for the masses. Don't fall for it."

The seats on the *Suki Moon* shuttle were pretty much like seats on a terrestrial aircraft, except wider, deeper, and much more comfortable. This was partly in order to accommodate the seats' anti-grav harnesses. There were only six seats across the width of the cabin, arranged in groups of two separated by two wide aisles. Obama wished he'd gotten a window seat. Through the cabin windows to his left, he could see the great curve of the earth's clouds already falling away below them as the aerospaceplane strained to escape the gravity well.

An Allura crouched down beside him. "I'll need your upper arm for the derma patch," she said. Her slippers were soled with a MicroVel that adhered to the carpets. Her haunches, Obama noticed, had a soft, humyn curve, and he shook his head slightly to rid his mind of the thoughts that Hector Kirmani's earlier words had injected into it. He rolled his sleeve up higher. It was definitely getting colder in the cabin. "You will notice some drowsiness, sir," said the robot, applying the patch. Up close, she really didn't look so much like Kim. And she had no breath to smell. In fact, she smelled of nothing at all. "It's important also for you to wear your complimentary game-cap at all times. Remember, the captain may need to use it in an emergency to require your attention."

"May I have a blanket?" he asked her. It. There had been a movement in the early '40s to obtain accredited minority status for robots, but it had come to nothing, though their humyn advocates continued to press for it. The robots themselves, however, just weren't interested.

"Of course, one minute. May I help you, sir?" she said to Kirmani, who had leaned forward to attract her attention.

"Are you ladies permitted a social life?" he asked her.

"A social life?" the robot asked blankly.

"One wonders what you do in your leisure hours," he murmured.

"I have no leisure hours, sir. I'm a machine. If you desire companionship, I'll be happy to direct you to the Sony Sales Department."

Through the cabin windows, the Earth's curvature had become pronounced. Tiny stray hairs from the stewardess's severely tied-back hair were floating freely, and behind her, Obama noticed that someone had let go of an inhaler that was drifting up toward the plastic ceiling racks. His clothes all felt as though they were gently billowing in a soft breeze rising from below. Deep beneath the white cloud cover, Obama could see the brown, distinctive outline of the Horn of Africa thrusting out into a patch of reflective ocean. He closed his eyes and fell asleep.

When Obama woke up, the windows were completely black. All around him, the passengers were dozing or gaming under their caps. The air inside the shuttle cabin had filled up with tiny drifts of debris — human skin-scale, lint from clothing, bits of food, and dust — and the thin haze created by this had been set swirling by the individual passenger air jets set into the overhead plastic racks.

"This is your captain speaking," said a warm, intimate voice in his ear. "We'll be approaching the UN International Space Station in, oh, about another half hour or so. Passengers to the starboard side of the craft should be able to view the station through the cabin windows until we make our final approach for docking. You'll find the gravity there to be half of Moon-grav, or about a tenth of what you're used to back home. Don't forget to take your hand baggage and any personal items along with you into the Space Station. Just a quick reminder that for most of you, there will be only an average layover of 45 minutes, so my advice is to find your departure lounge as soon as you can and check in at the gate. Enjoy the rest of your flight — and have a safe and pleasant trip to the Moon."

Obama took the opportunity, while he still had his complimentary game-cap on, to slip into Joyful Kalinga's skin and message "VJ Mechanou" over the Grid. VJ Mechanou was the pseudonym of the Romanian teenager who'd created the "Yaybo" hit video of Kalinga from cam-files at Casino Royale. Obama hoped that the message couldn't be traced back to him from this address. "Where is my Royalties money??" was the caption. Obama trembled slightly with the fear of discovery until he'd booted down again.

The interior of the Space Station turned out to pretty much resemble the onGrid social room where Obama, as Joyful Kalinga, had only a week before gone to a party. Except that this version had more billboard holos and corporate advertising and no gaming avatars costumed as demons or mutant droids or vampires. The real station had counter-rotating wheels to enhance stability and simulate a gravity of about .1 Gee. The vessel docking bays were in the large cylindrical central hub. Presumably that was where Eunice's humyn crew lived, though Obama saw none during the hour he spent there, only two types of robots: the Allura stewardesses, with their soft blue uniforms and caps, and the bigger, more rugged, genderless Endura workers, who were dressed in baggy orange safety overalls.

Obama found that there had been a dramatic improvement in low-grav toilet technology since the days of the first *Space Odyssey* sims, thanks to the miracle of the suction jet. After this happy discovery, Obama boarded the relay shuttle to Clarkesville. He watched the latest "*DeadSpace*" sim all the way to the Moon, pausing only to suck a pureed supper from tubes. He was already feeling more used to the weightlessness, so that when the *Queen Millennium* shuttle finally landed, he initially felt the lunar gravity as near-normal. Only, of course, it wasn't. On the Moon, you weighed one-sixth as much as you did on Earth and could jump six times higher, which is why Loonies, as native lunar citizens were called, had invented whole new forms of football, basketball, golf, and soccer.

As they exited, all the remaining passengers — Hector Kirmani had taken another shuttle to Mont Blanc in the Lunar Alps — were required to spray the same MicroVel griptight surface the stewardesses had used during the flight onto the soles of their own shoes, so that they wouldn't over-step and uncontrollably bounce up to the passageway ceilings. The lighter gravity induced a sense of general well-being, even euphoria. It was, Obama decided when he had finally checked into his hotel, like feeling slightly drunk all the time. He suddenly understood why people retired here. *Is Kim here already?* he wondered. *If not, will this be her final destination someday?*

The other reason people retired to the Moon was the luxury. 99% of the lunar colonies had been built underground, both to protect them from radiation and to conserve and stabilize temperatures, which, with no atmosphere, varied wildly on the surface from near absolute zero during the 15 days or so of continuous "night" to over boiling point during the 15-day "day." In any case, radiation-proofed glasspex was too expensive to use on a mass scale. Consequently, the surface domes had been constructed over kilometers of greenhouses, and, of course, the artificial Lake Serenity, but no one actually lived on the surface. So naturally, Obama had thought of living spaces here as cramped and dark — but nothing could have been further from the truth.

His hotel suite was nearly double the size of his condo back home, with high, light-filled ceilings. It was wildly expensive, even for a single night. The furniture was all made from stainless steel, carbon alloys, and cut and highly polished tektite slabs. Everything had to be heavier here, even the bed linens. Even given the high ceilings, Obama thought the suite would have been pretty claustrophobic if not for the hyper-realistic holos everywhere, some emulating windows overlooking underground parkland. There were even artificial aromas to enhance the illusion of the dark rainforest landscapes just "outside."

Yet it all somehow remained unearthly. Even the YouVee seemed different than back home, though there was only about a second and a half transmission delay from Earth. Obama decided that maybe the difference was because the Japanese had been the first lunar colonists. The morning news here was anchored by a holographic cartoon character called "Sailor Moon." Obama left the news on for the Pooka while he showered. In .17 Gee, jets of water were like soft, fat lazy warm blobs that clung to the skin. He had to use the ultrasound to speed them down the drain, and the combination tickled.

When the first lunar colonists had settled Clarkesville and Kubrick City, they'd pegged the Moon's UTC to Tokyo time, but with a 12-day week. So even though it felt like midnight to Obama, it was now almost 10 in the morning local time. He couldn't imagine what the colonists would do next month when it was mandatory to convert to decimal time.

He decided that he felt hungrier than sleepy. He'd been told that the Moon's hydroponic farms yielded inferior produce and that anything worth eating at its restaurants had to be imported from Earth. But after he'd gone down to eat at the Hyatt's main restaurant, he decided that there was very little real difference. The Mandarin Orange in-vitro chicken seemed the same as that at any good New York City restaurant, and the pickled vegetable salad and miso soup seemed slightly better. Sake, of course, was sake, wherever it was drunk, and here at least it was warmed to just the right temperature. For dessert he had "green cheese" ice cream.

The Hyatt was on the main concourse of Clarkesville, which overlooked Lake Serenity and LunaDisney. Hotels and apartment blocks rose up along it nearly 20 storeys high right up to the ceiling, which was covered in skylights. The dome over Lake Serenity was one of the great architectural wonders of the age, and even though the blackness of space was clearly visible through it, a slight atmospheric haze had formed beneath the glasspex, lending the scene something of the illusion of a sleepy summer's day on Earth. The lake's waters would be like the droplets in the shower, thick and viscous, almost as much gel as liquid. Obama tried to imagine what it might feel like to water-ski or float on it. Too bad there wouldn't be time on this trip to find out. Maybe he'd come back.

A holo of all the Moon's tourist attractions shimmered in the center of the table while Obama ate. It showed tourist trolleys snaking through the sidewalk cafes, through crowds of pedestrians, and over arched wooden bridges spanning the stone-lined canals. He'd arrived too late in the season for the Lunar Gran Prix and was too far from the Lunar Alps to visit the underground "North Pole Winter Holiday Village & Ski Resort" inside Mont Blanc, but there were always LFL games to see — in fact, there was one being held live in a local stadium that afternoon. Live sports events were rare on Earth these days, since they were so much easier to attend onGrid. But here on the Moon, the holo ads informed him, people were older and still valued sharing group experiences in person.

After his meal, Obama left the hotel and wandered around window-shopping for a while. Then he took a trip on a tour barge down the main canal into the Magic Kingdom. On his way back to the hotel, he remembered he'd left the Pooka behind in his suite. *Surely I couldn't be tracked down by the UNSS here on the Moon,* he thought. Yet he broke into a sweat anyway at the notion. So he made sure to bring the Pooka along that afternoon when he took the PTT, or Pneu-Tube Train, out to the Willow Precinct Liberry. The trip, which would have taken him 40 minutes on the Manacera City Retrorail, took exactly seven on the Moon. *Everything here feels so luxurious and clean and new,* he thought. *Maybe I should move here, too.* The place had that effect on everybody, apparently. Maybe it was the gravity. Of course, he'd miss real nature, especially the ocean and mountains. Beaches. Trees and meadows, even the rain. But since the advent of global cooling, he spent far less time outdoors being able to actually enjoy them.

If he found a good job here, he could be near his parents. And maybe find Kim again. They said that if you stood beneath the Millennium Arch on the main concourse here long enough, that sooner or later you'd meet everyone you'd ever known ...

The Liberry, which was in the middle of a grove of real willow trees in the middle of an underground park, was part of the Precinct's Traditional University campus. It was a big square building, constructed of pinkish polished Moon rock and some transparent mineral that looked like very pale quartz. It had, he was informed, the largest collection of Japanese literature preserved anywhere, including Japan. It also contained mirrors of most of the legacy data at Japanese universities and institutions. There were UN programs for the similar preservation of those of other nations and cultures, but of course, just like everything else connected to the UN, these programs were plagued by chronic budget shortages and inefficiency. It was true that the Moon, too, was a UN Mandated Territory depending heavily on Federal funding, but somehow things felt freer here. You could even open a little shop if you wanted to.

And everybody seemed so friendly. When Obama asked the Japanese student who helped him at the main desk of the Liberry's front lobby about this, she laughed shyly and gave him a flirtatious glance from the corners of her eyes. "It is because you are young, maybe," she said. "We are all used to only old people visiting us here."

"But you're young," he told her.

"There are only a few thousands of persons of my age on the Moon. Because, you know, we have to be raised in special heavy gravity when we are little. Like Earth's. Most of us are here together at this university. It's very boring. Do you have a girlfriend on Earth?"

"Well ... sort of, yes," he said. "I guess so, anyway. I'm married." Her manner changed perceptibly.

"This is all the information you will be needing for now, I think," she told him. "The robot will come and help to guide you if you become lost, Mr. Jones. And if you are needing any more assistance just speak my name, Tamiko, anywhere inside this building, and I will communicate with you by holo, OK?"

"OK, thanks." On his way down the pneu-tube ascensor he thought, *There are too many women in my life already.* He didn't need a Japanese Skoolgirl, or "Lolita," as they were called in Japan, "Lolitaism" being the actual name of a psychosexual syndrome listed in the World Psychological Association's latest *Diagnostic & Statistical Manual of Mental Disorders XXI.* It was part of Obama's job to keep abreast of all of these unfortunate illnesses, since their sufferers enjoyed automagic minority status.

Sometimes their conflicting needs could create bizarre legal tangles, on which the Department was sometimes called to depose. For example, if a sufferer from Japanese Skoolgirl Lolita Syndrome was driven by his illness to attempt to attempt to kidnap a real Japanese skoolgirl, and she injured him while resisting, then in theory she could be charged with a hate crime. However, as a womyn, she was also legally considered a victim. To obviate the dilemma, the UN provided blue-helmeted UN peacekeeper bodyguards to the families of skoolgirls who desired such protection, though most preferred to hire Japanese gangsters, or *yakuza*.

Since Japan's birth rate remained in precipitate decline, there was an ever-decreasing need for such protection. In fact, Tamiko was the first young Japanese person Obama had ever met. Aside from Simonetta Sato, of course. *If Simonetta grew up in that way,* thought Obama, *it might explain a lot about her behavior.*

Too many women in his life, except the only one he wanted. He sighed unhappily. Since the moment Kim had been taken away from him, his life had become nothing but a bad dream. Everything he'd done since had been like the actions of a laboratory rat clambering around a maze, pointless and frantic and futile. He'd achieved nothing. Maybe everybody was right. At some point maybe he really would need to just give up and start all over again. "And where better than the Moon?" whispered an ad holo in the ascensor. "Low grav, low pressure — and new low, low prices on villas and condominiums, thanks to the UN's new First-Time Buyers' Housing Assistance Credit. Sick of all the hassles of life Earthside? Feeling bogged down? Getting nowhere fast? Well, quit your worrying — up here on the Moon your cares will just float away ..."

Who knows? thought Obama treasonously, as he exited the ascensor onto his Liberry floor. *It might even be fun to hook up with a 'Moon Maid'.* He'd ask her to swipe iRists with him on the way out.

The data morgues of the Willow Precinct in no way resembled those of MAD. The GenBank collection was contained inside a single huge room, filled with helpful robot servitors and how-to holograms. Obama was looking for only the single data file collection, which was known as "HGP K6 SSWATZ28954172.1952-2022." Legacy Data translation machines stood at the end of each long row of gently refrigerated, waist-high, horizontal display bins. To use a translation machine, you simply slipped the storage media into it and the media were automagically detected, translated, and then ported to your iRist or onGrid account.

Why couldn't MAD have funding like this? thought Obama. Why did he have to work in such a miserably decrepit, ancient tenement of a building, filled with broken-down and outdated technologies and bored — or even worse, crazed and resentful — coworkers? Obama felt he could be perfectly happy spending the rest of his life at an institution like this one, helping to preserve the precious and vanishing humyn heritage for the future. Why not? It had already done him a lot of good just to get away off-planet for a bit. Some of this feeling, he knew, was just the giddiness of the lower gravity. But some of it was real. The question was, how much?

In the merest fraction of the time it would have taken Priska or Raffi, the Endura robot located and extracted the "HGP K6 SSWATZ28954172.1952-2022" disk and fed it into the translation machine. After a few minutes, the Endura swiped his iRist. Obama glanced at the data, then attempted to scroll through it. It was blank. None of the data was there.

He made the Endura remove the disk from the machine, then he himself fed the data back through and attempted to manually translate it, scanning it visually as he did. Blank. He removed other data containers at random from the bins and fed their contents into another machine. They were all blank. Obama looked around the huge, brightly gleaming, beautiful room. There was, as far as he could tell, nothing actually in it.

Tamiko seemed at first politely disbelieving, then terribly, almost personally, mortified when he complained to her about it at the front desk. But all she could do, aside from apologizing profusely, was to swipe him the iTooth of the Liberry's Director, a Mr. Ichinose, who did not answer his chimes. Obama left two messages, then went back to his hotel.

Where he spotted Park and Malek loitering inside the front lobby.

Maybe it was because he was so wired from lack of sleep. Or maybe it was just the pure adrenaline rush generated by sudden fear. But the moment he saw the two Security Service agents, Obama simply turned and walked back the way he'd come. Not hurriedly, but adapting his speed to that of the milling crowd of tourists around him and — most importantly, he thought — without glancing back and taking a look behind him. Were they following him? He hopped into a trolley-train as it moved past him, then hopped out of it again three intersections down. He ducked inside a souvenir shop, and stood watching in a reflective glasspex for any signs of pursuit. There seemed to be none. He glanced down at the top of the Pooka's head. Obviously, he'd strayed a little too far from her this morning — and for too long — but now they wouldn't be able to track him. Maybe.

He moved quickly, hopping the next trolley and ducking down into a station to take the pneu-tube out to the aerospaceport. He changed his reservations for an earlier shuttle out to the space station, and within a few hours was back at Eunice. Now he had a five-hour wait, since there were no shuttles back to Manacera City until the *Suki Moon* redocked. He didn't dare sleep or put on a game-cap, so he spent this time pretending to watch holo ads while actually scrutinizing each passenger who came through the lounge doors. He felt too sick and nervous to eat. What he would do if Park and Malek suddenly walked through the arrivals gate? Run? Chime Eunice security? He would have to face it if and when the time came.

Surely, Obama thought, if they had been hanging around his hotel lobby, it meant they hadn't known exactly where he was. Otherwise, they would have waylaid him at the Willow Precinct Station. Or anywhere else he'd gone today. Which meant they'd picked up his coms at lunch and had only just located him. Which maybe meant that now the Pooka was able to protect him again from remote scrutiny.

He'd made a swipe at the pneu-tube station, though. And there was that shuttle ticket switch. And biometric records of him going through all the gates between Clarkesville and here. *Don't let me down,* he silently begged the Pooka.

But how had they known he was on the Moon at all? Had they first traced him and then followed him here after he'd messaged the Romanian kid from the shuttle?

At just before 6 am Earth UTC, or 1 am Eastern Standard Time, the *Suki Moon* docked and released a flood of new passengers. An hour later the aerospace craft was ready to board. Obama was first in line. He was just strapping himself into his seat, one directly next to a cabin window this time, when the shuttle's last passenger arrived and sat down next him.

It was Simonetta. "Don't be mad, OK?" she said, laying a hand on his arm. "I have something really important to tell you, Bammy." The cabin doors hissed shut and sealed themselves. "I'm sorry. You aren't going to like this."

11.

"Yaybo, Mr. Kalinga," said Carmen Crowfoot in a husky whisper. "You literally cannot imagine how much I've looked forward to meeting you at last."

Actually, he could. She'd had a complete makeover for the occasion. This had involved getting 20 or so kilos of herself liposuctioned away and getting a glitter-rock pedicure. To show this off, she was wearing a pair of the latest open-toed aerogel-clogs, and, scariest of all, was sporting a new hairstyle. Her usual black cap of greasy, unkempt locks had been shorn and bleached into clumps of transparent spaghetti, punctuated by clusters of reddish tubes that resembled suction-cups attached to her scalp. Pathetically, she'd shed her motorized cart and was attempting to walk normally.

"Everyone does," Joyful Kalinga replied modestly. Obama was nervous about doing the voice. He was following Simonetta's instructions and keeping to the shadows as much as possible, so that his face would be less likely to be recognized. Disguised as Joyful Kalinga, he'd met Carmen on the rooftop parking lot atop the MAD building just after sunset. Obama had spent the workday in the building as himself, then "changed into" Kalinga in a restroom stall before taking the ascensor up to the roof after hours. Now he was terrified not only of discovery and arrest, but of Carmen's seeing through the charade. What could he possibly say to her if she did? Even if she didn't fire him, she'd make his life miserable forever after. The story would spread throughout the whole department like a virus, and he'd be a laughingstock for the rest of his career there. But Simonetta had given him no choice. Or wiggle-room, as Carmen liked to call it.

He and Carmen were standing, hidden from the few remaining parked aircars, on a balconied common area behind an arcade of ascensor doors. The balcony overlooked the bright lights of the city's downtown, which lay to the northwest. Stalled rush-hour traffic still streamed continuously on the streets far below, and a cold wind steadily blew exhaust fumes back in their faces. "Huff!" said Carmen. "I need to sit down!" She toppled onto a metal mesh patio bench that all but collapsed under her weight, its center sagging ominously halfway down to the ferro-concrete floor.

"What is it do you want from Kalinga, fat white lady?" Obama asked her.

"Oh, I'm not white! I'm a full-blooded Native American. Besides, I thought you Africans like your womyn fat." She giggled throatily. *Oh god,* Obama thought. *She's in heat. Not her, too.* For most of his life nobody had wanted him except Kim. Now it was like everybody did.

"OK, so what is it you want?" He had brought the Pooka along in his backpack for luck. Maybe it was keeping their conversation at least semi-private from all the bugs and crawling spider-bot cams that were probably lurking around them now. It certainly hadn't hidden him from Simonetta on the space shuttle a few hours earlier. But maybe that wasn't the Pooka's fault. Maybe Simonetta had been following Park and Malek. Or working with them.

"OK, what do you want?" he'd said to Simonetta when he'd first gotten over the shock of seeing her there.

"It isn't about what I want, Bammy," Simonetta had replied in a cold, hurt tone. "This is about what we both have to do to get what we want. And what you have to do is meet Carmen on the roof of the MAD building tonight disguised as Joyful Kalinga." She ignored his protests. "When you touch down, go straight home from the aerospaceport and pack everything you need to be Kalinga — clothes, make-up, whatever — into a bag or something. Then come in to work just like normal."

"What about security?" he had asked.

"Don't worry about security — that's all fixed. I'll be waiting for you downstairs anyway. And I'll coach you on the rest of this at lunch. It's really important."

"Important to who?" Obama had asked bitterly. "The Security Services?"

"Among others, yes."

"Well, if you're working for them, then you can tell me where Kim is."

Obama had been totally taken aback by Simonetta's reaction when he said this. She had suddenly and histrionically burst into tears. "Oh,

'Kim, Kim, Kim' — is that all you can ever say? Is that all you think about?"

"Well ... yeah. Pretty much." *Duh,* he'd thought.

She had turned in her seat and grasped both his jacket lapels angrily. The two of them had floated toward each other slightly, restrained by their zero-grav harnesses. A tear-drop detached itself from her face and drifted slowly across his vision. Another beaded on the tip of her nose. "Listen, Bammy: Kim was just something ephemeral in your life. Like, oh, I don't know, a cat or a dog. Or a mayfly or something. She was always going to go away and leave you — that moment in your life was always destined to happen. But you and I are different. We're intended to be together forever and ever. We were made for each other, get it? We belong to each other! I'm yours and you're mine. Can't you understand that?" He had looked at her then as if he were seeing her for the first time: the strained expression on her feral face, her eyes swimming with tears, her trembling chin, her waves of copperish hair escaping from around the game-cap wildly, like writhing snakes. Suddenly, he'd felt something like pity. She was clearly insane.

But what could he possibly say to make it better? His eyelids were growing heavy from the Gravinil patch, and he was already feeling drowsy. She'd leaned toward him so close that her Botticelli Venus face was all he could see. "Don't forget, Bammy. Tonight. On the roof. Carmen. Joyful Kalinga." She had spoken to him as though he were a baby, then kissed each of his eyelids as he fell asleep.

He'd woken up again when the *Suki Moon* had been just about to re-enter the Earth's atmosphere. But Simonetta was gone. She simply wasn't on the shuttle any more, unless she was hiding in the robot steward's galley or the cockpit. Or the luggage compartment. Obama had known this because he'd hung around and waited until the last of the passengers disembarked before he'd left the arrivals gate. Simonetta had somehow managed to vanish. From a spacecraft — while it had been in space.

This was, naturally enough, the first thing he had asked her about when he'd seen her two hours later in the MAD lobby. She just shrugged sullenly and said he must have missed her somehow. And now that he knew for sure she was sanity-challenged, he hadn't felt like calling her on it. But he hadn't believed her, either. How had she managed to disappear? And why? It had nagged at him all the rest of the day. He felt as if his subconscious was trying to tell him something, but he was too sleepy and stupid to listen to it.

"We want you to join our Direct Action team," Carmen was saying to him now, or rather to Kalinga, as she teetered dangerously forward, her arms groping at him like a she-bear's. She had, Obama noticed, made up her face to resemble that of a sad clown. "You see, MAD — my Department — is part of a coalition of other Federal departments and agencies at war with HHS, the Department of Health & Human Services. We're actually a pretty small player." She counted the others off on her sausage-like fingers: "The three biggest dogs on our side in this fight are the Departments of Peace & Non-Violence, Energy, and Education. Then there are a half-dozen others about our size. We here at MAD love your work — the HHS bombing was amazingly awesome — and we want you to be 'our guy' with the direct action group that's already been hired and put in place."

"Kalinga is getting bored now, because he can almost not understand a single damn word you are saying, woman. Who are these people you are talking about?"

She lowered her voice even further. "The Warriors of God," she told him. "You know, the radical Islamist terror group. They all hate HHS anyway, because they have a bunch of old Homeland Security spooks still working there. Plus the towel-heads are always feuding with Welfare & Social Services. On the other hand, MAD and Education are their biggest sponsors. So it was a perfect fit for us."

"And you want me to bomb buildings with these terror people?" asked Obama incredulously. He didn't have to fake his shock and disbelief. Carmen shook her head violently.

"Oh no," she said. "Not just bomb! That shit is just a side-show, anyway. No, we want you to be our executive agent on their action committee. You'll be participating in all the paramilitary decisions at the very highest level. And of course we'd expect you to act as our unofficial spokesperson while you pursue your YouVee career. In return I'm authorized to offer you full immunity as a North American resident with protected minority status. Plus, MAD is prepared to allocate a million Unos a year to you in a Swiss bank account. I fought for more for you, but hey, we're in the middle of a fucking budget crunch here." She made a dramatic mopey-face.

It was at that moment they felt the floor tremble beneath them and heard a loud "whump!" from downstairs. Obama knew by now exactly what this noise meant. Someone had just set off a bomb inside the MAD building.

"The fucking bastards!" exclaimed Carmen, struggling and failing to get to her feet. "It must be the WTC!" From below came the sounds of sirens whooping and a sudden smell of smoke. "We gotta get out of here! Don't just stand there — help me up, amigo!"

Obama lifted her out of her seat and they set off toward the parked aircars, with him supporting her as she hobbled uncomfortably along. "The WTC?" he asked her.

"The White Terror Commando — the rednecks who want the old US back. They're working for HHS. There just aren't that many terrorist groups out there to choose from any more." She paused in front of her aircar, a pimped metallic blue Revolvo, and swiped the doors open. "Get me into the driver's seat, and then let's get the hell out of here." The rooftop lighting was running on the emergency generators and had dimmed down to grey. Aircars would land and lift off now at their own risk. A warning siren whooped nearby as the car's exhausts started smoking.

"I can't," said Obama, momentarily forgetting to speak like Kalinga. "There might be people trapped down there."

"What?" she screamed at him over the racket.

He lowered his voice and roared, "Kalinga never run away from anybody! See you later maybe, fat lady!" He swiped open the door to the emergency staircase.

"But what about our deal?" she screeched after him. She sounded like a banshee in a D&D game onGrid.

The lights inside the emergency stairwells worked only intermittently even at the best of times, due to the constant rainfall inside them. Now Obama found himself in pitch darkness. "Damn, I wish I'd brought a flashlight," he muttered. The moment he said this, his backpack began to glow, casting a wide hunched shadow down the dripping cement steps beneath him. It was the Pooka — obviously she had the ability to light up in the dark like a lantern. *What else might she do if I just wish the words aloud?* he wondered. *Play music? Act as a GPS?* It was like being in a fairy-tale. Drops of condensation spattered on his head, and he made his way cautiously down to the landing on the next level. As he descended lower and lower into the building, the smell of smoke grew more intense, as did the electronic whooping of alarms.

The top floors appeared undamaged when he opened each of their safety doors in turn and peered inside them, though their sprinkler systems were all on and irrigating the carpets. It was hard to see much by the dim reddish glow cast by the Pooka through the woven Nitinelle fabric of the backpack. But he couldn't find another living soul the whole way down. It would take him hours to go thoroughly through the building — which, mercifully, tended to be deserted this late after hours anyway. Federal employees had little incentive to work late. Or at all, really.

But there were a few employees living in the second floor dormitory suites, he remembered. When he got there, he discovered that the second floor seemed to have been the epicenter of the blast. He could barely push the heavy staircase door open because of the plaster rubble blocking it. When he did, he found the corridor full of smoke, along with the overpowering odors of benzine and burning metal.

A nearby wall collapsed. There were fires still blazing wherever any combustible material remained, and a constant cascade of water dripped down from upper floors through huge, jagged holes in the ceiling. There were even larger gaps in the flooring, where virtually the entire center section had fallen into the lobby below, leaving twisted metal cables snaking out of the shattered concrete. Peering down through one of these enormous holes in the floor, Obama could see that part of the lobby floor had in turn crumbled under the impact of falling debris and fallen through into Data Storage.

By now he was coughing and choking uncontrollably. He tore off a part of his shirt and, after soaking it in water, wrapped it around his nose and mouth. This helped, but not much.

Obama gradually became aware of a high-pitched wailing noise coming from one of the hallways behind him. It sounded more or less humyn, but he couldn't be sure. It was coming from outside the middle ring of the building, close to the outer wall. But this section of the second floor was even smokier now, because the ceiling was relatively intact and therefore provided little ventilation. He set off down a second hallway in the direction of the noise, bent over almost double and keeping his face as close to the floor as possible so he could breathe in whatever oxygen was still left.

It was Priska. Obama had never been in this part of the building before, but he realized who it must be from the noises she was making. And the smell. He passed a closet which had been blown apart. The gorilla had evidently been throwing her used diapers into it for months.

He gagged and crawled away rapidly down the hall on all fours. Water was pouring down on him from the sprinklers on the ceiling. The doors of Priska's darkened suite were open, and the sound of wailing grew louder as he came closer.

Inside the suite, he saw that an ancient children's Jungle Gym had been constructed along the walls, and a few wooden bunk beds were anchored in the middle. The stench was even more overpowering here. Debris and rotting food were heaped everywhere, along with stacks of plastic toys and data storage containers. Priska was huddled under one of the bunk beds, crying and trembling.

There was a single window set into one of the walls. None of the windows inside the MAD building could be opened, however, so with the last reserves of his strength Obama wrenched loose a metal rung from a set of overhead bars and smashed it against the pane. It bounced back at him. It took several attempts before the double-glazed panels — real old-skool glass and not glasspex — cracked and then finally shattered. After he'd hammered out the sharp shards from the frame around it, Obama stuck his head outside and took in a few deep breaths of cold air. Smoke billowed out all around him. He felt an intense blast of heat from behind and turned to see the far wall suddenly engulfed in flames. The wall started to collapse. He had inadvertently injected a shot of oxygen into the second floor, and everywhere inside it fires were roaring back to life.

"Come on, Priska," he said, clambering over to pull at the form huddled in the darkened hole beneath the bed. "Come on, honey; we have to get you out of here. Priska doesn't want to die, does she?" *Do the higher primates even understand the concept of death?* he wondered. Dogs supposedly didn't, he knew — that had been one of the legal arguments against granting them minority status. Priska moaned and pushed his hands away. She was growing weaker, he could tell. Normally, one of her blows could break a wrist. "Come on, Priska," he said again, and managed to pull the gorilla's head around so that she could see him. The rain of water had stopped, and the room was rapidly filling up with dense smoke. "It's Obama, see?" He wrenched one of her front hands from her and placed it on his chest. "See? Obama." Priska nodded apathetically but gave him only a token squeeze. "Good girl. Let's get you out of there."

As he half-pulled, half-rolled Priska out of her hidey-hole, a plastic data container she'd been lying on tumbled out with her. Obama picked it up and read its spine: "HGP K6 SSWATZ28954172.1952-2022." He zipped it into his backpack, then wrenched Priska to her feet. Her

Fisher-Price "My First Symbols Keyboard" was lying on the bed beside him. He picked it up and looped its strap over her head, then turned and let her collapse onto his back. She wrapped her enormous furry arms around his shoulders and neck, and he carried her piggyback over to the window. He stopped and looked out of it.

Obama had assumed that he would find the place ringed by firefighting equipment, but there was none he could see anywhere. A few pedestrians stared up at him and waved, and he watched two news-bot cameras flying over in their direction from a landing CNN airvan. An airbulance circled overhead, lights flashing. He looked down. Immediately below the window was a thick ligustrum hedge and a crepe myrtle tree. That would have to do. He and Priska were only on the second floor; it was perhaps a 7 or 8 meter drop. He turned back to tell her, "We're going to have to jump, Priska. The hedge should break our fall." Her breath was hot in his face, and she started crying again. "Oh, stop being such a baby — you're probably better at this than I am!"

One of the pedestrians waved at him again and shouted something; he had no idea what. Nor did he care — he couldn't breathe at all now. His rib cage felt as if it were on fire. Obama clambered up onto the window ledge, crouched there until he over-balanced, then tried to jump just far enough to clear the side of the building. But with a 100 kilo gorilla on his back, his legs had no strength left in them, and he and Priska plummeted straight down into the ligustrum bushes and landed there with a loud crunch.

Somehow, maybe because Priska weighed more than he did, they'd twisted around during their fall, so that Obama had landed on top of her. The bush had fractured and flattened under them, but hadn't splintered. Which was probably what had prevented their being impaled, though they were both covered in scratches.

Obama couldn't tell if Priska was seriously injured or only badly winded, but he seemed to be unharmed. He clambered out of the hedge just as the airbulance landed and the Emergency Rescue crew raced over. "This is Tinkerbelle from Cartoon News!" chirped one of the bots while the other buzzed around Obama's face for close-ups. "I'm here at the scene of the latest alleged terrorist attack, along with 'North America's Most Wanted', Mr. Joyful Kalinga, who has just risked his own life to save that of a higher primate in a death-defying leap. Tell me, Mr. Kalinga, did you personally set off the bomb that has just devastated the Minority Assistance Building?"

"Call me Joyful, please," rumbled Obama. The smoke had irritated his voice into an unrecognizable rasp. He smiled a gruesome smile for the camera, exposing his false teeth. "Everybody mostly does. No, Tinkerbelle, I know nothing of that bomb. Whatever person who exploded this bomb did a very bad thing. Even now there are other minorities maybe dead or maybe just dying inside that place." He glanced around and saw the ER crew strapping Priska onto a gurney. They had fixed an oxygen mask over her face, but he was pretty sure she was OK. He could see her clutching the keyboard tightly to her, refusing all their attempts to pry it away.

"Tell me, Joyful — what goes through your head at a time like that? What was your very last thought before you jumped?"

"Oh, I would say the same as always. I think about sex. And money." The bot giggled encouragingly. The bot didn't actually look like Tinkerbelle; it just had her voice. Right now it was round and metallic. The Tinkerbelle visuals would be digitally added in the studio later. "There's talk of another hit video in the works, Joyful. Any truth to the rumor?"

"Oh yes, Tink, I think we be making a big deal for this very soon. But now Joyful Kalinga must sadly leave you," said Obama. "There are maybe other dead persons he must save." Picking up a loose chunk of concrete, he raised it above his head and hurled it through one of the first floor glass panels. It shattered and collapsed to the pavement, setting off yet another alarm.

"You're a big man, Joyful Kalinga!" Tinkerbelle trilled ecstatically. She would make CNN OneWorldLive! tonight. "Yaybo!"

"YeeeayyyeeaayyeayBO!" he roared for the cameras, then hurled himself back through the ornamental draperies into the MAD building before disappearing into the darkness within. He'd suddenly remembered that he needed a place to change back into himself before he could go home. Kalinga's black coat had caught fire in several places and was covered in white ash, and the alligator shoes were splitting apart at the seams. The first floor seemed as good a place for this makeover as any. Right now it was empty. And even though it was covered with close to 20 cm of water, it was relatively free of smoke outside the main lobby.

The Pooka switched her light on again without his even having to ask. The meeting with Carmen had gone far better than he'd dared hope — and now that the building had been destroyed, he probably wouldn't even have to come to work tomorrow. Things were definitely looking up.

It was weird, thought Obama, as he sloshed down the hallway in search of a restroom or private office, how much more cheerful and optimistic he felt whenever he was forced to turn into Joyful Kalinga. Kalinga, of course, was a horrible, even a vile and disgusting person — Obama had forced himself not to bathe before coming to work that morning, merely dousing himself in cheap cologne instead — but the terrorist character did exude something potent. For one thing, he had a contagious optimism about life. *And no matter how horrible they are,* thought Obama, *it really is fun to be someone else for a change.* The real Obama Jones would have been way too shy for a YouVee interview and probably wouldn't have thought of a single coherent thing to say. But Joyful Kalinga was never shy — and coherence wasn't an issue. He said whatever he wanted. He just waded in and took charge of situations, and people —even bots — seemed to admire that. Maybe Obama should have thought of doing this Kalinga thing years ago.

Although he'd never wanted to be anyone else, really, especially after he met Kim. Obama briefly wondered what she would have thought of Kalinga. Not much, probably. But at least she'd have been proud of him for saving Priska tonight.

The thought of Priska gave him another idea. He found a safe corner inside a ground-floor holographic exhibit dedicated to the life of Taichi Takashita — the first martyr of MAMAL, or Man And Manga Anime Love, who'd been so cruelly persecuted for attempting to legally marry a cartoon character — and changed back into being Obama Jones again, removing his tattoos and glue scars, and stuffing Kalinga's soiled, filthy clothing into his backpack. After he pulled his own clothing back on, he ducked down another emergency stairwell. He'd originally planned to loiter around inside until the fire-fighting robots, who were at long last breaking into the lobby through the front doors, could find and rescue him. Instead, Obama decided to try to go down two flights to the Custodial & Security level and check out Raffi's secret storage room. There was always the chance that Raffi or one of his friends had been trapped down there. And in addition, there was one last MAD thing he still needed to do.

The refrigerated permafrost was already breaking up in the halls. Floes of ice came floating down the knee-high river of water; sheets and stalactites crashed down from the walls and ceiling pipes. He'd have to hurry, or he'd drown. His breath came out in great clouds of steam, and a noxious fog, thick with the smells of burning chemicals and charred building materials, was rolling in.

A few emergency lights were still on, and there was just enough electrical power left so that the doors sluggishly opened when he swiped them. But how much longer would that last? The remaining lights were already dim and flickering. If he got trapped inside a room or locked out of a corridor, he really would drown.

He took a wrong turn, then retraced his steps. Finally, he found Raffi's storage room again. No one was there. Half the contents of the shelves were now floating in the water. Luckily, the disk-conversion unit he needed was still on its table. He put it in his backpack and left the way he'd come.

No one noticed him slip out of the building this time. *There's something to be said, after all, for being Obama Jones sometimes,* he thought. He was almost invisible. And that could be a good thing.

He took the Retro home. During the ride, just across from his seat up at billboard level the 11 o'clock holographic nightly news winked to life in miniature. "Yaybo," said Snow White gravely. "Tonight, yet another alleged terrorist bombing in the North American Administrative Area, downtown Manacera City. Yet another Federal building targeted. But in an incredible twist to our ongoing tale, a so-called villain turns out to be a real-life hero. Standing by with the details is our very own beloved Tinkerbelle."

"Yaybo, Snow. Just minutes ago, we personally witnessed an amazing death-defying act of unselfish bravery here on the part of the African-American 'Robin Hood', Joyful Kalinga, who saved an Affirmative Primate Employee at the Minorities Assistance Department from certain death inside this burning building behind me by leaping, with Priska the gorilla strapped to his back, from an upper floor window. Somehow they both survived. And not only is Joyful Kalinga the 'big man' he claims to be — he may very well be some kind of Superman! He actually got up and walked away from the scene — and was even unhurt enough to graciously grant us this exclusive interview ..."

The file footage of Obama's leap followed. It had been carefully taken from an angle which seemed to show him jumping down from a much greater height than in fact he had, and the speed of his descent had been slowed to add to the illusion. The interview which followed, however, was more or less as he remembered it. It was amazing, he thought, how different he looked when he was being Kalinga. He barely recognized himself.

Certainly no one else did. Two little girls of about 9 and 11, well-dressed and cute as buttons, were walking up and down his car, approaching each of the passengers in turn. Their mother was sitting at the rear nearest the doors. "Yaybo, Mister," one of them said to him. "Can you swipe me a Uno? I'll tell my momma you touched me if you don't." In the end he swiped each of them a Uno, feeling faintly outraged by having been gamed like that. *How would Joyful Kalinga have handled it?* Obama wondered — then decided he really didn't want to go there.

On his way out of the Harborplex Station, he suddenly had the irrational feeling that he was being followed. Unlike on the Moon, however, where spaces were smaller and brighter and there were fewer people, here on Earth it was harder to tell. He glanced back over his shoulder once or twice going up the segualator. There was something familiar about the shape of one of the figures following up from the platform. Was it Park? Malek? No, he didn't think so. His impression was that this guy was the wrong height. But UNSS had thousands of other agents and stringers. It could be anyone.

He hurriedly turned onto Arnold Avenue and accelerated his pace to a near run. *This is dumb,* he thought. *What's the point? They already know where I live. But in that case, why are they bothering to follow me?* Unless, he decided, it wasn't Park and Malek at all, but some new player in the Joyful game, like HHS. Could the guy tagging him now have picked him up leaving the MAD building?

Three blocks down Arnold, Obama turned off into an alley and looked back the way he'd come in a traffic mirror mounted into the corner of a building. The familiar shape materialized again in silhouette, walking purposefully behind him. Purposefully and patiently. Obama still couldn't see the guy's face. He got the feeling, though, that he really didn't want to.

He became aware of engine noise directly overhead. It grew louder, echoing against the brick walls of the alley, and a gleaming obsidian-black BeeMercedes floated down in a cloud of exhaust fumes and steam to land on the pavement just beside him. The front passenger side door swung vertically open, and Obama saw Siren Gunnarsdottir in the driver's seat, her white hair bathed in yellow-green light. She was wearing a glossy red Nitinyl raincoat that matched the color of her lips. "Need a lift?" she said. This time she wasn't smiling.

12.

"I just saw you on YouVee," Siren told him as she sent the Beemer into a dizzying vertical ascent. "Ever considered it as a career?" Once clear of the rooftops, the aircar slowed to spin and drift. Obama noticed the Princess — Siren's life-size Hair-Salon Barbie plastic bust — propped up in the center of the back seat.

"Where are we going?" Obama asked Siren.

"To your place," she said. It came out "yaw plyce" in her thick South African accent. "We have some info-trading to do, right? But I'm afraid I don't have very much to give you yet. Your wife has disappeared."

He was momentarily confused. Of course Kim had disappeared. That was the whole point. "What do you mean?"

Siren swiveled in her seat to glance at him. "Tell me something, Obama. I know it's an old-skool thing to do, but did your wife take your last name, by any chance? Did she call herself 'Kim Jones'?"

Obama shook his head emphatically. "No, no. Oh, wait, I know what this might be all about. My wife had her last name legally changed after her father left her mother. There was a lot of bitterness in the family. She had been Kim Blankenship before, but after that she became Kim Song."

"Which was the same name as her grandmother — Kim Frances Song?" They were approaching the blinking rooftop landing pad of his building. Obama hadn't been up there since the night they'd taken Kim away.

"Yeah, Kim Frances Song. What's all this about anyway?"

Siren didn't immediately answer. "Was there anything to connect your wife's grandmother to this address?" she asked him. The car landed with a soft bump, and Siren taxied it into a guest parking space. "Had she ever lived with you here, for instance?"

"No, she died right before we bought it. We used some of her bequest to Kim for the down payment, actually."

"Ah," said Siren unhappily. "I was afraid of something like that. This is typical of HHS — they summonsed and swore in the wrong Kim Song. They were after her dead grandmother all along, not her."

"So it was all just a big mistake," said Obama, feeling the first stirring of a vast sense of relief. "That's great! Can't we just sue them now and get her out?" He could hear an edge of excitement creeping into his own voice. But Siren was still shaking her head gloomily.

"No, the Feds never admit to making mistakes. And as you well know, lawsuits against any UN department take forever. There are still some on the docket from the last century. But here comes the really bad news, Obama — they really seem to have lost her. I meant what I said literally. They've mislaid her in the system somewhere. When they empaneled her they wiped all her biometrics, all her personal data, everything. The only physical records they have on file are those of your wife's grandmother. And of course, those are totally useless; they don't show her existing anywhere on Earth. There's no way to trace your wife now. She could walk through the security scanners downstairs in your lobby right this minute and not show up as anything, not even as a ghost. I won't stop trying to find her," Siren said, seeing the stricken expression on his face. "It's just going to take a bit longer, that's all. I'm sorry. Come on, let's go down to your apartment and take a look at the data files you found for me at MAD. You can feed me supper."

"Right, no garlic," Obama said, but his mind was on other things.

While they waited for the ascensor, he asked, "If she's not on Earth, then what about the Moon?" The ascensor arrived, and Siren gave a twisted smile as they got into it.

"I'd forgotten about your little weekend jaunt," she told him sardonically. "No, don't worry. Your wife's not on the Moon. Luckily for you."

"What do you mean?"

She sighed and shook her head again, as if to clear it. Then she stared at him hard. The ascensor door opened, they exited, and he swiped his front door open for her. "What is it about you that makes me want to tell you things?" Siren asked. "Such as the truth? It's not a problem I suffer from with anyone else. Right," she said as she followed him through the foyer into his living room. Lights turned themselves on as they entered. The place was a total mess, he saw. Everything needed straightening and cleaning. He hoped Siren Gunnarsdottir wasn't too fastidious. "You'd better sit down first."

"What?" he said. "Why?"

"Just sit down. This isn't something you're going to want to hear standing up." They took off their coats and he dumped them into a chair. She was wearing a soft white dress with its hemline cut very short. The dress was rumpled and so askew it was almost sideways. She had, he noticed, the longest, loveliest legs he'd ever seen in his life. They looked like silk. It was all he could do not to stare at them as she sat down. She reclined on the couch, and he sat in the other chair on the opposite side of the glasspex coffee table. She crossed her legs very deliberately. "Obama," she went on, "There is no Moon."

"Huh? What are you talking about? I was just there." He looked out the window over his shoulder. He had left the vertical blinds open, and the Moon was half-visible. It was full tonight and looked unusually swollen and bright, like a big orange balloon.

She smiled again. He was getting tired of those superior-looking smiles, especially when she had lipstick on her teeth. "Of course, the Moon exists. It's right up there in plain view. But the Moon Colony doesn't. It's all a political fiction."

"But you can see the Colony from Earth," Obama protested. "If I had a telescope here I could show you Tranquility Base and the dome over Lake Serenity. I've been to the Colony! I've seen it with my own eyes. People go back and forth all the time to see their relatives." But she was shaking her head again in that infuriating way of hers.

"No, Obama, what you could see through your telescope are just holograms under glasspex. There is a real space station, right enough; there are several bases on the Moon. But only a few robots live in them. Humyns can't for long because of radiation. Listen," she said, before he could interrupt. "What happened on your flight? After you put your Gravinil patch on, I mean?"

"I don't know. I fell asleep, I guess."

"Along with everybody else on board, except for the Allura robots. And what were you all wearing when you woke up? Game-caps. Remember what happened on the way back? You fell asleep again, didn't you?" She sounded like she was talking to a very small child. *As usual,* he thought. "And when you woke up?"

"Simonetta was gone," said Obama in a whisper. Suddenly everything that had been bothering him about the trip was starting to make sense. Only now he didn't want it to.

"She was gone because she'd never been there. The procedure is this: you take off on the shuttle from an aerospaceport and go into orbit. That part is real, at least — though at the very start of the program, they didn't even bother with it. They just processed everyone inside the aerospaceports here on Earth. But there were too many witnesses and too many awkward questions being raised, so now they do all the processing at Eunice."

"What do you mean — 'processing'?"

She re-crossed her legs. The whole situation was so surreal, he thought. Here she was, calmly trying to convince him that the Moon colonization program was a hoax — had always been a hoax — and the whole time all he could do was stare at her with his tongue hanging out. Did she have this effect on everyone? She must enjoy it, or she wouldn't be dressed like that. Or maybe she just used it to professional advantage. He didn't know anything about her at all, he realized, yet she seemed to know everything about him. Even the details of his shuttle flight back with Simonetta.

"As you must have realized by now, Obama, the whole false Moon experience happens onGrid, starting when you're on your way to the Space Station and fall asleep. It doesn't take place over the regular Grid but on the private one Sato built for the UN government. You'd already been there once, remember, after the second bombing? With Park and Malek? That Grid can only be accessed using special game-caps. They look pretty much the same as yours" — she gestured dismissively at his own, which was lying on the coffee-table right now between the two of them — "but they're a generation more advanced. So is the UNGrid. Surely you noticed how much more vivid and real the experience was. Right? But if you think about it, you'll realize you spotted some coding holes in it at the time. The data files at Willow Precinct, for instance; they didn't actually exist. They were just blank spaces. And do you really think there's any current technology — or enough UN money — to get that much water up to Lake Serenity and keep it from leaking and evaporating throughout the Colony? If there were, the place would be like a giant MAD building with mold growing everywhere and the windows frosted over. Your subconscious mind knew all this at some level, but you wanted to believe in it, so you did."

"Like believing in Tinkerbelle."

"Right, just like Tinkerbelle." Siren laughed. This made her whole body quiver beneath her dress, adding to Obama's torment. He felt as though he had millions of questions to ask her, but as long as he was staring at her like this, he was too stupid to think of them. He shut his eyes.

"OK," he said after a moment, still keeping them closed. "You said 'processed'. Obviously tourists and visitors like me come back to their real lives, unless this is just like in the 'Matrix' sims and I'm still onGrid – "

"You know how to find that out. Just say it. Go on, I dare you."

"Wiiboot. Detach. Wiiboot," he said, feeling foolish. Nothing happened, except that she laughed at him again. "OK, this is all real, I guess. Crazy and weird, but real. But what happens to the people who stay? My mom and dad are thinking of emigrating there. What would happen to them if they did?"

"I was really, really hoping you wouldn't ask me that, Obama," said Siren. "You sure you want to know? Why don't we have some supper first? You must be starving."

"No. No, please, just tell me."

"Just remember I warned you, OK? All right, at first, about 30 years ago, they used to just take emigrés up and shoot them out of the shuttles like torpedoes. The idea was to get the corpses out beyond the Lagrange points so that they could escape the planetary pull of both Earth and Moon. But of course, that didn't work out — the bodies kept getting recaptured and drifting around in orbit like shoals of dead fish in the Sargasso Sea. Some even fell back into re-entry and burned up like meteorites. So then Sato had a better suggestion: cryonics. You know what that is, right?"

"Freezing people so they can be revived later?"

"Right. So now all the old people are taken off the shuttle at Eunice and frozen in de-pressurized bays. Space is close to absolute zero in temperature, which is considered optimal in the so-called science of cryonics. Once they're flash-frozen, the bodies are hauled off to the far side of the Moon in secondary shuttles and buried there by the Endura robots in huge underground crypts. The idea, as you suggested a moment ago, is that someday the bodies will be revived and their brain cells, at least, restored to some form of consciousness."

"But why do all this? What's the point?"

"So that the rest of this planet doesn't starve. The UN has achieved a static, zero-growth economy and declining birthrate but still manages to grow less and less food every year. And old people live to be 100 all the time now. If the government didn't have the safety valve of the lunar Shangri-La to attract so many useless mouths to feed, the planet would be stuck in the same familiar cycle of starvation, war, and famine, just like in the bad old days. That's the thinking behind it, anyway."

"You sound like you approve of all this," said Obama bitterly.

"As it happens, I don't," she replied coldly. "You have absolutely no idea just how much I disapprove, in fact. But I'm not the boss of the human race. Maybe someday you'll be able to change things.

"For what it's worth, until Sato took power and pushed this — convinced Manacera to make it a strict government policy, complete with oversight and safety inspections — the UN government was behaving no differently than the Third Reich a century ago. Humans really are still just barbarous apes — present company excepted, of course. The UN and the Japanese corporations had all panicked when they'd run out of money and had to face reality, including face the anger of all the investors and taxpayers who'd been promised Moon colonies. So they created a fiction instead. It wasn't that hard to hide. By the way, did you know that there are onGrid cults that believe all lunar exploration has been a hoax since the 1960s?"

Obama stood up and looked out the window again. The Moon had risen higher in the night sky and changed color. It now looked blood-red, like an evil eye. He tried to imagine the lonely mausoleum under its surface, stacked full of frozen bodies by robots. "I'm sorry, Siren," he said, without turning around. "It was nice of you to tell me all this. I — I sort of suspected something was wrong, I just couldn't have imagined in a million years that this was the explanation for it. Does cryonics even work?"

"No," she said. "It's bullshit. It can never work; human cellular structure won't support it. Plus, it's based on an entirely false theoretical model of human biology and its relationship to sentience.

"Maybe Sato sincerely thinks it can work someday, I don't know. But it won't, not ever, and he really should know better. Hibernation will be technically feasible in the future, cloning is possible now, but not the resurrection of what amounts to flash-frozen meat. What the UN's doing is committing mass murder — but they probably genuinely don't realize it. The world government really is acting under the innocent illusion that they're doing something noble."

He turned and looked at her. "You seem awfully sure."

"Yes, I do, don't I? Being awfully sure of myself has always been my worst fault. How about that supper?" But somehow, when he was rooting around the freezer, surveying the stacks of frozen food inside it, he just didn't feel very hungry any more. Siren took over and exiled him back to the living room to set up the legacy data converter he'd stolen from MAD, so that the data file he'd found in Priska's room could be translated for her. He'd noticed she was always cold-bloodedly thinking several steps ahead. How much of what she'd told him tonight had been calculated, he wondered. How much of it was even true? His rational mind was still in a state of stubborn rebellion against what she'd told him.

The supper she prepared from his remaining store of Holi-foods hexes was sort of weird, too: a goulash of mushrooms and other vegetables she'd pulled out of various frozen meals and covered in liquids and protein powders. It tasted strange but wasn't too bad after you got used to it. Neither was her company, really. As long as he didn't stare at her too much. "Do I get to ask any more questions?" he said when they were finished eating.

She sighed again. "Sure." She wasn't very patient, either.

"OK, how do you manage to know everything? How do you know about the Moon? And everything that's happened with me, including the way Simonetta disappeared? And how did you know I'd found all the files you wanted?"

Now she was looking at him pityingly. "You really are tired and distracted, aren't you, Obama?" she said. "I truly thought you'd have figured that out more or less right away. Shit!" She turned her head toward the corner of the room where Obama had dumped his backpack. "Come on out!" she called. There was sudden movement inside the bag, like a kitten or ferret had been trapped inside, and then it tipped slowly over. There was an unzipping sound, then the backpack gave a final shudder, and the Pooka emerged, crawling on hands and knees, from it. She was no longer a frozen statuette, though she still seemed to be made of shiny plastic. But now she was walking.

"Can I talk now?" she asked. And talking, thought Obama.

"Yes, it's fine," said Siren. "Tell Obama why I know everything he does, hon."

"Because I tell her, that's why," said the Pooka, swiveling to look up at him. She put her blobby plastic fists to her round hips and stared up him with a certain air of defiance. Her voice was high-pitched and doll-like, with a slight Korean accent. There was something slightly menacing about her now. *She must be some advanced form of Sony robot,* thought Obama. This night just kept getting weirder.

"I'm sorry I yelled 'shut up' at you," he said after a moment.

"Oh, that's OK, Obama," she said. "I forgave you. Want me to sing or dance for you?"

"No thanks," said Obama. "Not now, anyway," he added hastily. The data converter had finished its translation, and Siren stood up and walked past him, hips swaying slightly, to swipe it onto her iRist.

"That's the lot, then," she said. "I'll be back in touch as soon as I find your wife for you. And Obama?" Siren adopted more or less the same pose the Pooka had a few moments before.

"Yes?"

"Please stop staring at me like that." He was struck speechless. "I'm sorry if you fancy me so much."

"Well, yes," Obama said, suddenly embarrassed and all on fire. He averted his eyes. "Who wouldn't?"

"Well, that's a nice compliment — and you're a nice boy — but don't. Just don't, all right? I'd only make you very, very unhappy." She put on her red coat and stood in the doorway. "Unhappier than you already are, I mean. You see, I just can't stand for any of — for anyone else to touch me. Anyone, under any circumstances, ever. And I didn't mean to be dressed this way — I was coming from another sort of meeting and didn't have time to change. I'm not very good with clothes. Goodnight, Obama." After a moment he heard his front door closing behind her.

The Pooka marched over to the couch. Her head didn't quite come up to the level of the cushions, but she grasped them in her plastic mitten-like hands and clambered up to sit in the indentation her mistress had made. And which was still warm, thought Obama, from her body heat. But Siren had made things pretty clear to him. Whatever happened, he couldn't ever say she'd led him on in any way.

He wondered what it would feel like to hate to touch anybody. Or to hate to have them touch you. But they'd shaken hands when they'd first met, hadn't they? So maybe she'd just meant sexually. Still, it was something he would have to respect. And he had no business macking on her anyway, especially not when she was looking for Kim on his behalf. He was just tired and freaked out. It had been a very crazy two weeks.

"Want to play a game?" the little robot asked him in the silence. He wondered if there was a polite way to make it shut up now. "Can I watch a DVD?"

"Hold on," he said, chiming his mother. "Hello, Mom? I just got back from my trip. Listen, don't ever go to the Moon, OK? Don't let them send Dad, either, not under any circumstances."

"Why not?" asked Lela. It was still afternoon there; he'd probably interrupted her doing something important. Like potting a plant. Or planting pot.

"Because you'd hate it, that's why. Trust me, Mom, it's lonely up there. It's cold. To be honest, it's a real dump."

"If you say so," she said dubiously. That was the trouble with his parents — neither of them ever believed a word he said.

13.

The next day Obama was given Liberal Leave, because the MAD building had been declared a Public Health & Safety Hazard. This meant that all employees were barred from entry and thus forced to spend the day off-premises, but the time off would be deducted from their annual leave. Of course, those employees above UNG Level 10 — which now presumably included Obama — could circumvent this by "neuro-commuting" from home using their game-caps.

Because the Federal Departmental coalition which included MAD distrusted HHS (which was conducting the formal investigation) and even suspected it of having planted the bomb by proxy in the first place, a ring of NYVs — Neighborhood Youth Volunteers — had been hastily brought in by the Department of Peace & Nonviolence to patrol the area around the building. NYVs were mandatory United National Service draftees, and in theory, everyone in the world who turned 18 was expected to spend the next year serving the public. Generally, however, only the poorest and most obese of minority and immigrant teens were unable to pay for the deferment vouchers that postponed and eventually discharged this public obligation while enabling those less advantaged to serve in their places. In return, of course, for credits to pay for their future educations.

Consequently, the NYVs now milling around in the streets ringing the MAD building in 8-hour shifts, clad in their distinctive red mao-mao caps and jackets, tended to spend most of that time playing iRist games or hanging around Mickey D's. Or stealing from passersby.

Meanwhile, inside the still-smoldering lower floors of the MAD building, a team of forensics experts had begun the grisly work of reassembling the wreckage into a semblance of its former structure in order to analyze the blast pattern. These experts had originally belonged to the old United States FBI and military agencies, but when those agencies had been disbanded, the personnel had been eagerly digested by the Federal Aviation Authority to augment its disaster reconstruction department. Groups of robot frogmen worked to clear the flooded lower levels, and a planeload of grief counselors had been airlifted in from the former Canada by the Department of Education.

Because it had occurred so late after hours, only six employees had been killed in the blast, including Little Mahendra Pollack and "Camille Lyonesse." What she had been doing in the squalid second-floor dormitories no one could say. A dozen or so more casualties had been hospitalized, most of them for smoke inhalation. Among this number was Priska, whose back and scalp had been badly burned — and who, when examined by a specialist, was found to have advanced cancer of the hip. This last was reported on "Have A Good One North America" by a breathless Lilo from "Lilo & Stitch."

Obama, even though he knew he would not be allowed to enter the building, went into work anyway. He'd been made so itchy and restless by Siren's visit the night before and so appalled at what she'd told him about the Moon he hadn't been able to stay home. Then there was the horror of the latest bombing attack — which, all the news cartoons kept repeating, could have been much, much worse if Federal employees had been offered more generous overtime packages. Obama felt as though he had to do something, had to warn the world about the secret cryonics program on the Moon — and somehow put a stop to the bombings that seemed to follow him around wherever he went.

He also didn't know quite how he felt about Simonetta's death. On the one hand, he had feared and pitied her. Her involvement with the Security Services and, therefore, with his torturers Park and Malek, made her an object of revulsion to him. And she'd been crazy. Her romantic fixation on him had clearly been insane — yet now he found himself kind of missing it.

What I'm really missing, of course, is Kim, thought Obama. He was lonely. Which was why he was feeling all these irrational and contradictory emotions. And Siren Gunnarsdottir's harsh rejection of him the previous night had hurt, too. Not that there had been anything to reject — he hadn't actually said a word. All he'd done was stare at her legs once or twice. Her dissing had just made him feel a little less than humyn, that was all. At least Simonetta had "fancied" him. When she'd been alive, anyway.

Obama's old gang had a hangout for emergencies and after hours: the Black Khat a block or two away, just across the street from Folger Park. You could sit in there half the day and get work done using your game-cap or iRist, and they didn't care just as long as you kept buying cheap caff. He found Scott Vega-Choi and FaLola Montoya already there this morning, seated at a hexagonal table cluttered with cups, holograms, and half-eaten doughnuts. The three of them were about as close to being workaholics as anyone in the Department, which merely meant that they were more than usually responsible about clearing their messages and submitting their status reports in a reasonably timely manner. And of course, Carmen was famous for being a slave-driver, which meant that she was always harassing her underlings by iTooth and creating a lot of budgetary cloud mapping. And taking credit for any work that anyone in her division actually got done.

FaLola, a middle-aged transsexual (or "Formerly Gender-Disadvantaged Person"), was the Administrative Associate for their "Go Team." Problem was, Obama wasn't sure if he was even on FaLola and Scott's team since he'd been promoted. He still hadn't received any formal notification of his promotion, but technically he should be a UNG-10 now and therefore eligible to neuro-commute, which was why he'd brought along a game-cap to the Khat just in case. So he was a little unsure of what his welcome from the others would be.

He was also worried that the Pooka might start chatting or climb out of his bag and somehow embarrass him in public. When he'd asked the little robot if she'd wanted to go with him into the office that morning, she'd climbed into his manbag without a word and was evidently still sulking inside it. But he wasn't sure how long that would last. On his way over to join his two coworkers he stopped and bought a Red-Eye, a peppermint-cola-nut-hempmilk swirl with injected Vitamin C, caff, and khat.

To his relief, his coworkers seemed happy enough to see him. "'Migo!" said Scott, extending a fist to bump.

"Yaybo, Obama," said FaLola. "Did you hear about Camille? All I can say is 'wow'." It was hard to know what They meant by this term, whether they were expressing great sorrow, horror, or even enthusiasm when They uttered it. "They" was the polite and departmental-mandatory personal pronoun used in referring to the transgendered, as some transgendered persons continued to express gender confusion or, occasionally, a desire to return to their previous state. But even those who were comfortable with their gender status preferred this neutral appellation, since it sounded so important and respectful. Admittedly, however, the use of "They" for an individual could be confusing, and Obama had to remind himself from time to time that there was only one of FaLola.

"Yes, I heard," he said, sitting down. The pedestals in Black Khat's were cushioned and way more comfortable than the ones at Mickey D's.

"You must be totally gutted," They said. "Wow, to lose Kim and then find love again — and then have to lose Camille, too ... It all just seems so romantic. In a really crappy way, I mean."

"Yeah, your life is totally like a sim, amigo," said Scott enviously.

"Actually, Camille and I weren't really all that close," Obama told them, feeling churlish somehow. "We were just ..." What? Good friends? Coworkers? Mortal enemies? Pushy, manipulative stalker and her prey? There must be a word in the Enriched language to describe what they'd meant to each other, but he really couldn't think of what it might be. "We just gamed together a few times."

"Fuck-friends." They nodded sympathetically ("they" meaning both Scott and FaLola this time). Obama sighed.

"More like buds," he told them.

"Have you heard the latest?" said FaLola, dramatically lowering Their voice. "A gal-pal of mine at the UNFAA says that UNFAA investigators think that Little Mahendra was behind the whole thing! They think he was secretly working on a bomb the whole time he was working at MAD, and it just went boom in his face while he was fooling around with it last night. Can you imagine? We could have all been blown up at any moment of the day all these past few months. It makes you pee yourself a little just thinking about it. Apparently, Little Mahendra was a member of the White Terror Commando. This is why I personally avoid all politics."

It was hard to get any work done with so much to gossip about. Obama tried to settle down with an evidentiary CAC hologram on the evils of Personality Profiling. This issue fell into the purview of the old "nature versus nurture" debate, which had become so bitter that extreme proponents of each side were in open warfare, particularly in academia. Cal-Davis, for instance, had been largely burnt to the ground by naturists only the year before.

The expert witness who'd prepared the CAC brief had tried to steer a middle course. Was there a genetic basis for an unpleasant personality similar to that which caused unsightly obesity — as opposed to "happy" or "baby"-fat — and ugly facial features? Or were the physically unattractive subjected to so much contempt and disdain in the course of their lives that they in turn became resentful, depressed, and rude, thereby worsening the cycle of abuse? Both, CAC believed. But in either case, the expert opined, hiring, firing, having sex with, or even marrying a person on the basis of either personality or physical prejudice, however positive, was unfair and thus should be made illegal and treated like any other hate crime.

While Obama pondered this crucial issue, he found his thoughts wandering. How, he wondered, had their physical appearances affected the personalities of Simonetta and Siren? Both had the kind of looks most womyn would give anything for. In fact, they were probably the two most attractive womyn Obama had ever met in his life, aside from Kim, who had a softness and grace about her that they lacked. Like Kim, Siren and Simonetta were also very intelligent, and it showed in their faces, a quality Obama had always found to be an absolute necessity for humyn beauty in any gender.

But Siren was cold and aloof and arrogant and, like Simonetta, highly manipulative. And both womyn were — or had been, in Simonetta's case — very secretive, a possible cover for deep dishonesty. Simonetta, he knew for sure, had lied to him. And she had been mentally ill, as well as possibly homicidal; he had no idea of how deeply she was implicated in Park's and Malek's business. Or even what that business really was. Had she known about the Moon colonization hoax? Of course she had — her father was Sato Shiseki, the man who had invented it. That made her an arch-villainess, on a par with one of the leading Nazis.

For all Obama knew, Simonetta had been standing right beside Little Mahendra Pollack when his bomb went off. He may even have been building it for her. How did that tally with "nature versus nurture"? Was the Sato genetic line inherently evil? Or had she just been trained to it by hanging with her dad?

Except for the coldness in her eyes, though, and a petulant, spoiled sort of look around her mouth, nothing in her appearance had really warned you of Simonetta's true nature. And with Siren, it was only those pale, icy eyes of hers and the abrasive manner that gave her away. Yet for all he knew, Siren might be even more evil than Simonetta. He only had Siren's word for it that the whole Moon colonization thing really was a hoax.

Maybe she was merely mistaken about it. Or was trying to trick him, for reasons of her own. Both womyn had grown up with every imaginable advantage in life, but was either of them actually any nicer than the most appearance-challenged person on the planet? *Less, in many ways,* he thought.

Look at FaLola Montoya. There was nothing in the least bit attractive about FaLola physically — quite the reverse, in fact — yet They were one of the kindest and most well-meaning people he knew. So maybe there was no link at all between appearance and personality. And if there wasn't, that sort of shot CAC's central argument to hell. Although, of course, CAC's attorneys, as well as Obama's boss, Norberto Zollto, would merely argue that FaLola was the "exception that proved the rule." Which was, Obama thought heretically, really just meaningless gibberish. Exceptions only disproved rules. But the whole existence of MAD was predicated on the expression. He felt totally confused. Maybe that was just the Red Eye.

"OK, Obama," said FaLola. "I've got you an appointment with your new Canadian grief counselor first thing tomorrow. This one is a real doctor, isn't that exciting? With a degree and everything. Mine even has a soft, downy beard, which I personally find soothing. Have you checked your iTooth lately?" He hadn't. This morning he'd noticed that the total of his unread messages was up to 229 (though none was from Siren). Which was nothing compared to Joyful Kalinga's messages. The last time Obama had looked, Kalinga had had many thousands. "And Priska's asking for you at the hospital."

"Priska? What does she want?"

"I have no idea. All I know is the hospital keeps chiming me, because Priska wants you to go visit her there. It's really the least you can do, Obama — she must be feeling really miserable and scared, poor thing. Take her some fruit."

They were right. "OK, thanks," he said. "I will, on my way home." He was too distracted to get any work done. Around lunchtime, after FaLola and Scott left, Obama ordered an almond milk-chamomile-vanilla honey shake laced with natural alpha-blockers, and opened the data file "HGP K6 SSWATZ28954172.1952-2022" on his iRist.

It was a big file, the biggest of all the series. Over two dozen family lines were represented on it, but by now only a few had the original Sugar or Sweet left in their names. Most had been diluted. The Sakarovs and the Zuckermans, for example, had intermarried and become the "Peaces." And a Covey had married a Jones of Knoxville, Tennessee.

And here *he* was, the very final entry in the file: Obama Peace Jones, born January 24, 2022, North Hawaii Community Hospital, Hawaii. The file included his genetic data and biometrics, and that was all — all the records ended at the time of his birth. And Simonetta's.

Because here she was too: Sato Yugao Simonetta, born January 24, 2022, North Hawaii Community Hospital, Hawaii. She was a half-hour older than he was.

Slowly, he realized: Siren Gunnarsdottir had sent him on a mission to recover his *own* genetic history. And Simonetta's. Who was apparently the granddaughter of the former Japanese premier, Sato Einsaku. He, Obama Jones, was descended from the Sweets and the Coveys. And the Zuckermans. Speaking of which, his own grandfather, Dr Ethan Peace, the former Eitan Zuckerman, had delivered both babies.

What was going on? What was Siren's interest in all this? Obama scrolled back through the data, but there was no mention of Siren. Nor of a Gunnarsdottir family. He ran a few searches, for Iceland, South Africa, Norway. Nothing. The only possible connection he could find was that the English name Sweet or "Sweat," as it was sometimes spelled, had originally meant "Swede." But that seemed a very tenuous connection indeed.

Why did Siren want this information about him and Simonetta? And what was it Simonetta had said on the *Suki Moon,* that he and she were "made for each other"? That they were destined to be "together forever"? Had the coincidence of their having been born in the same hospital ward at almost the same time been the cause of her bizarre romantic obsession with him?

Obama could think of no other rational reason for it. They were clearly not related in any other way. And why else would a woman as glamorous and wealthy and powerful as Simonetta have had any interest in him at all? None of it made sense. Nor did her death.

Could Siren have brought that about? Had something in the files he'd found for her provided her with some essential clue she'd needed to positively identify Simonetta and then have her killed? That made no sense, either. He hadn't even found this file on Simonetta until after the explosion, and besides, Siren had already known exactly who Simonetta was anyway. Siren had been the one to tell him.

Obama decided that the problem with his thinking was that he just wasn't being logical. Logic dictated that there had to be some information in these files that Siren Gunnarsdottir hadn't already known, which is why she'd sent him off looking for them in the first place. Something so important that she'd made a present to him of the little Pooka, a robot so new and advanced — from what he'd seen of it — that it had probably cost something close to the annual operating budget of the entire Accreditation Division to build.

By comparison, the frogman robots swimming around in the underground parking garage of the MAD building right this minute were little better than complex articulated toys. They had cams for eyes, pincers for hands, and could barely speak unless they had controllers. But each cost over half a million Unos new, which would buy you an imported luxury aircar. The Alluras cost two or three times that much. And the Pooka was more advanced than all of them.

So he was missing something big. Logic therefore also dictated that he go back through all the data, piece by piece, until he could figure out exactly what this information meant, beginning with his own and Simonetta's files and then those of their parents and grandparents. It might be his only chance to force Siren to find Kim for him. Because all other leads seemed closed off or shut down at the moment.

The file on his mother, Leleina Green Peace, born 1998, was brief and contained nothing he didn't already know. She had been born on April 2, 1998 at her father's "surgery," which had been in his house near Punaluu, Hawaii. Again, Obama's grandfather Ethan had delivered her. By contrast, Ethan World Peace, nee Eitan Zuckerman, born October 27, 1952, Serlin-Hakirya Maternity Hospital, Tel Aviv, the former Israel, had a much bigger file. His wife or partner's file, however, was missing. And aside from a note of her name, Niemi Kali Vagana, on Lela's birth certificate, there was no other record of Obama's grandmother and nothing on *her* parents.

Had his mom been a cloned tank baby? Obama already knew that his dad had a similar anomaly in his own family tree with the first Covey, who had appeared to have had no father. And his father's mother's records were also missing — there was only a note of her name, Adriana Terry Covey, and nothing else. Her parents were listed as Sarah Sweet and Bert Anson Covey, which meant they were cousins of some kind, however distantly related. The patrilineal Jones family records were intact, but only went back to 1960. None of this helped.

The Satos' files were equally confusing. Simonetta's mother had been an Italian porn actress, Anna Ciriani, who had enjoyed some popularity on the European internet in the early 'teens as "MadameWeb" and "The Sexy Professor of Pordenone." Incredibly, she had also been a Japanese language teacher, and was supposedly descended from the Cattaneo family — it was the most famous Cattaneo in history, Simonetta Vespucci, who had posed for Botticelli's "Venus" painting in 1475.

If life were like a sim, then Anna Ciriani had obviously been a trophy wife for the newly-rich and powerful computer programmer Sato Shiseki, but the truth seemed less clear. For one thing, they had both been fairly old when their daughter had been born. Simonetta wasn't an Aquarian baby, but a wombrat like Obama. Yet Anna had been in her early 40s when Simonetta had been born. And Shiseki, so far as Obama could tell, had been born in 1952, also on October 27 (like Eitan Zuckerman), in the Tokyo Women's Medical University, Daini Hospital, Tokyo, the former Japan. Which would have made him 70 when Simonetta was born. *And nearly 98 now,* thought Obama. Obviously he needed to read Sato's file again in more careful detail. And Goggle what he could onGrid.

Sato Shiseki was the illegitimate son of Sato Einsaku — the future Prime Minister of Japan, at that time a minor official in the American-installed postwar government — and a medical student, Watanabe Mitsuko. Einsaku had signed the birth certificate as the father, which had not been unusual in those days in Japan and which had proved in no way fatal to his future political career. The custom of having concubines or "minor wives" had only ended under the Meiji half a century earlier, and the unofficial practice that followed still carried little stigma — for myn.

Though their relationship was never mentioned in Einsaku's memoirs or official biography, other biographers noted the fact that Einsaku remained affectionate toward little Shiseki and sponsored him throughout his skooling and early career. And Sato Shiseki had been a child prodigy. He had graduated from medical skool while still in his teens and had become a doctor like his mother. He interned in hospital Emergency Rooms but had never practiced, returning to the University of Tokyo to acquire a PhD in Genetics. Aside from publishing a few research papers, however, it seemed that he'd done little with this degree, either, instead becoming a pioneer in the field of computerized medical imaging.

By the 1980s, Shiseki's theories of virtual fractal cellular replication were being used in early research into both humyn cloning and robot design. Abruptly he changed careers again, this time to become head of Sony's fledgling robotics division. By the time Simonetta was born in 2022, Shiseki had been already well on his way to finalizing the code that would become the foundation of the world-wide gaming Grid. And which would make him the richest man in the world.

Shiseki's hobbies, however, had always been the art and architecture of the Italian Renaissance. He spent nearly every vacation in Italy and had amassed one of the world's largest libraries of books and sketches from that period. He'd become obsessed with the face of Simonetta Vespucci, the most famous beauty of her age, who had married one of the "map of America" Vespuccis and become the mistress of Giuliani di Medici, the younger brother of Lorenzo, Duke of Florence. She was also the inspiration for several great painters, including Sandro Botticelli. And all this before dying in 1476 at the age of 21 of "consumption," as tuberculosis was then known.

Maybe Sato had seen Anna Ciriani — whom he seemed to have never legally or formally married — as a latter-day Simonetta when he first met her in Rome in 2009. Or maybe it had been her Cattaneo genes that had excited him. Viewed objectively, Sato's entire career seemed almost like a deliberate attempt to recreate Simonetta Vespucci — and even Obama, who knew very little about the subject, had noticed the uncanny resemblance when he'd first set eyes on "Camille Lyonesse."

Obama Goggled the Grid and saw that the first Simonetta's tomb had been rifled several times, most notably in the 1970s, when thieves had stolen jewelry, hair, and bones; and again in 2010, when most of the remaining hair and bones had disappeared. Obama had read that it was almost impossible to clone DNA taken from the corpses of historical figures. Such DNA was far too damaged and unstable. But what if Sato had found a way to accomplish such a thing? Reading between the lines of the Sato files, it really seemed that everything pointed to some kind of genetic program to resurrect a single idolized womyn: Simonetta Cattaneo de Vespucci. And if this were true, how would Sato Shiseki now be taking his "daughter's" pointlessly accidental death?

OK, thought Obama, *maybe that somehow explained Simonetta: she was the lifelong erotic-artistic obsession of a mad scientist.* But how did Obama Jones figure into all this? Nobody could claim he looked like anybody famous, beautiful or otherwise. He had the kind of face that most people forgot the moment they set eyes on it. He had no special skills or talents — other than the apparent ability to survive bomb blasts. *So far, anyway,* he thought. If he were a superhero, his secret super-power would be boringness. Nobody would rob any graves to get his DNA.

So why was he even in this file? Why had the Satos been so interested in him? And what about the Zuckermans? Had Ethan Peace been a colleague of Sato's? A rival? A student? What was the significance of the two myn having been born on the same day, just as he, Obama, and Simonetta had been?

Maybe the answers lay in the genetic code itself. The only problem was that, except for a college survey course on the subject and the garbage that came across his nBox, Obama knew next to nothing about genetics. He would have to go onGrid and find a filter or AI that would analyze and compare the actual individual DNA in all these files and then explain it all to him. Without alerting Sato, he reminded himself, into whose empire he would be trespassing.

Inside her bag, the Pooka was muttering again. Obama sighed and bought himself a Black Khat. It was going to be a long afternoon.

As of the year 2000, the total number of known gene loci on the humyn gene map had been 6270. At that time it had been thought that no more would ever be found, and by 2006, genome mapping had been declared complete by many scientists all over the world. But in 2011 several new loci had been discovered, and by the end of the decade the accepted total for all humyns had been 7168.

Running the most elementary analysis AI over the data files in "HGP K6 SSWATZ28954172.1952-2022" showed that both Sato and Ethan Peace possessed 7196 gene loci, as did Lela Green Peace — and that Simonetta and Obama had 7224. Their extra gene loci seemed to occur mostly in two specific regions: the major histocompatibility complex (MHC), a region on chromosome 6 essential to the humyn immune system across a spectrum of quantitative trait loci (QTL) found on other autosomes; and on two places on the X chromosome, a pattern indicating a relationship to physical health and strength. The AI informed him, "Over 50% of the MHC has been altered, creating entirely distinctive different haplotypes, indicating an extraordinary polymorphism and evolution of this region. Several of the new genes, particularly of the MHC class II and III regions, can be traced by sequence similarity and synteny to over 4 million years in the past, clearly predating the maturity of the adaptive immune system some 3 million years ago."

"So what does all that mean exactly?" Obama queried it.

The AI went silent for a few moments before it answered him. "I have no idea," it said at last.

On the way home, as promised, Obama bought a large bag of green *matoke* bananas and *akee* at Teeter Joe's, then took the Red Line to the Brookland Retro Station and rode the underground people-mover to the Manacera City Hospital Center stop. Priska turned out to be in a room in the same ICU ward where Obama had spent two nights only a week before. The same Allura nurse was even on duty — at least he thought it was the same one — but he couldn't tell whether she recognized him or not. It was always so hard to know with robots.

Priska, swathed in derma-paks, was propped up in bed surrounded by machinery and four blank walls. Because of the burns, she couldn't be hooked up to a game-cap, but her Fisher-Price My First Symbols Keyboard was lying in her lap. "Hi, Priska," said Obama. "I brought you some fruit."

The moment she saw him, the gorilla sat up furiously in bed and began typing. Because the keypad made synthetic animal noises, Priska's rapid typing first evidenced itself as a volley of barnyard grunts and bleats and howls. Someone had kindly hooked her keyboard graphics up to a digital blood pressure readout next to the bed; on it, Obama read, "i m not priska!" The letters were bright green and blinked.

"What do you mean, you aren't Priska?" he answered stupidly. "Who are you then?"

Moo. Baa. Quack. Woof woof. Baa. Honk. Oink. Moo. "i m simonetta," said the screen.

14.

"What?" said Obama. He felt like he was stuck inside a really frustrating game, crashing from too much 'Stim. "You can't be Simonetta. You're Priska."

"i hate these keys i hate these stupid hands and fingers! everything hurts! pls help me bammy!" Obama came closer and put his bag of fruit down.

"Please calm down, Priska," he said soothingly. "Wouldn't you like to turn on the wall holos? They have a nice, soothing rain-forest scene." This caused a fresh burst of frantic typing. Neigh. Baa. Quack. Woof woof. Maa. Honk. Oink. Moo moo. Baa. Miaow. Woof woof. Honk. Oink oink. Hee haw.

"fuck the rainforest!" it read. "i told u i m not priska u stupid clown! i m simonetta can't u read?" Obama sighed and sat down in the blue plastic visitor's pedestal next to the bed. The pedestal was very short, and his head barely came to the level of Priska's arms. "Why do you think you're Simonetta?" he asked. The higher primate never had a chance to reply. Obama heard a sudden wailing noise like a siren coming from inside his manbag, and suddenly the Pooka erupted from it, growing larger and reshaping itself into a new form. The molecules on its reflective plastic surface seemed to morph and flow like liquid until they coalesced into a more humyn-like shape, blank-faced, still colored black and pink and bright red but no longer quite resembling the chubby, jolly-faced little Pooka doll. This new creature looked a little like a humyn womyn — but even more like a killing machine. When it had, almost instantaneously, grown nearly two meters tall, it stepped daintily from the bag, darted forward to bend ominously over Priska's reclining form, and then wrapped a plastic hand like a vise-grip around the gorilla's throat.

Priska's eyes rolled back in her head, and her body collapsed as though she'd been drugged. "Pooka! Let go of her!" said Obama, shocked. The Pooka's face rotated around toward his own. The surface of Pooka's face swam again and reassembled itself into Simonetta's features, struggling with the effort to talk.

"Shut up!" the Pooka snapped in Simonetta's voice. "Just listen to me, Bammy. I don't know what's going on, but you have to help me, promise? Don't leave me here like this — you have to promise me you won't!"

"OK," he said in shock. "I promise."

"The last thing I remember is a really loud noise. I was in my room, and then everything just went white."

"That was a bomb, Simonetta. They're saying Little Mahendra set it off."

"Whatever. Then the next thing I knew you were carrying me to the window. Then I caught on fire, and we fell. Then you abandoned me. You shouldn't have done that, Bammy. I was so scared. It's horrible being stuck in here. Nothing works, my hands are useless, I can't even see properly. Everything smells gross and itches. And my body hurts so much." She started to cry.

"I'm sorry," he told her helplessly. Or rather, told the Pooka with Simonetta's weeping plastic face. He was hoping no one was going to walk in on them at that moment.

"Tell my father what's happened; he'll know what to do. Go onGrid and tell him everything. Tell him where I am. He'll fix this."

"OK."

"Promise?"

"I promise." Abruptly, the Pooka let go of the gorilla's throat and Priska/Simonetta fell back against the pillows.

"Obama, I really think you should wait for Siren to get here," the Pooka told him in her normal tinny little Korean-accented sing-song. "She'll know what this is all about. She's on her way now." The Pooka flowed swiftly back into her normal shape and disappeared back into his bag. He'd never heard of a robot being able to do that. By comparison, Alluras were as ungainly as rubber dolls. What had Siren called the Pooka? "A new technology"? It seemed far more advanced than any tech he'd ever read about. Where had it come from? And what was it really designed to do? Not just to babysit him, surely.

The monitors beside the bed were all loudly bleeping and chirping now. The robot nurse came running back into the room and silently peeled back the gorilla's eyelids to check them before readjusting her IV. "It's OK, she's sleeping now," she said. "I'll turn the rainforest back on, shall I?"

Obama picked up his Pooka-bag, as he now thought of it, and waited for Siren just outside in the hall. He didn't want to still be in the room if Priska — Simonetta — woke up again suddenly. The whole scene with her had seriously freaked him out. How was what he'd just seen even possible? He didn't want to think about it. He'd think about something else. He noticed that his bag seemed to weigh much more than it had before — it felt as though it had a bowling-ball or two in it now. As if the Pooka had a small nuclear reactor built into its body, he thought. He wished the Pooka had told him how long he would have to wait. He checked his iTooth. No new messages.

After ten minutes or so had gone by, the ceiling lights at the far end of the empty hospital corridor began to blink. He heard a clattering of high heels echoing down the hall, then a tall black-clad figure burst through the far doors and strode gracelessly toward him. He recognized Siren from her height and the way her hips swayed — she was wearing a head to ankle black silk *burqa* and gleaming black high heels. Her face was invisible, except for a splash of shadow. She couldn't get mad at him now for staring, he thought. Her hands were enclosed in a pair of long black leather gloves, and she was carrying a large pink and white striped cylindrical hatbox. She looked like an Arab princess from a fairy tale who'd just come from a shopping spree in Paris.

As she approached, all the lights in the hall above her dimmed and flickered on and off again, as if they were about to explode at any moment. *Please god, not another bomb,* he thought wildly.

Siren Gunnarsdottir stopped directly in front of him and pulled her *niqab,* the veiled part of the headpiece, aside. She looked exhilarated and strands of her white shoulder-length hair were tousled across her pink cheeks. "TNT," she said.

"'TNT'?" repeated Obama.

"Temporary Neural Transference Syndrome," she explained. It no longer surprised him that she already knew every detail of what he'd just experienced. "It's why Priska thinks she's Simonetta. It's a form of game 'haloing'. It's happened a few times when people who've been gaming together share some traumatic event at the same moment. Most often after airline crashes. One of them, usually the weaker personality, becomes neurally imprinted with the onGrid persona of the other dead one — it usually lasts only a few days. That's the likeliest explanation, anyway." It made sense. Priska always wore her neural game cap. And she was certainly the weaker personality of the two. There was just one thing wrong with the theory.

"I really can't imagine any way in hell that Simonetta would ever game with Priska," he said. "They hated each other." Siren pulled off the rest of her cap and hood and shook her hair free. Her pupils were wildly dilated, her lips parted over her gleaming white teeth. She looked like a predator on the trail of a kill, a jaguar, or a sleek white tigress. He wanted her now more than ever, and the thought made him look down at the floor in embarrassment.

"Well, I really don't want to consider the only other possibility," she said slowly.

"What's that?"

"That Simonetta is an alien." She frowned at the expression on his face. "No, I don't mean an undocumented immigrant. I mean a real alien, able to switch from one body to another during a bomb explosion."

"An alien? You mean like from a UFO or something? A monster from outer space?" Obama said. "Like in the sims?"

"Right. Just like in the sims. Except a lot more, well, 'alien'. There really isn't any other word for it. Language is so limited. A space alien, let's say."

Obama felt reality slipping dangerously away. Maybe Siren was as crazy as Simonetta. Or, he thought, as crazy as he felt right now, having conversed with a robot channeling a gorilla claiming to be Simonetta. So there was plenty of insanity to go round. He chose his next words carefully. "So there really is such a thing?"

Siren smiled this time, a terrible smile that chilled him to his bones because it was somehow so convincing. "Oh yes, my dear. It's just that, so far as I know, I'm the only true alien on this planet at the moment. Well, the only one in human form anyway. My helpers are only capable of operating machinery. Like the Princess. And your Pooka."

"So you're not really humyn?" Obama said, stammering very slightly. It was amazing how easy this was to believe. Obviously, he had totally become a crazy person.

"Nope. Not in the least."

"You just take on a humyn appearance? You can change shape?"

"No, we're not like the Helpers. We wear bodies like suits of clothes. Or as you wear skins on the Grid. Being shoe-horned into this body is sort of like ... well, like going down to the bottom of the ocean in a deep-sea diving suit, I suppose. Lots of heavy pressure, lots of discomfort and tight fits and jammed senses that feel like ringing in your ears or going half-blind would feel for you. Actually, that's the main reason I choose womyn to wear, because they're such a nicer fit. Softer and more comfortable. And durable. Plus it's easier to manipulate people using female pheromones. But honestly, I pretty much hate it in here.

"Look, I'd love to hang around and chat, but you'll have to excuse me. I have urgent business inside. I need you to go home now, Obama, go onGrid and do exactly what you promised the gorilla. Find Sato and tell him what Simonetta told you to tell him. Every detail — don't leave anything out. Except for what I've just told you, of course. In fact, please don't mention me at all to Sato. OK?"

"Sure," said Obama. He was getting used to being her errand boy. Or should he even keep thinking of Siren as a "her"? Did aliens have gender?

"Yes? Questions?" She paused before going into Priska's — Simonetta's — hospital room, stopped by the expression on his face.

"I — I was just wondering what you really look like."

That smile again. "Think ... the contents of your stomach. Transparent. With tentacles." Now she was laughing aloud at his reaction, exposing all those teeth again. "Don't worry, Obama — you people look revolting to me, too." She pressed the door open and went inside, swinging the hatboxes — Obama didn't even want to imagine what was in them — clear of the door frames.

On his way home, he changed his mind a dozen times about whether he believed her or not. He thought someone was following him again, but he barely noticed or cared. Because, while he still couldn't decide whether or not Siren Gunnarsdottir really was an alien from outer space, he was pretty sure the thing in his manbag was. When he got home, he took it out and asked it. "Pooka, where do you come from?"

"That bag?" The Pooka pointed back at it. Obama sighed. This wasn't going to be easy, obviously.

"No, I mean what planet do you come from?"

"We don't have planets, silly. Are you feeling hungry yet?"

"No thanks, not yet." Obama decided to persist. "Listen, Pooka. Please tell me about Siren. What is she, exactly? Is she really an alien from another planet — star system? She told me she was."

The Pooka shrugged its plastic shoulders. Then it turned on some music in its stomach and started dancing. "She is a visitor," it replied absently.

"Are you a visitor, too?"

"No, I'm a helper. But I'm not really here, so I'm not a visitor."

Obama summoned all the patience he was capable of. "How long has Siren been here?" he asked. "How long have you been helping her?" The Pooka seemed to like Afro-Tribal Transbeetles Pop — her plastic tummy was visibly throbbing with the drum and bass lines.

"Oh," said the Pooka, waving one hand vaguely at him. "I dunno. For some of your time, I guess." What other kinds of time were there? he wondered. And what had she — it — meant by "I'm not really here?"

He persisted. "When did you and she first come to this planet, Pooka? In humyn years?"

"In your years? Three years ago. 2047 CE. You know, this is one thing humyns are really good at, Obama — dancing! If I were you, Obama, I would do it all the time. But you're probably too old now."

"How old are you?" he asked her. "In humyn years?"

"In humyn years?" The Pooka stopped dancing for a moment and screwed up her face in an almost comical expression of calculation. After a while she relaxed and said, "I dunno. Forever, I guess. Obama, would you like me to make supper for you now?"

Obama sighed again. "OK, thanks."

"Oh, goody," said the Pooka, "I love playing with the hydrowave. But I hate all these stupid questions." She turned and trotted off to the kitchen. She and Siren both seemed fascinated by playing around in humyn kitchens. Maybe it was like making mud-pies for them.

While he ate, Obama went onGrid and Goggled alien visitations. There were hundreds of thousands of entries, many with glogs, or group journals, devoted to them. There were entire cults based around certain sightings or encounters with aliens, some of these nearly a century old. There was no mention of Siren or anything resembling her description of herself. But, incredibly, Sato Shiseki figured in at least one of these group journals. He was mentioned as having been part of an "alien breeding experiment."

According to this particular glog, Jewish lizard-like aliens from outer space had been grafting themselves into humyn bodies, beginning with the Rothschilds in 16th-Century Germany. The glog writers claimed that the late Sato Shiseki had been a descendant of these Zionist lizard creatures. And when Obama ran a search on the list, he found his grandfather's name on it, too, as Eitan Zuckerman. Neither he nor Simonetta was mentioned for some reason, but there was one other name on it that he recognized, that of Jose Manacera, the outgoing World President. According to the glog, any of the people on the list — or any descendant of them — was a lizard and had to disguise themselves as humyns using rubber masks and theatrical make-up.

Obama couldn't vouch for the others on the list, of course, but he was fairly certain he wasn't a lizard from outer space. Although anything seemed possible at that moment.

But how was he ever going to find Sato on the Grid again? What if Casino Royale wouldn't let him back in? And what if its reclusive owner ignored Obama even if he were allowed back in?

How had he met Sato the first time? Obama asked himself. As Joyful Kalinga. That meant he'd have to become Kalinga again, onGrid anyway. And it might mean having to track Gracia down again, too. He shuddered. Obama booted off, then rebooted into the skin of Joyful Kalinga. This time, he took the virtual Pooka along with him in a virtual backpack just to make her stop nagging. "But don't go killing anyone," he told her.

"Why not?" she demanded. "Nobody in a game is real."

"Good point," he admitted. "Well, just don't do anything until I tell you to, OK?"

Kalinga had several messages from Gracia Dal Costa, but they were all a week old. On the Grid, that was the same as an eternity. The messages were obviously intended to be part of the "confessions" package she'd sold to the O! holo network — a pair of erotic dreams she'd supposedly had about Kalinga, a demand to be on his next video, an offer of marriage when she turned 16. "Big Man is Back!" he captioned his reply, after some careful thought on its composition. "Marry you?

"I brought you this for a present," Obama said, handing her a large tube of honey-dew melon juice mixed with khat and caff. It was her favorite.

"Yum," she said politely.

"Priska, I need some old data deep-storage media from the HGP today."

Priska indicated an ancient YouFi port on a side counter. "Swipe it," she said. He had reformatted the long list Siren had given him the day before into a formal Intra-Departmental data request memo. Now he could only hope that all the proper clearances had been restored to his employee account.

A 3-Dimensional display unit over the counter showing a map of the storage facilities briefly lit up with dozens of tiny location indicator lights, then died. Barely any of the equipment down here worked any more. "Oh, lots of stuff!" said Priska, clearly upset. Complicated requests confused her, and Obama glimpsed tears in her eyes.

"Never mind," he said quickly. "I'll come back and help you find it." This was strictly against department rules, of course, which merely meant that it was an absolute necessity.

"OK," said the gorilla gratefully. She gave him one of her hands to hold and used the knuckles of the other as a third leg. She groaned intermittently as she led him down the hallway toward Deep Storage, moving arthritically, like an old womyn. But when, after endless huffing and groaning and checking and re-checking, Priska finally found the right storage room and swiped it open, its lights came on and Obama saw that it was completely empty. There weren't even any storage racks or containers left behind inside it.

"It's all gone?" he asked incredulously.

"Don't be mean," said Priska. "Don't be mean like the other two ones."

"What other two ones?"

"They were mean to Priska. She didn't like them." She became agitated, rising up off her front hands and making tearing motions with them.

"Two who? Who were they, Priska? Why were they here?" You had to be very persistent and precise with her. And cautious. She weighed 20 kilos more than he did and was incredibly strong.

"Just two bad myn. They wanted your stuff too. They looked like Raffi. Here, Priska will swipe you the memo." She waved at him wildly with her iRist. He looked at the tiny screen on his own and saw a single name. Camille's. Meanwhile, Priska's Aria holo had started screaming, "Raffi! Raffi!," while loud involuntary bellows escaped from the gorilla's own throat and chest. After a few moments of this din, Obama heard the clatter of feet, and a tiny figure, little more than half his own height, patiently trotted down the hallway toward them.

Raffi was a chubby brown elfin creature with slanted eyes and a pair of thick spectacles strapped to his bald head, along with various white plastic micro-com devices. Behind them, his eyes were slanted and his nose was running. Coming to a halt he said, "Hi, Priska! Hi, Obama!" A wide happy smile creased his face.

"Hi, Raffi," said Obama. "Priska needs your help. We're trying to find out about two men who came here on this date" — he swiped Raffi's iRist — "and stole all this data."

"OK, this is a matter for internal security, I believe!" said Raffi in his "official" voice, a startlingly deep rumbling like a blast from a fog-horn. Obama had learned that HEDs like Raffi were often fond of rhetorical flourishes like "I believe" or "I must say," which lent their observations the weight of a wisdom they didn't always possess. Raffi tugged at Obama's jacket until he followed after him. Obama turned to wave at Priska.

"Goodbye, Priska. Don't be upset, OK?"

"OK, Obama!" the gorilla called after him.

"She's been acting like quite the diva lately, I must say!" Raffi told him when they were out of ear- (and cam-) shot. Obama decided this was something Raffi had likely overheard somewhere. The little HEDS probably wasn't even totally clear on what the expression actually meant.

"She hates the cold, Raffi. It's hard on her joints."

"Oh, boo-hoo," replied Raffi, turning to scamper down an Emergency staircase. Feeling like Disney's beloved Alice, Obama followed him. But his mind was racing. Who had Simonetta sent down to seize the HGP files? Park and Malek? And why? "They looked like Raffi," Priska had said. Raffi had slanted eyes like Park. And his coloring was like Malek's. Of course, this had been a description given by a Higher Primate with bad eyesight. Obama would have to hope that Security would let him see the cam footage files.

9.

Internal Security comprised its own division at MAD but was, unsurprisingly, treated exactly like the other "lower divisions," which included the teachers and daycare aides, building curators, and even the robo-cleaners. This did little to endear the upper floors to the denizens of the deep, so that relations between them, echoing the temperature inside the MAD building itself, were rarely very warm.

The nominal Director of Security was a womyn, Keisha Garvey, who, like Norberto Zollto, was almost never actually in her office, so the real day-to-day running of the division was left to a "Rain-Myn," an extremely High End Autisal Person named Little Mahendra Pollack. Pollack's powers of memorization and total recall were legendary, but he was incapable of entertaining an opinion on any subject except his own and would fly into child-like temper tantrums when crossed or thwarted.

Obama had entertained a vague hope of finding Pollack absent at his post, but unfortunately Pollack lived in the building. On-site dormitories had been a fad in Silicon Valley during the 1990s and early 2000s, and the concept had migrated into the public sector. The UN had adopted the concept enthusiastically, and the MAD building had initially been constructed with an entire floor, the second, filled with dormitory-style sleeping cubicles and lavatories, centrally located kitchens and dining rooms, a gym, a swimming pool, and private suites with showers and bathrooms. Unfortunately, a UN Housing Voucher scandal had erupted in 2040 when Federal employees were exposed as routinely having cashed in credit vouchers for huge home financing and hotel allowances when they had actually been living in their own offices.

These days it was unusual for anyone at executive level to risk the stigma of living on-site. Consequently, the second floor at the MAD building had fallen into disrepair and was now almost deserted. Few of the appliances worked, the pool had been drained and was covered in mold, and robo-cleaners avoided the place. The only people living there now were a few of the hardiest PRIE hires, including Priska and Little Mahendra Pollack.

Just before he and Obama got to the main Security office, Raffi suddenly whispered, "He" — meaning Pollack — "scares me," and hid in a doorway. Obama found Little Mahendra inside the big Security room, along with a group of Security staffers, sitting at a long cafeteria table wearing game-caps and eating their lunches. Many of these Security personnel had been hired directly out of anger management work-release programs, since those who had once been scorned by society as "felons" were now protected by PRIE as well (excepting, of course, those who had been convicted of hate crimes). The very use of the term "felon" — along with terms such as "denigrate, "idiot," and "moron" — was illegal; Siren had technically been liable for arrest or citation for having used the word "moronic" the day before. But of course, as Obama knew all too well, no one was as foul-mouthed or verbally offensive as a female Federal employee, who was largely exempt from all legal accountability.

"What do you want?" Little Mahendra demanded as Obama walked in. "Little" was a misnomer; Mahendra was the tallest person in the building. He had vacant eyes and a shock of spiky hair. His features were doughy, and the black hairs visible on his wrists and neck were thick and prodigious. He shaved irregularly but lavished great care on his gleaming black uniform and body armor. The rest of the security staff didn't like wearing their helmets in the building, preferring to hang them at their belts, but Pollack always wore his outside his own office. He was rumored to collect guns, and each female employee at MAD was convinced that Pollack spied on her tirelessly in an attempt to compile a usable holographic nude image. Whether these allegations were true or not, Obama had no idea.

"We need the security-cam caps on these two guys," said Obama, swiping the memo at Pollack. Obama hoped he now had the "authorization" that Carmen had promised him. But Pollack didn't even query the matter; he simply flat-out refused to accommodate Obama's request, citing interdepartmental investigatory guidelines word for word in a rapid, sing-song tone. When Pollack came to the end of his first paragraph, Obama attempted to interrupt, but Pollack began to rock back and forth on his heels — a sign of frustration and incipient anger — and drowned Obama out.

Most newer security cams were stereoscopic. Multiple-angled images, seamlessly tiled together, formed the basis for holographic technology, though high-precision optical and CT-scanners were

OK, sure but only if I marry your sister too." This was followed by an invitation to connect. There was no reply. Maybe Gracia was just being coy. Or maybe Kalinga was adopting the wrong tone. Possibly she wasn't very romantic. Frustrated, Obama ported into Casino Royale.

But it was no longer quite the same place as last time. The more he explored it, the more differences he noticed. It appeared to be anchored in a virtual version of the city of Monte Carlo rather than Venice. There were superficial similarities — the casino was enclosed inside a similar cathedral-like domed building with palms everywhere — but garishly bright filaments of colored lights constantly snaked through the walls and ceilings at right angles to each other, and the noise level was set much higher. Both of these features were distracting, especially the music, which consisted of covers of classical favorites by a tinny Thai Girl Go Go band. There were no Allura robot croupiers, and none of the steward daemons responded to Kalinga's loud requests to speak to the owner.

"Know who I am?" he bellowed finally. "I am Joyful Kalinga! A big man!" It seemed to Obama that Joyful Kalinga's worldwide 15 minutes of fame was nearly over — onGrid, at least. The real world seemed to be lagging several days behind the virtual one in fad-time.

Finally one of the stewards spoke to him. "I'm sorry, sir, but I'll have to ask you to leave. We have a dress code for all our gentlemen guests. Tie and formal jacket."

Joyful Kalinga glared at him. "Are you crazy, man? You saying I must wear a tie to give my money away?"

"Those are the house rules, sir," said the steward.

"OK, OK, Joyful Kalinga will go soon — don't shit yourself. But he must talk to your boss man first." The steward grasped his elbow, and two others made their way toward him. Obama shook off the hand of the first daemon and in two long strides vaulted up onto one of the roulette tables. There was a gasp from the crowd, and the croupier halted the wheel. "Sato! Sato Shiseki!" he roared. "Kalinga have important message for you!" He felt hands suddenly grasping his legs and ankles. Several guests helped the stewards haul him down from the table and carry him out the main hall and through the front entrance. There they tossed him out onto the paving stones facing the Place du Casino. He got up again slowly, rubbing his backside.

It was evening — *l'heure bleu,* as it was referred to by the holographic virtual guide that was chattering over his head in three languages: "The Casino Royale, built in the restored shell of the old Monte Carlo Casino, is a majestic building consisting of an atrium paved in marble, surrounded by 28 Ionic columns made of onyx. Its numerous gaming rooms are decorated with stained glass windows, sculptures, paintings and opulent decorations and were used as sets for all the '007' sims and games. The casino also leads straight into the opulent Salle Garnier Opera House auditorium, visible to your left." Behind the casino, lit up a bright lemon-yellow, Obama caught the faintest glimpse of palm trees and the darkened sea in the distance.

A surprising number of avatars on the streets seemed to be simming rather than gaming; gamers ported everywhere instantly, whenever possible, while people paying for the cheaper so-called "reality sims," as opposed to the Holowood epics, experienced every moment of them realistically, whether they wanted to or not. Tonight there was a long line of ground cars crawling up from the Avenue de Monte Carlo, all filled with elegantly-dressed virtual tourists eager to gamble at the famous casino. Aircars, flashing their tiny lights, circled overhead, some landing to park around the green oval of the Place du Casino with its Maltese cross-shaped fountain in the middle. Obama unzipped his backpack. "You can come out now," he told the Pooka.

"Hooray!" she said, poking her head out like a small animal.

"What kind of weapons are allowed on this gaming level?" he asked her. Her face froze while she examined the Grid code.

"Nothing interesting — only10 and 20mm handguns, hunting rifles, knives. But you need legal permits from the Principality of Monaco and the UN, this says."

"What can you set me up with illegally?" Since they couldn't actually be robbed, shooting up casinos was a time-honored method of holding them hostage. At some point it began costing them enough money in lost custom that they would pay you to go away. Unfortunately, this had become so popular a crime in the early years of the Grid that most casino shootouts these days were just publicity stunts set up by the casinos themselves, because their virtual security was now too sophisticated to be intimidated by a real attack. Obama would need a major military arsenal to launch even a minor assault on the place. Furthermore, it had been years since he'd war-gamed, and his skills were rusty.

"I can get you anything," the Pooka said. "Are we playing a game now?"

"I think so. Unless you can think of some other way to get their attention."

"No, I think trying to kill them is the best way," said the Pooka, her shiny plastic features blankly reflecting the city lights. "But I would recommend that you let me serve as your body armor, Obama — then I can arm you through my gundam weapons rack. All you'll have to do then is point and click." Her surface started to shimmer, then to swim and melt, overflowing to the pavement like a puddle of viscous polymer paint. The puddle shivered, then moved toward his feet and encased them, flowing up his legs, instantly forming thick, articulated armored plates as it gradually covered his whole body. It engulfed his head, thrusting slimy wet tubes into his mouth, ears, and nose. And his anus and urethra. "Comfy?" the Pooka asked him. "I can easily give you orgasms this way while you're gaming, hee hee."

The offer, as much as the goosing she gave him, made Obama open his eyes with a start. His view of the casino was now overlaid with a slightly greenish panoramic operations screen, ringed with status icons. Right now it was loading and arming onboard weapons systems. "No thanks!" he said emphatically. The idea of autosex inside the Pooka was way too spooky to consider even for an instant. He had enough weird stuff to get used to already, he thought, noticing that his movements suddenly felt ponderous. When he held up his right hand to his face-plate, he saw that it was armored like a fat plastic armadillo. His left arm was basically a small tank, bristling with the noses of guns and portable missiles.

"OK, Obama," said the voice of the Pooka in his ear. "Be careful with our back-mounted MicroFusion Pack. It has to generate 100,000 Watts to power the HiFlo hydraulic systems built into the frame of the suit, and I'm not really sure how much impact it can absorb. Or how long it will last. The rest of me is made of a poly-laminate composite, the outer shell of which is capable of absorbing over 2500 Joules of kinetic impact. The 10 micron silver ablative coating can reflect laser and radiation emissions without damage to the composite subsurface. Isn't this fun? Humyns are so clever!"

"Don't you have weapons where you come from?" he asked her.

"Huh? What would we do with weapons? Oh, look, Obama — our first targets." Two of the casino security daemons had come back out of the front door and were walking toward him. Probably one of the guests coming from the rank of limousines had complained about his menacing appearance. Or perhaps it was because he wasn't wearing a tie. "Ooo, shall we kill them with the Gatling laser — or maybe a plasma gun?" asked the Pooka. "I just love having all these choices."

"We remind you that the use of any unregistered weapons within the Principality of Monaco is strictly prohibited," the holo over his head was chirping soothingly. "Instead, why not relax with a champagne cocktail at the Cafe Americano, sipping to the cool swinging sounds of live jazz? Or sample the specialties of the house at the stylish Restaurant Le Grill — "

"Shoot, Obama!" He raised his left arm and pulled the trigger. The outdoor entrance carpet erupted into flame, and the two security daemons quickly retreated back inside the front doors. The tourists started shrieking wildly and scattered. "I decided on the 'MasterBraun' flame-thrower," said the Pooka. "Don't be cross with me, OK, but you're over-aiming a little. Just point and squeeze."

"I'm out of practice," he said. He retreated back in the direction of the Cafe de Paris behind him and to his left, using a parked car for cover. A group of uniformed security daemons burst out of the doors carrying heavy black assault weapons.

"Halt!" cried the guide holo. "You are required to surrender all weapons immediately to the members of the *Compagnie des Carabiniers du Prince*. This elite para-military unit was originally formed to — " The flame-thrower blazed again, and two of the carabiniers burst into flame and lurched screaming around before falling to the pavement. The BeeMercedes beside them exploded. A spray of bullets bounced harmlessly off Obama's head. He slowly incinerated the entire front entrance area, then the Pooka rotated weapons and launched a small missile that exploded inside the hall, destroying several of the onyx columns.

"Not bad," said the Pooka. She sounded a bit disappointed, he thought.

Now they were drawing fire from a number of locations. He turned to his right — due west, according to his face-screen — and launched two more missiles at the Hotel de Paris opposite. The entire facade of the building crumbled into the street. There was a sudden eruption of garishly costumed gaming avatars — all carrying exotic weapons — from the front doors of the Opera House, which was directly attached to the casino to the east; Obama strafed them with Gatling plasma-gunfire, alternating with the occasional missile. A werewolf in a Nazi uniform aimed a handheld mortar at him, and the car in front of him blew up in Obama's face, bathing his suit in flaming ethanol. Bits of metal debris rained down on him like confetti.

The casino, noting his enhanced illegal weaponry, had probably put an instant bounty on him, and these were his fellow guests attacking him now, most wearing their favorite skins from other war-games. He could expect this interlude to last only a few minutes, however, until air-support arrived. He backed into the front lobby of the Cafe de Paris Casino, directly behind him, a sort of miniature pavilion-like version of the main one, and swiveled around briefly in order to incinerate a few hapless guests who were making a dash out of the main court toward the street. Glasspex exploded around him on three sides — obviously the paras had fired some sort of missile weapon at him, and tiny pellets of glass rained against his armor like a blizzard of hailstones.

He crouched behind a potted palm and strafed the area the missile had come from. Suddenly there was a blinding flash, and his monitor dimmed. A roar like a volcanic explosion picked Obama up and slammed him against the far wall. This was followed by a paralyzing blast of wind — and everything in the lobby not bolted down was blown out of the room as the interior walls collapsed. His vision returned slowly, and the systems check initiated as ghostly icons blinked around the edges of his vision, coming back online one by one. He picked himself up slowly and tried to use his right hand to feel if the back-mounted fusion generator was still intact. "What was that?" he asked the Pooka, as he clambered laboriously to his feet.

"Sorry," she said. "I switched to tactical nukes. I've always wanted to try one or two, just to see what would happen."

"Well, now we know." He walked over to where the front doors had been. The opera house was now a glowing crater, filled with swirling cinders. The skeleton of the casino still stood, though, and as he watched, one of its towers burst into flame and collapsed in very slow motion. The Cafe de Paris behind him was a blackened, smoking shell; street by street in the distance, the bright lights splashed across the night horizon like strings of blazing pearls were going out. The Pooka switched him over to nitevision.

A few scattered avatars, he saw, were slowly emerging from the doorways of shattered buildings and cellars and gingerly picking their way through the rubble of the *quartier*. It scarcely seemed worth the trouble of gunning them down. The haze was so dense that he could no longer see the dark silhouette of Monaco-Ville in the distance at all. If there had been a mushroom cloud he'd missed it.

A single, vaguely humyn-looking figure detached itself from the smoldering ruin of the casino and tottered across the street toward him. As it approached, he saw that most of its flesh and organs had been blasted away, and that it basically just consisted of charred bone and a few remaining muscles. It still had enough of Colonel Park Cha's face to be recognizable, though. It stopped in the middle of what had been the Allee de Boulingrins and called out, "You have a message?"

"Tell your boss his daughter Simonetta is at Manacera City Hospital Center. She's trapped in the body of a gorilla," Obama replied. The suit amplified his — Kalinga's — voice, so it sounded like a vocoder.

"Is this a joke?" Park yelled back.

"Just tell him what I say, fool!" Obama torched a little of the rubble close to Park's feet with the MasterBraun until the UNSS operative skulked away back toward the casino. *It's so hard to get through to people sometimes,* he thought, sighing.

"Could you do all that in real life?" Obama asked the Pooka after they'd booted off and were sitting back in his living room on the couch.

"Sure," she said. "I guess." Then after a moment, she added, "Obama, what does 'real life' mean, again? Exactly?"

15.

Obama had customized his morning YouVee shows to highlight any mention of Joyful Kalinga, so the headline "Big Man Breaks Bank at Monte Carlo" was the first news item he saw the next morning when he got up. Unfortunately, the virtual Monte Carlo he'd nuked had also been the official onGrid tourist site for the Principality, so Joyful Kalinga's attack on it was being treated by the Federal authorities as a real-life crime. According to the Disney cartoon character Clarabelle Cow, who had recently placed fifth in worldwide "Favorite Disney Character" polls — she was particularly popular in East Asia — Kalinga's wanton destruction of proprietary code had also triggered a number of viruses, which were now busily attacking the basic structure of the Grid itself. This was causing, as Clarabelle dramatically put it, "virtual radioactive fallout," and costing Sato Holdings LLC, the Principality of Monaco, and their UN-owned principal reinsurer, Lloyds of London, millions in lost revenue.

The Bally's and Harrah's online chains had reported a spike in new customers during the previous 12 hours, and there was speculation that one or both of the chains had hired Kalinga to destroy Monte Carlo. Clarabelle featured a Japanese Sato spokesperson saying through Babelfish, "It is unthinkable that security codes at this gaming level could have been hacked so easily without participation at the highest industry level. And the price for this act of wanton destruction is being passed on to all of us, the taxpayers."

World President Manacera appeared next on Clarabelle's show, reading a prepared statement. "Even though this monstrous act did not result in the tragic loss of actual humyn life, it still represents a frightening assault on the sovereignty of signatory states — and on the liberties of free citizens everywhere."

"Most terrifying of all," added Clarabelle gravely, "is the prospect that Joyful Kalinga might attempt to repeat this monstrous act in the *real* Monaco. Can this have been an innocent game gone horribly wrong — or was it a dress rehearsal for the real thing? We already knew that Kalinga is allegedly a hardened terrorist and bomber. The question now is, is he a nuclear-armed one? Will his next move be to hold the entire world hostage?" Behind her, a hologram of Joyful Kalinga's face looped over and over screaming, "I am a big man! I am a big man!" Suddenly, there were hundreds more messages on Kalinga's iRist, including a half-dozen from Gracia with pleading captions in very bad Enriched. One or two captions, like "All womyn worship a giant," had obviously been lifted from spamvertising campaigns. And "Want more sexy monstrus akshun, plz" had been ripped straight from the day's headlines.

But could he, Obama Jones, really take the whole world hostage? If so, then maybe that's what it would take for him to get Kim back. *But what would they do after that?* he wondered. Where could they hide? Maybe the alien, Siren, might help. But what would she want from him in return? And how was she mixed up in all this, anyway?

This was early on Threesday morning. When Obama arrived at work, he found the MAD building under siege. Someone on the Coalition of the Appearance-Challenged minority-status application jury — probably Rainbow Secakuku, Obama thought — had leaked the news that the rest of the panelists had refused to set foot inside the MAD building again after the bombing and now preferred to neuro-commute for the duration of the hearings. Some had, in fact, already gone home.

This news had been greeted with outrage by the CAC community. It was possible nowadays — indeed, in most cases preferable — for most people to neuro-commute to work, but ever since the discovery in the early '40s, first in Strasbourg, then in Geneva, that members of the European Parliament and later the World Congress had been using AI's and even looped holograms to represent themselves at their posts, it was considered a payment prerequisite for government employees and consultants to physically attend "meatworld" functions, simply to prove they'd actually been paying some slight degree of attention.

This present betrayal seemed particularly egregious to CAC, since several of the jurors were actually members of the organization and most had already taken bribes to assure the outcome of the hearings. Now these hearings seemed likely to be recessed or even abandoned. Consequently, hundreds of CAC demonstrators — real ones this time and not hired professionals — had been airbussed into town to converge on the MAD building. There they had come into conflict with the red-jacketed NYVs guarding the immediate neighborhood. Jostling and shoving matches had erupted, and by the time Obama emerged from the Retro Station across the street, an ineffectual sort of riot had begun. Derogatory racial and gender-oriented epithets illegal for nearly half a century were being publicly employed, much to his horror, and since HHS rarely, if ever, responded to the special 011 hate-crime abuse iTooth hotline, it appeared the offenses would go unpunished. Luckily, the YouVee news networks could be counted on not to broadcast the scene, since they had no wish to offend the government that funded them.

As Obama crossed the street, a barrage of OrgasMeal debris hurled by taunting NYV family members and hangers-on came pelting down both on him and on a pocket of particularly appearance-challenged demonstrators. The pavement was awash with dark, brackish water still being pumped out of the bottom floors of the building and deposited by hoses on the sidewalk outside, and several struggling combatants slipped down in front of him and fell wrestling into the water, liberally splashing him with muck.

Once inside the building, he discovered that only its top 18 floors had been reopened. The underground levels and the first four levels remained closed to everyone except emergency workers. The main lobby had been encased in heavy translucent Nitinyl curtains, and a series of hastily constructed metal catwalks led from the security scanners to the ascensors. The emergency stairwells had all been pumped clear, and electricity, heat, and water had been restored to much of the building.

Meanwhile (MAD employees were informed by iTooth), the forensics investigation and bomb-blast restoration on the lower floors would proceed for the foreseeable future. In fact, the entire 4th floor, which had previously housed the UN Disadvantaged Rehabilitation Initiative, was now to be used as office space, equipment storage, and emergency living facilities by the UNFAA forensics teams. Right now they were busy releasing thousands of crawling and skittering security cams and spy-bugs to replace those damaged by the blast and its after-effects.

In any case, UNDRI itself was an all but moribund departmental division. Its heyday had long since come and gone. From the early 2020's on, it had been a trend all over the world for social workers, inspired by the "Swedish example," to cut through red tape to get the unemployed onto welfare rolls by assigning them Intellectually Disadvantaged status. Families would even offer large bribes to case-workers to have themselves, their entire villages, or in some cases their entire tribes listed as such. At one point in 2034, it had been estimated that nearly one third of all the people on the planet were officially considered mentally subnormal, or mentally handicapable, both by their own governments and the UN agencies that increasingly supported them.

But in 2034, when the last few remaining rogue states — the United States, North Korea, Iran, and a half-dozen African countries — abrogated their independent status and agreed to World CommUnion, it was finally recognized that it was the Intellectually Disadvantaged classification itself that was abnormal. To avoid the social shock that would follow a formal declaration that 95% of ID UN citizens had been wrongfully diagnosed, it was decided instead to create UNDRI, a jobs and social skills retraining program that would allow the Formerly Intellectually Disadvantaged to be gainfully reintegrated into global society.

This decision was one of several bitter battles that MAD proceeded to lose; it had meant the gradual disappearance of millions of minority clients who had fallen within its purview. As a sop, UNDRI had been assigned to MAD, but every year its budget had been cut as more and more FIDs disappeared from its rolls. By 2050, a victim of its own faux success, the Disadvantaged Rehabilitation Initiative had shrunk to just a few dozen employees overseeing a number of programs devoid of participants. After the bombing, it was decided by Norberto Zollto to quietly terminate the division altogether. Its employees would be assigned, or as they put it, "sacrificed," to Carmen.

There were two very depressed Hindus already seated inside his cube when Obama reached his office on the 14th floor. The carpets were still sodden, in spite of the portable dehumidifiers and space heaters everywhere, and the ceiling tiles were stained with soot and water damage. Some of the cubicle walls were already warping. "Meet your replacements from the 4th floor," Scott told him. "I guess they're assigned to our team. Carmen says I'm Go-Captain now."

"Congratulations, Scott," Obama told him. "You totally deserve it. Where am I supposed to work, though?"

"I dunno, 'migo. Better ask the boss-lady."

But when Obama iToothed her, she merely said, "Fuck you, Obama. No seriously, get over yourself. I've got real problems. I have to absorb all these 4th floor losers today — I'm even having to retrain a new AA, 'cuz Camille croaked on me. So I've got nothing left to give. Take it up with Operations." *It's just her way of mourning,* thought

Obama. He debated the wisdom of telling Carmen that Simonetta had temporarily survived as Priska, but decided against it.

The conference hall had fared even worse than the 14th floor. Its interior reeked of smoke and mildew. A damp, dark haze hung in the air. Water damage had stained the circular walls a yeasty organic brown, and had so affected the room's subdermal smart-wiring that the holograms of the other jurors sometimes flickered on and off. Obama was the only real person there, and it occurred to him that he could simply use the empty space as his own office, and no one would ever know. Conversely, he could also just go home. How long would it take, he wondered, for anyone to even notice he was absent and fire him? Or would he just keep getting promoted in absentia like Norberto, until he ended up as director of the whole department?

The morning began with a presentation by CAC's legal counsel, seemingly unaffected by the demonstrations outside. Their first submission was on the topic of Looksism or Appearance Oppression. For millennia, went the CAC argument, humyn males, with the complicity of their "brainwashed female hostages," had constructed a false standard of attractiveness for both genders. Radical CAC members had in the past therefore demanded the creation of a UN agency for the formulation of Appearance Equality where persons with "Alpha" or "Gamma" levels of attractiveness would be required to undergo cosmetic surgery to achieve a uniform, or "Beta" status. This demand had in turn given way to the even more radical concept that ughliness was in fact a new form of beauty — and that Alphas and Betas, therefore, should all be forced to surgically become Gammas.

More moderate voices within the movement, however, were now willing to trade these hard-line demands for formal UN recognition that Appearance Oppression consisted, not merely of discriminating against the traditionally unattractive, but in noticing the distinction at all. That admission of culpability was a necessary first step toward reparations and full equality under the law. But it was at this point that the otherwise seemingly reasonable demand ran into trouble with the distinguished panelists. It was true that several were already members of CAC and so felt loyalty toward its aims, particularly those who had accepted large sums of funding from it, but because most had a history of investment in other equally praiseworthy causes, conflicting interests were beginning to collide with bewildering ferocity.

People's Tribune Cao Ding informed the rest of them — through the signing Babelfish interpreter, Babelpus — that she was uncomfortable assigning any of the guilt of Appearance Oppression to womyn. All oppression, she argued, including the rape of Nature herself, was rooted in the eternal male abuse of womyn. Dr Plassnik objected. This was outmoded thinking, rooted in "hetero-sexism," she pointed out. Lesbians and the formerly gendered had already liberated themselves from it and objectively viewed "looksism" as a universal humyn right, not merely restricted to males. LaDonna Slaughter-Townley countered that this argument was "logo-centric," logic itself being a system of non-intuitive — and therefore anti-female — thought, imposed by male tyranny. "Nature is female," she declared, "The very term, 'knowledge', was created as an act of oppression by myn."

"We're straying from the topic," interrupted Dr Khan. "Ughliness is non-gender-specific. Look at me!"

"We're all pretty damn sick of looking at you!" snapped Rainbow Secakuku. And so the day passed.

Late in the afternoon, after everyone else had booted off, Obama was startled by what he assumed to be a hologram of Norberto Zollto in black satin pajamas, but which turned out to be real when he tapped Obama on the shoulder. "A word in your dusky shell-like ear, Obama," said Zollto in a near whisper. "I'm holding a private meeting with Khan and Secakuku tonight over supper. I think it might be most instructive if you tagged along. We'll see what we can salvage from this fiasco, eh?"

Surprised, Obama got awkwardly to his feet. He'd never been invited out to a meal by the MAD boss before. Of course he'd been invited, along with half of MAD, out to Zollto's yearly senior staff retreats at his palatial home overlooking the Chesapeake Bay, but that wasn't quite the same thing as an invitation to a private dinner.

Zollto was one of the new "Unocrats," a class of UN officials who by dint of privileges, inflated salaries, padding of expense accounts, and bribes from corporations and special-interest groups, had become ostentatiously wealthy "buzzers" (as rich people were generally called by the poor, because of the vulture-like way their aircars looked from inner-city neighborhoods). Norberto Zollto's home, for instance, was a former bed 'n' breakfast hotel with 18 bed and bathroom suites, two dining halls — one outdoors inside a permanent pavilion — several kitchens, a wine cellar bought and reconstructed from a monastery, and a perfect replica of a Victorian English tavern on the ground floor, complete with stained-glass windows and a six-meter-long polished oak bar. He also owned a loft in Manhattan. In town, he kept a suite at a local hotel and, as Obama discovered when the two of them stepped out of the ascensor tower onto the rooftop parking lot, a chauffeured white Cadillaire limousine and a private bodyguard. Shepherding Obama toward the idling aircar, Zollto told him, "Right now the two of them" — meaning Khan and Secakuku — "are blocking any kind of compromise."

"Oh? Why?"

Zollto waited until they were both enclosed inside the back seat of the limo, which had a glasspex privacy screen separating them from the driver and the bodyguard in the front seat, before saying, "To be perfectly frank, Obama, it's because Khan and Sekacucu are both notorious sexual predators. Which is the only reason they're even still here in Manacera City — they've been shacked up in a hotel suite for the past week rutting like a pair of wild pigs in heat. I imagine it must like watching a World Fight Club Smackdown; I wish they'd sold tickets. I admit I've personally been all agog to see which of them will emerge the winner." Obama made a face at the thought, then realized guiltily that he was being a "looksist." But it was too late; Zollto had caught his expression. "Yes, comical picture, isn't it? But really, it's time for you to grow up a bit, and I say this for your own good. In our racket — public service — sex is increasingly just about power, the higher up you go. And advancing one's career, naturally. Why else do you imagine anyone would actually have sex with Carmen? Now there's a truly revolting picture for you. But people do, I've heard. And incredible as it may seem to your innocent eyes, both Khan and Sekacucu actually think they're perfectly hot. Or let's say they've separately subscribed to that fiction, anyway, by dint of sheer hard labor in the bedroom. More to the point, they like their partners to be physically attractive — excepting, of course, this particular liaison. Hence their bigotry against the appearance-challenged. Khan is a famous cocksman, you know, despite the silly pink goatee and the little pot-belly. I've tried to inveigle him into bed myself, but alas, he isn't bi."

Through the darkened limo window, Obama watched as the Cadillaire made its approach to the rooftop landing pad of the Ritz-Hilton Hotel, which towered over the ruins of the old Federal Center on Pennsylvania Avenue. Zollto leaned forward, as if fearful of being overheard, and murmured conspiratorially, "Strictly *entre nous*, Obama — and this is to go no further — I'm personally against the CAC petition myself. It's just one damned minority too many, in my opinion. Though of course, that's only my unofficial opinion. I'll tack my professional sails to whichever way the prevailing winds are blowing. I've never really minded embracing the halt and the lame and the blind and the retarded, metaphorically speaking, of course. I don't really even mind the apes, though heaven knows they smell godawful

— but, call me an old queezer if you like, I really think I draw the line at CAC. Were you watching the demonstrators outside the building today? Did you see the ones with mountain goat-horn implants? And tropical disease-induced scaling? And the womyn with all that pubic hair all over and no noses? Some of them actually made poor Priska look like a beauty queen. One shudders to imagine what the employee cafeteria will look like in a year if this goes through."

Vorace, the rooftop restaurant at the Ritz-Hilton, was the most expensive in Manacera City. In fact, it was the most expensive in the North American Federal Administrative Area. Obama had seen the restaurant on YouVee but had never been inside. Its menu, which consisted mostly of endangered species, was part of a green global awareness initiative to heighten awareness of these species by eating them, and a single meal there could easily cost 1,000 Unos or more. Luckily, as Norberto Zollto, explained on his way in, this was a business meal and could therefore be expensed.

He had left his bodyguard behind with the car. While they waited for the teenage Thai hippy-hostess to locate their party — her naked breasts were day-glo-painted with the words "hippy" and "hostess" — Zollto suddenly said, "This seems as good a time as any to have a word with you about your future with us, Obama."

"Oh?" said Obama. He assumed "with us" meant "with MAD," not his future with his three fellow diners that evening. Or the humyn race in general. But neither would have surprised him at that moment.

"You know," his boss went on, "I've always had such tremendously high hopes for you. To be frank, I always thought you'd be filling my shoes — well, flip-flops — as Department Director someday. But much as I hate to say it, Obama, you've disappointed me."

Their hippy-hostess interrupted. "Your party is waiting for you, gentlemyn. I take you now, please follow me." So Obama would have to wait to find out how he'd disappointed his boss. Did he care? He decided that he really didn't. Today, he thought with relief, might well have been the last day he ever set foot inside the MAD building.

A few weeks ago, that prospect would have filled him with a certain sense of panic and even sorrow. He would at least have missed Scott and FaLola and all the other friends he'd made there. But they'd all made it plain they could get along perfectly well without him. The building was now a toxic health hazard, and the job itself had become nothing but a corrupt joke. Certainly Norberto saw it that way. Maybe it really was time for Obama to move on and start over.

The decor of Vorace had been interwoven with holos and the night sky overhead to create the illusion of ancient temples and beaches under the stars. Blue marble columns rose around stone-lined circular jacuzzis set halfway up a flight of stairs. In their centers, carved jade dinner tables had been mounted 30 centimeters or so above water level. For privacy's sake, each of these "feeding pits" was surrounded by holograms of an empty beach at night, through which the humyn waiters and waitresses disconcertingly emerged and disappeared.

Before climbing up to their pit, Norberto and Obama were led to cabana-style changing stalls. These were decorated in a sort of Moorish modern brickwork motif and warmly lit by tiny orange spotlights.

"I don't want to leave you behind," Obama muttered to the Pooka as he undressed. He was getting dangerously addicted to the feeling of personal safety she gave him. The little machine poked her head out of her bag and stared at him.

"OK, I can be your swim-pants, hee hee," she said, and flowed up his bare leg to sculpt herself into a rigid facsimile of a pair of swimming trunks. Her round shiny face beamed inscrutably out from over his crotch, like a medallion. If anything, Obama felt overdressed — and gratefully so — when he joined the others in the jacuzzi.

Dr Khan and Ms Sekacucu ("Please call me 'Rainbow'"), who were already sampling a crème brûlée of soft shelled turtle foie gras with Tonga beans, were wearing only the most minimal of caches-sexes, while Norberto, perhaps in a last valiant attempt to pique Khan's interest, was entirely nude. "Oo, I see they're still serving king cobra steaks in coconut soup," Norberto said, watching the menu holos. "Or you can have them fried with garlic, chili or oyster sauce if you're interested, Obama. None of this is in-vitro, you know — all wild, as nature intended." Warm jets of water played over Obama's legs and belly as he half-sat, half-floated in his tiled corner.

"The mousseline of macaque brains with morel mushroom infusion sounds delicious to me," said Dr Khan. "Fancy a 1961 Château Haut-Brion with that, Rainbow?" Khan had, Obama noticed, hennaed his considerable body hair to match the shade of his beard. Obama looked quickly away, but found the sight of Rainbow's sagging semi-nudity equally disturbing. Might Kim look like that someday? He hoped not.

While they flirted with the menu, talk turned to the CAC hearings. "It's over," Rainbow brutally asserted, slapping a hand like a side of ham on the tabletop. "CAC just fucked itself up the ass with this last demo. They've given us the perfect excuse to walk away from the table." Norberto tried, not very energetically, to talk them round, but she and Khan remained as hard-boiled as the sea-turtle eggs they were eating. They could, they said, count on the support of Plassnik, who despite the emergence of the Neo-Punctuated Equilibrium, or "Punk Eek," Movement in Aesthetic Philosophy, remained a loyal member of the looksist old guard. Their fourth ally on the panel, Norberto admitted at last, would of course be Obama Jones. His reluctant vote would be that of the MAD establishment.

"Although I've just been forced to tell Obama how disappointed I've been with his job performance so far," Zollto blandly announced to them all. "Our young amigo seems to utterly lack any kind of killer instinct."

"Oh dear," said Khan, fixing Obama with a patronizing gaze from behind his blue spectacles. "What can we do about that?" It was on the tip of Obama's tongue to mention that he'd just nuked Monte Carlo the night before and that all he had to do now, in fact, was unleash the plastic toy now grinning at his groin in order to reduce the entire room to a pile of smoking cinders, but the problem was that Zollto was right. Obama did lack that instinct. And he wasn't sure he wanted it.

"Suggestions?" said Zollto.

"Kill Carmen," said Rainbow. "I hate that stinking fat bitch. Ayub, I think I'll go for the civet cheeks with Périgord truffle and a 1955 Château Latour. The Haut-Brion would be kinda dry with that, don't you think?"

"Rainbow doesn't mean you should literally kill Carmen, Obama," explained Zollto. "She means you should destroy her professionally and then take over her job. You'll have to do that anyway before she gets rid of you. You're a threat to her now."

"Don't tell me what I mean," said Rainbow, bursting into gales of laughter. Long, leathery-brown, and large, she likely weighed about half as much as Carmen, who, Obama thought unkindly, must have been one of the few persons Rainbow Sekacucu could get away with calling fat. With a straight face, anyway. The two womyn, he'd heard, had once been bitter rivals on the Council of Native American Nations.

"Supplanting her," Dr Khan added judiciously to Obama, "would certainly prove a number of things about the sincerity of your own ambition." *As well as being convenient for Norberto Zollto,* Obama perceived with sudden clarity. Obviously, it was Zollto who saw

Carmen as a threat. "How exactly would you suggest our young amigo here go about this project, Norberto?"

"Oh, let me count the ways," smiled Zollto, but the waiter arrived before he could. In the end, Obama had the near-extinct blue-fin tuna with scallops and black truffle and then for dessert, an Imperial gingerbread pyramid with caramel and salted butter ice cream, all with a 1967 Château d'Yquem, which was, Dr Khan insisted, far too inappropriately fruity for the fish, but which Obama stubbornly enjoyed anyway. Unfortunately, he was throwing it all up a few short minutes later.

He'd gone back to his cabana to change so that he could go to the bathroom, and was startled to find Siren Gunnarsdottir — or the alien inhabiting the body of Siren Gunnarsdottir, to be precise — waiting for him inside. Tonight she was all dressed up as if for a party. Her pale hair was worn high in a bun held by glittering butterfly pincers, one of which had the Princess's face on it, and she was wearing formal sequined eyeglasses and a short-short blue ball sheath dress wrong way round. With matching high heels, of course. The glimpse of her creamy thighs made Obama, already full of the Château d'Yquem, visibly totter. "You'd better sit down, Obama," she said. Her expression was severe in the orange-ish glare.

"Why, what's going on?"

"I can't stay long — I need to get back to guarding Prisca. I should have sent a holo, but I wanted to tell you this in person."

"What?" He felt confused. Why exactly was she "guarding Prisca?" He sat down heavily on the little inset stool. The Pooka flowed off and resumed her normal shape.

"Let's get him dressed," Siren told her, and the two of them started tugging his clothes onto him until he stopped them.

"What's going on?" he demanded.

In reply, Siren put her arm around him. "I've had some terrible news, some worse news, and some even worse news, Obama," she said. "Well, the exact order of those may vary from a human perspective. Which would you like to hear first?"

Obama sat down heavily again with his pants half-on. "The worst news, I guess," he said. "From my own perspective, I mean."

"OK," said Siren unhappily. She reached down and stroked his cheek. *What the hell is going on?* thought Obama. *She's an alien — she hates touching humyns.* "Obama, there's no easy way to say this. Kim was in the Federal Courthouse building with you the day the bomb went off there. In fact, she was in a room only a few meters away from you at the time. The blast killed her. She's dead, Obama. I'm so sorry." She continued to stroke him until he shook his head violently.

"No!" he said. "You must be wrong!" But he knew better.

The alien said nothing. He felt a tugging at his pants leg and looked down. It was the Pooka. "Never mind, Obama," she said. "You'll always have me."

That was when he vomited.

16.

After she'd cleaned them both up a bit, Siren grasped him firmly by the shoulders and stared into his eyes. Her irises expanded and contracted like a camera's. "Get a grip," she said. "I know this has been a terrible shock, but you need to act like an adult for me now, Obama. Believe me, there are still worse things that could happen."

"Not for me," he mumbled. And started to cry. She slapped him. Hard. "Hey!" he said.

"Sorry," she said. "But wow, I could develop a taste for that. Humyns get to do all kinds of amazingly primitive things. Look, I need to get back to the hospital now, it's important. And I'm taking you along, too, because I want to keep an eye on you. OK?" He nodded. "You," she said to the Pooka. "In the bag." They ran into the rest of Obama's party — Norberto Zollto, Dr Khan, and Rainbow Sekacucu, in the hallway outside the restrooms. The three stopped and stared wide-eyed at Siren, who was dragging Obama along by one hand.

"Obama!" said Zollto. "We were wondering what had become of you."

"This poor baby is feeling awfully sick to his tummy right now," said Siren smoothly in a broad American accent. "He's allergic to seafood. And it was so mean of you all to let him eat it. Hi. I'm Obama's new fiancee, Barbara Dahl." She shook hands with each of them in turn.

"His new fiancee?" said Khan. "What happened to the old one? What an extraordinarily lucky young fellow he is. I had literally no idea his taste in womyn was so excellent."

"Amazing," said Zollto. "I had no idea either. You must come to our next MAD function, Ms Dahl."

"I look forward to it," Siren cooed. Even Rainbow was leaning forward, lips slightly parted, with a sort of panting look on her face. *Pheromones,* Obama thought. *Siren is doing it again.* Her face had actually changed character, even appearance, with the new voice, as if she'd suddenly become an entirely different person. Was this a trait of her species, to have no real physical characteristics of their own but only to mimic those of others?

"We do apologize. Care to join us for drinks?" Rainbow asked hopefully. Siren gave an exaggerated pout of disappointment.

"Oh, we really can't. *Quelle dommage*, but we need to pop Obama straight into bed. Some other time?" And then, almost miraculously, they were free and outside in the cold fresh air of the rooftop.

"What does it feel like, to change your personality so easily?" Obama asked her on the way to her aircar. Anything not to think about Kim.

"You tell me, 'Joyful'," the alien answered cruelly.

Once they were airborne, Obama said, "Does your species have genders?" He felt desperate to keep the conversation going. He'd talk about anything, just so he wouldn't have to sober up and think. He had known about Kim all along, he told himself, somehow, somewhere on some level deep down inside himself. He'd known he'd never see her again right from the start, the moment they'd taken her away, in fact. But to have been so physically near her and not to have even realized it was, well, there was no word he could think of to describe it. Horrible. Devastating. Heartbreaking.

He'd come so close to being reunited with her when she'd died. If only he'd had the Pooka a little sooner. He could have smashed through walls, burst into buildings, laid waste to whole cities, if need be, to get Kim back. Instead he'd allowed himself to be sidetracked into a dozen false diversions and distractions. And now it was too late.

"Each of us is our own gender," Siren was saying.

"How do you reproduce, then?" He and Kim had talked about having children. But it was too late for that now, too. For anything. The knowledge struck him again like a vast hammer blow

"Oh, we don't do that much. Basically, when you live forever, there's not much urge to procreate. Besides, there are already billions of us in existence — and we don't get along with each other all that well." Beneath them as they flew by, the lights of the city blinked and twinkled against a black night of unbearable loneliness. "Our species, as you call it, is highly evolved, Obama. But evolution is the result of constant and intense competition. When we were still at the primitive planetary stage humans are stuck in right now, we were always at each other's throats. No two of us could meet in the flesh, so to speak, without either instantly feeling an irresistible attraction or an overpowering urge to kill each other. Am I making any sense? Good.

"Well, even today, the same reactions persist inside us, only we've learned how to control them. In fact, we've bred violence right out of ourselves. Still, we only meet each other remotely or else cloaked in the most elaborate of physical disguises — any contact more intimate than that is begging for trouble. We're too passionate. With us, emotions last forever. So we spread ourselves out across the universe in order to avoid having any. We might become either become eternal jealous lovers or mortal enemies — or both. And since we're now totally incapable of killing each other — or anybody else — hating each other is miserable and pointless. Much smarter just to stay out of each others' faces and send e-cards at Xmas. So to speak."

"You have names, right? What do you call yourselves?"

The alien looked amused. The glowing green cross of the hospital landing pad came into view, and the car changed course. "Of course we have names. But not in a spoken language like yours. So, I guess you should keep calling me Siren. Originally, we evolved in an ocean a bit like yours, and my 'real' name means something sort of like mermaid anyway."

As they landed, Obama asked her, "What about the Helpers?"

"The Helpers are the oldest, most mysterious race in existence. Even we don't know everything about them. Think of them as, I don't know, nannies or nursemaids to the rest of us. They love children — that's why they're always playing games with us. And inhabiting our toys. Come on, let's go inside and see if we've caught anything. The Princess was busy while you were puking your guts out."

The big landing pad in front of the hospital ER-ICU wing, the one with the green cross, was reserved for incoming airbulances. Ordinary aircars landed in the smaller satellite-pads that ringed the main one like an electronic drum-kit. Obama and Siren were walking down a dimly lit cement walkway leading from her parked aircar to the front doors when, suddenly Siren cocked her head. Obama heard the sounds of several muffled explosions, and then the hospital alarms all went off at once. At that moment, Siren's forehead blossomed with dark crimson jelly, and her entire head was flung back. A loud crack echoed across the parking lot.

Before she'd even hit the pavement, the alien was encased in a new skin of pink plastic as the Princess flowed protectively around her. *Too late,* thought Obama. He had flinched away, so the second shot, milliseconds later, missed his own heart but caused a piercing white-hot pain in his right shoulder and upper arm. This time, he barely heard the sound of the shot — he was too busy being hurled backwards.

The Pooka encased him instantly, too, so that he didn't even feel the impact of landing on cement. His eyes remained open. The shell of the Pooka over them was no thicker than that of a contact lens; as he watched, Siren jerked abruptly to her feet. Now she looked exactly like a shiny, naked Barbie doll. Her head swiveled from side to side, and then she set off at a run. Her legs spun into ultrafast motion, faster even than the Allura's knitting had been that first night he'd spent here himself; then Siren became a near-invisible blur as she smacked into the Emergency Room's glasspex doors and smashed through them. Meanwhile, his shoulder and arm were numb. He sat up suddenly. Several bullets bounced harmlessly off him, and there was a tinkling noise as the one inside his shoulder was suddenly expelled, bouncing onto the cement. The Pooka suit yanked him abruptly to his feet and set him off in motion after Siren. "Come on, get moving!" it said in his left ear. "We haven't got all night."

"What about my shoulder?" he asked.

"I'm repairing it as fast as I can!" snapped the Pooka. "It would help if you'd stop bleeding." Inside the ER, lights were blinking on and off everywhere, and Obama noticed a number of patients huddled against a wall behind a barricade of chairs. More bullets clattered against him, and something burst noisily against the side of his head. He turned. Several black armor-clad SWAT troopers were crouched in a side doorway firing at him with assault weapons. He pointed at them, and a long, very thin thread of sticky translucent plastic shot out of his index finger. With incredible speed, it whipped itself around each of them in turn, elongated, then suspended all three upside-down from the ceiling, where they hung swaying like insects suspended inside a spider's nest.

"Siren won't let us kill anything," the Pooka muttered plaintively. "So this isn't gonna be any fun. As usual." The hall leading to Priska's room was deserted, but filled with debris and scorch-marks, as if it had been the site of an attack. The Allura robot nurse lay spasming in a twisted heap halfway down it, her electronic entrails spreading across the floor-tiles. Several more fiber-cocoons were hanging from the ceiling. A room burst into flame as Obama raced by.

The walls and doorway around Priska's room were coated in a white, oozing plastic that appeared to be digesting the marks of a major explosion. However, as though this barrier were no more substantial than a curtain of milk, they passed through it and into Priska's room.

Inside, the hospital room now looked like a bat-cave. Or the lining of someone's throat. Wet plastic oozed and dripped from every surface, and the lights were on emergency power. A dozen or so cocoons hung from the ceiling, and Siren, still wrapped in her Barbie armor, was examining the face of one of them in the beam of a pink light the Princess was projecting from her tiara. A tear seemed to have escaped her left eye, right beneath where she'd been shot. "Recognize him?" she asked Obama in his other ear. The man looked a bit like Colonel Park, but wasn't — though it was a bit hard to tell, since he was upside-down.

"No," he said.

"Dr Wong Kyu-Bong, according to his ID badge. He's the one who made all this mess." Behind her, he caught a glimpse of Priska lying lifeless and bloody on her face in the bed. The back of her head and neck all the way down to where her shoulder-blades met had been cut open.

"Why did they do this to her?" He felt sick at the sight.

"I'll explain later," said the alien. "This is all my fault; I should never have used poor Priska as bait. Come on, we're wasting our time. Let's get out of here before they send in more troopers." The moment she spoke, the plastic on the walls and ceiling swirled and boiled away until it had all evaporated. "And I shouldn't have distracted the Princess by taking her along with me," she added.

"My bad," the Princess said. "I waited too long for Sato to get here." Siren picked up her striped hatbox, and left the room quickly, Obama close behind. At some unheard command of hers, their armor shaped itself into orderlies' loose light-blue clothing, so that from a distance the two of them resembled hospital robots. Carrying a hatbox.

"What were they looking for?" he tried asking again when they'd safely reached the aircar. The alien sighed and slammed her door shut. A faint column of smoke was visible above the ICU wing.

"You really aren't thinking straight tonight, aren't you? Use your brains, Obama. Sheesh! What do you think they were looking for?" The aircar lifted off as a torrent of paramilitary vehicles began spinning down to land on the pads and hospital roof. "Simonetta."

It took him a moment to comprehend the implications of this. "So ... Simonetta really was— is — an alien?"

"A very, very illegal alien," said Siren. "She shouldn't have been here. She shouldn't even exist. She shouldn't have been able to crawl inside Priska. Yet all of the above happened. I don't understand any of it. Yet."

"Where is she now?" he said.

"In a safe place," said Siren. "I extracted her as soon as you left yesterday. But I should have medevac'ed Priska out right away and left a dummy in her bed instead. I feel awful about this. I was expecting a much higher-tech assault, to be honest. Humans still always manage to surprise me." She started crying again. After a few minutes she blew her nose. *It really isn't the kind of behavior you expect from an alien,* thought Obama. "Well, the poor thing wouldn't have lived more than a few more days or weeks, anyway. Her cancer was so far advanced."

"Can't you cure cancer?" he asked her.

"Could have — but wouldn't. I'm not here to interfere." So what was she here for? he thought. So far, he didn't have a clue.

The lights below resolved themselves into a familiar pattern, and Obama realized that he and Siren were now circling his own rooftop. Aircars were fast. That was the only thing he regretted about not stealing Carmen's job from her — or cashing in Kalinga's winnings, either; Obama would have liked very much to have owned an aircar. But he was planning to quit his job tomorrow, and that meant he was going to be poor. Potentially, very poor.

"The thing I don't understand," he said, "— well, the biggest thing, anyway — is exactly what Simonetta wanted from me. I just don't get it."

"Your body? Marriage? Food?" said Siren. He couldn't tell if she were being sarcastic or not. The aircar landed with a bump, and Siren turned and looked at him with an intense expression of motherly concern. The Princess had peeled itself from her face and become a fur coat, and Obama saw the bullet wound had healed completely, as if it had never been. Just like his shoulder. "Listen, Obama, this is important," she said. "I want you to pack up whatever stuff of yours that really matters to you and be ready to move out of your apartment by had straighter teeth, been taller, or maybe cleaned her room more often, her father would have stayed.

No, the facts were all they needed. As she talked, she watched her audience for signs of recognition. Soo studied the picture and listened with interest and sympathy. Bones was harder to read. His beard covered his face like a mask, from his throat almost to his eyes. His only response to the photo was a shrug, though some of the hostility faded from his eyes.

Hotshot's reaction was different. He almost dropped the picture after barely a glance. For the first time, he lifted his head and looked directly into Lennie's face. Fear screamed from his eyes. Whatever he knew couldn't be good.

"So here I am," Lennie concluded. "I know it's an old picture, but I was hoping someone would recognize him and tell me where he might be." She looked directly at Hotshot, but he had gone back to staring at his feet.

"Sorry, honey," Soo said. "Ah'd like to help, but cain't say Ah recognize your daddy. Bones and Hotshot, though, they been traveling longer and harder'n me. What about it, boys?"

"Can't say I've seen him," Bones said. "Can't say I haven't, either. Nice fish, though. You take the fillets and cook them up in tinfoil with some butter, fresh lemon, salt, maybe some basil or marjoram, and you got a tasty dinner. Or fish stew. I made a fish stew once that—"

Junkyard nudged him with his foot and the big man broke off, muttering to himself. Lennie never took her eyes off Hotshot. Tension had drawn his shoulders high, and he kept swallowing as though he had a fish bone stuck in his throat.

"What about you?" she said softly.

He didn't answer right away. Lennie waited, driving her nails into her palms to keep from yelling at him. Blinking rapidly, he glanced up without meeting her eyes. "Can't say I've ever seen him before, either."

"Oh, come *on*!" Lennie shot to her feet. Hotshot cringed under his blanket, looking miserable and more frightened than before, but she didn't care. "You know something. Something bad. You've got to tell me—it's my father!"

Hotshot only hunched lower, as if he were trying to hide behind the fire. "Don't know nothin'."

His lips clamped together as though he planned never to open his mouth again. Lennie took a step toward him, fists clenched. She opened her mouth, ready to start yelling. Junkyard put up a hand to stop her. "Mood you're in, you'll just scare him more."

He squatted next to Hotshot. "It's okay, Bob. Nothing can hurt you, here."

The bald man snorted. "Lot *you* know. I'm not sticking my neck out to tell you anything."

He pivoted on his seat, putting his back to Junkyard. His reaction hit Lennie like ice water. She forgot her anger and watched numbly while Junkyard rested a hand on Hotshot's shoulder.

"Come on, Bob. Help the lady out. Tell her what you know."

Hotshot gave a short shake of his head and rose from the cement block. He shuffled across the jungle and crawled back into his box, pulling the cardboard flap closed behind him.

Bones whistled low. "Check his seat for a puddle, Junkyard. I think Hotshot peed his pants."

Junkyard ignored him and spoke to Lennie in a low voice. "I'd sure as hell like to know what your father was into, to get a reaction like that."

"Me, too." Lennie rubbed the tattoo surreptitiously. She laughed bitterly. "I suppose we'll try to talk with Hotshot later—right after we talk to Bill."

"Maybe so. There's always the poetry reading. There'll be a lot more 'bos there, tonight. If you can get any of 'em to talk."

Soo watched Lennie and Junkyard cross the parking lot, hands on her hips, her concern apparent in the s-shape of her brows. When they turned a corner, she strode back to her truck to unload supplies.

Bones O'Riley hoisted himself up from the log and leaned over the pot to check the stew. He dipped a finger and stuck it in his mouth. His face twisted in disgust.

"Shit soup."

He pulled a box from his breast pocket, extracted a large pinch of dried leaves and crumbled them into the pot. He gave the stew a stir and leaned over the steam for a sniff. Shrugging, he dumped in the remaining contents of the box.

"Shit soup with flavor."

Nodding in grim satisfaction, he stumped back to the wooden crate and crawled inside.

Flies buzzed around the empty jungle. A breeze sent a napkin tumbling into the fire for a brief, bright ending. Nothing else moved.

Then there was a scrape of denim across pavement and a grunt. The Ragman squeezed out of the space between battered garbage cans. He peered around. If anyone was looking, they might have puzzled over the yellow glint in his eyes. But no one was looking. He sneered and strutted away from the jungle, a paint-stained bandana trailing from his back pocket. When he reached empty pavement, he hesitated, glanced around, and disappeared into shadow.

Fenrir waited in the smoky darkness. The hollow old man stood behind him, ignored. Fenrir had no need to hear the Ragman's report. He had watched One-Eye's pawn through the Ragman's eyes and listened to her story with the Ragman's ears.

A cruel grin twisted the gangbanger's mouth. "Do you want me to kill her?"

Fenrir considered. It might be prudent. Unlike her father, a nervous, weak-willed man who had fallen to Fenrir ten years before, the daughter had proven herself surprisingly resistant to his control. She could pose a substantial nuisance. And he would not need to touch the Ragman's mind to push his hatred of the woman into murder.

But the Ragman was not a fit executioner for this subject. He would kill her by ordinary means. A waste. It would be more useful for her to be bound in the remnants of Fenrir's own bindings, with a bronze blade thrust through her palate, as One-Eye had done to him millennia before. It appealed to Fenrir to use One-Eye's own tool as another gauntlet thrown at his feet. Would the coward face him then, when the last of his champions was dead?

But Fenrir felt an odd, almost instinctive reluctance to order her execution. She could become dangerous, yes, but the depth of her emotions made her both valuable and vulnerable. Surely he could make better use of her alive.

"No," he replied. "Do not harm her."

"But she—"

Fenrir growled and felt the Wolf rise into his eyes. "I said *no*."

The Ragman flinched and fell silent. His expression remained hard and uncaring, but Fenrir sensed the fear crawling across the surface of the gangbanger's mind. Satisfied, Fenrir forced the Wolf to recede.

"Find Monte." The growl in Fenrir's voice was as smooth as a purr. "Tell him to meet me at the warehouse at seven o'clock tonight. I have a job for him."

Then, seeing through the Ragman's eyes, Fenrir watched himself

"Oh, she won't do that," said the Pooka tartly. "She's way too patient with you."

Kalinga's iTooth chimed. It was Carmen.

"Yaybo!" she said, in a voice bursting with excitement. "3 am. Black Khat, King Street Station, Alexandria. Order a Joyful Khat and ask if you can have it in vanilla. Then just follow instructions." She disconnected.

"Will you mind being Kalinga's black coat, too?" he asked the Pooka. "I lost it in the fire."

"Grrrr, I hate being clothes. They make so much extra work for me. I have to process the molecules from airborne contaminants — then I have to excrete the stuff I don't use."

"Excrete?" asked Obama.

"Well, sweat it out, anyway," said the Pooka. "That's why I always look so shiny. And clothes aren't shiny. So I have to hold it in for hours."

"I'm sorry, Pooka," he said, slipping on his backpack. "I know I've been a lot of trouble for you lately."

"That's OK, Obama," she said brightly. "I don't mind doing it for you." He wasn't sure, but he thought Joyful Kalinga's clothes gave him a hug.

He turned off the last of the apartment lights by waving at them, then closed the front door behind him. It auto-locked and recoded. Would he ever be back again, he wondered. It had been his home — and Kim's — for two years. But now it was time to move on. *It's time,* thought Obama, *for some pay-back. Joyful Kalinga-style.*

As he exited the Marbela and set off down the deserted street, Obama's mood was nihilistic. His plan was simple: he would infiltrate the Warriors of God terrorist organization and use their own weapons to take out as many of them as he could. If the Pooka could protect him, that was fine — if not, then he'd do as much damage to them as he could before being killed himself. He'd just been shot by a high-powered assault rifle. It hadn't hurt so much. And, realistically, what did he have to live for, anyway? Without Kim, his life was meaningless. It sucked anyway, he realized. He now hated his job. He had no friends — unless you wanted to count a couple of alien entities as friends. One with tentacles. Not for the first time it occurred to Obama that maybe he'd just gone crazy with loneliness and made them up. Whatever, he thought. At least he could make his life — and maybe death — have some kind of meaning if he did something to help rid the world of evil, cold-blooded killers like the Warriors of God.

But he would need to be way smarter than he'd been acting lately. The alien was right. He'd behaved like a big baby right from the start of all this. He'd thrashed around with no plan or purpose or real information, doing whatever occurred to him at the moment. Just like he was doing right now, said a small voice in the back of his head. Something really stupid, like Siren had made him promise not to do. OK, fair enough. He was acting stupid all over again. But this time he'd have to smarten up big-time while he was doing it. The Warriors of God were obviously tough, cruel-minded professionals — they'd have to be, in order to survive enemies like Park and Malek. So they weren't going to be impressed by Joyful Kalinga or cut him any slack just because he was in the news all the time. Obama would have to out-think them. So far, he'd been dumb, but really lucky. In terms of staying alive, anyway. Now he'd have to be smart *and* lucky.

And here was a good example. It was just before 2 am, when the last Retro trains ran. The streets, unlike those of New York or LA, were completely empty. So it was really easy for him to spot the people who'd been following him around for the last few days. Obviously, because the Pooka was now jamming all the coms around him, they'd decided to keep track of him the old-skool low-tech way.

Usually there were three of them, hanging a block or two behind him in relays, riding the Retro car just behind his, always wearing the same kind of overcoats that Park and Malek had worn. Sometimes these guys wore hats, too, and in the daytime, sunglasses. They followed him whether he was dressed as Obama or Kalinga — which implied they already knew that both were the same person. Which meant that Simonetta had told the UNSS about him. Or that the UNSS was secretly taking its orders from her — or Sato, her "daddy," as she'd called him. Which also meant that if Simonetta really was an alien from outer space, then so was Sato.

But that was Siren's problem. *My problem is the tail following me down the street right now,* Obama thought, forcing himself to be logical again. It might be that they weren't UNSS, for example, but HHS. Or were working, not for UNSS or HHS at all, but for the same coalition of agencies that MAD belonged to, the coalition that was sponsoring the terror group's bombing attacks on their rival. In which case, it would make no difference if they followed him or not.

But if they were UNSS or HHS, and he led them straight to the Warriors of God, that would solve all his problems at once. He slowed his pace to make sure his tails didn't lose him. There was a rustling noise coming from the pavement all around him, and Obama realized it was sleeting. He was grateful when he reached the shelter of the station.

"You don't have 6 fingers on each hand, do you?" demanded the indecently-bronzed holographic goddess shimmering iridescently inside his Retro car. "Or 6 toes? Of course, it would be cool if you did. But most of us just have 5 — like me." Charmingly, she unveiled them each in turn. "And that's why we humyns only count to ten. It just feels so natural! So guess what? Starting on the first of Humida, we'll all be converting to the new decimal time, with 100 seconds in each minute and 100 minutes in each hour. And best of all, we'll be switching over to the new 20-hour decimal day! Remember, after that date, old-fashioned time will be completely useless — be sure to automagically reprogram so you can keep the new time. Like me!" There were three other people on the car with him, all immigrant Retrorail workers slumped over in their seats asleep.

The Black Khat at the King Street Station was underground and mostly empty. A second Joyful Kalinga musical hit, "Breakin' da Bank," was playing while a holographic version of the "big man" sprayed transparent 3D tactical nuclear missiles around the room from a shoulder-carried launch-pad. One flew through Obama's chest as he walked in. "Try our new Joyful Khat energy drink now — and get a second one free!" screamed the subliminal text-crawl. "Your *linga* will love it!"

The barrista wandered with insolent slowness over to his table beneath the milky blue-green glare. She was a short, slender girl, with Medusa hair that curled like gleaming black wires. The artificial kohl around her big black eyes was created by a pattern of tiny tattoos, and dark, angry veins showed beneath her sallow skin. "Yes?" she demanded contemptuously. Obama gave her his widest filed-tooth Joyful grin.

"I maybe try me some that Joyful Khat, sister," he told her. "But I want it with va-nil-la." He licked his lips in a manner which he hoped conveyed obscene lasciviousness. But it was late, and Obama was tired, and he suspected the gesture had fallen flat.

The girl cocked her head to one side, and a faint flicker of something, Obama couldn't tell what, seemed to spark in her eyes. "Vanilla is for white myn only, 'migo. I'll show you what kind o' sweetness the black myn likes." She made a motion, and Obama followed her inside the counter and through to the kitchen. The girl put on a dusty grey coat with a hood and tugged at his arm. They went out through a back service door into a concrete stairwell filled with uncollected garbage and dead leaves, then up onto the street.

The sleet was falling more heavily now, and tiny pellets dusted their shoulders like sugar and melted in her hair. Their breaths hung in the air. Headlights blazed, and a huge ancient dark green recycling van rumbled noisily to a stop beside them. It stank. A door opened, the girl said, "Get in," and pushed impatiently at his butt as he climbed up. It was a four-door cab, and he was in the back seat. She pushed him again and he slid across behind the driver. The girl followed him in and slammed the door behind her as the truck rumbled away, sleet glazing the windows and refracting the street-lights. Beneath one of them Obama spotted one of the myn who'd been following him, black-gloved finger pressed to one temple as he spoke into his iTooth.

A figure leaned back at him from the gloom of the "shotty," or front passenger seat: a pale twitchy-looking guy wearing a game-cap and mirrored monitor-glasses. He extended his fist for a knuckle-butt. It was the same guy from the first Black Khat, the Iranian black-hat hacker Scott had originally hooked him up with. The bumper with muscular dystrophy. "Call me Freedom, man," he said.

17.

So it was Freedom who set off the Madam's Organ bomb, Obama thought. He'd noticed at the time the way the guy had abruptly left the building just before the bomb had gone off. What Obama still didn't get was why Freedom had set it off. And, as the garbage truck pulled away from the curb, it occurred to him to worry that Freedom might recognize Joyful Kalinga as the Obama Jones he'd met that day. If so, so far Freedom had given no sign of it. Could he also have been responsible for the bombing that had killed Kim?

"Did you know you brought a tick with you from the subway?" the hacker asked him accusingly. Obama shrugged, arms spread wide and expressively.

"People always be following me everywhere, man," he said in a booming tone. The girl interrupted in a burst of some other language, Farsi, perhaps, and Freedom replied in it. After a moment, Obama realized he'd understood what they'd just said: "Does he have any other bugs?" and "No, he's clean. No coms noise." But he'd always been terrible at languages — the Pooka must have been piping Babelfish into his neural receptors using skin conduction. And what about his shoulder? He should be really feeling it right now. He'd even seen the bullet, huge, flattened and misshapen by the impact — it should have smashed the bone. Yet he felt no pain or stiffness from it, and there wasn't even a scar. SWAT teams usually used higher-tech weapons, too — laser dazzlers and ADS, or Activity Denial Systems. There hadn't been any of that stuff at the hospital before the snipers started firing real bullets at them, so Obama assumed the Helpers had jammed their electronics.

"I'm his sister, Xina," the girl told him in Enriched Standard. The dark, bearded driver wasn't introduced. Obama somehow got the impression from her manner that Xina was in charge here. Was she really Freedom's sister? Or did she just mean sister in a colloquial sense?

"Yaybo," he said politely. "I am Joyful Kalinga, the man from MAD."

"We know who you are," said the girl. *Uh oh,* thought Obama. He didn't like the sound of that. He didn't like the look of controlled excitement in her eyes, either, as if she were keeping some important secret. It crossed his mind to ask where they were taking him. But he didn't, because Joyful Kalinga wouldn't have.

He didn't know Virginia well and quickly became lost, since his iRist GPS was turned off. He'd been to Alexandria once or twice before, though; it was a small satellite city of very old buildings, many of which had been rehabbed during the Big Boom, then gradually repaired with external ducts and pipes and structural supports during the Depression that had followed. Alexandria hadn't been affected by Seven-Eleven.

Once a tourist trap, the town had retooled in the '30s to become a local center of microbreweries and microfactories and the microwave weapons industry, which were collectively known as Microbiz. They all relied on a viral technology called Bubble Tech. But near the river, untouched by the Bubble, the buildings became darkened ruins. They turned off North Union Street into an alley that ran between two overhanging brick hulks almost down to the waterfront. "Torpedo Factory" said an old sign on the side of one of them.

The truck scraped against a sooty wall and rumbled, idling to a halt. "This way," said Xina. She and Freedom opened their doors and clambered down onto the broken pavement, then ducked inside a gap in the bricks. The driver turned and motioned Obama to follow them. When he did, he discovered the sleet was turning back into drizzle.

"Come on, hurry!" said Xina crossly, grabbing his arm. He felt the Pooka stiffen and shake the girl's hand off. Xina looked startled for a second, then turned away. They followed her brother's awkward, hopping gait, across a yard filled with smashed bricks and chunks of ferro-plasticrete, into what had once been a parking garage. A battered plum-colored Nissair airvan idled beneath a section of collapsed roof, and Freedom swiped the side-doors open. There were more brief exchanges in Farsi — "Is this the guy?" and "Any sweeps?" and "No, all clean" — before Xina bundled him inside it.

"Let's spin!" she said to the driver when they were strapped in. The Nissair — an "Electroflite" (said the logo on the dashboard fascia) — took off slowly, rattling and shaking like a tin can. It was one of the first airvan models ever made and the oldest car Obama had ever flown in. It gave a single sickening lurch as it cleared the roof of the garage, then flew low over the river into a bank of fog before slowly rising up into an air-traffic lane heading east.

During the entire journey, which lasted about an hour, the driver said only one thing: "No lights and no coms." Meaning inside the cab. The van's own dashboard screens were lit up with tiny glowing lane and routing beacon icons that passed by them in the dark like invisible tracer bullets. This time of night there still wasn't much air traffic coming over the river, though the bridges were busy with groundcars. This changed when they turned north into Maryland, and suddenly there were more and more cars and vans in the air around them. Including a few Federal troopers. The driver was trying to intercept their WiiFi iTooth signals manually, and occasional bursts of static or garbled coms transmissions filled the van.

Still no one spoke. Freedom remained hooked into the Grid, and the girl just gazed impassively out the window. From time to time, she would turn to stare at Obama for a moment with what he thought was a speculative look in her eyes, as if she might open her mouth and say something important or menacing to him. But she never did.

They took the bay route to the south of Baltimore and flew over open water. The crosswinds batted the Nissair around dangerously, and Obama wondered if the Pooka could save him from drowning if they went down. After a few minutes, they were over land again on the Delaware side, then skirted Wilmington before crossing over into New Jersey. Over Camden they descended into a thickening haze of brown-green smog; north of the city he could see occasional gas flares on the ground.

In 2027 a "dirty bomb" — a radioactive device commissioned by AMAL, the new revolutionary Islamic government of the former Egypt — had been detonated in Linden, New Jersey. The prevailing winds had been predicted to be southwesterly, in which case the radioactive cloud would have swept over Newark, Staten Island, and then Manhattan, its presumed target. However, a classic "nor'easter" had unexpectedly developed and, instead, the radioactivity had contaminated central New Jersey before dissipating south of Trenton. Princeton University had been evacuated and later completely relocated to Piscataway.

Over the following decade, the deserted area had been resettled by immigrants from the former Iraq. Older Muslim residents as well had increasingly returned to the region that had once boasted the largest number of mosques in America and was now known as "iRockistan."

Its principal industries had become warehousing, food preparation, oil refining, and petrochemical production.

Then, in the late '20s, had come the first shock of European re-glaciation, and poorer Scandinavian and northern British refugees had flooded into the area, a pattern that had continued for the next decade. There had once been large Muslim minorities in many of the refugees' home countries — in fact, several urban centers like Leeds and Malmo were Muslim-majority — but most had returned to their Locations Of Origin during the late 'teens as the cold weather had dramatically worsened.

The UN had poured money into the state of New Jersey to build tower-blocks, factories, and box-malls extending from Edison to Camden, and the whole region, which had once been a crumbling, poisoned wasteland, was now a repaved instant slum. But thanks to the Gulf Stream and the treatment of ARS — Acute Radiation Syndrome — with Novamune, it was now a relatively survivable one, especially since the radiation had disappeared so quickly: 99.9 of it within the first few weeks. Social conflicts, however, had arisen almost instantly between the new Caucasian-European immigrants and the Muslim natives; these had turned into sporadically bitter gang warfare. Which was why they were flying over the minarets and apartment blocks and oil refineries of Trenton at this moment. This was the Warriors of God's power base.

And things really were different here. Obama spotted only one holographic billboard after they left Camden, on a highrise building below: a political ad for a Pan-Islamist Party (AQI, or Al-Qaeda International) candidate for People's Tribune in the coming elections. The ad featured a thinly veiled fashion model smashing what appeared to be a bottle of wine.

They followed the old Pennsylvania Turnpike, turned off at Levittown, and recrossed the Delaware River, plunging so low over it that they were almost skimming the black, murky water as they entered Trenton. There was an old steel bridge to their left with the words "Trenton Makes" painted on it in giant white letters; the rest of the sign had been spray-painted over in Arabic along with a few swastikas. The van slowed, stalled, then began to spin, and landed with a jarring bump on a patch of land beside the river.

"Out," said the girl. Once outside the van, Obama saw they'd landed in a sea of hardened mud in the middle of an old abandoned sports stadium. Crumbling rows of bleachers, and a few peeling advertisements on its gap-toothed wooden walls, were faintly visible through the gloom. Dimly lit traffic overpasses and MagLev bullet train tracks snaked overhead, and he saw holo signs for the Trenton Tunnel. They waited in silence in the dark.

After a few minutes, a string of bright lights coalesced down the parkway from the north. This resolved itself into a motorcade of groundcars which descended a ramp from the opposite direction, then turned back around to enter the stadium grounds, headlights and ground-fog lamps blazing. It was a convoy of armor-plated Toyota pickup trucks and old Lincoln limousines. Several of the vehicles were decorated with strands of fiber-optic lights, others had machine guns mounted into their beds. The convoy drove up to the Nissair van, then stopped with an electronic whooping noise.

A number of young myn with assault rifles, their faces wrapped in long scarves, leaped down from the trucks and stood guard while an older myn approached. He was dressed in a dirty white robe beneath a leather jacket and had a long black beard streaked with grey. He shook hands with Freedom and Xina in turn. They all murmured *"Assalaamu alaikum"* and kissed each other on the cheeks. Then it was Obama's turn. *"Assalaamu alaikum,"* the man said. "I am Imam Osama Chebli."

"Yaybo," said Obama disdainfully. "I am Joyful Kalinga." A Joyful Kalinga, who, he decided, was not impressed by anything he'd seen so far.

"Come," said the imam, after they'd shaken hands. "You must ride with me." The three of them followed him into the second Lincoln limo in line and got in. Behind them, the van elevated unsteadily into the air, landing lights circulating. Obama felt like it was somehow his last link with reality. Or safety. He was now deep in enemy country.

"You people surely very strapped," Obama said, as the motorcade went back up the ramp to the freeway into the first orange glow of dawn.

"Strapped?" asked Chebli, confused.

"You know, man — all fusked up. Got lotso guns."

"Ayin barg," Xina murmured. "Armed."

"I am a man of peace," said the imam firmly. That seemed to end the conversation. Within a block or two they turned off the freeway onto an empty street marked Lalor Street and into city slums. Then a right and a left into an alley, and the entrance to the Riverview Mosque, a newish building that resembled a bombproof concrete fortress with a minaret/observation tower. It was bathed in lights. "Before, this was a cemetery for unbelievers," said Chebli. "Their polluting bones are all gone now. Only the faithful remain. We were on YouVee with our rebuilding plans — maybe you saw us. We won the 'Model Mosques' contest show." Obama shook his head, as the motorcade drove down an underground ramp into the car park. The reinforced metal gates slammed shut behind them.

A warren of rooms lay beneath the mosque's main level, and Obama was told to follow Freedom into one of them, a bare, windowless dormitory room with two camp cots inside it. "We'll be meeting the others later," Freedom said, throwing his sack on the floor and flinging himself onto one of them. "They are some mean muthas. Better get some sleep now, 'migo."

There was a barely functional bathroom, lacking all ultrasonics and modern hydraulics, just down the hall. There were dead mosquitoes floating in the toilet bowl. The mosquitoes in this region had become famously huge and predatory after the radiation blast, just like the ones in Manacera City. While Obama was flushing it, the Pooka said, "There's a weapons arsenal at the other end of the basement."

"Shhh," he said.

"Don't worry, only you can hear me," she told him.

"But they can hear me."

"So, pretend you're crazy. That shouldn't be too hard for you — amigo. They've already swept you three times for bugs, anyway."

How does a crazy person sleep? Obama wondered, lying on the hard cot. *Poorly,* he decided. He was finding it impossible to sleep at all, in spite of his fatigue. His thoughts returned over and over again to the events of the day, and all the things that had happened that he still didn't understand, like his shoulder being repaired.

He tried to re-order them in his mind. Firstly, Siren had used Simonetta — trapped inside the body of Priska — as bait. Bait to lead her to Sato. Simonetta, like Siren, was an alien, and since Simonetta viewed Sato as her "daddy," it seemed obvious that Sato was an alien, too. All three, he noticed, used human names beginning with the letter "S" — maybe that was how the alien lizard myth had gotten started online.

For a few minutes he examined the implications of Sato's potential alienness. Was the Grid itself, which Sato had invented singlehandedly, an alien invention? Or was it merely a crude approximation of one? Were Sato and Simonetta even the same species of alien as Siren? Did they come from two warring races? Or two factions of the same one waging some sort of bitter civil war? Obama felt embarrassed to be falling back on the cliches of sims and old flat-screen films, but really he felt he had no other frame of reference.

There was something about Sato and Simonetta that kept worrying the back of his mind, the way your tongue keeps going over a chipped tooth. It was this: just where exactly did he, Obama Jones, fit in? Sato had "bred" Simonetta, that much he knew from examining the HGP records. Bred her the way you'd breed cattle or a prize dog. But obviously it was only her body he'd been breeding; Siren had said her race was immortal, or at least had been around forever. No, that wasn't right — it was the Helpers who'd been around forever. But Siren had seemed to imply that her race never died, and she was already pretty old, too, at least from the way she talked. Which meant that Sato and Simonetta probably were, as well.

So they'd been breeding all the people in the files as human "skins" for themselves, or maybe even for other aliens who had yet to arrive. Or invade, or whatever. So that meant that he, Obama, had been — or even still might be — destined for that fate. All that lovey-dovey stuff from Simonetta might have been to tempt him into being impregnated with an alien who would take over his body as Simonetta had Priska's, and kill him in the process. Possibly even Sato himself, since all his humyn bodies would surely die within a normal humyn lifespan. But maybe by some other alien? Maybe Simonetta had even believed that Obama had already been impregnated by it. Or with it. The thought made him shiver. He felt slightly sick and turned over on his side.

And here was another thing. OK, he knew for sure that Sato and Simonetta had been breeding humyn bodies to use as hosts, right? So presumably that meant that Siren had been doing the same thing all this time, too. Which meant that Siren was just as evil and ruthless as the other two, didn't it? Or did it? She'd genuinely cried over Priska — and she hadn't even known her. It made no sense. Maybe she was evil but really sentimental about animals. Although, of course, higher primates weren't legally animals.

Tiny lights blinked and chased each other across Freedom's dark monitor glasses as he lay on the cot opposite. It was impossible to tell if he was asleep or not. Obama must have dozed off watching them, because the next thing he knew Xina was shaking him awake. There were two young guys with her, both moving as if they had guns under their coats.

"This is Habib," she said, indicating one, "and Hijack," indicating the other. "They are both in our cell." They glared at him. Habib was heavy, dark-skinned and bearded, Hijack taller, reddish-haired, and freckled. Both, from the way they let her order them around, were obviously in thrall to Xina, thought Obama, when they were all having breakfast together in the cafeteria. Breakfast was toasted pita with butter, apricot jam, olives, Laughing Cow cheese, and black coffee, served by an old myn with no front teeth. Obama was told to say *"Shukran, shukran"* for "thank you."

"We'll be meeting the others soon," Xina said to him, waving off his attempts to question her. "They are not all part of the Warriors of God, but represent a number of important Resistance groups. The one you must be careful with" — she lowered her voice — "is 'Joker': he is the Emir of Trenton. And he's a Chechen, so don't piss him off. Because during the meeting upstairs, we will be put in the back of the hall where we can't advise you anymore — they say we are Shia and Alawi and so won't allow us to pray with them. But we're not actually religious."

"You are not religious?" said Obama. "But you are in the Warriors of God?" He rolled his eyes, Kalinga-style.

"We believe in the Resistance. The United Nations world government is a Satanic abomination and must be stopped before they send everyone to the Moon to die." It took a major act of will for Obama to keep his jaw from dropping open with surprise. How did Xina know about that? Was it common knowledge in the Resistance movement? Or was it just a Grid myth she'd read on a glog somewhere? Or was Obama Jones the only person on the planet who hadn't suspected the truth? He started to quiz her about this, but they were interrupted by a *mujahedeen*, as Chebli had referred to them, with orders from the imam. It was time for their meeting.

The main prayer hall was up a flight of stairs, beyond a prayer courtyard and water fountain, both roofed with thick bullet-proof glasspex. Inside the hall, which was ringed by several round marble columns, about thirty people sat or kneeled, most on cushions. Xina, Obama noticed, had put on a head-scarf. There were several other womyn in the room, all wearing veiled *burqas*. About half a dozen of the myn had their faces concealed, as well. Xina tugged at his arm, and he sat to the left of the imam.

Piping his iTooth through a local amplifier, Chebli took over the meeting, speaking alternately in Arabic and Enriched Standard. One by one, he introduced each of the attending groups, some of which were represented by only a single person. Most were AQI or Warriors of God, although there were Black Muslims from Newark and Detroit and even a few White Muslims — Albanians, Chechens, and Swedes — from Toronto, Dearborn, Michigan, and Jersey City. All said "*Assalaamu alaikum*" and bowed their heads in turn.

Finally the imam came to Joyful Kalinga. When he was introduced, a ripple of comment went through the room. Obama rose to his feet to tower above the rest, hands on hips, jaw stuck out pugnaciously. These were the people who had ruthlessly and cold-bloodedly killed Kim, he told himself. And dozens, maybe hundreds, of other innocent victims. He didn't want to meet or pray with them — he wanted to kill them all as quickly as possible. "Enough talk. Where is the bomb?" demanded Joyful Kalinga. His voice rumbled and echoed around the big hall.

And died in the sound of mocking laughter. A white guy strolled laughing into the prayer hall through its wide arched entrance, followed by two others. He was in his late thirties, but his hair had turned prematurely silver, though still black on the crown. He was wearing an expensive satiny black tracksuit, had an oversized head, and huge, improbably broad shoulders, though his legs were short, even stumpy. He would have been classically handsome, except for a cartoon-like, almost lumpish, exaggeration of his features and a permanent look of petulance on them.

As he came closer, Obama saw there was something slightly psychotic in his manner, too, as if he might at any moment fly into a violent, murderous rage. Carmen shared this apparent trait, which, Obama had always felt, largely explained her career success. But Carmen didn't have a large handgun tucked under one armpit. The myn stopped and gave Obama an affectionate clap on the shoulder.

"The *abed* is impatient, is he?" he said in Arabic. The Pooka obligingly translated the derogatory racial slur. Then in accented Enriched, "Don't worry, amigo, I like you." He smiled, showing dog-yellow teeth being expensively rescued by orthodontic braces with tiny diamonds in them, and held out a huge hand. "Djokhar Hadjibaeyev. But you can call me Joker, jiggah. These are my main soljahs, Mukh and Bashir. Maybe they are not on YouVee all the time like you, but they are seriously tough amigos, too. They are always saying to me, 'Joker, we want to meet this Joyful Kalinga sometime and party with him.' Right? Now, look at this, squaddies — here he is! In the flesh!" He tried to crush Obama's grip when they shook hands. This, evidently, was the Emir of Trenton.

The meeting that afternoon in many ways resembled those of the CAC accreditation application panel, except for prayer-breaks, at the end of each of which Obama was instructed by Chebli to just say "*aameen*" over and over ("You must end each phrase with '*aameen*', my friend — this is very important!"). Both the terrorist talks and the CAC review seemed to drag on forever, and both seemed to be a lot of empty discussion over, essentially, nothing at all. As in the CAC accreditation meetings, there was the same sense of deep internal wrangling glossed over by a common canon of liturgical language and pre-agreed policy, the same sense of violent personal hatreds forced into expedient alliances by the power of money. And most of all, the same sense that Obama was missing out on what was really going on.

Were they just making up their minds whether or not they could trust Joyful Kalinga? he wondered. Sometimes he caught groups of them staring fixedly in his direction — but what were they really thinking? Malevolence, calculation, even blank curiosity seemed the most likely explanations, but Obama had no way of telling for sure. Until they put a bomb in his hands. Or a bullet in his back.

Carmen had claimed that Kalinga would be the MAD representative on the direct action committee, but so far, at least, there had been absolutely no mention in the discussion of any sponsoring Federal agency or, in fact, any overt future act of terror at all. Instead, there were simply complaints about other groups in the room not living up to their "obligations of honor" and how cheated they all were by unbelievers who never paid their bills. There was a great deal of discussion of the "caliphate," by which they seemed to mean an Islamic North America freed from the control of the United Nations, or "Zionist World Government." The HHS police were called "Zionist Crusaders," and the innocent victims of previous attacks, such as the Federal Courthouse bombing, were referred to as "Jew dogs." Including, presumably, Mrs. Housmanzadeh.

Correctly interpreting these terms, once they were translated by the Pooka, presented no problems to a career MAD bureaucrat like Obama. In fact, he became so hypnotized by the conversation that he totally failed to notice when, at last, it turned to him. "They are asking, what is it exactly that you are bringing to us?" said Chebli, turning to him suddenly. Obama stared at him stupidly.

"Bringing to you?" he said, uncomprehending. It wildly crossed his mind for a moment that he should have brought gifts for everyone — gold cuff links, maybe, or expensive iRist enhancements, or a Vespair for the "emir." But that couldn't be what they meant.

"What do you bring to the table, big man?" Joker loudly interrupted, holding up four fingers. "Our brothers from Toronto hook us up with kif and bhang. Our brothers from Dearborn import raw opium cake direct from Herat. Our brothers from North Jersey sell us girls. What do you provide for us if you want to join the family? You are not even a believer, so why should we trust you?"

Carmen hadn't filled him in on this part of the deal. He was going to have to improvise. What did MAD have to offer hardened terrorists, anyway, aside from lots of electronic application forms and minority vouchers as well as protection from ethnic profiling and other hate crimes? "What is it you are needing the most?" he asked.

Several of the older representatives gravely conferred. He heard the words "*ajjan*" and "*almajthoob*" muttered. At last one of them turned to him and said, "We cannot commission any more bombings until we have some more 'iddies' or similar retarded persons to carry the bombs. We used our last one in the Federal Courthouse attack. We have no more now."

"Oh yes," said Joyful Kalinga with a great happy smile of relief. "Oh my, yes. I can get all of these you want. We have many of these people!" At last, here was something positive the Minority Assistance Department could bring to the terrorists' table ...

18.

There were many moments over the next few hours and days when Obama regretted not having killed — or at least attempted to capture — the leadership of the Warriors of God when he'd had the chance at the meeting in the Riverview Mosque's main prayer hall. Foolishly, he'd assumed he'd have several more opportunities when they were all gathered together. This was not to be the case. But he hadn't realized at the time how rare, even unique, the occasion of this meeting had been. In addition, there had been three other compelling reasons why he had done nothing at the time.

The first was that he had had no real idea of how the Pooka would have reacted if he'd asked her to arm him so he could start blazing away. Which is what, he decided in retrospect, he should have done. She'd acquiesced, with great bloodthirstiness, to arming him during his attack on the Casino Royale, but that had been onGrid and not real. And at the hospital, she'd reacted to being shot at by disabling the SWAT team non-violently. But he'd had no idea in this case if she'd go that far at his command. They hadn't gone over these things in advance. Obviously, they needed to, but so far, at least, there'd been no opportunity.

Besides, what would he have done with the terrorists once they were all hanging upside-down from the ceiling, assuming the Pooka had taken things that far? Call HHS? And what would have happened then? Even if he had been able to legally prove these people had been involved in the bombings that had killed Kim, which he couldn't at this point, the most they'd get would be a year or two of anger management. No, they needed executing. Before they killed again and again. His original plan of making sure that the bombs they supplied him with went off prematurely was still the best one.

The second reason he'd done nothing at the meeting in the Riverview Mosque's main prayer hall had been something Xina had said about the UN taking people to the Moon to kill them. How had she known this? He'd needed time to question her about it. He had a feeling it was important.

And the third reason had been something he hadn't known at the time and wouldn't find out until much later, but which had manifested during the meeting as a vague sense of inhibition he'd felt about taking action. In the end, that inhibition would prove to have been the most constraining of all.

Still, afterwards, Obama blamed himself bitterly that things just seemed to go on as usual. It was little consolation to reflect on the fact that if all of these thugs were somehow magically removed from the rackets they ran — the drug-running, prostitution, extortion, torture, murder, and political terrorism these people engaged in as a normal way of life — their rivals and underlings would simply fill the vacuum. This was the kind of sociological detachment you were taught at MAD, but which was impossible to feel any longer once violence had touched you.

For Kim's sake he had wanted to become a kind of superhero vigilante for justice. But he'd already flunked the first test. And everything that happened the rest of that first evening only made him feel worse.

The meeting finally broke up after the electronic muezzin called the sunset prayers at about 6 pm. Joker Hadjibaeyev then insisted that they all come back with him to his restaurant, The Casbah, but several of the other leaders, including Imam Chebli, declined. Joyful Kalinga was not so lucky. Freedom and Xina's squad seemed to have appointed themselves his watchdogs, or maybe they'd just been assigned to keep an eye on him. Either way, they insisted on going.

Habib handed Obama his backpack, re-closed after an obvious search, and escorted him back down to the parking garage. Another motorcade was forming, idling in a cloud of noxious exhaust fumes, with several of the same vehicles from the morning, plus a few restored old Hummers. "This one," said Xina, and Obama was bundled into a brand-new cream-colored Beemer limo, one of two in the middle of the convoy. Joker's gang, obviously, was far wealthier than Chebli's. Car doors slammed shut in staccato, the garage gates re-opened, and the motorcade got under way, exiting back onto Center Street, then taking the parkway north into the downtown area.

The day was gunmetal grey, in the upper teens centigrade, but with snow flurries whipping against the windshields. The sun was setting a few degrees above the river's horizon to the left with all the angry colors of a rotting egg-yolk. The convoy used police sirens and the occasional rifle-shot out of car windows to force the sparse traffic aside; then, after exiting the parkway into the War Memorial and passing Peace Street, employed the sirens and rifle-shot as devices to assemble a crowd.

Most of the huge abandoned buildings in the neighborhood were the ruins of the former state capital complexes, but a few blocks around East State Street and South Warren were still occupied by rows of old townhouses. The town was a world away from Manacera City or New York, thought Obama. There were no tall buildings and few digital advertising billboards. Lights showed in windows behind blackout curtains and plywood boards. Dishes and gun emplacements were mounted on rooftops, and almost every porch had an electrical generator on it. Wiring cables and duct hose, even PVC water pipes, snaked everywhere between buildings and down from ancient line poles. There were no robots hovering at intersections, and traffic and street signs were all haphazardly pre-digital. He spotted a few spy-cams, but there was no way of knowing who they belonged to.

The convoy stopped, and Joker and his bodyguards got out. A young blond-haired boy, dressed in expensive Italian clothes, came out of one of the houses with another pair of mujahedeen wearing masks and baseball caps and an old woman in a black *chador*. Then the boy embraced Joker, who waved at the rest of the convoy to get out of their cars as well. "My son, Adam," he said proudly, when Obama and the others joined him. "Beautiful boy, huh? We walk from here, OK?"

A few dozen people had gathered on the broken sidewalks to watch Joker and his people parade down the middle of the street, followed very slowly by their cars. "Give me your gun, papa!" Adam demanded. Joker removed his from his armpit-holster, then with a wink, removed the ammunition clip and put it in his jacket-pocket before handing his son the gun.

"He wants to shoot everybody!" he said, laughing. Adam was already pointing the weapon at anyone who caught his eye, and Obama could hear its action clicking loudly every time he pulled the trigger. As they passed, a few myn and teenage boys emerged from houses to shake hands with Joker, who occasionally passed custom iRists to them or swiped theirs with his.

Once the local "emir" would have handed out wads of cash, thought Obama, but of course money hadn't existed for the last 30 years. Nowadays, everyone was taught in skool how evil money had been, but Obama had never really been able to see the difference between obsolete paper money and the Uno "social credit" swiping system. People like Norberto Zollto and the Satos — and Joker Hadjibaeyev, apparently — were still just as rich as ever.

Sometimes the emir's generous mask slipped, though: with some of the supplicants, Obama noticed, his face would lose its look of good humor and become cartoonishly enraged. Then he might shove or pummel them or slap their faces while they knelt on the pavement in front of him. "His pushers and pimps," murmured Xina, though whether or not she disapproved in any way he couldn't tell from her tone. It was equally likely she was boasting.

Following Joker's lead, the party turned off onto South Warren, where there were brightly lit buildings, restaurants, Sharia law offices, a few small grocers, a 24-7, a Uno-Mart, an Omar's Garden, a Mickey D's, an old Starbucks now covered in AQI posters and used, said Xina, as a "community liaison office" or neighborhood interrogation center, an erotic belly-dancing club called Beliza, and Trenton's largest and only comfortable hotel, formerly a Marriott and now the Jumeirah iRock Trenton. Joker's restaurant, the Casbah, was on its 12th and top floor. A row of new plane trees with lights strung across their branches lined the sidewalk outside, along with a number of advertising holos.

The Jumeirah hotel chain, which had originated in the former Dubai, was the most luxurious in the world. The Jumeirah iRock Trenton was no exception. Entering it from Trenton's South Warren Street was like stepping onto another planet. The lobby was vast and ringed by a holographic night desert scene. In one corner, a sleeping Bedouin was endlessly stalked by a looped lion beneath a glittering moon. Overhead, a glowing atrium, ribbed like a honeycomb made from raw rock, rose up to the roof. The room was ringed by white Tuscan columns and doorways framed by ornate Moorish arches with gold-embossed Arabic geometries. "Do you belong to our Sirius Awards Program, sir?"asked the Allura robot at the front desk when she swiped Obama his room number.

"He is my guest," Joker interrupted. "All are my guests tonight! Come, you'll have time to see your rooms later — first we will smoke together and relax." And he shepherded them up a marble spiral staircase with a wrought-iron gold leaf railing, leading up to a second-floor hookah or *shisha* parlor that shimmered like a blue aquarium. The parlor shared a massive glasspex wall with the indoor swimming pool, and was lined with brass water pipes outfitted with colored plastic tubes that glittered like undersea pirates' treasure.

Obama started coughing the moment he walked into the parlor. He had never smoked before in his life. Few North Americans had — it had been illegal for decades. After world governments had been forced to take over the insurance industry, both no-fault health and fire insurance requirements had gradually outlawed the carcinogenic practice, even in private. Nowadays, traditional drugs like marijuana and cocaine were usually enjoyed dermally or sublingually, though social aerosols were still popular with teenagers at parties. Obviously, the hotel had obtained a "unique case" or United Nations Endangered Cultural Activity (UNECA) Special Exemption, in order to allow smoking.

In some ways, Obama reflected, as he sat down on a wide leather couch next to Freedom and Hijack, the entire city of Trenton, with its emir and Sharia and clan-based economic system and lack of Federal oversight, was sort of a giant UNECASE. This suddenly struck him as unfair. What if every community were allowed to run itself like this? It would lead to city-states and even new countries springing up — and the whole criminal cycle of war and hunger would start all over again.

Luckily, it was only a few minorities that continued to demand this sort of special treatment, and no doubt they would eventually grow out of it with increased educational opportunities. *If, of course,* thought Obama heretically, *they don't blow everyone else up first.* That was what he was here to put a stop to, even if it meant going outside the law. Which would make him no better than they were. He felt dizzy. The smoke was already giving him a headache.

The swimming pool was mammoth, easily the size of a large public pool. For the past decade there had been a fad for "live" pools, even inside large bathrooms. Such pools contained plant-life, a pebbled or living sandy floor, sometimes snails and small fish, and filters and microbial protein skimmers to keep the top layers of water fresh. But the pool inside the Jumeirah iRock Trenton contained a living reef. A dozen different brightly colored coral colonies rose up from the oolite floor, covered in luminous flower-like zoanthids and waving sea-mushrooms. Exotic species of anemone and snails and tiny fish inhabited the slightly murky lower depths, while a few hotel guests lazily swam above them.

It seemed slightly obscene to fill up the space beside this brilliantly-lit natural vista with smoke. But there was no getting out of it. Even Xina had pulled one of the pipes close and was hunched over puffing away at it. Obama Jones had never smoked before — but Joyful Kalinga almost surely had. In a sense, this was another test. Maybe, it suddenly occurred to him, by design. He would somehow have to get through it without coughing or choking or hurling or showing any other signs of weakness. Could he do it? He had no idea.

Joker elbowed his way past Freedom on the couch to grasp Obama by the nape of the neck. "My friend, I will share with you the best *tobamel*, my own blend. Let the others smoke the cherry or the mint flavors. They are good enough for women and the *misli'i* — the queer boys. In Chechnya we like our *ma'sal*, that means 'honey', with *kif* and tobacco. You African jiggahs love to smoke your *ganja*, isn't that right? Well, this is very much like that." He put a sticky dark-gold wad into the bowl at the very top of the water pipe, then lit it with a burning piece of charcoal. He put the mouthpiece of the hose to his protuberant lips and inhaled noisily. The blue water inside the jar at the hookah's base bubbled. He exhaled, then put his arm around Obama while he poked the damp mouthpiece at him. "You try now. You know, usually I kill people for money. But you are my friend, Joyful Kalinga! I kill you for nothing!" He laughed uproariously at the ancient joke.

But Obama needn't have worried. It was Joyful Kalinga who inhaled deeply, who held the lungful of foul-tasting smoke like a deep-sea diver holding his breath and then blew it extravagantly back out again into a floating smoke-ring. "Delici-ous," he boomed. "Not strong like *ganja*, but good enough for white boys! Ha ha!"

It was strange, thought Obama, as they took the ascensor up to supper at the Casbah a little later, how Kalinga's personality just seemed to take him over at times like that, doing things he would never think of doing. Saying things it would never occur to him to say. Even knowing things that he, Obama, didn't know. Maybe this was what it felt like being invaded by an alien, the way Priska had been by Simonetta. So far, at least, Joyful Kalinga had been respectful and obliging about disappearing when he wasn't needed. But what if he decided, one of these days, just to stay and take over permanently?

Rows of long tables filled Joker Hadjibaeyev's enormous private dining-room at the restaurant. The tables were covered in red cloths and silver place-settings with white origami swan napkins rising from their centers. A VJ wearing a *kufi* occupied one corner of the room, playing polyphonic Chechen pop tunes over-sampled with electronic throat-singing. A slightly overweight girl belly-danced in front of him. Holographic vistas of Caucasus mountain scenes covered one wall, while carcasses of sheep, still covered with a stubble of wool, rotated on spits inside three huge open-hearth brick ovens.

About thirty guests had filed in, some of them from the earlier meeting at the mosque. When they were all seated, Joker rose to his feet to address them. *"Assalaamu alaikum,"* he said. "Welcome — and Allah's blessings on you. Tonight, as my honored guests, you will all be eating traditional delicacies of my country, Ichkeria. That is what we call the land of 'Chechnya' in our language. I will help to prepare with my own hands. This one is called *Korta-Kogish.*" He picked up a blowtorch and strode across to one of the sheep, thoroughly burning the wool off it with the flame. A smell of singed air filled the air. He was joined by two young women wearing head-scarves, one of whom took over the blowtorch, while the other imperiously directed several of the restaurant staff in boiling a number of other dishes.

Joker sat down directly across the main table from Freedom, flanked by his "soljahs," Bashir and Mukh. Bashir was seated across from Obama. "I offer all of you *nokhchallah* tonight!"Joker bellowed over the music. "In Chechen this word means friendship that lasts for all life. We have a saying in my country: 'Better to hurt a friend or a brother than an enemy, because you will see your brother again in Paradise to apologize. But your enemy will be roasting in hell, so you can never make things good with him again!'"

When the first sheep was cooked, Joker sawed off its head and presented it to Obama, insisting that he sample the brains. Obama found them sickeningly sweet, and they spoiled his appetite for the mutton. His mother had been a hippie vegetarian, so he still didn't often eat red meat, anyway. But he liked the cottage cheese pancakes and corn flour griddle-cakes the two women served as side dishes.

"Those are my two wives," Joker said carelessly to Obama, indicating them. "Do you like women, or are you *misli*, too?" This was a deadly insult, but Obama, as Kalinga, let it pass.

"I have three wives. But I do not know where they are now. One is dead, this I know for sure." To his astonishment, Obama found that tears were escaping from his eyes, running down his falsely scarred cheeks and dripping, hot and salty, into his mouth. Everybody at the table stared at him. Xina, in particular, had an expression on her face he couldn't fathom. Beatific, maybe? Her black eyes were shining.

"Don't worry," said Joker after an embarrassed silence had fallen. He cleared his throat several times. "I get you a new woman tonight, my friend. Maybe you like a Swedish one, like my top wife. We buy lots of girls from Swedesboro. They are very sexy, but stupid. Argue all the time."

"Djokhar Emir, will you give me a woman if I cry, too?" asked Bashir in a mocking falsetto.

"Maybe I give one woman to both of you and then you fight to see who fucks her, huh?" Joker said, unsmiling. It was obvious to Obama that the emir had decided to delegate the task of directly challenging Kalinga to one of his bodyguards. Joker was too smart, or maybe too old, to want to chance it himself.

Or maybe his attention span was just too short. He was hyperactive, like a child. He couldn't stay seated for long, but constantly got up and down from the table to circulate among his guests while they ate. His son, Adam, seemed to be infected by his father's restlessness, and ran around the room waving Joker's gun, loudly accosting the diners and snatching food from their plates. Joker ignored this behavior until the boy stole a sausage from his own plate. Then he stamped his feet loudly and shouted, "Bastard!" He and Adam both laughed. The boy sat back at his place, but now his face was beet-red. Something about Freedom's blank stare from behind the black wraparound monitor glasses annoyed him, and he began stamping and even kicking at the Iranian hacker's twisted feet under the table.

Then Adam made the mistake of throwing the greasy sausage back. Perhaps he had been aiming for his father's plate, but it hit Joker on his left ear instead. "Bastard!" Joker screamed again, and rising suddenly from his chair, stamped on the child's foot. Adam howled, and Joker hit him back-handed, knocking him onto the floor. Blood poured from his son's nose. The mother, the Swedish "top wife," came flying across the room and grabbed the screaming child protectively. Enraged by the sight, the Emir of Trenton started kicking them both as they crawled across the dining room floor.

When he heard the sound of a rib cracking, Joyful Kalinga said, "Enough." Along with several of the other guests, he'd half-risen from his seat. Now he stood up fully and pushed his chair back from him. Across the table, the two bodyguards had also risen to their feet and pulled out handguns. There was a rustle of activity from behind Obama as other guests hid beneath their dinner tables. In order to show his contempt, Kalinga belched loudly.

Joker Hadjibaeyev stared at him, speechless and purplish with rage. He made furious, kung-fu-like waving motions with his arms while Bashir and Mukh carefully aimed their weapons at Kalinga, who merely smiled and fluttered his eyelashes. "Big man," he said mockingly to his host. "Big man ..."

The lights went out. In the darkness and sudden silence, Bashir fired two loud, rapid shots into Joyful Kalinga's chest. Obama crumpled heavily to the floor. The lights came on with the emergency generators, and the wall behind Joker Hadjibaeyev, blank now of holograms, suddenly collapsed and fell away down into the street. Simultaneously, there was a blinding flash of light, then a loud roar that seemed to pick Joker up and fling him bodily, tumbling through the air in slow-motion, at his guests.

Most of those standing at his table were blown over with him, crashing heavily into the tabletop. Food and dishes and shattered glass spun everywhere. But the explosion felt very different than those employed by Xina's gang. This one had been a military smart-bomb with a limited directional blast area, designed to neatly take down the wall. It had just been Joker's bad luck to be standing so close to it. Obama heard Xina's voice beside his ear. "Help me move him, Kourosh," she said in Farsi. The lights had gone out again, and the ceiling sprinklers came on.

"I'm fine," Obama said. A loud wailing noise all but drowned him out. "I can move by myself." He rolled further under the table.

"But he was shot!" Freedom — Kourosh — said. "I saw it."

"They missed." Two intact bullets fell out of his coat pocket and dropped clinking to the floor.

"Come on! Let's get out of here! "They are coming!" Xina said in a fierce, low tone, and in a half crouch began dragging Obama by the shoulder lapel toward the door. Guided only by the glow of the ovens, she scuttled along the wet floor like a crab, followed by Obama, absurdly clutching his backpack, then Freedom, then Habib, along with a dozen other fleeing diners. Hijack stood just outside the doorway, covering their retreat with an automatic rifle.

"Who's coming?" asked Obama.

"HHS, stupid. SWAT teams in flying suits."

The gaping hole where the outside wall had been began to fill up with a glaring light from the street, and the silhouettes of black figures became visible against it, flying into the room like big ungainly bees. Hijack let off a burst of gunfire past Obama, Xina, and the fleeing diners as they straightened and raced down the hallway, slowed by Freedom's limp. Behind them, the doorway where Hijack had been standing blew up. "*Gai!*" said Xina under her breath. Sounds of screaming filled the passageway, followed by a cloud of plaster dust. "In here!" she said, and they turned into a service area. Inside was a laundry elevator, and beside that, an unmarked emergency staircase. They hurtled down it, their breath coming in ragged gasps. When they got down to the second floor, Xina stopped them. She and her two comrades turned on tiny flashlights embedded in their caps.

"Kourosh?" she said.

Freedom peered around into nothing and nodded, "The building's surrounded. They're all over the parking garage below the lobby and the parking lot in the back."

"How about the lobby?"

"Yeah, a few," he told her.

"Can you hack anything parked here, bro?" Habib asked him. A pair of maids came hurtling past them in the dark, cursing.

"Any aircars?" Xina added impatiently.

"Maybe," Freedom answered, after a few moments. He was frantically searching the Grid, hacking into military systems, looking for any vehicle parked nearby, preferably an empty one, that could be broken into remotely, started up, and then coaxed into the air.

"Well, have something waiting outside the front door in 5 minutes," she snapped. "Hovering about a meter up, OK?" Then to Obama: "Gimme your backpack, amigo."

"Why?" he asked. He'd forgotten he still had it.

"I'll show you why, just gimme." She wrenched it from his grasp. "This way," she said, and they followed her out of the stairwell. She led them back into the hookah parlor, which was now deserted, and set the backpack down on a table beside the panoramic vue-wall that looked into the swimming pool. She unzipped the bag, played with something inside it for a minute, then re-sealed it. "Come on," she said. "Now we need to find some mattresses. They use smart-foam ones here, right?"

They found two of these in the guest-rooms just down the corridor. Xina made her companions strip the mattresses, drag them out into the hallway, and stand them up on their ends facing the way they'd just come. "OK," she said. "When I say 'go', lower them into the water."

"What water?" said Obama.

"This water," said Xina, and signaled with her iRist. The floors and walls shuddered, and a second explosion, this one much louder than the first, rocked the building. This was followed by a roaring noise, and then the sound of splashing and an overpowering odor of brine. The thin beam of Habib's flashlight picked out a cascade of salty swimming-pool water spilling violently out of the hookah parlor.

"You blew up a living reef?" Obama asked her incredulously. "You must have put the bomb in my backpack when we were at the mosque." The bomb had also destroyed, he realized, the last link he had with Kim: the holo-projector from their marital altar. Now only his heart would be able to conjure up her image. The rest of her was gone.

Xina smirked at him. "Insurance," she said. The water began rapidly filling the corridor. "I had to be sure you were the one we were after. Kourosh, you ride with Habib. Obama, you ride with me. Pretend it's a sled, and steer for the main staircase. Go!"

They went. In the near-darkness, they flung themselves headfirst onto the mattresses and kicked them into the cold water. For a moment or two the mattresses eddied backwards, then picked up momentum from the current and began floating toward the main landing. The roaring got louder. The mattresses sagged into the water and spun slowly before being picked up and hurled down the grand marble staircase. They hurtled down the stairs on a raging torrent into the lobby, sweeping past a pair of SWAT-team troopers struggling in waist-deep water filled with a muddy mix of sand and coral. A few fish still swam in it. A shot came from somewhere, then another, as the mattresses spun around and around in the main lobby. Xina, Obama suddenly realized, had called him by his real name ...

The current picked them up again and propelled them in the direction of the front lobby doors and then out into the night. An unmanned black HHS airvan, sirens flashing, hovered just above the flood, its side doors open. Habib got to it first and hauled Freedom up into the cab. Obama and Xina's mattress sank to the pavement the moment they both sat up, and they abandoned it in the water. Bullets slammed and ricocheted all around them. "Go! Go!" Xina was screaming. Before they were even inside it, the vehicle was spinning straight up and then away. They clambered inside and slammed the doors closed.

The van took a direct hit from a hand-held rocket-propelled grenade, and half the glasspex in it exploded, turning into snow behind the protective metal window grills. The vehicle shuddered. The spindrive rattled and throbbed and almost stalled, and they instantly lost altitude. Several more RPGs rocked them from behind. The airvan was armored — otherwise, they would never have survived the first hit — but the extra weight would bring it down very quickly. How long had they known he was really Obama Jones? he wondered. Had they known all along? Or had something given him away? Did it change things?

Xina said rapidly in Farsi, "Get us close to East State Street, and Joker's people will hide us."

"Why did they come after him?" Obama asked her, tumbling over hard against the cab wall as Habib manually executed a steep right turn. Xina's slim form slammed up against him, as she grasped at a hand-grip. Through the van's rear windows, he could see searchlights whipping across the sky and the flashing sirens of pursuing aircars. Beneath them — only a few meters below, as they veered along at the level of the rooftops — the city had gone dark, individual lights reappearing slowly as the generators switched on.

"They didn't. Joker's been paying them off for years. They were after us. And especially," she added in a husky rasp, "after you."

"Why me?" The Pratt & Whitney drives suddenly shut off and the airvan went horribly quiet. It glided smoothly for a moment or two, skimmed a few treetops and utility poles, snapped a heavy bough, then spun into a near-empty parking lot and hit the ground, scraping the asphalt with a sound like an electric lathe. The van kept on sliding and screaming, losing pieces of itself, until it came to a dead stop against a dumpster. Smoke poured from the engines. An airbag inflated.

"Because you're the one everybody's looking been for, Obama. You're the chosen one, the leader of our resistance movement."

19.

Xina, thought Obama, *is crazy. Even crazier than Simonetta.* Which really should have come as no surprise to him. *What kind of girl joins a jihadist terror cell, anyway?* Especially as a career choice, since she claimed not even to be religious. Right now she was acting even weirder than usual, trembling, covered in sweat but refusing to take her coat off, staring at him like she was hypnotized, claiming he was some kind of messiah — and arguing bitterly with everyone else. *Maybe she's coming down with a mutated designer flu,* he thought. *IRockistan isn't exactly a healthy place to be.*

They were half-lying, half-sitting on some of the mattresses that covered the rough concrete floor in the basement of the safe house they'd been sent to. These mattresses were not smart-foam — in fact, they didn't seem to be any kind of foam at all. Xina had barely moved since they'd arrived there. Habib had carried Kourosh back upstairs so he could try to rig an electric line down to the basement in order to play an important hologram message for Obama. Kourosh — Freedom — had injured his leg in the crash and could barely stand or walk; one of Joker's *mujahedeen* had pushed him all the way down East State Street and across the railroad tracks to Chambers Street in a wheelbarrow stolen from a construction site, a distance, guessed Obama, of a kilometer or two. Only Habib was healthy. And Habib, judging from the glances he kept directing at Obama, would have happily killed his new "leader." Only Xina stood in his way. And Xina was either sick or crazy. Or both.

"Why me?" Obama asked her again.

"Because. You'll see why, just be patient. He recorded a holo just for you. It explains everything better than I can."

"What does it explain, exactly?"

"I don't know," she said. "I haven't seen it."

"And who is 'he'?" It was the third time they'd had this conversation.

"You'll see." This with a secretive smile.

HHS was looking for them, Joker's soljahs had said. Right now, the HHS peacekeepers — or "peacies," as they were commonly called — were being pinned down by a counterattack near the site of the airvan crash. But of course the HHS owned the air. Xina's party would be safe for maybe 24 hours, the *mujahedeen* told them, maybe less, depending on what kind of microwave weapons HHS committed to the fight. And how serious they were about the search.

Very serious, said Xina. Right now, there was a second pitched battle going on at the mosque. They could see the lights crackling to the south, and hear occasional serial pop-pops-pops or louder RPG crumps. Nobody had heard anything about the fate of Joker Hadjibaeyev and his family, even whether they were alive or dead. Most of the other guests in the dining hall had just surrendered. They would be released again in days or weeks.

The *mujahedeen* had stared curiously at Xina's gang while they were relating this, like, "Why didn't you just do that, too, and spare us all this trouble?" But the *mujahedeen* were under orders to help them, and they did. Xina and her three companions had been given automatic rifles, red and white checkered *keffiyahs* to wear as disguises, and had then been led — or wheelbarrowed, in Kourosh's case — to the safe house. Without the GPS in his iRist, Obama had no idea where he was.

He tried again. "How did you know I was Obama Jones?"

"He told us," she said. "He" again. Obama felt like strangling her. "But I wasn't sure until I saw you cry. Your Kalinga act is very good. It's as if you really are a different person. Kourosh was completely tricked."

"And if I really had been Kalinga, you would have exploded my backpack and killed me."

"Sure," she said, yawning as if with boredom. Then she was seized by a fresh fit of trembling. "But it wouldn't have mattered anyway."

"Are you OK? Are you sure you aren't sick?" asked Obama, for the fourth or fifth time.

"I'm fine," Xina said impatiently. Though the basement room was cold and dusty, she had refused a blanket. Aside from the mattresses, the room was bare of any other furniture except for a kerosene hurricane lamp hanging from the low ceiling. Obama shuddered to imagine how many roentgens of radiation must still be measurable down there. None, according to the UN Department of Energy, of course, just like in Manacera City. But Obama wasn't sure he trusted the DOE any more. He could only hope the Pooka was protecting him from the radiation as she had from Bashir's bullets.

The rest of the old brick townhouse was little more than a gutted shell, with rotting floorboards covered by rat droppings and holes in the outside walls. Hidden in the farthest corner of the basement there was a tiny ancient bathroom with no door, no light, rusting pipes and darkly discolored water in the sink and toilet. In response to his muted complaints about not being able to bathe, the Pooka had begun absorbing and recycling his sweat and skin-scale, but he still felt itchy. A sudden thought struck him. "What do you mean, 'it wouldn't have mattered anyway'?"

"Because, stupid, either way, even if we'd been wrong, as long you really were Obama Jones, you still couldn't have died," she said. "You're indestructible. The bullets didn't kill you, either."

What did she mean, "indestructible"? He had thought that life with terrorists would at least be simple, but it just kept getting weirder and weirder. "Huh?"

"I guess you still don't know. Look, I'm sorry to be the one to break it to you, but you're the product of a genetic breeding experiment. He told us all about it. I mean, please don't tell me you never noticed — you never had any broken bones when you were a kid, right? And I bet you never got sick, either. And all your cuts and bruises just healed themselves? You were bred over generations to be some kind of, I dunno, superman. Indestructible. That's why we had to test you with those bombs. To make sure it had really worked."

Now that she mentioned it, some of what she was saying was sort of true — he had always been a whole lot stronger than the other kids. He'd had to be careful not to hurt anybody in kindergarten. But his mom would never have let him play competitive sports even if they'd still been allowed any more in skool. When he'd wanted to try out for an illicit summer football league once, he remembered the huge fights he and his Mom had had.

And it was true he was healthy as a horse; Kim had always teased him about it. So what? Lots of people were, since everybody had free health care. It was rare for anyone at MAD to really need their two months a year of Personal Choice days for illness alone, though naturally everybody took them anyway. Of course his coworkers were always coughing and sneezing, but that was from climate change. He'd never really thought about it.

But all this was probably just more of Xina's craziness. His thoughts were spinning again. "You mean the bomb blasts were just to see if you could kill me?" he asked her with real horror in his voice.

"Yes. Kourosh didn't put the first bomb in the right place because we didn't have a martyr to carry it out. So we had to do it all over again at the HHS building. It was nothing personal," she added, apparently upset that he might be angry with her. "We just had to be sure you were the one. We were told to do it that way. But don't take it personally — we were carrying out a hit on HHS anyway."

So what that meant was that Kim — and all those other innocent victims — had been killed by a bomb meant for him, Obama! Not even meant for him, really, but merely as a test for him — a bomb not even set off out of genuine political or religious conviction. A bomb set off to see if he really was a superman!

What made the situation even more tragic was that Obama knew perfectly well he wasn't. The only thing that had been stopping the bombs and the bullets aimed at him had been dumb luck. And, of course, the Pooka. Simonetta had been a product of exactly the same genetic breeding experiment, and that certainly hadn't stopped her from being blown apart by Little Mahendra's bomb.

Yet Obama had seen the genetic records for himself. He hadn't understood them, but there was no doubt that both he and Simonetta had been given extra genes — genes that did seem to be for things like strength and endurance.

Habib suddenly appeared on the rickety wooden stairway. He and Xina kept their weapons under their arms at all times; Obama and Kourosh had left theirs on a mattress. "We've connected it to a neighbor's generator," he said. "Kourosh thinks he can make it work." He came all the way downstairs and placed a small holographic projector, a black box about the size of a soap dish, on the concrete floor in front of them. After a few moments, a hologram sparkled to life above the little projector, then sputtered and collapsed in iridescent pixilation. A moment later it came back on.

" — Jersey's most serious outbreak of civic violence in the past year," a blurry Snow White was saying. "HHS peacekeepers have sealed off Terrestrial Intrastate Highways 195 and 295, in addition to Route 1, and all air traffic has been rerouted from entering the city. If you're planning to over-fly, just a reminder to use the Delaware River detours north and south at Air-95." She was joined by an avatar of Joyful Kalinga. "The UN authorities now believe they have succeeded in tracking down the world-famous terrorist, Joyful Kalinga, to an address inside the city. If you've seen this person, please do not attempt to apprehend him on your own. Instead, use one of the 'X11' series of iTooth numbers to contact HHS. Kalinga must be considered armed and extremely dangerous, and may now be masquerading as a known alias of his, this person, Obama Peace Jones. " A spinning representation of Obama's real face was superimposed over spy-cam night-vision scenes of the ongoing gun battles between Joker's local Islamic militia and the HHS "peacies."

Obama sighed. There was no going back now. Kalinga's iTooth had nearly 20,000 messages in it, which made him wonder if there were a maximum limit. But when he checked Obama's iTooth, he saw that all his messages had been sealed by court order. *This must be the work of Sato,* Obama thought, *in revenge for Simonetta's death or disappearance or whatever really happened to her.* Death and subsequent alien abduction, technically. But Simonetta had known all along that Obama and Joyful Kalinga were the same person, so presumably Sato knew, too. And whoever it was who was directing Xina's gang. *Not Sato,* he fervently hoped.

Obama could feel the noose tightening. And now he had no normal life to go back to — he would spend the rest of it, however long that might be, in the company of crazy people like Xina and Kourosh. And gangsters like Habib and Joker Hadjibaeyev. It didn't even bear thinking about. He found himself actually missing his old, everyday life at MAD.

Habib went upstairs again, then returned, carrying Kourosh on his back. "They're jamming me," Kourosh complained, as Habib dumped him down onto the mattress next to Xina. "And my cap-cam battery died. I'm blind now." With a slight shock of surprise, Obama realized Kourosh meant it literally. The guy really was visually-deprived. *That's why he's a bumper and uses his game-cap and glasses to navigate everywhere with.* He'd probably never been able to have the bio-CCD retinal implants because of his muscular dystrophy. Obama felt he could almost forgive Kourosh his murderous acts, because the poor kid probably had never been able to perceive the difference between reality and the Grid. Almost — but not quite. Obama wasn't going to be deterred from his revenge by pity.

"We'll just have to get out of here ourselves, then," Xina told Kourosh in Farsi. "Don't worry, we'll find a way, brother; we always do. The important thing now is to get Obama to New Mexico." Then in Enriched: "Let's run the holo, OK?"

"New Mexico?" said Obama.

"He wants to meet you," said Xina.

The holo came on. Because it was prerecorded and wasn't being wirelessly holocast over YouVee, the image was sharply ultrarealistic and life-size. It was that of World President Jose Manacera, who looked exactly as though he were lounging on a white leather couch in the room in front of them. "Hello, Obama," Manacera said.

President Manacera had been born in Mexico, but had moved with his undocumented immigrant parents across the border to Truth or Consequences, New Mexico, when he was 3. He was a small man in his late 60s with a big head and rough hands. His hair, which he kept dyed shoe-polish black out of a self-admitted sense of vanity, was thinning across his scalp. His brown, weathered "mestizo" features, which were slightly larger-than-life, were exceptionally ugly, yet so kindly and gentle that they radiated a deep and genuine attractiveness to those of all ages and genders.

He'd been president of the planet since Obama was 12, and before that president of the former United States; he'd first been elected in 2030, after passage of the 28th Amendment, which had allowed non-native-born Americans to become president. Obama could remember how sometimes President Manacera had been beamed directly into his elementary skool class — just as he had been to many classes simultaneously across the then-nation — to read stories to the children for an hour. Now it somehow seemed to Obama to be very natural, even comforting, to have Manacera suddenly appear in their darkened hide-out like this.

"I guess you're wondering what I'm, I mean my holo, is doing here right now, huh?" the president was saying with a rueful smile. "And I guess that deep down, being a real square-shooter, you're pretty shocked and horrified to learn that I'm the one behind the recent wave of bombings in Manacera City. Yep, I own up to it, and I take full responsibility. Just give me a minute, and I'll try to explain why." He sighed heavily, and then seemed to gaze directly at him.

"You know, Obama, sometimes we have to do terrible things in life according to what we politicians call the 'greater good' concept. But when we do, it can get all too easy for us to forget there are real individual humyn lives involved. Fact is, I've had to resort to such tactics — I've had to start up the Resistance movement that Xina and her people are part of — for a simple reason. What I'm going to tell you now, Obama, is classified top secret and known only to a few dozen people on Earth. And it is this: an honest-to-god terrible existential threat hangs over our planet right now — the threat of an alien invasion.

"Yep, I know how nutty that must sound to you, amigo — but take it from me, it's the gospel truth. You yourself are a product of the aliens' long-term plans. They've been breeding a new race of superhumyn bodies to 'wear,' as they call it, because they're physically a little like jellyfish and need a skeletal structure to walk around in our gravity with. And that's where you come in. You're nothing but a suit of clothes to them, and when they get inside a person — and the process requires a complex surgical operation — the real person dies.

"Somehow you got away from them at birth, and that's why they've been after you all this time. If you are seeing and hearing me now, it means we got to you first, thank your personal god." Manacera's voice was underscored by a faint sound of gunfire. At first Obama thought the gunfire was on the holo, but then he realized it was real.

"Now you may think that all I have to do, as world president, is snap my fingers to instantly assemble an army to take care of this threat. Sadly, that just ain't so. I may be UN president, but that's basically an empty title these days. Personally, I'm virtually powerless. HHS is completely infiltrated by alien stooges. Even my own UN Security Service is! All I can do is reach out to a few dedicated freedom fighters, like these brave folks who've just rescued you, and try to inspire them to wage a just war in our cause. The cause of all humynkind, Obama.

"As you probably know, I'm currently involved in a bitter election contest right now. I can't serve a third term as president, so I'm trying to lead my party as prime minister. Right now the opposition seems pretty well set to beat us. Now I won't lie to you — the aliens are pulling the strings on this one. My probable successor in this office, Senator Ho of the New Party, is a decent, straight-up kind of guy, but he has no idea what he's dealing with here. My big mistake was in trusting the chief of these aliens, who masquerades as a Japanese scientist named Shiseki Sato. And he's got Ho in his pocket. Sato was the one who convinced me to take over the Moon colonies when they went belly-up financially, and then ran the whole damn program himself. And then just a few years ago, I found out it was all a sham. The whole time, Sato and his alien cohorts had been running nothing but a great big cemetery up there. That's right, Obama, millions of our people, mostly old folks, have gone to the Moon dreaming of a new life, only to be slaughtered like turkeys at Thanksgiving." Genuine tears came to his eyes, and President Manacera stopped to blow his nose.

"That's why I'll do anything, sacrifice anybody, to stop them. Because the aliens plan to do the same thing to Earth next: turn it into a kind of theme-park for their own entertainment while they assume humyn form. And, believe me, when they 'assume' humyn form, it's always to make an 'ass' of 'u' and 'me'. You can't trust a word they tell you. They'll lie to you the same way they've lied to me. They must be stopped, whatever the cost.

"Once we beat them — and I'm hoping and praying you'll join me in this desperately important venture — then I'll be the first to voluntarily go before the court of world opinion and stand trial for my crimes. But I think even you, Obama, will be willing by then to see that I have at least acted in the best interests of humynity." He paused. The gunfire seemed to be getting louder.

"As you know, I keep a so-called presidential ranch down here near Truth or Consequences, and I guess the place is aptly named. Everything I've just told you is the honest truth, amigo — and I'm certainly prepared to take the consequences. Xina's instructions are to get you down here to New Mexico by hook or by crook, so that I can fill you in on everything I know about these space invaders and what we can do to destroy them. Then it will be your war, Obama. I'm too old and tired and useless to lead it any more. After you take over the reins, son, I reckon you'll find yourself saying and doing the same kind of things I've had to. And maybe, just maybe, when you do, you'll forgive your old Uncle Jose just a little."

The hologram lingered in the air for a few seconds, then vanished. There was a rattle of small-arms fire nearby, then the sound of a missile or mortar shell exploding. "We need to get out of here," said Habib urgently. "The Crusader pigs will be going house to house soon."

"They're in no shape to travel," Obama said, pointing at the other two.

"I'm fine!" snapped Xina, getting to her feet. Her eyes looked glassy, but the sweating and shivering had stopped. She'd put something in her mouth and swallowed it while they'd been listening to President Manacera. "This town will be surrounded by checkpoints now. We'll have to find the hospital. Follow me, and do as I do. No talking."

"You're the superman," Habib told Obama with a sneer. "You can carry Kourosh." *Fair enough*, Obama decided. *At least I'll be doing something useful.* He found, when he'd crouched down to pick him up, that the hacker kid was light as a feather. After Obama straightened up, he slung Kourosh over one shoulder. Xina and Habib picked up the extra rifles, and they all trooped up the stairs and into the darkened back yard of the derelict rowhouse.

The lights were out all over the city, but overhead, the night sky was pierced by searchlight beams from HHS aircars drifting amid occasional flashes of brilliant light. These were "dazzlers," microwave beams designed to temporarily blind combatants on the ground. Xina had told Obama that the real danger, aside from bullets and explosives, was from ADS, or Active Denial Systems, which used acoustic emissions to disrupt the central nervous system. ADS caused people to go into convulsions, crap themselves, or even have seizures.

Xina led them on a zig-zagging path down alleys, over fences, and across back yards, pausing and crouching in doorways or against tree trunks whenever an aircar passed over them. She did this in silence, using hand signals and pointing. Xina seemed to be working her way south, parallel to Chambers. Perhaps because the Pooka was doing most of the work of carrying Kourosh, Obama barely noticed the weight. What bothered him most, side from the constant fear of being attacked from the sky, was the ongoing feeling that he really didn't have a clue what he was even doing in Trenton any more. He'd just wasted another perfect opportunity to avenge Kim while they were all down in the basement together. He could have picked up one of the assault rifles and simply shot the three of them. Why hadn't he? Instead, he'd done nothing. And now he was a wanted person with every peacie on the planet looking for him — looking for Obama Jones, now, and not just Joyful Kalinga. Worse, he'd become helplessly dependent on Xina and the survivors of her little squad to smuggle him out of the city and help him somehow survive, even start a new life. He should have listened to Siren and just waited for her to pick him the previous morning instead of running off to play "cops and robbers," as his dad had used to call it.

On the other hand, Obama thought, *if I hadn't come to Trenton on my own, I'd probably never have received the holo message from President Manacera.* And discovered that the president himself was the person responsible for ordering the bomb attack that had taken Kim's life. As he followed Xina through the dark streets, Habib trailing silently behind — to keep an eye on him? — Obama mulled over the president's statement in his thoughts. The Pooka had told him that Siren was the only "visitor" on Earth, meaning, presumably, the only alien from outer space, yet President Manacera had claimed there was an alien invasion, which implied a lot more aliens than just one. Had he been telling the truth? Had he been lying?

Or had Siren been lying to Obama all along? It was true, she had seemed truly shocked and surprised to discover that Simonetta — and therefore Simonetta's father, Sato — was a fellow-alien. But hadn't Siren also killed someone by taking over her body? If so, that made her just as evil as Sato and Simonetta. Of course Sato had obviously done it over and over again, since, according to the files anyway, he'd been breeding humyn bodies for hundreds of years now. If he were launching an invasion, it sure hadn't happened very fast. Or on any big scale.

On the other hand, maybe Manacera knew lots of things that Siren hadn't told Obama. Or did he? Maybe he was just a crazy paranoid old guy, trying to hold onto power by inventing an invasion scare and tricking gullible young people like Xina and Kourosh into following him. And now he was trying out the same act on Obama.

And that, Obama finally decided, was the real reason he had to stay with Xina and not just vanish into the night, as he wanted to do. Only Xina could lead him to President Manacera. And then Obama might at last have the opportunity to pass judgment and take revenge on all of them at once. In the meantime, he was having a great deal of trouble standing the very sight of them.

Through a copse of trees on Hamilton they could see lights glowing at the intersection with the larger Chambers Street. On the left lay the Central Trenton Madrassah, on the right a hospital, with the name "Mikeel Jackson Charitable Islamic Medical Center" in glowing Roman letters beneath the Arabic. Both of these buildings were functioning with their own emergency generators. As the four revolutionaries watched from cover, a long column of black, sleekly armored HHS ground troop carriers rumbled past, going north. There was no other traffic on the roads.

After the armored Hummvees had disappeared, Habib and Xina briefly conferred, then told Obama to stay put with her brother. "We need a car," Xina whispered in his ear. The only parked cars on the streets that Obama had seen since leaving the downtown area were the rusting frames of old burned-out hulks, but Habib thought he'd spotted a pair of drivable cars in a backyard garage they'd passed. He and Xina retraced their steps to go back and look for them, and a few minutes later Obama heard the sound of glasspex being smashed, followed by the piercing electronic screech of a security sensor. A few minutes later, a jacked-up Ford Escort replica with a hydrogen engine came bouncing across a nearby front yard and hurtled into the street.

The tires squealed as Habib gunned the engine and pulled the wheel into a tight turn, then came to a dead stop in front of Obama.

Obama opened a back door and piled inside with Kourosh. As he did, a bullet suddenly smashed into the back windshield, leaving behind a hole the size of an orange and a web of cracks. Habib accelerated violently, then skidded as a second shot from behind took out one of the rear tires. "Go! Go!" Xina called out, aiming a burst of automatic fire back at the darkened house. The car slumped to one side, and the shot-out tire flapped noisily on the surface of the road. Its hubcap detached itself and rolled clattering alongside them before skipping onto the kerb and disappearing.

Habib turned right, then left, as the car limped across the oncoming lane into the hospital's main entrance. The dimly-lit lobby in front of them had glasspex side panels covered in rusting security bars, and an automagic door in front, patched with plywood, slid open as they drove by. A four-storey concrete parking garage loomed directly ahead of them. They smashed into the barred traffic barrier at its entrance and came to a dead stop. Habib backed up and rammed the barrier again. On the third try, the Escort, its retro front grill mangled and headlights dangling out, tore through the metal gates and over the sawtooth directional barrier in the floor. Instantly, the remaining three tires blew out.

The car kept on rolling, flapping and skidding on the cement, the noise of its screaming tires echoing loudly back from the walls. Slowly they climbed a long series of ramps higher and higher into the garage. By the time they emerged onto the open roof, they were scraping along on the car's wheel-rims, and sparks were flying out behind them. Habib twisted the car into a U-turn, and the car briefly flew into the air over the speed-hump at the entrance to the airbulance landing pad before coming down with a crash.

A single airbulance was idling there. Its crew — two myn and a womyn with dyed blond hair, Iraqi or Palestinian, all wearing body armor, steel helmets with green crosses, and jackets over their orderly uniforms — were standing at the rooftop wall railing, drinking hot cups of khat and pointing out flashes of gunfire and aircar lights in the distance. They turned to see what the all the racket was about. Habib stopped the car, and he and Xina got out in a hurry, their weapons hidden under their coats. "You stay here," Xina said to Obama.

"Emergency! *Momkin almusada!*" she yelled imploringly at the airbulance crew, waving her free arm at them. When she and Habib came close enough, they pulled out their rifles and motioned the medics over against the railing. Speaking in rapid Arabic, they made the driver kneel with his hands behind his bowed head, then told the other two to take off their clothes.

"Just down to your uniforms, we don't want your underwear," said Habib. When the two had complied, he shot the half-naked medic in the heart. The myn toppled like a stone.

The womyn began crying and screaming, "Laa! Laa! No, please!" over and over again. Xina pulled the womyn's hair hard with her free hand, then blew her brains out against the base of the wall. The womyn's legs kicked for several long seconds on the cement floor while she voided her bowels. Obama gagged.

Habib put on the green-cross helmet and motioned the driver into the airbulance, then climbed into the passenger seat, still pointing his assault rifle at him. He tossed the rest of the dead myn's clothes on the floor. Xina, meanwhile, took off her own clothes and put on the womyn's before returning to the Ford Escort where Obama was still waiting with Kourosh. He found himself flinching away from her.

"No time for that now," she said, annoyed. "Come on, move! We're doing this for all for you. Habib has a wife and two children at home he may never see again because of this mission. We have given our lives to this cause — those people could not be allowed to identify us. Kourosh, take off your clothes now. Obama, carry him to the gurney in the back of the airbulance. Our story is that he is a blind person who has been shot by the *mujahedeen*, OK?" Once her brother was strapped in under a blanket, Xina smeared the dead womyn's blood all over his shirt, then attached an oxygen mask and an IV to him.

"Your turn now," she said to Obama, throwing him a folded Nitinyl bag. "Turn this body-bag inside out and then get into it under the gurney. Zip it up from the inside. Then stretch out there and lie still. If we are stopped, don't move or make any noise, OK? If HHS catches you, you'll spend the rest of your life in a tank with a game-cap on. If that's what you really want, then make a scene and get us all killed. If it isn't, just shut up and let us get you out of here."

There seemed nothing more to say. The gurney had been locked in an intermediate position, about half a meter off the airbulance floor. Obama just barely managed to fit beneath it. He zipped the bag over his head and face and heard the rear airbulance door hiss closed and the sound of call codes crackling over the coms in the front seat.

The airbulance lurched into the air suddenly, while Habib grilled the driver. "What are the choices when you call this in?" Habib demanded.

"Critical, regular, or non-critical emergency," the driver told him in Enriched.

"Tell them the middle one. Say we have someone with a gunshot wound, bleeding badly. We want to take him across the river to a Pennsylvania hospital — got that? Say anything else and I shoot you. You saw what happened to the others. I can fly this car myself; I only need you for the coms. So be very careful what you tell them."

"*Inshallah*," the myn said. "But I am having to clear this with the HHS authorities. We are under martial law here now." And then, into his iTooth: "This is X-Ray-Sixer-Three-Eight at Facility 83 Mikeel Jackson MedCent NJ. Requesting clearance for a Priority 2." After a few minutes, when clearance was evidently granted, he went on, "This is a Signal 3, en route Facility 109 Bryn Mawr MedCent, PA — I have an AM, Code 10-15. Class 1. Yes, Class 1, he's critical but stable. OK," he said to Habib, switching back to Arabic. "We can go now. They say to follow Chambers to South Broad Street. There is a checkpoint at 295. Then we can cross the river. If I do this for you, my brother, you will not kill me?"

"I swear it," Habib said in the same language. "*Bismillah, ma-salaam.*" Obama knew he was lying. The driver probably did, too. He turned on the vehicle's sirens anyway, and it picked up speed.

"Pooka?" he whispered, very quietly inside the body-bag in the dark.

"I'm here, Obama," the Pooka said inside his auditory nerve. He hadn't been so happy to hear anyone's voice in weeks. Even if it wasn't a humyn one. Especially at this moment, if it wasn't a humyn one. Suddenly, he wasn't so sure he even wanted to be a humyn being any more. Right now, it seemed like a pretty terrible thing to be.

20.

Xina and Habib killed the airbulance driver the second time they landed. This was somewhere in Pennsylvania. They had touched down earlier at the 295 checkpoint, where there had been a perfunctory scan before they'd all been waved through (or so Obama had assumed from the darkness inside his body-bag). He, he'd had to remind himself, was what they were really smuggling out of Trenton. With their contacts there, Xina's squad could probably have found other hideouts and out-waited the emergency. They were putting their lives — and those of everyone they came in contact with — at risk because of him. But it didn't matter. They were cold-blooded murderers anyway. If they hadn't had him they'd have found some other cause to kill for.

After crossing the river, they'd flown west for about 20 minutes — 20 of the soon-to-be-obsolete analog minutes — until they'd landed the second time. And that was when Obama had heard the single shot.

He struggled out of the bag and opened the rear airbulance door. They'd landed in a frost-covered field somewhere off Air-76, the old Pennsylvania Turnpike. In the false dawn, Obama could just barely make out the pale, huddled shape on the ground, already being stripped by Habib. "You promised him," was all he could think of to say. Habib ignored him. "There's got to be no more killing from now on," Obama went on. "Otherwise, I'm walking away now."

Habib straightened up and strode over to stare at him mockingly for a moment before tossing the dead myn's green cross helmet at him. It hit Obama's stomach and bounced onto the hard ground. "We'll take orders from you when you've proved yourself a good leader," he said in Arabic. "But not before." Did he realize Obama could understand him, thanks to the Pooka? No. He was just being deliberately insulting by speaking a foreign language. Xina popped up at Obama's elbow, her teeth chattering with the cold.

"We gave him time to make his peace with god," she said. "It had to be, Obama. We couldn't leave him alive to identify us — all the innocents whose blood we shed are martyrs in our war against the aliens. You must realize this. We need you to be a warrior now. Or is Joyful Kalinga nothing but an act?" Suddenly, she collapsed against him. At first he thought she was merely being dramatic and manipulative, but then he felt that her face was on fire.

"She's burning up with fever," Obama said. "She's sick."

"I'm fine," she insisted.

"Well, don't just stand there," said Habib in Enriched. "Pick her up and put her on the airbulance cot. Maybe she needs medicine. You know how to fly the machine?" Obama shook his head. "*Khawal!* You are no more use to us than a baby!" Habib told him contemptuously. "You are soft and weak and make us hold your hand the whole time." He spat. For an instant, Obama actually felt ashamed. He carried Xina back to the airbulance, where he found Kourosh recharging his cap and glasses in the front passenger seat.

"Where are we, anyway?" Obama asked Kourosh, after he and Habib had tucked Xina into the cot over her protests, and given her a Paracedrin patch.

"Someplace called 'Valley Forge'," replied Kourosh. None of them had ever heard of it.

With Kourosh navigating they now made much faster time, since he was able to bypass checkpoints and EZ-Pay toll-scanners by hacking into them. They bisected Harrisburg and York, then turned south on Air-81 and skirted the Allegheny Mountains. It was the first time Obama had been outside the North American Federal Administrative Area since his honeymoon. The NAFAA, of course, was one of the largest "blue zones" in the world, but even though their route nominally lay over the protective "green zone" of the Shenandoah foothills, similar to those which surrounded most of the world's major urban areas, there was more than a hint of "red" wilderness visible in the mountains to the west. Everywhere below them, brightly-colored tiny houses and strip-malls and churches and highways spread out like toys, clinging to green hills and yellow fields. This struck Obama as almost unbearably beautiful and old-fashioned, like an Xmas calendar from his childhood.

As they flew south, the sun rose to the east, to the left of them, and the outside temperature began to climb dramatically. This was typical of ice-age summer weather — there might be a frigid spell, as there had been in the Northeast for the past two weeks, even snow and sleet and midsummer morning frost — and then the front would break up and the heat would return. Often accompanied by the hatching of vast numbers of mosquitoes. This morning, according to the weather-bot reports they were picking up, the Cascadian clipper that had been parked over them all month was being pushed north by a bubble of hot air coming up from the Gulf of Texico.

In the back of the airbulance he could hear Xina muttering feverishly to herself in a mix of Enriched, Farsi, and Arabic. Everything the Pooka translated from this was gibberish. Xina seemed to think she was in a donut shop with her mother. At about noon, her fever broke, and she sat up and began to make sense again. *Or at least,* he thought spitefully, *as much sense as she ever makes.* He'd been hoping she'd just die.

He couldn't force the horrific image out of his mind of Xina's white-knuckled fist bunched in the blond womyn's hair, before she'd put the barrel of her rifle to her head and pulled the trigger. These people had killed Kim and Mrs. Housmanzadeh with equal callousness and brutality. And what was he doing still hanging with them right now, just sitting there doing nothing, riding passively along inside a stolen airbulance as if they were all some kind of dysfunctional psycho family off together for a summer vacation?

Xina, to give her credit, was right. He seemed to have surrendered all initiative the moment he'd stopped being Kalinga. Maybe he, Obama, should "resign" and let Joyful Kalinga take over permanently. It was as if Kalinga had all the force, all the dynamism, that he, Obama, obviously lacked. He'd just sat there while those people had been killed in cold blood in front of him — in fact, in a way, their deaths had really been his fault. Xina and Habib had committed them in order to get him out of Trenton and to President Manacera's ranch. How many more innocent victims was Obama prepared to watch die in the name of revenge?

Kim was the last person who'd have wanted that. In fact, she was the last person who'd have wanted him to kill even these disgusting people in order to avenge her. He'd had several opportunities to do that, and blown them. *Obviously, I'm not seriously capable of it,* he decided. Maybe he should seize his next chance to walk away from the terror group and disappear before they got to New Mexico.

Up to now he'd just been reacting to events instead of trying to control them. But even without money or an identity, Obama Jones might still be able to survive on his own. He had the Pooka to protect him — and maybe Siren, too. Maybe the alien would forgive him for having disobeyed her instructions. But was she telling him the truth any more than Manacera was? It was impossible to know.

Habib landed the airbulance in the Shenandoah Valley somewhere near Harrisonburg, VA, for lunch and gas. There was a row of fast-food restaurants serving both Air-81 and the old Terrestrial Intrastate Highway that snaked through the range more or less below it. There was a Mickey D's, with a "Reddie Rockabilly" rather than the blue-zone "Urban Gangsta" motif Obama was used to; a "WiiFresh," a "Bro' King," and a "Big Booby's" restaurant with a huge hologram of the beloved cartoon character outside in front. They ate at the Big Booby's, where the waitresses, mostly local teenagers, had submitted to temporary steroline injections — which caused their breasts to be inflated to nearly 4 times their natural size — before being spray-clothed over with clingy wet-look Syntex.

Without even inspecting the kitchens, Obama could spot at least a half-dozen open UN human-rights and health code violations, but nobody seemed to care. The food was greasy, bland, and contained what he suspected to be multiple illegal animal parts, but he was hungry and ate it anyway. They all did, even Xina.

When they were done, Habib insisted on stopping at each of the other chains to order carry-out meals to take with them. He was using the iRist of the dead driver. Then they stopped again at an S-Mart near Harrisonburg, where Habib bought a large food cooler, gallons of water in hexahedrons, flashlights, tarpaulins, camping equipment, thermal socks, gloves, and parkas, and several tubes of red spray-paint. It felt really weird to Obama to be shopping off-Grid. Once outside in the parking lot, Habib threw the stolen iRist onto the pavement and ground it to pieces under his boot. "You have any accounts we can use now?" he asked Obama.

"No, mine is frozen. And Kalinga's is too hot."

Habib nodded dourly. "We can't use any of the others, so we're on our own. Unless Kourosh can think of something." He and Obama sprayed the green crosses of their helmets and the sides of the airbulance bright red; then, under Kourosh's direction, altered the airbulance's bar and number-codes. No one passing by seemed to notice or care, though surely, Obama thought, there would be security cams recording everything.

He asked Xina about this once they were under way again, and she shrugged. "This is an invisible 'green line'," she said. "The UN would like to control everything everywhere, all the time, but it can't.

We're not in the red zone yet, but very close — even here people do as they like. Eat what they like, buy and sell what they want, don't pay VAT taxes. But we are also still inside the green zone, so they are used to brown faces and won't report us to HHS unless we create a disturbance. But we'll have to be very careful south of Knoxville."

"Why is that? I thought the HHS was weak there."

"It is — but the Volunteers are everywhere," she told him. "They run most things in the red zones. And they don't like Muslims."

The "red zone" was the polite term for the vast expanse of America that had only indifferently — and times actively rebelliously — accepted the UN Mandate. This area generally included the states of the former Confederacy, minus south Florida and northern Virginia, plus southeastern Ohio and western Pennsylvania, large areas of the plains states, and the so-called "Mormon Rift." Naturally there were large blue and green enclaves within the red, mostly major cities like Atlanta and Dallas and even Salt Lake City, as well as university towns like Knoxville and Gainesville or Missoula — but in general, the "reddies," or red-necks, lived their lives as independently of the federal government as possible. Though, as was often pointed out by YouVee, they were always surprisingly "ready" to accept UN farming or small business subsidies.

This had resulted in infamous scams, like that of the "bovograms." Most of the continent's agricultural work was done by robotics, but a growing number of small farmers earned extra subsidies — which were distributed on a per-animal or even per-vegetable basis — by spreading over their acreage holo-projectors displaying fake cows in order to deceive Department of Agriculture (UNDOA) satellites and auditing bots.

In fact, reddies — half of whom, ironically, were by now African-American or Hispanic — had become as welfare-dependent as many of the immigrant "meanies," or minorities, of the blue zones. The reddies' truculent cultural separatism had been held in check by this fact, as well as by the long tenure of President Manacera, who had always managed to pass himself off politically as one of their own, the "last of the good ole boys" as he often put it. But now he was to be replaced as world president, so no one knew how restive the region might become.

To complicate matters, most of the former United States' military bases had once existed inside the red zone, and when the US armed forces were absorbed into the United Nations Department of Peace & Non-Violence in 2034-35, vast amounts of military hardware, including ammunition, tanks and even aircraft, had gone missing, presumably looted by a sudden new underclass of unemployed veterans.

Might these be used in some future insurrection? No one knew. Paramilitary groups like the Minutemen, PROGUSA (Provisional Government of the USA In Exile) — or its famous violent splinter group, the White Terror Commando — had generated a lot of sympathy across the so-called "Gun Belt," but not much active support — so far, at least. If that changed, many political analysts were doubtful that HHS could contain an actual armed rebellion, especially since so many of its employees, drawn from this region of the continent, would probably feel divided loyalties. It was these very loyalties which had caused the usurpation by the Department of Health and Humyn Services of the prerogatives of the Department of Peace & Non-Violence (DPNV) in the first place.

The story of the DPNV was perhaps the most unusual of any department in the history of world government. First proposed in 1792 by Dr Benjamin Rush, one of the "Founding Fathers" of the United States Constitution, the concept had been given fresh life in 2001 by US Representative Dennis Kucinich and adopted by the United Nations in 2019. The mission of the new UN agency had been, among other things, the replacement of conventional military training and use of force by teaching violence prevention, particularly against womyn, children, and minorities; the employment of conflict resolution skills and mediation by the military; the dismantling of violent gangs and "gang psychology;" the rehabilitation of the prison population by replacing jails with anger management teaching facilities; the strict banning of non-military as well as military weapons and weapons of mass destruction (WMDs); and the banning of all violent crimes against animals.

At the time this mandate was adopted, the largest military entities in the world, aside from the former United States and North Korea, had been the former China, Russia, India, Pakistan, and Turkey. This latter group had contributed the bulk of the UN peacekeepers — peacies or Blue Hats — who had earned such detestation during the mini-wars of the 2020's. By the early '30's, the outright failure of these forces to maintain order, and the enormous backlog of lawsuits and cases against UN military personnel at the World Court in the Hague, had caused the ceding of all authority for UN peacekeeping to the DPNV, by that time the largest UN agency.

At the same time, responsibility for law enforcement on a daily basis had devolved to the Department of Health and Humyn

Services, which had begun to recruit its peace officers locally. In the former United States, the bulk had been drawn from former military personnel, and by the time CommUnion had been finally completed in 2041, most of the UN peacekeepers in North America were reddies. This had manifested itself in HHS' relentless rivalry with other agencies and most particularly in their semi-successful campaign, in concert with Slavic and Han Chinese personnel on other continents, to force DPNV — who by now consisted mostly of idealistic, college-educated European and North American gays and lesbian womyn — to honor its own mandate and completely disarm. Thus had begun the bitter inter-agency rivalry that had raged for the past decade in every one of the Federal Administration Areas on the planet — Brasilia, Sydney, Singapore, Hong Kong, Kiev, Geneva, Cairo, Lagos, Mumbai, Istanbul, and Tokyo — resulting in intermittent street warfare in several of them.

So far, the NAFAA had been spared. *How much longer will that last?* Obama wondered. He'd always been aware of the friction, especially since he'd come to work at MAD. It would have been impossible not to have been. Everybody was familiar with HHS's unprecedented expansion and strong-arm tactics. But he'd never have guessed in a million years the extent of MAD's senior-level involvement in open violence through its minority contacts.

They spotted their first Volunteers when they crossed the old state line between Virginia and Tennessee. Originally, these had been Voluntary Redundancy Careers Counselors, an organization formed to assist former US military employees in their awkward transition to civilian life as world citizens. But the Volunteers had instantly begun to function as an organized police force throughout the South, where the HHS was notably inefficient and corrupt. They were commonly found near green lines, where they patrolled the air-lanes as well as the terrestrial ones, on the prowl for smuggled goods, particularly cigarettes, drugs, and weapons.

They also stopped cars, looking for wanted criminals and terrorists. Whenever Obama and his companions spotted any of the distinctive orange and grey Hyundair cruisers, Habib put the airbulance siren lights on, and the Vols left them alone. Obama wasn't about to tell the others that ever since they'd left the hospital in Trenton, the Pooka had been cloaking their coms signals; otherwise they'd probably never have gotten past that first checkpoint. It was better to let Xina's gang think their escape had been due to a combination of luck and HHS incompetence. And, of course, there had been plenty of both.

Their flight crossed the Blue Ridge range, following the course of hollows and valleys that lay between the heroic rocky cliffs of the pine-covered mountains, peaks covered with melting snow. Here the towns looked even more like toys nestled against the mountainsides. Some of the toy towns were even girded by toy trains. He wished Kim could have seen these vistas — how she would have fallen in love with the sight. Instead, he was forced to share it with Habib, who despised it, Kourosh, who couldn't see it, and Xina, who was indifferent. "How did President Manacera know that Kalinga and Obama Jones were the same person?" he asked her at one point.

"I don't know. You had some agents following you in Alexandria. Maybe they figured out who you were, and he read their reports. Maybe," she went on, struck all at once by the idea, "they even tailed us to Trenton, and that's why the hotel was attacked."

"A whole lot of maybes," Obama said dubiously.

"That's life," she told him. "A lot of maybes." She coughed loudly.

"How did he first contact you? How long have you been working with him?"

"He found Kourosh on the Grid about, I don't know, maybe a year ago. Before that, we were with a local Warriors of God group in NoVa, before that with a drug gang. All of the Resistance groups in America began as drug gangs, you know," she said. "Oh yes, it's true. The militant Muslim movements here come from a single organization that moved from the former Colombia to Caracas, Venezuela over 40 years ago — and we still control all the heroin here through them. They were called FARC. The WTC comes from a rival cartel from Medellin, Colombia that's even older than ours. That's why they still control all the cocaine. And ever since they joined with White Power groups in this country, the meth.

"In the early days most of our military trainers spoke Spanish, they were originally Muslims from North Africa or Lebanon. At least that's what we've always been told." She began coughing again and had to lie down. "Pretty funny, isn't it? The president of the whole world having to depend on people like us! But you're different, Obama. You're not like Habib and me. You're a good man and much braver than you think, so you can inspire people. You could be the great leader we need to save the planet — if only you will learn to make yourself be hard."

Obama thought of several sarcastic replies to this. But he said nothing.

The sun was setting as they reached the end of 81 where it joined 40 east of Knoxville. His dad was originally from Knoxville, but Obama had never been there. He felt a stab of disappointment as they turned south on 40 over the old TVA lakes to the Great Smoky Mountains Green Peoples' Park. He would have liked to have spent a few days in the city as a tourist. Instead of being lost in the dark in the middle of nowhere, as they now were, looking for a safe place to spend the night.

The mountains, their tops studded with pines, loomed immediately ahead, blacker than the night sky. They were flying blind with all their lights and coms blacked out, guided only by Kourosh, who was plugged into a single small micro-sat, the kind a group of local farmers or hobbyists had probably launched into orbit from a back yard. They turned left off the remains of a parkway and followed a creek south, skimming just above the level of the trees. After they passed over the wreckage of a deserted ranger station, Kourosh allowed Habib to manually use a single searchlight mounted on the driver's-side door to steer by.

Former national parks like this one were no longer government-maintained. After CommUnion, the old National Park Service had been disbanded and replaced by UN Eco-Trustees or greenies. Most of these were lawyers or student volunteers. The few who actually showed up in remote and unglamorous places like Gatlinburg, Tennessee, were part of the Biodiversity Activist Movement, which believed in introducing a bold new range of foreign species into ecological backwaters. The most disastrous of these introductions had been those of the Chinese northern snakehead, which had depopulated most of the Great Smoky Mountains fishing streams, and the Brazilian nutria in the marshes. Wolves were a particular favorite of BAMmers worldwide, and here they had exterminated most of the native coyotes and were even being blamed for the gradual disappearance of the black bear.

As the airbulance followed the trail of a creek deeper into the forest, Obama imagined he could hear one or two wolves howling in the distance now. Occasionally, the searchlight would pick out the reflecting eyes of animals beneath the tree-cover, but he decided these were probably deer. They passed through a gap in the piedmont, then slowed to spin over the wooden ruins of an old campground. They landed in a clearing in the middle, stirring up a cloud of dust and leaves.

Despite the earlier heat of the day, the moment the doors were opened they could feel the chill of the night air. There was a sudden roar of cicadas and bullfrogs and a smell of pine and leaf mold and human waste from the old latrines nearby. A row of crumbling wooden A-frame cabins was visible in the moonlight, but even though one or two still had their roofs intact, Habib decided they were likely full of snakes and rats. Obama helped him set up one of the tents they'd bought that afternoon. He hadn't been camping since he was a kid in Hawaii and was clumsy and kept dropping things in the dark. When an owl hooted at him, he tripped over the remains of an old sign that said "Injun Creek Campground." Overhead, the waning Moon was brightening. Venus, the evening star, was brilliantly visible below it, and there were stars splashed everywhere across the night sky, a sight Obama had never seen in the city.

After they were done with the tent, they draped the tarps over the airbulance. Xina would sleep inside, since she was too ill to leave it. Kourosh stayed put in the front passenger seat, still fiddling with the coms. They had no other way to disguise the vehicle from the air — the trick with a hologram wouldn't work, because it was a well-known fact that being inside one caused an unpleasant tickling sensation from the electron flow. Besides, it would be too bright for Xina to sleep.

At midnight, after they'd all eaten the last of the OrgasMeals, Kourosh received a transmission from President Manacera. Kourosh called Obama into the cab. "He wants to talk to you," Kourosh said. Tonight, the world president was reduced to a small, grainy talking head on one of the dashboard flat-screens. "The micro-sat can't handle 3D," explained Kourosh. "The signal is super-weak, anyway. It could go out any time."

"Hello Obama!" the president said, with his usual avuncular affection. "I hear you've been having a pretty rough time of it."

"Yes, Mr. President," Obama said. "It wasn't easy getting out of Trenton."

"Well, tomorrow night I'll have you all enjoying the comforts of civilization again. I've uploaded fresh account data into Freedom's iRist — you'll be able to buy gas and food without being traced the rest of the way. I've also reserved a couple of suites for you folks at a Personal Choice Day's Inn outside Amarillo tomorrow night. You should be able to make it there pretty easy from where you are right now. The night after that you'll spend here with me at the Presidential Ranch. I apologize for the trouble we've put you to."

"No problem, sir," said Obama. He felt as if everything he was saying to President Manacera was false or a deliberate evasion. A few weeks ago, he would have felt thrilled and honored to be having this conversation — and proud that the president of the world trusted him. But so much had changed since then to shatter Obama's normal view of things. Now he trusted no one. Except, perhaps, the Pooka.

"Son," Manacera said, "I know you probably have a ton of questions you want to ask me right now. About the aliens, for one thing — how I found out about them in the first place, where they come from, what they really want, and so on and so forth. If I were you, I likely wouldn't have believed a single word of what I told you on that holo message. So while I've got a minute — and I've got your attention — I'd like to tell you a little story and then answer a few of your questions, if I may."

"Of course, Mr. President." Mosquitoes had begun to find them, even inside the airbulance, and Obama slapped at one whining near his ear. Kourosh was listening in, and Xina had gotten up from her gurney and was watching from the jump-seat just behind. Obama assumed Manacera had no secrets from them — or none, at least, that he planned to expose in the course of this conversation.

"I want to tell you how I first came into contact with the alien who calls himself 'Sato'," the president went on. "This would have been in 2025 or so, when I was just about your age. Right after the nuke attack on DC. It happened near Roswell, where I had come to practice. I'd moved there just out of law skool thinking I was quite a hotshot." He chuckled at the memory. "Well, I guess there's nothing like small-town life to cure you of that crazy delusion. Anyhow, I'd decided to run for the state assembly, and I'm on my way back from canvassing in the boonies — some chicken BBQ at Bottomless Lakes — when suddenly I spot something falling out of the sky. So I pull off the highway and go over to have a look.

"Now I know what you're thinking right now. You're thinking, 'OK: Roswell — UFO falling out of the sky — that old coot Uncle Jose is as nutty as a fruitcake.' Don't bother denying it, Obama, because it's what I'd be thinking too if somebody spun me a story like this. Except that it wasn't a UFO. It was one of the very first prototype aircars. I'd seen 'em on satellite TV — that's what we had back then instead of holovision — so I knew what I was looking at. This one was all busted up with smoke billowing out everywhere and this Japanese gentleman slumped over the wheel. So naturally I got him out and drove him into town to the hospital. Only, halfway there, he says to me, 'Jose, I'm fine. I was flying here just to meet you anyway. I'm an alien from outer space, and I'm pretty much indestructible.' So I figure the crash had done something to his head, and I decided I better, you know, humor the old guy. Well, I say 'old' — he must have been about the same age I am now.

"Only, when he kept talking, I realized he wasn't concussed or crazy or anything. Or if he was, then we both were. Because he started telling me stuff about my life no one else could have known. He knew everything about me, even about my parents and their lives down in Mexico and why they'd changed their name when they came to the US. Stuff like that. But the thing that really convinced me was that he had this big cut on his forehead that was bleeding and I'd been trying to mop at with my handkerchief while I drove the car, and as he was telling me all this, the wound just magically healed up all by itself. Right in front of my very eyes. And in the weeks that followed, believe you me, I saw a lot of other things that convinced me beyond any shadow of doubt that he really was an alien being from another galaxy. He said he'd come to Roswell specifically to find me, because he had a special mission that only I could carry out.

"Basically, that mission was to do exactly what I went ahead and did, if you've been following my career at all. First, state senator, then governor, then president of the USA, then world president. I admit I couldn't have done it without his help. But so help me, Obama, I swear to you all I thought he ever wanted was peace on Earth and a tranquil and lawful political progression. I'd have never gotten mixed up with him otherwise. The Moon and the invasion business all came as a big shock to me when I finally found out about them.

"See, what Sato told me was this: he said that his race were like 'space shepherds.' They would come to a planet and gently nudge the most promising species into evolving sentience. He said they'd first come to our planet about 4 million years ago or so, back when we were still basically just apes. Then, inside a very short time, his people had used their superior alien genetic techniques to evolve us into modern humynkind. If they'd left us to our own devices, we'd still be like chimps, he said, because look at how little they'd evolved all this time. I guess that made Sato a kind of god or something — well, not 'the' Creator god, I mean, but at least a sort of godfather to the humyn race.

"So basically, these 'shepherds' were still with us up till about 6,000 years ago and then, through some kind of terrible medical accident or plague, they all lost their humyn bodies and had to be placed in cryogenic cold storage somewhere on the Moon. Which their kind can be revived from, by the way — unlike ours. Something to do with cellular structure. So now Sato was the only one left on the planet, all alone here and separated from the rest of his race. He didn't even know where they were hibernating. Can you imagine what that must feel like, being all alone for 6,000 years? I can't.

"Now, his race can live forever, but in order to function here on earth, they had to be inside some kind of body. And since his human bodies died every 70 years or so, Sato had to constantly be migrating from one to another. He told me there were only two ways of doing this: either he had to invade a womyn's womb during sexual intercourse, fertilize and inhabit the fetus, then come to term normally, be born, grow up, and so on; or else he could be transplanted by a complicated medical operation that basically destroyed the brain of the host humyn. And of course, for millennia, there was no way that could happen, since humyn medicine was just too primitive — though he said that he had been able to train doctors in ancient Egypt to perform the surgery. But generally, he'd had to reincarnate the old-fashioned slow way.

"That's why the alien, as Sato, became a genetics expert. His clinics helped to invent and develop the cloning process, and by the time I'd met up with him, he was already successfully creating clones and perfected humyn stock for migrating into. These were genetically advanced, so that whatever that had wiped them out before couldn't happen again. That's what you are, Obama: one of the perfected host bodies.

"And as soon as I put him in charge of the Moon, Sato must have found his lost companions and started putting them into the new bodies he'd bred for them. How many got transplanted I don't know. There could be dozens. There could be hundreds, even thousands. You could have met some already yourself, Obama — they might have appeared to you as an unusually attractive womyn, for example. Have you met anybody like that lately? Someone who tried to recruit you?"

"No, I don't think so," Obama lied. He'd never been a very good liar. He hoped this didn't show on his face over the tiny dashboard cam — maybe, he thought, the events of the last two weeks were teaching him to do a better job. But would he be able to keep it up when he met Manacera face to face? Behind him, Xina was having a coughing fit.

"What about Simonetta Sato?" the president asked him slyly.

"Oh, right. Well, I didn't know about her at the time. I didn't put two and two together until you told me about her father."

"But you were there at the hospital when Simonetta spoke to you from the body of the gorilla, Priska. I read the UNSS report. Then you contacted her father, Sato, for her — so you must have had some kind of relationship with her."

Is that what all this is really about? wondered Obama. *Simonetta again?* "I thought that was just Temporary Neural Transference Syndrome," Obama told Manacera. "It's a form of game haloing where a dominant personality takes over for a while after there's an accident while two people are gaming. I didn't think for a minute that Priska was really Simonetta. Or that Simonetta was really an alien. I only started thinking that way when you explained everything to me in your hologram the other night."

President Manacera nodded reluctantly. "Makes sense," he said. "So you really have no idea what happened to Simonetta Sato — or where she is now? She could be the key to this whole damn sorry business. If we only could find her."

"I'm sorry, Mr. President, I really don't. Besides, I thought Sato told you there were only two ways an alien could take over a humyn body, surgery or sex. And Simonetta was blown up by a bomb. So there's no way that could have really been her."

"Unless Sato was lying to me," said the world president somberly. "It certainly wouldn't have been for the first time. Or the last. Maybe he's perfected some new technique so that the aliens can now migrate directly into another host if their current body gets killed accidentally — drowned, for instance, or exploded like Simonetta. A third way. Anyway — not your problem, son. Thanks for your time, and I'll be meeting you in person the day after tomorrow. *Vaya con dios,* as we used to say in these parts. That means, 'travel with your own personal god'. Goodnight, amigos!"

As he zipped up his sleeping bag next to Kourosh in the tent, with Habib standing the first watch seated on the roof of the airbulance, it occurred to Obama that President Manacera had employed exactly the same executive trick that Obama was already used to from Norberto Zollto. Manacera had begun by saying he would answer Obama's questions, but instead, the president had done all the talking.

21.

By the time they got to Amarillo, Texas, it was seriously hot. The temperature had climbed into the mid-30s C, and the land beneath Air-40 had a dry dusty look to it, even though global cooling had caused this part of the continent to become greener over the past decades. The city, which had once been the national capital of cattle-slaughtering and packing, had reinvented itself as "RotoCity, North America," due to the spin-drives now manufactured there for the aircar industry. It was also home to the "Cadillac Ranch" and the "World's Biggest Steak Theme Park," which they passed on their way to the Personal Choice Day's Inn just off the terrestrial Intrastate 40 (formerly the historic Route 66).

The neighborhood was called Rich Husbands Estates — a Rick Husband had been an astronaut from Amarillo, and once upon a time the local airport had been named for him, but over the years the proper spelling of his name had become corrupted. When they swipe-checked in, the front entrance hallway greeted them with a merry roaring holographic fireplace and a chiming song:

"Happy Choice Day

Happy Choice Day

May the calendar keep bringing

Personal Choice Days to you ..."

Originally, the motel chain — North America's most popular — had been two: Holiday Inn and Day's Inn. But in compliance with the United Nations Freedom From Religion Act of 2028, the former had been legally forced to drop the word "Holiday" from its name, since it contained the root word "holy." Similarly, "God" had become "my or your personal god," and "Christmas" had become "Xmas." Xmas carols had been carefully altered to comply with the new regulations so that they could be cleared for inoffensive public performance. Naturally, Muslim holy days remained exempted.

The universally-mandated term for all vacation days and former public holidays was now Personal Choice Days, and this became the new hospitality corporation's name after merger.

President Manacera had reserved two suites for them, but Habib insisted they use only one — two, he said, would be impossible to secure or defend in the night. To Obama, however — in spite of the cramped conditions — the suite felt like heaven (or, more properly, his own "personal vision of an afterlife") when it was his turn to take a hot shower. *This is probably a relief to the Pooka, too,* he thought, as he watched her, briefly restored to her original form, sweating in a corner of the sculpted ultrasonic stall. He still hadn't heard a single blamey or reproachful word from her, which automagically made her better company than almost any humyn womyn he'd ever known, except of course, Kim. When he was drying himself off, he discovered a hand towel stuffed into a laundry bag soaked in dark, almost purplish, fresh blood.

When he got out of the bathroom, it was to find the other three glued to the Cartoon News Network. There were holos of tiny black HHS troop carriers in the streets of Manacera City, along with a larger one of the elegant, carved mahogany features of Vice President Terrawati giving a speech.

" — this unprecedented action forced on me and the rest of the Cabinet by the irresponsible and illegal behavior of President Manacera," she was saying. "I wish to take this opportunity to reassure every citizen of this great planet of ours that the suspension is temporary, and that full civil liberties will be restored — including election campaigning — just as soon as the current situation is fully under control."

"That was United Nations Vice President Coco Terrawati, speaking live from Geneva, Switzerland," said Snow White gravely. "To recap the extraordinary events of our top breaking story: early this morning peacekeepers from the Department of Health of Humyn services were forced to take World President Jose Manacera into custody, following shocking revelations by his own Security Services that the president has been secretly plotting violent revolutionary activity with suspected super-terrorist, Joyful Kalinga, also known as Obama Jones." Here holograms of Kalinga and President Manacera appeared, one over each of her shoulders. "This marks the first time that civil liberties have been suspended in the history of the United Nations. At present, President Manacera's exact location is undisclosed, but he is known to be on his way to the North American Federal Administration Area to face impeachment proceedings. A motion for his impeachment has already been made and seconded in the Assembly of People's Tribunes in Geneva and is expected to reach the Senate floor by tomorrow. Meanwhile, 'Killah Kalinga,' as he has come to be known in popular urban culture, has still managed to evade apprehension, though HHS is said to have a reliable lead as to his whereabouts. For more on the story, we go to our own Jiminy Cricket at Rockettefeller Center, New York. Jiminy, is this a coup?"

"*Khara*! We need to get out of here — now!" Habib suddenly shouted. "Quickly, quickly! You — he pointed at Obama. "Take Kourosh on your back again!" Within seconds, Habib and Xina had grabbed their weapons and were bursting out the door to the room in a half-crouching combat stance. The degree of their toughness and training continued to amaze Obama. Kourosh climbed Obama's back, wrapping his arms around his shoulders, and Obama reflexively made stirrups of his arms before following the others out the doorway.

"You've left our rifles behind," Kourosh said. Ahead of him, the other two were hurtling down the hotel hallway, overturning metal trolleys and sending the three Uzbeki and North Korean maids screaming into the laundry room.

"No time," gasped Obama. He heard more screaming behind them. Then he was running, trying to catch up, toward the front entrance hall. The doors slid open for Habib, tried to close, re-opened for Obama, the hotel AI loudly complaining, "We are sorry — there is a problem with your account. Please — " then they were outside into the heat and dazzling sunlight.

A gold Toyotair was parked just in front of the main *porte-cochere*, doors wide open. Its driver, a dark-haired young woman, was helping her small son out of it. Suddenly, she saw Habib and Xina bursting out of the Inn with their weapons and began tugging her child away toward the parking lot. A gunshot rang out; Obama felt an impact like a punch against his kidneys, and Kourosh slumped against him. Kourosh's arms went limp, and he lolled back like a rag doll. Several more shots exploded around them. One chipped a piece of stucco from the column beside Obama's head, and sent it flying against the aircar like a stone.

"Let him go!" screamed Xina. "He's dead, stupid!" Obama let Kourosh slide to the ground. Kourosh hit it hard, and rolled over, his glasses smashed and mouth open. He lay very still. Xina used the open passenger side door as cover and squeezed off a round of return fire at an orange aircar parked near a dumpster, siren lights idling. It had the words "Texas Ranger Careers Counselors" painted in white letters on its side. She hit someone. There was a muffled thump as he fell to the asphalt, and all firing stopped for a moment.

Habib, meanwhile, had reached the young woman and her son and was trying to wrestle both of them toward the car with one arm, using them to shield himself from the Rangers' car. "No, no, please! Let him go!" she was shrieking as she tried to pull away. "Please just let my son go! I'll do anything!" Obama charged Habib from behind, bowling him over, and the woman half-picked up her child and scuttled with incredible speed behind a parked groundcar. Several more shots were fired, and Obama realized that there were at least one or two more of the orange aircars landing around them. Without thinking, he slipped into the driver's seat of the Toyotair.

"You have killed us all now," Xina said bitterly, sitting down beside him. "We can't get away without hostages!" Obama slammed his door shut and started up the aircar's spin-drive engine. Habib had bounced to his feet and was firing rapidly in each direction before diving head-first into the back seat. "You don't even know how to drive this thing." She evidently wasn't going to waste any time mourning her brother's death.

"Pooka," said Obama. "Get us the hell out of here!"

"OK," the Pooka said inside his auditory nerve. She constricted the clothing slightly around his limbs and sent neural-stimulation electrons pulsing directly into his brain's muscular control centers. Suddenly, feeling like a marionette, Obama found his left hand clamped to the center-column spinwheel, while his right grasped the joystick. His right foot descended heavily onto the gas throttle pedal on the floor, and within milliseconds the vehicle was spinning straight up and banking backwards, presenting its under-chassis to the shots aimed at them from the orange Hyundairs, which were rising sluggishly after them with their sirens shrilling.

Sweat instantly sprang from every pore in his body as the Pooka killed all the extraneous electrical systems that were draining engine power, including the air conditioning. The car continued to arc backwards and upside-down until she put it through a series of spins that sent it hurtling back east just above the terrestrial I-40.

In order to deter RPG fire, the aircar hugged the rush-hour ground traffic on the highway at a height of only a half-dozen meters or so, just enough to skip over freeway signs and light posts. If they were shot down, they would fall directly on top of ground commuters. As they raced along, skating up and down at slightly different elevations with manic speed, the Pooka occasionally turned the car completely over along its longitudinal axis. Obama had never flown a car before, but he had played enough racing games onGrid to know that what she was doing was impossible even for the best professional humyn drivers.

Occasionally, Xina and even Habib involuntarily screamed or whooped with fear as the vehicle approached a sign-tower at a dizzying 400 kph, only to squeeze beneath it upside-down a meter or so above a triple-decker tractor-trailer rig. Their orange pursuers, pushed to max speed above them and strung out further from the highway, had been joined by several white vans with military mods: side and bottom gundams with visible rocket-tips. "White Terror Commando," gasped Xina when she could catch her breath. "Now we're really fucked." She lapsed into another coughing fit, and Obama glimpsed blood when she took her sleeve away from her mouth.

"We need a hiding-place. We can never outrun them," Habib said from the back seat. He had fallen back onto it from the ceiling, and was strapping himself in at last. The kid's toys had been flying all over the cabin, banging each of them in the head and piling up against the rear window.

"Hide us," Obama told the Pooka.

She peeled off from I-40 over the Western Plaza Mallplex, hanging them all upside-down again and sending the toys flying. The Toyotair crossed I-27 and skirted the west side of the Tradewind Aerospacedrome. Two of the white vans released rocket-propelled grenades at them at this point, whose microprocessors the Pooka must have reprogrammed. Both curled back to detonate about twenty meters in front of each of the vehicles that had fired them, causing them to slow significantly. It occurred to him that she could have simply made them all explode in their cradles, and he wondered at her restraint. Was she awaiting instructions from him?

The Pooka seemed to have more trouble with stray bullets than she did with RPGs. Several times Obama felt them hit the plexiglass rear of the car, and once he heard a tail-light shatter. When this happened, she increased the nauseating elevator-like movement up and down. They buzzed over a golf course, hugging it so low that their displaced air knocked over a few golf carts, and steeple-chased across the Loop Road. Then they turned due south, still closely pursued. Now they were over green farmland, pocketed with tiny round lakes.

"I thought you said you couldn't fly," said Habib in wonder, as they skittered beneath some ancient utility lines and then briefly below a canopy of tall trees. "Is this Pooka your personal god?" *Maybe in a sense,* thought Obama. It wouldn't hurt for them to believe his instructions to be prayers. An explosion shook the ground beneath them, rocking the Toyotair from side to side. *There isn't really much difference between instruction and prayer at the moment, anyway,* he decided.

A second explosion kicked up a huge cloud of brown dust from a field directly in front of them. When they'd blown through it, Obama saw a dramatic change in the landscape ahead of them, a line of rugged red mesas rising up from the green earth around an enormous jagged gouge. Then they were over a long, narrow dark lake bordered by hundreds of docks and boat-houses and bungalows, skimming so low that they left a wake behind them in the water below. They shot up the ramp of a big green spillway that dammed a small creek and skipped over it into fields filled with scrub trees. Robo-farmed cash crops grew everywhere; before global cooling, this had been dusty and semi-arid steppe.

"Want me to hack their computer systems?" the Pooka asked Obama.

"Please," he said. Two of the orange cars bumped into each other and quickly disappeared from sight.

"Oops," she said. That just left the two white vans far behind them, which obviously had logged off their onboard systems and were now being operated manually.

The Toyotair had left the farmland and was flying over white chalky rock and red clay deposits studded with scrub and sagebrush. They passed over a small agricultural station and followed a winding creek into the mesa. The Pooka turned aside several more missiles and lowered the car to treetop level. They turned south to follow the main river, the Prairie Dog Town Fork, which had originally carved out the Palo Duro Canyon. Once they crossed Route 217, they were into the former national park. Huge, multicolored, eroded rock formations towered above them as they hugged the canyon floor just above the waters of the river, passing through the ruins of campgrounds and ranger stations, now covered in lush vegetation.

They were nearly 100 meters below the crest of the mesa, following the twisting meandering river with dizzying speed as the Pooka squeezed everything she could from the spin-drives. The two airvans were distant specks high above, trailing them like a pair of vultures. The airvans wouldn't dare try to navigate the canyons without their computers — and would have been swiftly left behind even if they had. All they could hope to do now would be to track the Toyotair by eye from a great height.

Suddenly the car turned due west into the setting sun and followed an old mule trail up into the walls of the escarpment. Below, the hot red rocks reflected the sunset like charcoal in a cauldron, the vehicle's long shadow stretching and snapping across them like a slithering black Syntex ghoul. Their pursuers had disappeared from sight. After a few kilometers, the spinner engines began to choke and shudder."Pooka, what's going on?" Obama said. "Were we hit?"

"Nope. We're out of gas. Sorry, Obama," said the Pooka. "Next time steal something with a full tank. See that hole in the rocks just on the other side of the trees? That's a deep cave — you'll be safe in there." She set the aircar down with a bump in a small valley that looked like the Garden of Eden. "I've scrambled their GPS and convinced their computers we're halfway to Lubbock, but they'll probably come back and spot this machine soon. So we'll need to run, OK?"

Obama opened all the doors. "Come on," he said. "We have to get out of here. There's a cave up in those rocks." It lay at the foot of a huge hoodoo that rose up above them like a high castle tower. It was easily the tallest formation in the whole range.

But Xina was coughing again. "You'll have to leave me," she said, cradling her rifle. "I can't walk any more."

Habib shook his head. "Shit," he said in rapid Arabic. "Give me your gun, Xina. You're too weak to even pull the trigger. Stop being an idiot and let the unbeliever carry you up to the cave." To Obama he said, "Carry her. I'll hold them off when they come."

"Hurry," said the Pooka in his ear. "They're coming back."

"OK," Obama said to no one in particular. He picked up Xina like a baby, and instantly the Pooka sent him into the same hyper-motion run that she had the night of the attack at the hospital. He raced along, nearly faster than the eye could follow, through the bushes and trees, across the rocks near the pond, and up the sloping face of the mesa. The cave entrance was nearly halfway up, a height of 40 or 50 meters, but Obama traversed it in seconds.

He paused inside the deep shadow of the cave mouth. In the faint pink light, he could see the last rays of the sun sparkling gold on the distant roof of the car. Xina started coughing again when he put her down on the rocky floor. Her skin was hot and dry to the touch. "I'm thirsty," she said.

"There's nothing to drink," he said.

"You could get me some of the pond water," she said. "It wouldn't matter anyway — I'm dying."

"Don't be so dramatic," he said. She started laughing, but it turned into a retching coughing fit.

"I've been dying for days," she said when she'd finished. "I got shot when we first escaped from the hotel in Trenton. Remember that? Inside the HHS van? The bullet hit a rib and must have nicked my lung." She opened her coat, and he could see the dark blood soaking through her grubby shirt to the side of one breast. "It feels infected to me. I had some opium from the *mujahedeen* that I took for the first two days, and I was taking antibiotics in the airbulance, but now I'm out."

"Why didn't you say anything? We could have taken you to a hospital."

"Because I had an important mission, stupid! I had to get you to the president." Xina snapped and then spat up blood. "And we've failed. Truly, I think it would be too late for me even if you could get me to a hospital now. I just wish I had water." *Kim died without water,* thought Obama. *Xina doesn't deserve my pity.* He heard a distant noise of engines and left the girl's side to look back down at the canyon floor in the gathering twilight. He saw a pair of headlights in the air high above, followed after a few seconds by another. The WTC vans had found them. A searchlight came to life from the first one and started sweeping the ground from side to side until it picked out their car. It looked empty from this distance. Habib must have gone to ground somewhere nearby.

"They've found us," Obama told Xina. She shrugged. Her hardiness was amazing. So was that of Habib. Out there in the dusk, the terrorist was preparing to trade his life for theirs. The lives of an "unbeliever" myn he hated and a dying womyn he probably loved. Xina grabbed at Obama's hand.

"Don't let them take me alive," she said. "Promise me? Kill me first."

"OK, now you really are being dramatic," he told her. "I have no way of killing you." It was ironic, however, that she was now begging him to. Instead of answering, Xina handed him a hunting knife she pulled from her boot. It looked well-used. Suddenly there was a loud explosion outside, one that echoed for 10 or 15 seconds against the distant rock walls and then back again.

"Go see what they did," she commanded him. He absentmindedly put the knife in his pocket.

"Ouch," said the Pooka angrily.

"Sorry," Obama said.

Outside, the canyon walls were lit by the flickering of the burning Toyotair. One of the vans had destroyed it with a rocket, probably to make sure it wasn't booby-trapped. Or to make sure it couldn't be made mobile again. Obama briefly felt a stab of sorrow for the little boy's toys. Then he realized that if he hadn't acted on impulse earlier, the little boy might very well be burning inside it now, too. *Xina and Habib might have many admirable qualities,* he thought, *but they are atavisms, throwbacks to an earlier age. This one holds no place for them. It would be much better off without people like them. Maybe with better educational opportunities and no more Trentons the future will be free of terror and murder. Or maybe not. Maybe humyns are just naturally violent.* The two airvans spent a few more minutes searching the floor of the canyon, then suddenly turned and flew off.

"They were just given orders to stop searching until daylight," said the Pooka. "They don't want any visual confusion. Someone wants you alive."

"Just me?"

"Yes. Just you, Obama. Their instructions are to kill the other two."

"Who's giving them these instructions?"

There was a momentary silence while she digested all the data she had gobbled up. "Interesting," she told him finally. "Colonel Park."

A few minutes later, a flickering light became visible, slowly working its way toward Obama up the rock-strewn incline from the valley. It turned out to be Habib, carrying a couple of flaming tree-branches like torches, both rifles slung across his back. "How is she?" he asked when he was near enough.

"She says she's dying," Obama told him. Habib nodded.

"Yes, I saw the wound this morning — I think she may be right. If she really is dying, then she'll be cold and will need a fire. I lit these from the burning car so we could build one inside here. This looks like it was used as a hearth," he said, pointing out a shallow hollow in the rock to one side of the cave-mouth. It was filled with dead leaves and charred humus. "You should clear it out while I gather more wood from below."

"You think that's wise? Someone might see it."

Habib shook his head. "No, no one else is here except the coyotes. The humyn dogs will wait for daylight to try to take us." He gave Obama a shrewd, calculating look. "They want you alive, I think. If you were wise, you'll leave before dawn. With your strength and your powers, I believe you could escape from them if you wanted to. I've never seen anyone fly a car like that. Now I understand why the president wanted you — I didn't before."

"Thanks," Obama said. "That's good advice." In the flickering light he saw the glint of tiny eyes deeper inside the blackness of the cave. "What are those?" he asked, startled.

"Bats or maybe mice. We should hope for bats, because mice always attract snakes. And bats eat mosquitoes. But both carry rabies." Habib stood over Xina, who was lying curled up on her good side, facing away from the entrance. "How are you feeling, my dear?" he asked her in Arabic.

"Much better," she replied in Enriched. "But I'm thirsty. And horny."

"Don't worry," he told her. On his way out he said to Obama in a low tone, "I'll bring water back for her, too. She needs it. She's burning up with fever again and is delirious." While Obama dug out the hearth with Xina's knife, Habib made several trips, coming back with more wood and several scorched car parts, wheel rims, and caps filled with water, which they set to boil. Habib used the glasspex from the head and tail lights to cool the water for drinking. "Has she made her peace yet with Allah, do you know?" he asked, after Xina had fallen fitfully asleep.

"I don't know," Obama said. "She told me she wasn't religious." The two of them were sitting to one side of the fire just out on the lip of the cave, Habib still cradling one of the assault rifles.

"It's important anyway." He frowned. The night, still warm, was alive with rustling noises, the din of crickets and the occasional distant yipping of coyotes. It smelled of sage, creosote bush and wood smoke. Overhead, the dark satin sky was brilliant with stars, the Moon and the planets even more clearly visible than they had been in Tennessee. *Almost,* thought Obama, *as if I could reach up and grab them.* He wondered which star Siren and Sato had come from. Habib caught his glance.

"Xina and Kourosh are Persians, so they are Shia, but I am Alawi," he said. "From Syria. Do you know anything about my religion? It is like no other sect of Islam. You see those stars above us now in the sky? We Alawi believe they are the souls of all the people who have gone before us."

"That's very beautiful," Obama told him, moved in spite of himself.

"My religion is the oldest in the world, from long before the time of Muhammed, from a time when there were many other names for Allah. We believe that each man lives seven lives on Earth, then he goes to live in the heavens as a star. Women are like dogs, however — they have no souls. The best they can hope for is to be reborn as a man." After a few moments he added softly, "Xina will make a very good man. She is as brave and beautiful as a tiger."

All this bickering and warring over a god, thought Obama, *when the closest thing to a real god humyns have ever had is Shiseki Sato. Or an alien being who calls himself Shiseki Sato. At least if President Manacera is to be believed.* From behind them inside the cave, Xina called something out, and Habib rose and went back to talk to her. When he returned, he said, "She wants to speak with you. We'll need another way out of this place before daylight — while you are talking, I'll go and try to find it." He lit another branch from the fire, then walked back down the rocks into the Moonlit canyon.

"I'm feeling much better," said Xina, when Obama approached her. She was sitting up and holding her gun. "I'm still going to die very soon, however. I can feel it. But there's something I want you to do for me first, Obama. Consider it a last request, OK?" The firelight chiseled the planes of her face into the features of an enigmatic ancient mask; her black eyes glittered with fever.

"OK," Obama said, squatting down in front of her. "But I need to ask you something."

"No, first I want you to make love to me." She started unbuttoning her shirt. To his horror, Obama's first reaction was one of intense arousal. This feeling, however, lasted only an instant.

"Huh? What are you talking about?" he said churlishly, pulling away from her. This was the person who'd helped kill Kim, who'd murdered other innocent victims in cold blood in front of him. Plus she was deathly sick, grubby and unkempt. And clearly — more clearly than ever — psychotic.

"Look," she said piteously. "I'm dying, Obama — get it?" Her chin began to tremble like a little girl's. "All I want before I go is to have something wonderful happen first. I want to feel somebody's arms around me, even if I can't feel anything else. I want to feel beautiful. Please fuck me, is that so much to ask?" Now he felt deluged by other emotions. Disgust, mostly. Hatred, even a faint sense of glee that she was dying. But mixed in with it was something else. Not compassion, exactly. But pity. Xina, he thought, had a fine, sharp mind and a kind of beauty. She'd wasted both, lavished them away on the crazed, violent fantasies of her grandparents that in the end had left her with nothing. *Nothing but a fever and a raging thirst,* he thought. She started coughing. Her body shook with it, became wracked by it. Her breath smelled like an open grave. A thin stream of black blood leaked from her mouth.

Obama took the rifle out of her hand and put it aside. Suddenly she stopped breathing. The color drained from her face, and her eyes bulged from her head as she fought for breath. A loud, hollow gurgling noise rose up from her throat. It sounded like a drain being cleared. "Do something, Pooka!" Obama said in a panic.

"What do you want me to do?"

"I don't know. I need to ask her some questions before she dies." A thin sheath of molecules flowed out of his coat cuffs to encase his right hand, which then grasped Xina's throat tightly. At the same time, the shape of a womyn's head blistered up in the crook of his left elbow, becoming life-sized. The surface of the face swam with liquid plastic, then coalesced into Xina's features. "Hello, Obama," it said, sounding surprised. "Goodbye, Obama."

"Wait! I need you to tell me something! Who really planned the bombing attack on the Federal Courthouse Building?"

"I told you. We all did. Me, Kourosh, Habib, Hijack."

"And that's the truth?" he said.

"I'm not going to lie to you at a time like this," the plastic bubble calmly replied.

"OK, who carried out the plan, then? Who actually went to the building and put the bomb there?"

"Habib and Um Ali." The voice was getting weaker.

"Um Ali?" Obama asked.

"The little iddie girl. Imam Chebli found her for us in Trenton. Habib and I trained her, and she took the bomb inside the HHS building strapped to her waist. Listen, Obama, I need to go now, OK?"

"OK, Xina. Goodbye."

"Do you think they'll be waiting for me?" her voice whispered, no louder than a sigh. Then the plastic face went blank, and the Pooka deflated it. Would who be waiting for her? Obama wondered. Phillip and Kourosh? Or had she meant the ghosts of all her victims?

"What the devil are you doing?" It was Habib, standing in the entrance. He moved swiftly across the cave floor, staring down at Xina. Obama stood up, and Habib jabbed the barrel of his rifle into his chest. "You killed her," he said furiously. "I saw you do it."

Obama lost his temper. He felt it leave him almost physically, replaced by a baleful, icy calm. "No," he said. "I didn't kill her. I wish I had. But now it's your turn, Habib."

"If I shoot you, it will do no good, will it?" Habib said. "The bullets won't harm you?" Incredibly, he seemed unafraid even now, merely analytical. All his emotions seemed to have centered on Xina and their cause. *And most likely his family,* Obama thought. "Well, I have to try anyway. I hope you understand." Habib squeezed the trigger, and a burst of deafening automatic fire blasted against Obama's left nipple. He couldn't decide whether it actually hurt or merely tickled. The bullets bounced around and fell clinking to the floor along with the spent casings, the noise echoing loudly inside the cave like a chiming holo jingle. A flock of bats, disturbed by all the racket, burst from the inside of the cave, making both myn duck and almost bowling them over, before flapping wildly around the fire and disappearing out into the night. Obama took the gun from Habib and pointed it at his forehead. Habib bowed his head and began to recite prayers in Arabic.

"Let me know when you're ready," Obama told him, caressing the trigger with his index finger. "You know why I have to do this, don't you?"

"No, I swear it, I don't."

"You killed my wife in the Federal Courthouse bombing." Habib nodded solemnly at this, as if in agreement.

"*Inshallah,* I didn't know. OK, do what you must do, then — any time is good. I'm at peace with Allah now." Obama tried to squeeze the trigger. Nothing happened. He strained but couldn't move. He could feel the veins swelling out of his temples. His face became bathed in sweat, and he could hear his heart racing, pounding in his chest and ears. He couldn't make himself do it.

"Oh for god's sake!" he said, disgusted with his own impotence. His anger returned in a dizzying rush, and with both hands he bent the barrel of the assault rifle into a "U" before handing it back to Habib. "Go on, get out of here," he said, his voice choking. Habib looked at him wonderingly.

"You can't kill anyone, can you?" he said, shaking his head with withering contempt. "I don't think you're really a man at all. With enemies like you, the aliens will easily take over the Earth. But I suppose that also means you didn't strangle Xina. What were you doing to her?"

"Listening to her last words," said Obama.

"May I ask what they were?" Habib inquired politely.

"She asked if I thought others were waiting for her."

"OK, thanks." Habib sounded disappointed. He squatted down and closed Xina's open eyes, removed her coat, and spread it over her head and upper body like a shroud. Then he muttered a few words of prayer over her before he retrieved her undamaged rifle and checked his iRist. "4:22. The White Commandos will be back here soon, within the hour. *Assalaamu alaikum,* Obama."

Obama said nothing. He gave the mujahedin a fifteen minute start, then followed him down the rock-slope to the canyon. He walked past the pond and the smoldering shell of the aircar and found the mule path. It was just before dawn. Overhead, far beyond the black silhouette of the hoodoo, a pair of stars became brighter, then moved in the sky. Then they turned into a pair of headlights. They came closer. Obama stopped and stood still on the trail. Something dark with a stripe, a skunk perhaps, scuttled across the trail in front of him.

He felt utterly drained, utterly passive. He'd barely slept for the previous four nights, couldn't remember the last time he'd eaten a meal. He'd come to the end of his search, had found those responsible for killing Kim, had had them in his power — yet had still been able to do nothing. *Habib is right,* Obama thought. *I'm not a "real man." What's the use of my continuing to look for Manacera or Sato or anyone else, since I'm too weak and stupid to do anything about them?*

Kalinga would have pulled the trigger. Kalinga could do anything; he'd proven that in Trenton, eating sheep's brains, smoking, threatening Joker Hadjibaeyev. Kalinga would have had sex with a dying womyn without a second thought. *Though perhaps not Xina,* Obama decided. *She was too weird and crazy even for Joyful Kalinga.*

He watched with dull eyes as the aircar lazily drifted over him and started circling before making its descent. Who was in it? he wondered. Colonel Park? Sato? White Commandoes? He had no idea. What did it matter? He was at the end of his quest — and had been found wanting. He could still feel the cold titanium of the trigger against his forefinger. He'd wanted to pull it with all his heart and soul, yet he'd been unable to do it. As for turning Manacera and Sato over to the authorities — the HHS, for instance — well, the idea was ludicrous on many levels. No, he'd had his chance, and he'd blown it. He wouldn't get another.

He idly wondered if the Pooka could protect him from Colonel Park. He knew she could stop bullets — but could she stop an RPG? Or a direct hit by a missile? She must have some limits. He wondered if he could summon the energy to overpower Park, or whoever this was, and hijack his aircar.

The car spun down and landed in the tall grass nearby, scarcely making any noise or stirring up much dust. It was a little pink VW Ladybug with yellow hippie flower decals painted all over it. The passenger door swung open, and the cabin lights came on inside. There was a young womyn sitting alone in the driver's seat. When he came close enough to make out her face, he found that he recognized her. With only the faintest sense of shock he realized that she was Jonessa Qali, the most famous sim star in the planet's history. Looking like a youthful cross between Nefertiti and Brigitte Bardot, she leaned slightly forward in her seat as he approached the open gull-wing door and, exposing most of her molasses-colored breasts and with full pink lips wetly pouting, said, "Need a lift?"

He assumed she and the car were some kind of advertising holo. But what was it doing all the way out here in the middle of nowhere? "OK," he said. *What the hell.*

22.

However, he was wrong. The car wasn't an ad holo. He could feel the heat of the spin-drive engines, smell the fumes from the exhaust. He reached out and touched the fiberglass edge of the door — real, not a hologram. Jonessa Qali looked at him impatiently and drawled in her rich, distinctive, British boarding-skool voice, "Get on board, bozo, we haven't got all night."

Only she couldn't possibly really be Jonessa Qali. For one thing, she was far too young. The real Jonessa Qali had lived in seclusion in Patagonia or someplace saving whales and penguins ever since she'd turned 40. This womyn — girl, really — couldn't be older than 20, if that. For another, encounters like this only took place on the Grid. And this was real life — wasn't it?

The real Jonessa Qali had made her first flattie in 2017 and instantly became an overnight worldwide sensation. Her mother was a famous Falasha fashion model, her father a half-Parsi, half-Portuguese Mumbai multimillionaire. Jonessa had grown up in Goa and Lisbon before being sent to skool in Hertfordshire. She'd run away when she was 16 to live with a soft-porn film director, who'd made her an international star the following year. She'd left him for the co-star of her first mainstream vehicle the year after that, moving to Hollywood to launch a long and successful career.

Qali had been widely considered to be the most beautiful womyn in the world, with the most perfectly feminine body. When holographic dramas had begun to replace the traditional flat-screen films in the early '20's, she'd been one of the few major stars to make the transition, since she had never needed surgeries or body doubles — both having proved to be fatally apparent in the new medium, which resulted in the abrupt ending of a great many show business careers, much as sound had once destroyed those of silent-screen stars.

But the worst had been still ahead for the industry. In an era of worldwide economic stagflation and studio cost-cutting, the next technological advance, that of the Simulated Immersive Media (or "the sim"), had been even more brutal on aging stars.

A sim differed from a holodrama or a flattie — or an onGrid game — in that the subscriber — or sometimes many thousands of them at once — inhabited the onGrid consciousness of a single character. These were cast in a tightly-scripted drama or comedy in which the action was neurally compressed to appear to take place over days, weeks, or in some cases, entire lifetimes — even though only a few hours might pass in objective time. In sims, every detail of the actor's or actress's life was shared, even down to the banal routines of everyday life. Dozens of these simmed characters might intersect inside the same drama, with the subscriber able to choose from a variety of roles; hardcore fans might even try to experience a sim over and over from the consecutive perspective of every single character in it.

Unlike games, however, actions and dialogue in sims could not be altered by the subscriber, only passively experienced. Even so, this reality could become so seductive that people became addicted to particular sims or the actors in them. Often, in fact, popular actors allowed their daily lives to be shared by fans within so-called "reality sims," and there had been legal cases where hardcore fans had actually become violently convinced that they themselves were the real actor or sim character.

This kind of "haloing" was a common after-effect of violent gaming, as well. When the viewer was inside a sim or game, all awareness of their real identity could ebb away, leaving them convinced for some time after they had disconnected that they were still inside the sim or game. Adding to this problem were malicious hacks or "mods" to sims that could hijack subscribers by user command and install in the sim alternative characters, endings, and scenes, usually pornographic.

Such hacks or mods were called "Logic Bombs." Several actors had been successfully sued by studios for participating in sim modding, and the industry participated in a vigorous copyright detection and protection program in partnership with the United Nations Holographic Arts Council and HHS. Some of the stiffest civil sentences under UN law were handed out for "crimedia" violations.

Qali had been by far the most popular sim star in the world during the 2030's. She had combined the artless grace and cruel sensuality of a young girl with the wisdom and droll gravitas of a passionate, vengeful goddess. Every womyn in the world had wanted to be Jonessa Qali. Her youthful beauty became, if anything, softer, more supple, and more alluring with age. Almost all of her sims involved at least one lengthy scene in front of the mirror where she merely put on makeup or washed it off again. And several scenes of her languidly bathing, often in an enormous tub ringed by scented candles and sex-toys.

Even more than her trademark pouting lips, ripe, athletic figure and dark brown skin, Qali's most arresting feature had been her mismatched eyes, one a dark, olive-like brown, the other a startling bright blue. Again, this unusual attribute was, natural, and not the result of retinal surgery or lenses, just as her dark, thick, wiry brown hair had a natural gold highlight that no amount of studio artifice could quite emulate.

Jonessa Qali's face had only one classical imperfection: a deep, masculine dimple in her chin. This feature became so popular that for nearly a decade it was the top cosmetic request of teenage girls altering their appearances by having them "surged."

Unfortunately, Qali's private life was nowhere near so successful. A brief early marriage to a Finnish director had ended in a miscarriage and divorce. A succession of brief affairs with fellow-celebrities of every gender had resulted in a great deal of negative publicity, along with several suicide attempts by jilted lovers — successful in the case of one, the actor, bare-knuckle boxer and Country-Western Swing-Rap artist, Frady Boy Puckett. In addition, an African baby adoption had resulted in an emancipated-minor lawsuit when the child had reached the age of 5.

In 2039, Qali had suffered the first significant flop of her career, followed by a domestic accident requiring surgery. Soon after, she had discovered lines in her face, and, sickened by the sight, abruptly retired from sim-making. Long active in the Aquatic Mammal Emancipation movement, she had become a notorious hermit, living inside a vast tropical AquaBioDome on the brutally cold and windswept Patagonian coast, along with her whales, dolphins, and a devoted staff of Allura robots. From this refuge, in addition to becoming a Zoroastrian fundamentalist, she'd become a leading advocate of the rights of wild animals to be provided natural psychotropic anti-depressants (like Sam-E and MOO-sulfate) as an alternative to the commercial ones animals had increasingly ingested from human waste products in the world's water supplies.

A year before, Obama had seen a few seconds of Qali on YouVee, captured naked and living in the wild inside her 'Dome by a bot-camerazzo after her "Natural Meds for Quadripeds" campaign had kicked off. Her wild mane of hair had been stringy and grey, her breasts and belly sagging, and the famous skin that had once thrilled the world's sim-addicts had become heavily wrinkled. Quite obviously, the young womyn sitting scowling at him in the front seat of the aircar was not the real Jonessa Qali. So who was she?

He sat down tiredly in the passenger seat and swiped the door closed. "There's a terrorist killer somewhere out there in the dark with a high-powered rifle," he told her. "And he's desperate enough to steal this aircar. So we'd better get out of here pretty quickly, miss." Instead of replying, she started laughing so hard that her eyes teared up. She was wearing a sort of Nitinelle memory-cloth version of a traditional skoolgirl's uniform: an open white blouse with a disarranged Syntex tie, knee-socks, and a pleated thermochromic plaid skirt that changed colors whenever you touched or breathed on it. He could also see epithelial thermochromic skin cell tattoos all over her arms, knees, and throat, similar to the ones he wore when he was being Kalinga. His, he realized, were fading away completely now.

"Oh golly, Obama," the girl said, when she'd caught her breath again. "I owe you an apology. I completely forgot you didn't know who I was. The Pooka did, though — and she should have told you."

"Hee hee," his shirt said out loud.

"Siren..?" he asked.

"Like it?" Jonessa Qali — Siren — preened, extending bangled brown arms. "I was in the mood for a change of clothes."

"Why? What made you choose this, um, appearance?"

"White wasn't working for me."

"You can't go anywhere on the planet looking like that," he sensibly pointed out. "You'll get mobbed for autograms whenever you do."

"Well, duh, I guess I better not go anywhere on the planet, then!" Siren said, lifting the Ladybug into a vertical spin. *She even sounds like the young Jonessa,* thought Obama. *Maybe it's in the genes.* He hoped she wouldn't be driving like a teenager, too.

Of course, there had already been successful attempts to illegally clone Jonessa Qali, attempts that had resulted in a number of criminal prosecutions. However, as far as Obama had ever seen on the Tattloid shows, none of the surviving clones had ever possessed even a modicum of Qali's rather modest acting talent. And weirdly, he'd always thought, none had even really looked that much like her, either. Siren, however, did. A convoy of military-looking air vehicles slowly came into sight below them as they continued to ascend. "Sorry I took so long to get here. The operation took longer than I thought."

"What operation?"

"Most of what Manacera's been telling you about us is rubbish, Obama," said Siren with a sigh. "But one part is true, anyway. A surgical operation is required to transfer me from one humyn body into another. It's also true that I can't just crawl inside one and take it over, as Simonetta seems to have done to Priska. If, for example, I was suddenly stranded here on Earth with no helpers, the only way I could survive would be to gestate another body inside my own womb and migrate into it at birth. Or I could train a team of doctors into performing the surgery, as Sato has apparently done. But even that wouldn't actually kill the host body — if I transferred into the body of the real Jonessa Qali, for example, she would experience the intrusion in the same way she would a sim. In other words, she'd experience everything that was going on — including my thoughts — but passively. And if I left her body, she'd go back to being herself again. That seems to be what happened to Sato's last host, the homeless guy you kept running into outside the subway station. Sharing a mind with Sato for a while seems to have driven him crazy."

"But he was way younger than Sato," said Obama.

"Exactly. That means he was a clone. That's what this body is, Obama — just a clone. I grow mine in plastic tanks hanging in my closet. It takes about 4 to 6 weeks. I made this one from a few cells I scraped off a pair of panties I bought at a fan glog.

"And just so your delicate sense of ethics isn't outraged, my clones are 'clean and green.' They have no brains. Well, no parts of the brain that can handle much except autonomic body functions like breathing or heartbeat, anyway. If I don't use my clones, they can never be born. That's just so that I won't do to them what Sato did to his. But Priska was OK. She was back to being herself again once the Princess and I removed Simonetta from her. That's why I was so upset when the UNSS team killed her. I totally wasn't expecting that."

"What did you do with Simonetta?" he asked her. The sky had been lightening with the dawn as they ascended — now the Ladybug's windows darkened again, and he realized they were passing through clouds. "I didn't know an aircar could go this high."

"They can't," said Siren. "This isn't an aircar. And in answer to your question, I'm taking you to see Simonetta now. The bitch won't say a word to me. Maybe she'll talk to you."

He peered out the window. He could see blue-green-greyish swirling mist through the glasspex; then, suddenly, they were rising above the cloud cover. The car had stopped spinning. "If this isn't an aircar, then what is it?"

"The Princess, of course." For the first time he noticed a flattened Barbie face on the Spinwheel column in place of the VW corporate logo. It winked at him.

"You mean you could have turned into an aircar, too, the whole time?" he asked the Pooka.

"Sure," she said.

"Well then, why didn't you?"

She laughed her little tinny laugh again. It vibrated against his stomach. "Because you never asked me to, silly," she said.

It began to feel cold inside the little cabin, and the Princess turned her internal heater on. Obama realized he was getting light-headed from the altitude. It seemed as though everything Siren told him only stirred up more questions than it answered. He felt his head was exploding with fresh ones — but he was having a lot of trouble keeping them straight. *Wait a minute. Something she said about Simonetta.* "So Simonetta can crawl from body to body — but you can't," he slowly said to Siren. "Isn't that what you told me? So, that means ..."

"That means Simonetta is a different sort of alien being than I am," Siren answered with a mocking grin. "Well done, Obama. That's part of the reason she and I aren't communicating too well. Aside from literally hating each other's guts, that is. To be exact, Simonetta is a hybrid, a combination of the humyn race and mine. Sato seems to have created a whole new life-form."

"So there's no alien invasion?"

Siren gave a derisive snort. "As if. No, I'm the only other one of my kind here. The only visitor. I think. Remember when you asked the Pooka how many of us there were here? She said one, right? Well, she was telling you the truth, as she sees it — she and the other helpers don't consider Sato to be a visitor any more. They think he's gone native. That's why they abandoned him here 6,000 Earth-years ago. I suppose I'd better tell you the whole story." She flipped the nose of the

Ladybug straight up as they climbed into the stratosphere, and Obama saw the Earth curving on the distant horizon. Below them, he glimpsed all of West Texas spreading out like a Goggle holomap.

"Of course," she went on reflectively, "for all I know Sato may have created thousands of Simonettas. So maybe there is an invasion going on, sort of. Technically, they wouldn't really be aliens, though, would they? Anyway, that's one of the things I'd like you to find out about from Simonetta. How many of her there are."

"What makes you think she'll tell me anything?"

"Well, for one thing, because she keeps asking after you," Siren said sourly.

"Are we headed into space?" he asked her.

"Yup. But don't too excited, we aren't going far. Not to another star or anything, I mean. You haven't had your shots, haha." He began to feel giddy again before the cabin pressure adjusted.

"So you're a kind of, I dunno, galactic cop? You're here to arrest Sato and take him home?"

"Fuck, no. You've been watching too many old flat-screen films, Obama. Our race doesn't have a government or authority or any organization at all, in fact. I know it's hard for you to understand because you've grown up here on Earth and humyns are so obsessed with their primal pecking orders, but we're not like that. We're all too old. Try to imagine us as a race of, well, hobbyists. Amateur enthusiasts. Observers. Tourists."

"Visitors," suggested the Pooka.

"Visitors really is the best word to describe us," Siren agreed. "Not guests. Just visitors. We don't have any laws, but we do have, well, sensible precautions I guess you could call them. And Sato seems to have broken every one in the book. For one thing, we never allow ourselves to interfere with another species. To be honest, I've only tracked Sato this far out of sheer bloody embarrassment."

The stratocumulus clouds were thinning dramatically, and the world was slowly turning blue as they slowly exited the stratosphere. Obama guessed they were about 60 km from the ground. The car was getting hot again inside. He yawned. "We'll be there in about half an hour," she said. "You could nap if you like." She put her hand on his knee. He still felt very confused by her identity change. Confused and wary. It amounted to a lot more than just a change of clothes — it was even more disorienting, in fact, than a gender-change, which was really no big deal these days. But if the alien had been alluring before as "Siren Gunnarsdottir," there was no question that she was now overpoweringly attractive as "Jonessa Qali," irritating as this new persona was. The cabin was full of the scent of her.

"No, that's OK," he said. "Tell me about Sato."

Sato, Siren told him, was one of the "amateur enthusiasts" she'd mentioned earlier. In fact, as far as personality traits went, enthusiasm seemed to be his most distinctive, particularly since he came from a race of beings that possessed very little.

One of Sato's enthusiasms was what humyns might call astrobiology. He'd arrived on Earth at about the time Manacera had said, 4 or 4.5 million Earth-years before, which had made his sojourn here a lengthy one even for immortal beings, who might live forever but, said Siren, generally had pretty short attention spans. Helpers were another matter. Patience, and an almost boundless craving for amusement, were their most defining characteristics, so that when Sato had arrived, it was Helpers who had done most of the actual work for him. Most of what they had done had involved gathering data and physical samples.

Helpers, however, could not invade living creatures — they had no physical form, but were just electrical energy patterns. Getting inside his subjects was Sato's scientific technique. Over the millennia, he had compiled an enormous number of immersive "vital samples" from his trips down the gravity well into the skins of the wildlife which inhabited the Earth. These samples had been similar to human sim data except that they had covered an animal's entire lifetime. Sato had seen and felt and heard and tasted and smelled everything in the animals' lives exactly as they had, which had been, he had felt, the best type of scientific data-gathering there could be.

He had been particularly addicted to experiencing the life-cycles of certain strains of hominids, coming to know first-hand every aspect of their lives: the migratory hunting and gathering of the extended families, the thrill of violent predation and conflict, the passion of mating, the affection of the family and the joys of motherhood. And because his migration from body to body took place in the womb — alternately his own or his mate's — he had experienced this primitive way of life more thoroughly than any of the so-called super-apes native to it, since he had lived life after life in their company. As one of them.

But somewhere along the line, Sato had grown bored. And instead of losing interest and just drifting off somewhere new, as Siren would have done, he'd become frustrated. He'd been in communication with a few of his fellow-beings who had explored similar hobbies, and from the tone of his messages, it had been clear he felt that several species on the planet, notably those that humyns nowadays termed Australopithecines, had been on the verge of achieving true sentience.

At some point, it seemed that Sato had stopped waiting for random radioactive mutation to bring this evolution about — a process which might have taken eons or never occurred at all — and had begun instead to actively genetically manipulate the creatures. He had been, Siren, guessed, lonely. But so what? Her race, she said, was built for loneliness, it was what they were best at.

They'd even made it into an art form. The oldest existing work of drama in their culture, preserved from the time they had recently emerged from a methane sea and still lived on their home planet, was about a pair of beings, possibly lovers, who were interrupted by the arrival of a third party on their equivalent of a sandy beach. The exquisite nuances of this encounter, the permutations of every possible relationship among the three of them, each possessing their own unique and individual "sex" (if sex could be considered a universal attribute), were explored in bursts of primitive, overwhelming emotion. A bit like humyn opera, in fact. In humyn terms, the production — the alien equivalent of the *Bhagavad-Gita* or the Ring Cycle — had a title which could be translated as something like "The Disturbing Interruption" or "A Vague Feeling of Being Observed." And it went on continuously for several months, though its dramatic action took place only during the course of a single one of the planet's nights. The basic theme of the work was the preferability of infinite loneliness to acute social embarrassment. And if anything could be said to summarize the instinctive philosophy of her race, Siren said, it was that. They were a bit like the British.

Except, it seemed, for Sato. His actions proved he was different, a true maverick. His visits back to his base, which Siren urged Obama to imagine as a sort of Park Ranger Station for the entire planetary system, had become fewer and fewer. When he had returned, it had been only to conduct bio-genetic experiments with the terrified, screaming hominids he'd abducted from the planet. His helpers had become more and more uncomfortable with this, and so he had begun to do the bulk of his work on Earth.

Finally, it appeared from the station's records, Sato had been able to construct the precise sequence of loci he'd needed in order to produce a stable genetic mutation. He had successfully created the immediate ancestors of what would later become known to the humyn world as the hominid fossil AL 288-1, otherwise known as "Lucy."

At that point Sato had been on the planet nearly a million years. His absences from the base station had become longer and longer, and over the next few million years his helpers had begun to drift away. The last one had deserted him around 4,000 BCE, leaving him with no way to get off the planet again or communicate with his fellows. By then, Siren said — according to his helpers — he'd become completely insane. He'd gone native. Worst of all, he'd started to kill, an act long thought no longer possible by any of Sato's race.

Furthermore, in the absence of his helpers, the only way now left for Sato to migrate bodily had been sexually. Gradually, over the centuries, advances in humyn science, many of which he himself most likely had clandestinely instigated, had allowed him to resume his genetic experiments. But this time with a different purpose, Siren believed. Because by now, his loneliness must have been too great to be borne any more, his confusion and loss of identity, after so many reincarnations, profound. Now Sato wanted company. He wanted love. So he'd set out to create a new race, mixing his own DNA with that of humyns. He had set out to create a race of Simonettas.

"It was," said Siren, using terms she most likely had dredged up from what remained of Jonessa Qali's imprinted personality, "as if he'd created the dog, fucked the dog — and then tried to marry the dog."

"Thanks," said Obama. "Speaking as a dog."

"Sorry," she said insincerely.

"Anyway, I prefer to think of Sato the way President Manacera described him, as a 'shepherd.' You know, feeding his flock, protecting his flock, maybe sometimes culling a few of his flock ..."

"Tending his flock by night?" asked Siren, smirking.

"OK, OK. It's just really weird to imagine that, all along, the Judeo-Christian god has really been just an alien mad scientist experimenting on us."

"Look, bozo, get serious!" she snapped. "Sato isn't a god. He's not even that great of a scientist. He didn't create the stars or the planets or even a single blade of grass on them."

"No," said Obama. "But apparently he created me." That shut her up. He was starting to miss the old Siren. At least she'd never called him "bozo."

The solar system's "Park Ranger Station" was inside Phobos, the larger and closer of Mars's two Moons. Once they had cleared the Earth's mesosphere, it was nearly pitch-black outside their windows, windows which now seemed to Obama to be extremely frail. It was at that point the Princess began to pick up speed. Helper starships, Siren explained, contained antimatter scooped up from collapsed stars, and were capable of what she called "zero light-speed," which meant that they could travel between galaxies in a matter of minutes and between stars nearly instantaneously. The Princess and the Pooka, however, were much smaller, because they had downsized for local traffic — they could only reach "half-light," which, Siren explained, was just a general term. In reality, it only amounted to about 2 per cent of zero-light. But it was still fast enough to get them to Phobos before she'd even finished her explanation. It hung in front of them now like a charcoal cinder against the giant orange-red billiard ball of Mars.

As they approached the planet Siren asked him, "When you were a kid wasn't there a fad for fake gray plastic rocks that people left near their front doors with an extra set of keys inside them?"

"Well, actually my mom didn't believe in locking anything. And most of my friends had electronic door-locks," said Obama.

"OK, I guess I'm mixing up my Earth history then," she said. "Whatever. Think of Phobos as a fake rock. With the keys to Earth hidden inside." Up close, Phobos did indeed look like a fake rock, a small 26.8 × 22.4 × 18.4 kilometer asteroidal object in the shape of a pockmarked cigar stub. It had first been briefly explored by the (all unmanned) Soviet probe Phobos 2 in 1989, the Russian Phobos-Grunt in 2010, then by the Japanese Gulliver 1 in 2019 and Gulliver 2 in 2036. None of these had found evidence of underground ice, but had established that Phobos was a Mohr-Coulomb body, or galactic rubble-pile, filled with caverns. A small surface station had been left behind by the last mission as a springboard for a future manned landing on Mars itself. Which, of course, had never taken place.

The tip of the cigar was the huge, hollowed-out Stickney Crater, which was surrounded by the streaks and grooves of impact eruptions and ejecta from Mars itself. Many of these streaks glimmered like snail trails. This was the tip of the cigar. The Princess ducked down into it, and they were plunged into darkness.

Her headlights came on. At the floor of the crater they passed through what appeared to be volcanic ash-colored rock straight into a long, twisting umbilical tunnel which deposited them inside a vast cavern. The walls, ceilings, and floors, covered with gently waving, luminous extra-terrestrial fungi and carboniferous mono-cellular crystal colonies, looked to Obama a little like the floor of the living-reef swimming pool in Trenton.

The light was heavy on the ultraviolet. Inside the cab of the aircar, their teeth and eye-whites and the nylon threads in Siren's Nitinelle fabric glowed like LEDs. "A third helper named Laputa inhabits this station," she said. "'Laputa' means 'the Prostitute' in Spanish. We're inside her now."

"Hi, Obama," Laputa said from a dashboard speaker. She sounded cross. The Princess landed on a sort of elevated pad in front of a sort of landing bay with an arched entrance. She popped open her doors and air from the outside rushed in, warm and gelid, smelling of ozone, ouzo, and burning oolite. It reminded him a little of Hawaii. If Hawaii had been dark, underground, and in orbit around the planet Mars.

"Are all the Helpers female?" he asked as they got out, and his shirt laughed again.

"The Helpers have no gender," Siren said, walking briskly into the landing bay. She was wearing brown patent leather skool shoes that clacked noisily on the polished stone floor and echoed from the walls. "Sato just preferred to feminize them while they were working together. Besides, 'it' sounds so lifeless and ugly in Enriched. I mean, would you want to be an 'it?'" Behind them, the Princess dissolved from Ladybug form into that of a nude, anatomically incorrect life-sized Barbie doll, and followed them inside.

"And the Pooka and the Princess and the Pros — Laputa — were the ones who were here with Sato? I mean, before he went crazy — millions of years ago?"

"Sure," she said, and abruptly came to a stop. She turned around and faced him, and he realized that the circle around them had become a sort of ascensor that propelled them instantly to another level of the station. Though whether up or down he had no idea. "Well, the Pooka and Laputa were, anyway. The Princess has always been with me. It was the two of them who found me and nagged me into coming here in the first place. They were pretty pissed off at him."

"So you're an astrobiologist like Sato?" he asked her.

"No fuckin' way." Siren laughed. "Actually, I hate science. My specialty is drama. Which humyns really are awfully good at." Now they were inside a vast room that reminded him of the main hall of the beneath-the-ice Swedish International Arboretum, which he'd visited on his honeymoon. It was defined on three sides by translucent amber smart-walls glowing in places with tiny lights, through which other layers of wall could be glimpsed. One of these contained a wide, darkened doorway. Overhead, bright, greenish light filtered down through strata of white marbleized ceiling, as if deflected from far above by skylights through thick crystal. Objects which might be rocks or plants or, conceivably, furniture were contained inside elevated ledges carpeted with white volcanic oolite that ran along two of the walls.

The third wall was simply a window onto Mars itself, big and brilliantly visible now against the black backdrop of space. A bright light off to one side was, Obama assumed, its second Moon, Deimos. *Deimos,* he knew, meant "dread" in ancient Greek. *Phobos* meant "fear."

"Simonetta's in there." Siren pointed at the open doorway. "I'm not going in with you. I really can't stand being anywhere near her, and believe me, the feeling is mutual. She'll stay much calmer if you go in there alone and try to talk to her. Just don't — I don't know, don't let her think you'll help her escape or get her too excited or anything, OK? To be honest, she scares the shit out of me."

"She scares you?"repeated Obama stupidly. He felt exhausted. "Why?"

Siren slumped slightly and suddenly looked like a forlorn skoolgirl standing alone in the middle of a darkened, empty museum. "She's just so new and different from us. And strange. I guess what I'm trying to say is, I find her primitive and predatory and amoral. To be perfectly honest, I'm always a little frightened she's going to burst out of there and then burrow into me through my mouth or anus or vagina or however it was she got into Priska. You'll understand what I mean, maybe, when you see her. She's sort of terrifying." *Great,* thought Obama. *Because my day just wasn't scary or dramatic enough...*

"What do you want me to say to her?"

"Oh, I don't know — I can't think straight on the subject anymore." She sounded cross and petulant. *Hijacking the body of an 18-year-old has obviously been a mistake on her part,* thought Obama. *She should have gone for somebody stable and middle-aged. And smart.*

"Pretend it's like a date or something. Get her to talk about herself. Ideally, what we'd like to know is where Sato is and what his plans are. And of course," she added, "There's the jackpot question."

"Which is?"

"Which is," Siren reminded him, "'Exactly how many Simonettas are there out there?' Come on, Obama, get with it — this is important!"

The room was dark, the tiny lights embedded in the walls glowing very faintly like stars or strings of Xmas lights. A huge columnar tank in the form of an elongated cube, looking a bit like an aquarium, extended up to the ceiling from its base, a slab of polished black rock as high as Obama's waist. The tank was filled with a murky, organic liquid that appeared alternately blueish and brownish in the dim radiant lighting, rather like Qali's eyes. It reminded him of amniotic fluid.

In the middle of this murk floated a thing that looked a little like a cross between a jellyfish, a small squid, and a human brain trailing its ganglia. It was a translucent reddish-pink capped with reflective silver; darker browns and blacks pulsed like lights through ephemeral conduits resembling arteries and veins, changing location constantly like violent electrical lightning strikes. The creature had no distinguishing features aside from its ganglion-like tentacles: no eyes, no ear-holes, no gills or mouth or visible internal organs. It was about the size of an over-ripe medium-sized grapefruit.

"Simonetta?" he said tentatively.

The grapefruit's reaction was instantaneous. It immediately splayed itself against the transparent wall, tentacles spread, and remained there quivering, as if glued. The wall, Obama noticed, which he'd assumed to be glasspex, seemed to have no thickness, as if it had been spun from 2-dimensional molecules. Remembering what Siren had just said, this notion made him distinctly uneasy. "Is that you, Obama?" The voice was that of the Prostitute, translating and retransmitting vibrations from inside the tank. "I can't see anything. I don't even know where I am. You've got to help me!" There was a suggestion of a fluttering membrane that struck Obama as faintly vulvular in the middle of the pink, porous skin plastered against the window.

"Is that you, Simonetta?" he asked, feeling nauseated. He forced himself to stay standing there in front of her.

"Well, duh, who do you think it is? Am I still in the hospital, Obama? Is Daddy here? I can't feel anything, just wetness."

"What — what do you remember about being in the hospital?" he asked her. Waves of pain washed over him, as if Simonetta were broadcasting her own emotions directly into his body. "What's the last thing you remember?"

"I don't know. An explosion?"

"Do you remember being inside Priska?" He was gasping now, almost doubled over with muscle cramps.

"Ewww, gross. What are you talking about, Obama? Please stop bullshitting and help me! I need to get out of here."

He found himself beside her tank. He closed his eyes and put his forehead against it — it felt cool to the touch. "You're the one who's doing all the bull-shitting, Simonetta," he told her. "You know what happened. The explosion destroyed your body and you escaped into Priska's. Now you've been taken out of Priska and put into a tank. So stop lying to me."

"OK." Her tone had changed somehow. He opened his eyes and pulled away. She was still only centimeters away from him. "So you know all about us. Did Daddy tell you?"

"No."

"Wow, I kept telling him you were smarter than he thought. Maybe that's why I wanted you so much. And that's why he kept trying to kill you — because I love you, I mean. But I protected you, Obama," Simonetta said hurriedly. "I saved you from Park and Malek. And Daddy wanted to freeze you on the Moon — that's why I showed up on the shuttle. To save you. You have to believe me." He cast his mind back for a moment. Had Sato tried to kill him? He remembered the marksman on the hospital landing pad, the impact of the bullet. Someone had given him orders to kill. And Park and Malek had had orders to break him — they probably would never have let him go if the biometric info on him hadn't differed from that of Kalinga.

"I still don't understand," he said. "Sato was trying to kill me because you thought you loved me?"

"I didn't think I loved you — I did love you. I still do, even if you are being so weird and mean to me right now. I had to disobey him just to track you down in the first place. He didn't want me to."

"But why?" he asked her. "Why did you track me down?"

"I thought you said you knew everything," she said, sounding puzzled and annoyed. "Because we were created to be together, that's why. To mate and have babies. Because we're twins! Daddy made us compatible with each other so we could reproduce someday. You're exactly the same as me, Obama."

The moment she said it, he realized it must be true. He felt the conviction deep in his gut, as if he and Simonetta had always been linked together there somehow since the minute they were born. *"Telepathically" or whatever,* he thought. *Linked in some way.* He'd heard that twins sometimes were. But he couldn't stand to look at her any more. Was that how he, Obama, really looked? Exactly the same as Simonetta? Were they identical twins — or were there minor differences? He didn't want to know. He was an alien, too — the horror of that reality was enough. He turned and stumbled toward the door.

"Only, Daddy got jealous," she whispered somewhere in the murk behind him.

23.

Siren was still standing exactly where he'd left her in the main hall, looking even more miserable, if possible. "I'm sorry, Obama," she said the moment she saw his face. "I mean, that you had to find out like this. I kept meaning to tell you."

"I feel sick to my stomach."

"OK, I'll show you to your room. You can lie down and have a rest." She took his hand. Surprisingly, hers felt coolly comforting. "It's not so terrible being who and what you are, you know," she said as they sank — or maybe rose — through the floor. "There are benefits." She led him down a darkened hallway. "And by the way, just for the record — I don't doubt that she loves you in her own special way, but it wasn't Simonetta who saved you from Park and Malek, actually. It was me. I faked Kalinga's biometrics so that they had to release you." He stopped.

"You mean you've known all along I was, you know, an alien like Simonetta? And like you, I guess."

"Yes and no," she said. "Yes, I had my suspicions right from the start, but I was only sure after I spent some time with you. I could sort of feel you in there. And yes, you're like Simonetta, superficially anyway. But no, you aren't exactly like me."

"Well, what do you look like, then?" Was he imagining it, or had her dark brown face turned slightly scarlet? Siren hesitated for a moment, then waved at the wall.

"Laputa will project an image of what I look like for you. Think of it as a sort of CAT-scan." A life-like hologram suddenly filled the wall, a tank filled with the same fluid that surrounded Simonetta. In it swam a different kind of creature altogether: smaller, paler, softer, more transparent and filled with light. Filled with something else, too, that he sensed rather than could define intellectually. Intelligence, maybe? Joy? Compassion? These were just impressions, things he couldn't put into words, and for the first time he became aware of the vast, almost infinite number of things he had yet to learn.

"Wow," he said involuntarily. "Is that really you? I wish I looked like that."

Siren hung her head like an embarrassed child. "It's just an identity-sac. Eventually we'll evolve into beings like the Helpers, probably, with no physical bodies at all. You and Simonetta are a few billion billion years younger than I am, so don't be too hard on yourself." She touched the wall again, and suddenly they were both standing inside a Ritz-Hilton hotel luxury suite. It looked sort of like the fake room he'd stayed in on the virtual Moon, only much larger. There was a change of clothes on the enormous emperor-sized bed, a pair of baby-blue Softrete pajamas, fluffy white socks, and dark blue tartan bedroom slippers on the Axminster carpet beneath.

"I can make a nicer room for you if you like, Obama," said the Prostitute's voice eagerly. "I'm only allowed to see Earth from YouVee transmissions, but I could create a new environment for you based on any of your favorite shows. There's only a 3-minute time delay." A Cartoon Network News holo flickered to life at the foot of the bed, an ad for a Medically-Assisted Surcease of Suffering, or MASS, suicide clinic. These had fallen on hard times recently because of the Lunar Retirement program. Obama swiped it off again.

"Thanks," he told her. "This is great."

"Can I change into something else now?" interrupted the Pooka abrasively. "I'm so tired of being these clothes." Obama could see why Sato had begun to think of the Helpers as feminine. When they were around each other, they were like Siamese cats, whiny and competitive.

"Sure."

She melted off him and reformed herself in what he thought of as her "big Pooka" shape, leaving him wearing only his boxer shorts. "You stink, amigo," she said, wrinkling her plastic nose.

"The bathroom's over here," said Siren. "Why don't you get cleaned up and take a nap? Then we'll have some breakfast together whenever you're feeling better."

"That might take a while," he told her. "I have a lot of other stuff to digest first. What do you plan to do with Simonetta, exactly?" Now he just felt numb. He was an alien. He felt as he had right after Kim had died — every time he was distracted for 15 seconds or so, the new reality would re-descend on him with twice the weight of misery as before: Kim would still be dead. And from now on, no matter what else he thought about, he would still be an alien. He would always look like that thing in the tank. Always and forever.

"I don't know what else to do with her," Siren said unhappily. "I guess I'll just keep her here for now. I really can't just let her go. She's not like you in at least one key way, Obama — like her father, she's able to kill. She was happy enough to send people off to the Moon for years before you came along. Or to send Park and Malek along to deal with them. You may think she's just a spoiled daddy's girl, but to me she's ..."

"She's what?"

"A monster," Siren mumbled. She sounded ashamed of herself.

"I'm just like her," he said.

Siren's furious reaction surprised him. "No, you're not!" she hissed. "Don't you dare say that! You had every reason to kill Habib in the cave — but when it came to actually doing it, you couldn't. Simonetta or Sato would have pulled the trigger. They'd have enjoyed it. You're not like them — you're one of us! Look, I'm really sorry I had to put you through all that. I wanted to jump in and rescue you over and over again. But I had to find out what you'd do in that situation, Obama. I had to be sure of you."

"So everything I've been through was basically just one big test?"

"In some ways, yes." She kissed him on the cheek. "And you passed. Listen, Obama, there's something else I'll tell you. I don't have to, but I will." She handed him a towel. "That's the first time I've ever revealed my, you know, real physical self to anyone. Ever. For our race that's sort of like a humyn woman showing herself naked to a man, only it's a way, way bigger deal." Her face was on fire again, and she couldn't meet his eyes. Her voice was pleading. "Like a million times bigger. It must mean I really, really trust you, OK? So can we cut all the 'monster' crap? Does it actually matter what we look like?"

Which was pretty funny, he thought in the shower later, coming from someone who'd just stolen Jonessa Qali's body. He actually laughed out loud, until he remembered he was an alien and got depressed again.

What was he expected to do, anyway, now that he was an alien? What would his new life be like? Would he spend eternity as some kind of parasite, hopping from body to body, unable to experience anything unless he was wearing a humyn or some other, even more disgusting alien form, like a suit of clothes? And what was the alternative? Being stuck inside a tank like Simonetta certainly didn't look like much fun. *Obviously,* thought Obama, *I need to know exactly what my options are. I need alien careers counseling.*

Once in bed, he found he couldn't sleep. One of his walls shared the same window view of Mars as the one in the main hall, and it occurred to him that he could fly down to the planet's surface now, if he wanted, even walk around it inside the Pooka. He could be an interstellar tourist from now on, maybe even a "visitor" to other star systems like Siren. But that kind of loneliness held no appeal for him — maybe that was one of the differences created by his humyn side. The planet shone too bright in his eyes, filling the darkened room with a russet glow, until he asked the Prostitute to black it out. Did aliens really even need sleep? He had no idea. "Take a nap," Siren had said. All he seemed to do lately was what Siren told him to. *How am I going to explain all this to Mom?* he wondered, right before he fell asleep.

When he woke up, he was ravenous. The Pooka beamed at him benignly from his bedside table. It was almost like being back home again — except now the time on her tummy clock made absolutely no sense to him.

"What do you — we — I — eat now?" he asked Siren over breakfast or lunch or maybe midnight supper. It was impossible to tell. They were inside a sort of cafeteria near the main hall, seated in a pair of floating round chairs that were like soft half-bubbles. Between them was a round table of polished white rock with a wine-glass stem base, covered with what looked like real food from a real Parisian restaurant. The window provided a glorious view of the sun, a blazing pin-prick in the far distance, against a sprawling starscape.

"What do I eat?" said Siren. "This, preferably. As long as I'm in this body, anyway. I admit it tastes a lot better in Paris, though maybe that's just me. OK, OK, I know what you mean. We can survive on anything, Obama. Hydrogen atoms. Silicates. Methane. Any kind of chemical garbage. But as long as you keep amusing them, your Helper will stay with you forever — and they're wonderful cooks. Try the asparagus Bearnaise." She sinuously leaned forward to serve his plate, her soft brown breasts moving beneath her pink pajama top, and Obama imagined how he would have felt at 14 if he'd been fed by Jonessa Qali in her PJs. In fact, he'd had several sex fantasies that had started out pretty much exactly like this. *But this is just as phony as any adolescent fantasy,* he reminded himself, *little more real than Sato's Moon colony. We aren't really eating in a restaurant at all. Phobos Station is just a plastic shell animated by an electrical energy field, and Jonessa Qali is an alien squid. And so am I.*

The asparagus, however, seemed real enough. Though he was more in the mood for the quiche Lorraine and warm raisin bread. And the fresh chocolate — the former France had a UNECASE exception to the legal ban on the substance. "So what do we do now?" he asked her between mouthfuls.

"What do you want to do?" she said, sucking on an asparagus tip.

"I want to turn the clock back," he said. "I don't suppose the Helpers are time machines, too?"

"I wish!" she said. "I'm afraid that's another Earthling flattie fiction. There's no such thing as time travel. Other races have blown up their star systems attempting it. What's your second choice?"

"I guess ... stopping Sato." She nodded approvingly.

"That won't be so easy," she said, "considering that neither of us can actually kill anybody. It might be a little like fighting tanks with flowers. But maybe you'd feel better about yourself if we tried. You're awfully attached to Earth, Obama. However confused and freaked out you may feel about things right now, it is your home, and you'd be crazy to give up on it just because you've discovered some of your internal organs don't look quite the way you thought they did. Because that's all it really amounts to, you know — try to think of your alien self as just some new organ you didn't know you had. Like a really disgusting-looking pancreas or something. One that never showed up on a scan before."

It was sensible advice, and along with the meal, made him feel a little better. "What about the changing bodies part?" he asked her. "And the living forever?"

She shrugged. "Cross those bridges when you get to them."

"And I was wondering earlier — do we sleep? I mean when we aren't inside humyn — or other — bodies?"

"Do we sleep? Do we sleep? Amigo, we can sleep for centuries. Millennia. Eons," said Siren. "In fact, I do wish darling Simonetta would shut up and fall asleep right now. She's been howling away non-stop ever since we got here."

"Really?" he said dubiously. "I can't hear anything."

She nodded. 'It's not audible. I'm sure you're aware of it some level, though — it may be partly why you're so upset. For me, it's the equivalent of listening to a humyn baby screaming all night. It's driving me bonkers. Any more questions?"

"OK." He indicated the starry sky outside. "Which of those do we come from? Originally, I mean." She put down her fork and squinted.

"Well, none of them, actually," she said. "We're from another galaxy that isn't visible from here." She pointed. "It's somewhere on the far side of the Horsehead Nebula over there. A really long way away. I wouldn't recommend that you try to swim there." She bit into a lemon tart. "Although, I suppose, if we both started now, we could make it in a few trillion trillion years. That's actually a pretty romantic idea."

"I'm sure our ancestors must have written an opera about it," he said, and she spattered her tart all over the table.

"Golly, Obama," she said when she stopped choking, "That's the cutest thing you've ever said to me! Almost witty, even! Even a totally alien way, I mean."

"Look," he said irritably. "I know I'm just a baby to you. I know I'm primitive and ugly and telepathically disadvantaged. But I would really appreciate it if you didn't patronize me."

To his astonishment, Siren looked like he'd just slapped her. She seemed almost like a different woman now she wasn't Icelandic-Afrikaaner or whatever any more. "I wasn't patronizing you!" she protested. "OK. To be perfectly honest, Obama — it wasn't just the cutest thing you've ever said to me, it was also the cutest thing that anyone's ever said me, all right? I haven't had many 'relationships,' I guess you'd call them. In fact, this is actually the first time I've ever been this physically close to another member of my species. In the same room, or whatever."

"But you're billions of years old," Obama blurted.

"Thanks for reminding me. As if I wasn't feeling fucking old enough."

After that, he didn't see Siren all the next day, or for whatever passed for a day on Phobos, which appeared to orbit Mars several times during the course of the Martian day. When he asked the Pooka if Siren had left the station, she said, "No, she's just avoiding you."

"Huh? She's avoiding me? Why?"

"I guess because you pissed her off, Obama," answered the Pooka. She sounded amused. Apparently even aliens from distant galaxies could still have lousy luck with dating. Who knew? Obama felt guilty for having brought the subject up, so he penitently spent part of the morning or afternoon or whatever it was trying to dig more information out of Simonetta. It was horrifying; there was really no other word to describe it. Every time he got anywhere near her, even in the same part of the station, he got depressed and nauseated — and if he spent too much time with her in the "tank room," he started feeling outright suicidal. It reminded him a bit of his relationship with his first girlfriend in college. He'd spent most of junior year trying to talk her into allowing him to break up with her.

In some ways it was easier doing this with Simonetta than it had been with his girlfriend because Simonetta was at least stuck inside a tank. Even so, she was still pretty scary, especially when she hurled herself against its walls at him. She seemed to only have two moods: clingy and pleading, when she told Obama that they were the only two of "Daddy's children left" and so had to mate for the survival of their race; and panicky and ferocious, when she demanded that he let her out or else Daddy would arrive someday with an army of "his other children" and rescue her.

Sometimes it seemed to Obama that he was even beginning to be able to hear her psychic screams himself, but he decided this might just be the power of suggestion. Whenever he was safely away from her and able to recover enough to be halfway objective, what he found most depressing of all was how little either of them — he or Simonetta — knew about anything. It wasn't just their alien heritage they were ignorant about; neither of them had been very well-educated even by Earth standards. He had a BA from a commuter state university and a useless, two-year MA in Social Studies from NYU that had qualified him to be a mid-level bureaucrat for life at a UN agency. Simonetta had a BA (he thought) from some ski party college and had then gone to work for a spy agency.

He knew that she had been a viciously clever, shrewd, and manipulative operative at MAD, but talking to her on an intellectual plane was like spending an evening on a blind date with someone who could barely speak Enriched and had never read a book in their life. Sato hadn't tutored either of them for the kind of romantic destiny that Simonetta kept imagining for them and their children — and what those children would be like, Obama didn't even want to imagine. In fact, aside from spoiling Simonetta and keeping her in a childish, dependent state like a pet, Sato seemed to have preferred her to just stay ignorant and stupid. Several times Obama wondered from some of the things she let slip if her relationship with "Daddy" was or had been a sexual one — but he really didn't want to go there. He was having enough trouble keeping his meals down when he was anywhere around her.

As far as bargaining for information with her was concerned, his worst problem was that he really had nothing to offer. He couldn't let her go; he couldn't even lie to her and pretend he could let her out of the tank, because Siren, for whatever reasons of her own, had strictly forbidden it. He couldn't bribe Simonetta with food or clothes or access to YouVee; she had no senses.

The only thing she wanted was a body. Siren probably had some extras gestating in a closet somewhere, but she wasn't about to give any of them away to Simonetta. Considering Simonetta's violent nature, as well as her talent for hijacking other people's bodies, that would be like handing a humyn prisoner a loaded TOW missile system. A talent he, Obama, must share, come to think of it. He idly wondered what it would feel like physically to do something like that. Horrible and disgusting, probably, like everything else connected with alienness. He hoped he'd never have to find out.

It was incredible that Sato had survived all those thousands of years without that ability, instead having to hope that each fresh body he was born into was naturally fertile and would survive at least until adolescence. For him, it must have been like a high-wire act with no safety net.

Obama asked the Pooka what would have happened to Sato if he'd ever failed to reproduce and reincarnate. "He'd have had to wait until his host body died and then was either burned or decomposed. Then he could have crawled off in search of some body of water to hibernate in. Then he'd have just had to wait until another visitor came along. Or until one of us helpers found him. Or until the Earth was consumed by the sun and he was able to float off into space." *No wonder Sato went crazy,* Obama thought. *That could be my fate, too, so far away from Earth, if an accident should happen to suddenly wipe out Siren and her helpers. It might be Simonetta's, too, now, since she's both immortal and impossible to let loose again on the general public.* When he realized this, he felt pity for her for the very first time. *Surely it might be possible to rehabilitate her somehow,* he thought.

The next time he saw her, he gave it a try. "Don't you ever feel any remorse for killing people?" he asked her.

"What people?" she wanted to know.

"You know, helping Sato send all those poor people to the Moon?"

"Well, you just said yourself they were poor. And old. They couldn't afford to live on Earth any more — they were just a drain on the planet's resources," said Simonetta. "Besides, we never actually killed them, we just froze them and stacked them up underground. They might be revived later."

"But that doesn't work. It never will."

"We don't know that. It might work someday. At least we didn't saw off their heads, like they used to do in the olden days. Come on, Obama, this is boring," she said in the plaintive tone that, even through the medium of the Prostitute's voice, he was coming to recognize heralded a tantrum. "Let's talk about us."

"But, Simonetta, there is no us," he said wearily. "We've been over this over and over."

"But why?"

This time he lost his patience. "Because I've met someone else!" he snapped. He briefly had time to wonder if this were true before the sheer psychic blast of Simonetta's fury physically knocked him backwards a few steps. This time, he could definitely hear her howling, somewhere deep in his gut. It was then that it first occurred to him that by metaphorically throwing him into a shark tank with Simonetta Siren might be training him, as she would a small child, in telepathy. Because he'd definitely just heard his first word in "alien."

There were no days and nights on Phobos, but the Prostitute observed a cycle of alternating 12-hour brighter and dimmer lighting periods inside the station. After a lonely supper of leftovers inside the cavernous, deserted cafeteria, he was watching the news in bed when there was a knock on the door. It was Siren. She was wearing misbuttoned canary-yellow Softrete pajamas with animated circus animals on them and was carrying the Princess in the crook of her arm like a Teddy Bear. Her wiry hair was freshly combed and pulled back by a plastic headband. "Can I come in?" she said. "I'm bored." *This is as close to an apology as I'll get,* he guessed.

"Sure," he said. "Did you bring popcorn?"

She brightened. "What a great idea. Is that what you usually do at bedtime?"

"Oh yes, every night," he lied. The Pooka obligingly turned herself into a popcorn popper, and he and Siren propped themselves up with pillows in the middle of his emperor-sized bed, which was the size of a small barge, while the Pooka popped the popcorn and they ate it. The scale of the room, as well as their eating loudly with sticky fingers and spilling kernels all over the place, made them look like a pair of bad little children, he thought.

"Incidentally, there are two things I need to discuss with you," he said to Siren. "First, I think we should give Simonetta some kind of neural-net, so she can go on-Grid on Earth while she's stuck in the tank. As long as she's this confined, she's going to keep on acting insane. Plus, it would be humane, or whatever the alien equivalent of that is, to give her some kind of distraction. She can't do any real harm — she doesn't even know where she is or what's happened to her. In fact, she still doesn't even know who you are. And if we set the Prostitute to spy on Simonetta while she's on the Grid, Simonetta might even lead us straight to Sato and we could overhear what they say to each other. Of course, we'd have to spoof our source signal here."

Siren nodded gravely. "What about the 6-minute transmission lag?"

"Six? I thought it was three. Oh yeah, duh — there and back again. Hmmm," he said chewing. "This needs caramel topping and peanuts next time we do it. If we put 'Stim in her tank time will compress itself, and she might not even notice the lag."

She stared at him. "Very devious. I'm starting to see the resemblance to your father for the first time. Joke!" she added quickly, catching sight of the expression on his face.

"Sorry, I just spent most of the day with her. Well, in 15-minute bursts, which is about all anybody could take. So my sense of humor is pretty much shot."

"It's not a bad idea. I'll discuss the technical problems with the Helpers. It does seem a little cruel, though, to give someone who's stuck in a sensory deprivation tank for the foreseeable future a drug that actually has the net effect of slowing time down," Siren pointed out.

"Yeah, but at least it would shut her up. Thanks to you, I can hear her all the time now, too."

"OK, done," she said. "Laputa's taking care of it now. What was the second thing?"

"This," he said, swiping the sound back on the giant YouVee holo of Snow White at the foot of the bed.

" — the mutineers are believed to be led by Colonel Nguyen 'Tommy' Ng, who has long been suspected of ties to White Terror groups in his native Texas. While we cannot confirm at present that Jose Manacera has actually joined the HHS mutineers in Manacera City yet, reporters for the Cartoon News Network have confirmed that he definitely escaped protective custody earlier today in New York City, after the People's Senate in Geneva had voted overwhelmingly in favor of bringing articles of impeachment against the disgraced world president. Our Manacera City bureau chief, Clarabelle Cow, has more on the story."

"Good morning, everyone," said Clarabelle. "Snow White, here's the latest on the dizzying series of overnight developments that have sent armed troopers back onto the streets of the North American Federal Administration Area, this time against the direct orders of Acting President Terrawati. What we know is this: just before midnight our time, Health and Humyn Services peacekeepers of the Executive Protection Division met secretly with senior members of the president's own Security Services somewhere just outside the United Nations Unity Complex in New York City. At stake was the orderly transfer of executive power from the indicted President Manacera to his former vice president and now Acting-President Coco Terrawati. Ms Terrawati is trailing badly in the polls and thought to be in danger of losing next month's presidential election to the New Party candidate, Senator Ho Me Shaw.

"But what came out of this clandestine meeting was something that none of us in the media had anticipated: a broad agreement among the membership of both the NAFAA-based HHS forces and the UNSS that the arrest and detention of President Manacera and the seizure of power by Acting President Megawati were unlawful. Well before dawn, many of these units had left their barracks to take up key positions around Federal buildings in both Manacera City and New York at the direction of Colonel Tommy Ng. Shockingly, the so-called 'soft coup' that had peacefully taken place just two short days ago, now seemed in danger of being over-turned by a real-life counter-coup.

"But as daylight broke this morning, it became clear that these renegade HHS troops were not to be entirely unopposed. Corps of loyal HHS forces flown in from overseas during the night, joined by a coalition of trained peace-keeping units belonging to the Departments of Peace & Non-Violence, Energy, and Education, had moved into position to support the acting president and preserve the peaceful transition of power. To make the situation even more complex and volatile, the specific crime President Manacera stands accused of involves having ordered the bombing of the UN Federal Courthouse filled with HHS employees."

A smaller holographic projection now ran over her shoulder, showing President Manacera saying, *"I guess you're wondering what I'm, I mean my holo, is doing here right now, huh? And I guess that deep down, being a real square-shooter, you're pretty shocked and horrified to learn that I'm the one behind the recent wave of bombings in Manacera City. Yep, I own up to it, and I take full responsibility."* The segment had apparently been taken directly from the personal message recorded by Manacera which Obama had viewed in the basement in Trenton.

"So you'd think that the HHS rank and file, more than anyone else, would be joining in the general sense of outrage against the indicted president," Clarabelle went on. "But less than an hour ago, the insurgent forces released the following statement from Colonel Nguyen 'Tommy' Ng from their Interdependence Avenue, SW, Manacera City headquarters." The holo of Manacera was replaced by that of Colonel Ng, a serious-looking man of about 40, with thick black hair and the softening bulk of a former high-skool football player.

"After careful review," he was saying with a distinct Texas twang, as he gazed directly into the holo-cam, "Our forensics experts have determined that this holographic message purporting to show President Manacera confessing to a heinous crime, is in fact, a fake. The rush to judgment and denial of due process in this matter has been so flagrant an abuse of power that it calls into question the very Articles of Common Union that this great planetary government is founded on. We peacekeepers for the Department of Health and Humyn Services feel we have no choice but to act in the best interests of the people, as well as in the spirit of the original UN Charter, and demand the reinstatement of our rightfully elected Chief Executive. We call upon our Cuban and Chinese fellow-peacekeepers, who have been rushed into the NAFAA by Vice President Terrawati and her partners in this deception, to immediately lay down their weapons and return peaceably to their own Admin Centers."

Obama's first impulse, of course, was to dismiss Ng's statement as a blatant political lie. Then he thought, *But what if it isn't? What if Ng is right and the holo really was a fake, one of Sato's tricks?* In fact, what if Sato had been leading Xina and her terror gang on all along, using faked transmissions of President Manacera? It was just the kind of stuff Sato would easily be able to program. Or maybe the whole thing had been a hoax set up, not by Sato at all, but by his wily opponent in this power struggle, Manacera himself? That way, Manacera could create enough chaos to cancel or postpone the general election — and then be seen to be exonerated of responsibility for it at the last moment.

Clarabelle Cow, at least, seemed to share Obama's doubts. She glared disapprovingly at the fading holo of Colonel Ng before continuing, "You may recall that this admission took place during a series of communications between President Manacera and the notorious terrorist and video rap artist, Joyful Kalinga, who has now completely disappeared after last having been seen in Texas. What you may not know is that for 6 years, Kalinga adopted the persona of a quiet, respectable, hard-working Minority Assistance Department employee named Obama Jones. We go now to our favorite local reporter, the beloved Tinkerbelle, who is on the scene with several of his former colleagues. Tink, what do they have to say about the cold-blooded killer who once masqueraded in their midst?"

Suddenly the hologram shifted to the street outside the MAD building. Scott Vega-Choi and Raffi stood flanking Carmen Crowfoot, seated in her Rascal. All three were wearing steel helmets painted a bright blue and scarves around their throats. Behind them stood a dozen red-jacketed NYVs guarding the front entrance, carrying assorted weapons. Tinkerbelle fluttered nervously in the foreground.

"Thank you, Clarabelle," she said. "Kalinga's former colleagues continue to be shocked, horrified, and frankly frightened for their very lives, as you might imagine, for there is a very real fear among Federal workers here that this self-confessed African voodoo magician and international terrorist might be back someday bent on revenge. Director Crowfoot, did you ever have the slightest suspicion that mild-mannered Obama Jones and Killah Kalinga were really one and the same person?"

"No, Tink, I didn't," husked Carmen tearfully, dark Gothscara streaming down her face. She was fully made up for the interview. "And I was probably closer to him than anyone, including his many wives. I'll be honest. With me, Joyful Kalinga engaged in a pattern of deceit over the years that's left me feeling violated — both as a womyn and as one of North America's original inhabitants."

"I always thought there was something bogus about him," growled Scott. "And I'm totally not surprised he's been doing his dirty work all along for the tyrant and war-criminal Manacera."

"Missing your old life?" Siren asked from beside him. Obama couldn't tell whether she was being sarcastic or not.

"Not so much," he told her. His old life, however, seemed determined to follow him everywhere. Even to the Moons of Mars.

" — tell those HHS goons from us they better not try anything," Raffi was bellowing to Tink in his startling basso profundo. "They'll be sorry if they do, I believe!" He shook his child-sized fist. Obama noticed that Raffi's helmet was on backwards. Who would force a little HEDS to go to war? The Federal government, he thought, was no better than the Warriors of God.

The cam-bot pulled back so that viewers could see that a crowd of about 50 people, mostly Neighborhood Youth Volunteers, but also a fair number of MAD employees, CAC activists, and passersby, were gathering to link arms on the sidewalk in front of the building between the bollards and the barricades. They began raggedly singing the UN International Anthem, "One World," as Tinkerbelle flew up close to the lens to announce, "Clarabelle, I'm getting word now that the first of the Chinese and Cuban HHS relief forces are breaking the insurgents' blockade even as we speak, in a bold bid to liberate this section of the city. I'm told we'll be able to see them coming into sight at any moment now." The camera-view shifted to look south toward G St SW, as the first of the gleaming black armored troop-carriers turned right on their way from the old Marine Barracks.

The crowd cheered. Obama recognized the spot where the cam-bot was hovering, just above a little piece of enclosed greenery between the Mickey D's and the DOTARD Building directly across 6th Street from MAD. DOTARD was the Department of Times and Relative Dates and was responsible for conceptualizing and supervising the entire planet's impending shift to digital time. The Analog to Digital Time Act was hardly a popular measure — it had passed the House of Tribunes in Geneva by only three votes, and President Manacera had been widely expected to veto it. But he hadn't, possibly because of political concerns over the general election. Obama had the feeling that the HHS mutiny might be, at least in some small part, a reaction to this.

And suddenly he became aware of something new in himself: his own reaction to it all. What had Siren said yesterday? That humyns were good at drama? Watching the crowd, which included several of his former friends and coworkers, milling around singing and cheering and clapping and striking defiant poses for the YouVee cams, Obama realized how utterly severed his relations now were with them and with their world, the humyn world. He could never go back. They thought of him now as a monster, an imposter, a killer. Ironically, the imposture part had turned out to be the only true part of that description — but none of them, not Carmen, not Scott or FaLola or any of the others, would ever be able to guess that he really belonged to an alien race. One far gentler and less violent than their own.

He was having trouble believing that any of the people he saw on YouVee actually were serious, or even believed the portentous pronouncements they were themselves making. Already, he felt removed from the dangerous melodrama of these events — detached, almost indifferent even, except for a nagging sense of worry and embarrassment. He felt like the only person he now had anything in common with in the whole universe was Siren.

He turned to look at her now, propped up against the pillows beside him, her pajama-clad legs crossed like a little girl's, as she stared raptly at the holovision, points of reflected light dancing in her glittering, mismatched eyes. *But this isn't the real Siren either,* Obama reminded himself. *She's really just an alien brain-parasite with tentacles. And so are you, amigo, so are you.* Maybe they were right. Maybe he was a monster.

.".in other news today the Con-Global Index lost nearly 300 points in overnight trading in New York. This marks the 15th straight losing day for the market — analysts blamed last night's sharp downturn on the ongoing constitutional crisis, as well as news of growing job losses." Suddenly Snow White stopped. "We're just getting word that shots have been fired outside the MAD Building in Manacera City. Repeating, we can now confirm that shots have been fired, and a conflict of some kind has erupted. We return you now to local coverage and Tinkerbelle."

Instantly, the hologram became skewed and slightly distorted. They were peering out from ground level at a tilted angle as though the cam-bot were hiding in the shrubbery. There were loud sounds of screaming, punctuated by the echoes of gunshots. Tinkerbelle's face, huge and fisheye-distorted, suddenly filled the room.

"Behind me, the last of the MAD employees have returned inside the building, as a fire-fight has now broken out. I don't know if you can see what's going on." She retreated, so that a section of the street was visible, and now Obama glimpsed several bodies lying in it, most wearing red jackets. "As the supplemental UN peacies arrived in their troop-carriers — they're the ones behind me in the blue helmets — they were fired on by insurgent HHS peacies, who have tied red ribbons around their own helmets. Right now they seem to be out of camera range on the rooftops of other buildings. Several of the loyalists were hit — you can see them lying in the street — and a number of the NYVs have thrown down their weapons and run off. I know their peeps will be concerned about them."

"We've established an iTooth Friends and Family Hotline you can chime into for instant updates," Snow White interjected. "We'll be flashing that number for swiping in just a few moments. In the meantime, Tink, what's the exact situation? Are you under fire right now?"

"Yes, I am, Snow." Tinkerbelle looked up. "Can you get a shot of this?" A loud explosion went off nearby, and the hologram shuddered and rocked. There were a few bursts of brightly colored "fairy dust" pixel static, then the projection went black.

After a few seconds, Snow White reappeared, staring off to one side. "Save yourself, Tinkerbelle!" she was calling out urgently and dramatically. "Get out of there now, girlfriend! Be well! Be safe!" After this benediction, she turned back to her audience. "That was Tinkerbelle, reporting live from the battle going on just south of the Federal Center. We now have reports of other gun battles going on in other parts of the city. Will this mean war? Stay with our ongoing coverage of the current constitutional crisis — we'll return after these words." Of course, her audience knew perfectly well that Tinkerbelle wasn't a real person, just a holo projected by a flying bot, and could not, therefore, be killed. Nonetheless, Snow White's concern felt momentarily heart-warming.

"Had enough for now?" Obama asked Siren, and swiped the holo off when she nodded.

"Are you very upset?" she asked him.

He shrugged. "A bit. Not as much as I thought I'd be. I just feel like there should be something I could do to stop it."

"I don't know for sure," she said, "but I'm guessing that must have been a little how Sato felt when he first started meddling in humyn affairs. It makes it a little easier to understand his motives when you're forced to watch humyns bumping each other off for no apparent reason."

"Right. Only what's going on now is his handiwork. I know it is." She shut him up by putting the tip of her index finger on his lips. The top button of her pajama tops had come undone, and he could see one of her brown shoulders gleaming damply in the dim light. Looping lions leapt through flaming hoops on the soft yellow material covering her breasts, and clowns tumbled down her thighs.

"I hope you weren't planning to actually get any sleep tonight," Siren purred, staring deep into his eyes. He forgot he knew how to breathe. The thought of sex with her was both too tempting and too scary to even imagine. But sex, it turned out, wasn't quite what she had in mind. "Because we have to leave right now. Come on, Obama — get dressed! Chop chop!"

He inhaled again. And then breathed out. "Where are we going?"

"Back to planet Earth. Your idea about putting Simonetta onGrid was a good one — but you only thought it half-way through. We'll have to cut her off and hack into her skin ourselves the moment she makes contact with 'Daddy.' Which means we'll have to be back on Earth ourselves in order to do it. Sato would immediately notice the 6 minute lag-time in her responses. Eventually he'd figure out from it that she was on Phobos. He'd have no way of getting here in a hurry, of course, but it would certainly alert him to the fact that the station has been reactivated. Which would imply the arrival of another visitor, even though he doesn't know me. But he would infer someone like me." She sat up briskly and swung her sock-clad feet off the edge of the bed. "And then he would guess what his ex-helpers might have to say on the subject. And so he'd immediately do the wisest possible thing, which would be to go deep underground and stay there so far and for so long we'd never find him."

Obama found himself oddly reluctant to get out of bed. "The Helpers seem to have near-infinite powers," he said. There was a note of petulance in his voice, he noticed. "Why can't they, I don't know, cover the Earth invisibly and image everybody on it? You know, the way Laputa did to you in the hallway. That way, you could spot exactly where Sato was. And you could see if there were any other hybrids like me and Simonetta." He was proud of this idea and so was crestfallen when she burst into laughter.

"A week or two of living with your own Helper, and you're ready to rule the universe," Siren said, still grinning. "The only problem with your idea is that much radiation would sterilize the entire planet. We'll view it as our last resort, OK? Joke," she added, as she walked over to the clothes closet.

"By the way, when I say we will have to hack into Simonetta's skin onGrid, I actually mean you will. Neither I nor the Helpers dare have any contact with Sato, for obvious reasons. So I'm afraid that only leaves you, Obama." Siren returned and tossed a heap of clothing onto the foot of the bed. "Try these on for size," she said. "We'll need to hurry — I want to be Earthside and onGrid within the hour. That's when I'm letting Simonetta out of her cage — virtually speaking, of course."

Obama sighed and got out of bed. He picked up the top article of clothing — it was a black Arab *burnoose*. Beneath it was a white silken *thobe*. "Where are we going?" he asked her.

Siren paused in the doorway to unbutton the rest of her pajama top. He caught a glimpse of dark nipple. "Well, where do you think? Isn't it obvious? Tokyo, of course!" she said, then disappeared.

24.

They were used to Arabs in Tokyo, Arabs clothed from head to foot in raw silk, their faces veiled, and eyes hidden behind thick sunglasses. At least the Allura robots at the front desk of the Jumeirah GranNipponjin Hotel were used to them. Nearly 70% of all the robots in the world were to be found in the former Japan, which proudly proclaimed itself the "Robotic Society." Such was the degree of public admiration for them, that in addition to the landmark Hiroshi case, where a Japanese scientist sued to legally adopt as a son the android he created as his own exact double, followed by the gangster Koma Kudi's notorious lawsuit to allow him to marry the Jay-Pop robot diva Akio Robo, there had also been dozens of applications by young Japanese men and women for "Robotic Status." However, all of those working at the GranNipponjin, both male and female in their general appearance, were genuine robots.

The hotel, the most luxurious and expensive in the city, was in the West Tower of the Tokyo Station City in Marunouchi. Obama and Siren's penthouse suite, the Imperial, overlooked the Imperial Palace Gardens, with the palace itself visible just beyond a row of cherry blossom trees on the other side of the eastern moat. In addition to bullet-proof glasspex and bedside security alarm sensors, the suite featured a cocktail lounge with a 20-meter long bar and a mahogany dining table, a liberry, a Steinway grand piano, a 4-meter round revolving bed with ceiling mirrors, walls inlaid with mother of pearl, onyx bathroom floors, marble baths, tiger shark skin upholstery, and an indoor waterfall. The suite could be accessed by either a private ascensor or a front door leading to a common floor foyer. The hotel also contained a basement living-reef swimming pool so enormous that it featured a pair of whales employed as full time pool lifeguards.

"Like it?" asked Siren when they were all alone and she had removed her veil. All alone, of course, except for their Helpers, each of which had taken the form of an *igal*, the blueish headpiece woven from sheepskin and goat-hair that held their hoods in place.

"How much does it cost a night?" asked Obama, flabbergasted.

"If you have to ask," Siren told him, "then you can't afford it. I thought you'd like it!"

"Well, sure. It just seems ... well, I thought we were trying to stay anonymous," he added weakly. The sight of the mirrors above the bed had unnerved him.

"Sorry, anonymity costs 50,000 Unos a night here," Siren said. She smiled at the look on his face. "Look, Obama, seriously — I just thought this place looked fun. Our race has no tradition of money or shopping. That is usually the reason why we visit backward little planets like this, not to create evolutionary chain reactions. Or start wars."

"Yes, but the money for all this doesn't come out of thin air. Money is just a way of measuring the worth of our labor, anyway — when we let the Helpers hack into the world's credit agencies so we can stay at places like this, it's just the same as stealing. Credit has to come from somewhere."

She looked as though she were dealing with a child again. "But Obama, I just pay for things the way your world government does. By charging everything to bankrupt accounts!"

If Siren is really interested in experiencing money and shopping, thought Obama, *we've certainly come to the right place.* Tokyo had reinvented itself as the Year-Round Kurisumasu Shopping Capital of the world, due to the UNECASE exception extended to its heavily Christian South Korean minority, which had been allowed to retain the "Kurisu" in "Christmas." There were Kurisumasu decorations everywhere. Most traffic intersections featured sparkling lights in the shape of snowflakes and giant red-and-white-striped candy canes. There was even a city-wide muzak jingle that subliminally played 24 hours a day, called "Let's Do Shopping". Its refrain was:

"You always window-shopping

But should start stopping to buy!"

So Tokyo was a great place to shop in, although much changed from the way it had been even fifty years before. Once the largest city in the world, Tokyo — along with the rest of the former Japan — had suffered a dramatic drop in its population during the previous half-century, due to a negative native birth rate and the exodus of vast numbers of its elderly citizens to a life of low-gravity luxury on the Moon Colonies. Their places had been taken by several million refugee South Koreans and Taiwanese, as well as sizable wealthy expatriate colonies from the Arab Gulf States, the former Israel, the former Finland, and Siberia. But despite this, the population of the city's greater metropolitan area had shrunk from a one-time high of 33 million to less than half that number now. Thanks to the Tsushima Warm Current, the former Japan had been spared many of the horrors of the re-glaciation brought about by the mini-ice age, but even in Humida, the hottest month of the year, the weather was crisp and cold. And Mount Fuji was now covered in snow year-round.

The suite's wraparound full-length window gave Obama a stunning panoramic view of the city at sunset. Immediately to the south were the bright blinking multicolored lights and gigantic hyper-real holograms of the Ginza Strip, where the beloved monsters Godzilla and Rhodan eternally rampaged between stalling streams of rush-hour air traffic. Farther off to the southwest loomed the delicate glasspex spires and winged buttress skyscrapers of Rippongi Midtown and Akasaki Hanging Garden City, looking like rows of Xmas, or rather, Kurisumasu, trees. This resemblance was heightened by the aircraft collision poles that stuck out everywhere like fiber-optic filaments above the ghostly, constantly-shifting billboard holos of young teenage girls, cartoon characters, and aging Holowood stars advertising aircars, smart-appliances, alcoholic products, sex-aids, and almost any other consumer product imaginable. There was even a holo of the real Jonessa Qali, evidently made some years before, endorsing a personal scent. It was called "Thugra" and contained a potent natural hallucinogen. Obama caught himself wondering how she might look in the bedroom ceiling mirror. *Don't be crazy,* he told himself. "OK, she's out now," said Siren, from behind him.

"Simonetta? Where is she?" Her eyes glazed over. The Princess was acting as a game-cap for her.

"She's at the Casino Royale. What there is left of it in functioning condition, anyway. You do realize, don't you, that they've never quite been able to get the codes virus-free since you nuked the place?"

"Hee hee," said the Pooka from his *igal.* "I was in a hurry, sorry." The vibration of her laugh tickled his scalp.

"Simonetta's looking for Sato there now. Come on, Obama," Siren said impatiently. "We're in a hurry. Let's get going." She was, he thought, starting to sound a little like Xina. What was it about him that attracted bossy women? Or in this case, bossy aliens from outer space?

Was it all his own fault? Maybe there was something intrinsically wishy-washy or hesitant in his character that made them act bossy in response. He couldn't decide.

"Where are we going now?" he asked her.

"Downstairs. 'Let's do shopping.' And Obama?" She paused and then suddenly kissed him hard on the mouth. "There's nothing hesitant or wishy-washy about you. You're perfect. It's me —I'm just tense and distracted. I'm sorry I sounded so bossy." She was looking deep into his eyes as she said this, and he could feel the blood roaring in his temples.

"You can — read my mind?" he stammered. She nodded, her expression tender and, he imagined, sympathetic. *Literally empathetic,* thought Obama. She kissed him again briefly.

"You'll be able to read mine too, someday," she whispered into his ear. "I hope you'll like what you see there."

On the way down the private ascensor, while Siren veiled herself again, Obama began to inventory all the embarrassing thoughts he'd had since he'd met her. How many of them had she overheard? Was there a distance limit? Surely if you had this power, you should ask permission before you "listened in," right?

"Wrong," she said immediately, as the ascensor doors opened. "I can't control what I overhear that way. Not in your case, anyway." They were now inside the main level of the Tokyo Station City shopping mall, which was about the size of downtown Trenton. Crowds hurried past them on their way to the pneumatic commuter trains on the lower levels. There was a smell of stale body odor, lavender bath oil, marinated garlic, fried fish, and citrus-scented cleaning fluid in the air. Tokyo was almost as modern as the Moon, or at least as modern as the fake Moon colony appeared to be — only dirtier and far more crowded. "You're broadcasting like Simonetta, at full blast," she said, as they fought through the commuters. "Like a humyn three-year-old who's just learned how to talk. The only way for me not to overhear you would be to leave the room."

"Is that why you kissed me?" he asked her. "Because you knew I'd been thinking about you that way?" He wasn't sure, but he thought she squirmed at the question. It was hard to tell beneath the full-length *burqa* she was wearing.

"I guess," she said reluctantly. "Actually, I always thought kissing a human would be totally repulsive and disgusting, but I figured I'd give it a try for your sake. It's my fault it's been on your mind lately, anyway, because I've been trying to copy the way human women flirt. You know, to make you like me. How was I, by the way?"

"Great," said Obama.

"Thanks. I practiced with some sims. Bear in mind I can only read the thoughts on the surfaces of your mind. It's not like I can simply scan Simonetta's brain or something and learn everything she knows that way. Basically with her, all I can hear is the emotional noise she makes, plus her constant worrying about herself. Like coms chatter. And of course, all her cunning little plans to fix things. And get revenge on us. Over here, Obama, we need to find a skin shop in the arcade."

"What about ordinary humyns? Can you hear their thoughts, too?"

"Yuck!" she said. "Now that's really revolting stuff to have to listen to all the time. Especially in crowds like right now. Even worse than Simonetta sometimes. Here we are." Just as Roman-alphabet public signs had been mandated everywhere, Enriched Standard Language, or ESL, was the official language of the UN and was required in all skools on the planet. However, the Japanese had little natural aptitude for Enriched and preferred just to use Babelfish instead.

This had resulted in constant mistranslations and malapropisms, especially on YouVee, as well as an infinite variety of hybrid phraseology on shop signs, which were also illegally projected with Kanji and Kana lettering. The stuttering faux-neon sign over the shop they were entering read, "Sexy Rubdown Lady Skin & Game Parlor" in several languages. It was the commercial gaming skins for sale that interested Siren, apparently.

"Ever 'bumped' before?" she asked him as she swiped through a life-sized sample display of them.

"Not since college," he said. "Why?"

"Because we need to now," said Siren. "She's here."

"Who's here? Simonetta?"

"She couldn't find Sato at the Casino. Now she's here in virtual Tokyo. Just outside the station exit, in fact. Here, boot into this."

In 2018, Tokyo had been the first city in the world to construct a virtual real-time replica of itself , using a combination of 3D modeling and a mapping service called Google Earth that had been accessible over the old Internet. Google had once been a giant company in the days of the old Internet. But after going into receivership when the Grid had first become popular, Google had managed to reinvent itself as a 2D informational tool for monitor glasses, resulting in the name change to Goggle. Now the Internet had evolved into the Grid, but Tokyo still remained the most realistically mapped place on Earth, its everyday and virtual versions matching each other so ideally that it had become a favorite destination not only for local bumpers — those gaming in the virtual environment while inhabiting the corresponding real-life one — but also for virtual gamers and shoppers from all over the world.

In fact, sales to onGrid foreigners were so brisk that most store clerks — like the middle-aged Korean womyn at the Sexy Rubdown Lady Parlor — wore their game-caps and monitor glasses 24/7, just as Kourosh had, in order not to miss any of their possible customers in either reality. Obama had heard that even most mid-priced prostitutes now did this, as well. Hector, the guy in the seat next to him on his first shuttle flight, had complained that sex was now becoming prohibitively expensive "if you want to see their eyes."

Prostitutes, of course, had become a protected minority early in the '20's and were often touted as one of the very few growth industries under UN world government. It was, very properly, a hate crime to refer to members of the adult services industries in a derogatory manner. On Earth, Laputa's very name would have been illegal.

Siren had chosen a pair of "twin-skins" for the two of them. A twin-skin was a package of commercial onGrid characters bundled with matching real-world costumes. The characters she had chosen were among the most best-selling in the world. They were taken from the successful British time-travelling spy-thriller sim series, "The Chronos Killers," which featured the long-legged and glamorously lethal Vera Pim, clad from head to high heel in tight black leather with zippered crotch, eye and mouth-holes, and her partner, the dapper, debonaire, but amnesiac assassin, Ed Hat, who wore a bland white stocking mask beneath his black homburg.

With the help of the Princess and Pooka, who altered shape to emulate monitor glasses, Siren and Obama hurriedly changed into the skins inside a stall in the back room, then booted up onGrid through their Helpers. Instantly, Obama's vision was overlain with that of the Grid version of the shop's changing-room, in this case a blandly textured box, the two versions prismatically refracting slightly where they overlapped and ghosting where they didn't. He and Siren exited the parlor quickly and, already dizzy and slightly disoriented, took the segualator down to the main concourse. A minute later they walked out onto the antique red-brick station's front steps.

They were too late. Simonetta, whose skin was now that of the cruel gaming dominatrix Fall-From-Grace Katana — famed for her constantly swaying hips, her trademark whimper of "Coming!" when introduced to a fresh victim, and her orgasmic screams whenever she was temporarily killed — had just ported away from the sidewalk outside the Central UnEx-Post Office. Porting, of course, was something bumpers couldn't do.

"Damn!" muttered Siren.

"She's going to the Ginza," said the Princess, and electronically hailed an aircab, which swooped down from Gofukubashi and hovered in the entrance roundabout in front of them as they piled in.

"Ginza," said Siren to the blond Finnish cabbie, and they ascended in a cloud of exhaust the night air had made as visible as steam. It was turning colder. "Why would she be going to the Ginza?" Siren said to Obama. "Surely that's only for tourists."

They turned left in front of the Sony Building just as Godzilla swiped at them with an astral paw that made Obama tingle slightly as they passed through its holographic electron flow. Here the traffic was so sluggish that Siren asked the driver to let them out the first place he could stop. Inside a long Lexair limousine stalled in the lane next to them, Obama caught a glimpse of the pale, pinched face of a Lolita, one of the 12-to-16 year old adolescent girls so pampered and prized that they couldn't be allowed out in public unguarded for fear of being kidnapped. Their underwear was sometimes auctioned off on iBay for fantastic sums, and according to the Tattloids several of the wealthier ones had run off with their *yakuza* bodyguards. This Lolita, huddled between two darker male shapes, was wearing a white mink coat over her skool-girl uniform and vomiting into a bag.

"Here OK?" the cabbie asked, pointing at the roof of the brilliantly lit Mitsukoshi Department Store, whose walls were covered in shimmering holograms. Lines of aircars circled it slowly, waiting for spaces.

"Forget it. Just let us out in the street," Siren told him.

"If you say," he said. Seizing an opening in the traffic of a few centimeters, he spun down and deposited them in the dead center of the grid-locked 4-Chome Intersection while the traffic-bots squawked at them in Enriched and Japanese. Obama and Siren were almost bowled over several times by low-flying airscooters as they made their way through the groundcars to the moving sidewalk. Behind them were the huge Wako and Mitsukoshi Department stores, the Wako still boasting its antique, historically protected store-fronts.

Bumping had been invented in the former Japan, and Tokyo had the highest percentage of bumpers in the world. Some, especially teenage boys, never took their caps and glasses off even to bathe, so the Japanese had invented a wide range of accessories to accommodate them, such as waterproof anti-bacterial helmets, inflatable bumper pads, and an infinite variety of haptic — touch-sensitive — dildonics.

A few of these accessories had been adopted by non-bumpers out of simple self-protection. The most popular was the full-body prophylactic suit called the "Mr. or Mrs. Brobby," which looked a bit like a huge, inflated condom. In addition to providing physical padding at rush-hour and on subways, Mr. or Mrs. Brobby was also a cultural response to the traditional fear of germs being spread by immigrants and tourists. Pale pink and padded at belly and groin, with white goggles and ear-pods and big round inverted red rubber nipples where the nose and mouth should be, the Brobbies had become such a fetish item among both bumpers and ordinary Tokyo commuters that some even wore them during sex at home. About a quarter of the pedestrians on the Ginza were wearing them now. There were also, Obama noticed, half a dozen other womyn dressed as Vera Pim and at least one more Ed Hat.

A holographic snow had started to fall, and the bright colored lights and moving holos of the Ginza reflected wetly up and down Siren's black leather catsuit. As they stood on the static sidewalk island, Obama looked up and came to a dead stop as they stood on the static sidewalk island. "Do you see what I see?" he asked Siren. Directly in front of them stood the garishly bright New San-ai Dream Center, a slender 12-storey crystal advertising tower covered with holograms and lenticular LEDs etched into its glasspex windows. It was the single most expensive piece of real and virtual estate in the world, as well as a notable tourist attraction. Atop it, floating just above the Bulgari holo, was a giant holo Santa, slowly waving.

"What?" asked Siren, momentarily distracted. Simonetta was somewhere among the constantly shifting groups of virtual pedestrians in front of them which overlaid the real ones. The two crowds existed in a writhing, incompatible visual turmoil in Obama's double-vision, the onGrid tourists constantly walking through the more solid real-life citizens or hovering and swooping around them like demons, visible only to the bumpers and ignored by everyone else. Keeping an eye on Simonetta would have been nearly impossible, even at this short distance, without the Helpers to track her.

"Sato Claus," said Obama, pointing up at the holo, his fingers enclosed in one of Ed Hat's signature white leather strangling gloves. "Look, it has Sato's face." There was a small crowd of tourists and shoppers ringing the first floor of the San-ai, which functioned as a sort of giant kiosk, waving at holo reproductions of themselves waving back and watching news bulletins on the YouVee monitors. Occasional miniature sonic booms of sound from these swept over them as they crossed the main street. "Sato Foundation World Headquarters" read a small gold-leaf sign in one of the building's second-floor windows. The offices looked darkened and empty. Obama noticed tiny drops of real-world drizzle beading on Siren's suit and wondered if she was cold. Maybe not — she seemed to have perfect body control. On the way into the hotel, she'd changed the color of her eyes back to the original Siren's pale icy blue. Now they matched again. Maybe she was getting bored being Qali.

"I'm fine," she said. "Let's save the Sato office for later and keep following Simonetta for now, OK?"

This wasn't as easy as it sounded. Half a block ahead of them on the people-mover, a ghostly Simonetta, dressed in a frilly black bra and gartered stockings, thick black-rimmed reading glasses, red leather bondage-wear with belts and clasps, was getting off the sidewalk every few minutes to stop and talk to groups of youthful male bumpers. She was carrying a furled whip. Following her involved — in addition to being pushed and jostled by the crowd — continuing to hop on and off the rolling surface well behind her, while keeping her in sight the whole time; then huddling together against the store-fronts pretending to window-shop for diamonds and designer iRists. Several times they lost her visually, but of course, the Helpers had a tight lock on her onGrid, even to the point of recording all her conversations. "She's found a guy," the Princess informed them suddenly.

"For what?" Siren asked her.

"Oral sex, she said."

The ranks of the crowd briefly parted, and they spotted Simonetta just ahead of them at the intersection, dragging a Mr. Brobby away from a gang of three or four others who tagged along behind the two of them, calling out coarse words of encouragement from a distance. Simonetta and her bumper friend crossed Chuo-Dori and disappeared inside the huge glasspex-box Matsuzakaya Department Store, where a row of huge penguins dressed in Santa suits were line-dancing on the roof high above singing,

"The pleasing faces of our sales-persons

Will surely make you wish to purchase

Many popular items from our store"

in the chiming electronic song tones so popular in Asia.

Siren grabbed Obama's white-gloved hand with her black-gloved one and dragged him across the street after Simonetta and her Brobby, dodging the beeping groundcars. A traffic-bot flew down angrily to intercept them, but the Pooka disabled it instantaneously, and it crashed at their feet like a dead pigeon. They dashed inside the titanium-framed main entrance beneath the crimson and gold awnings, then turned the wrong way and got briefly lost in the Pet Department.

"Bloody hell! Where are they now?" Siren snapped.

"In the restroom in Lolita & PreTeen SmartWare," the Pooka replied. "Just follow the yellow Rascal Trax."

"I'm sure she's spent many a happy girlhood hour on the toilets in there," muttered Siren, as they crossed back out of Pets and into the Center Way. Like swarms of buzzing fireflies, tiny holograms flew out of the racks of clothing they hurried past; if you opened your palm to any of the little holos, it would grow full-sized and deliver its sales pitch. Allura robots representing both genders stood on little floating pedestals spraying underwear and cocktail dresses onto themselves, then modeling the automagic stretching and shaping capabilities of their instant clothes by dancing demurely with leering holographic space monsters. "Fruit-favor single-malt?" asked a humyn sales-girl, handing out samples.

At the entrance to the Lolita Bootique, they found their way blocked by four Mr. Brobbies. "No bumping, prease," one said. His onGrid avatar was that of Gamera.

"Bumping not arroud," said another, giggling. The two then began deliberately bumping into Siren with their padded bellies.

"Hey!" said Obama, and moved to defend her. The other two got in his way, using their bellies and inflated arms to block and shove him. The Pooka and the Princess both flowed into action beneath their clothing, and their attackers were bounced aside. One fell heavily, upending a display of Kurisumasu eggs that hatched little trees. Another smashed through an edible rice-paper dividing wall. All at once, half-clad Allura robots began leaping down from the pedestals all around them and applying choke-holds to the Mr. Brobbies.

"Wow!" said one of the Mr. Brobbies happily and went limp in the arms of his captor. "You can sex with me now prease?"

One of the Alluras delivered a stern lecture to them about public courtesy, while another embarked on a long apology to Siren, offering her a voucher for discounted shopping. But the Princess hacked into her, cutting her short, and the robot froze. "Look," said Siren to Obama, pointing across the aisle. The fifth Mr. Brobby, Simonetta's date, was sneaking out through the Why Not Yacht Department in the distance, his big red rubber mouth-nose prosthesis disturbingly awry. "You follow him," she said. "I'll stick with Simonetta."

"OK," he said.

"Don't worry, I have footage of what they were up to from the security cams," the Pooka told Obama on his way out. "This is the virtual version. The real-time one just looks stupid." She started playing it in one corner of his monitor. The effect of watching a tiny Mr. Brobby on his knees in a tiny toilet stall nuzzling a tiny translucent seated Simonetta with her skirt hiked up and a whip in her hand was one distraction too many for Obama as he tried to follow the real-life Mr. Brobby through a crowded department store he was seeing simultaneously onGrid and off. Through a face mask and a pair of virtual reality monitor glasses.

"Please turn it off. I'm getting dizzy again. Plus it's kind of disgusting." Was he becoming as prudish as Siren? Maybe it was his growing alienness talking. Or maybe what he was watching really was just kind of disgusting. It was the kind of thing kids pranked each other with at his high skool, and he hadn't really enjoyed watching it even then.

"But she made him write something down on a piece of paper," protested the Pooka. "In the real world, I mean. Don't you want to watch?"

"No thanks. What did he write?" asked Obama, following his quarry back out the main entrance and onto the sidewalk again.

"We can't tell, actually," the Pooka confessed ashamedly. "The resolution wasn't good enough." Straight ahead of them, the Mr.

Brobby was re-crossing the street. Obama and the Pooka followed him back down the Chuo-Dori to the Sai-An Building and watched him go inside.

"What's he doing now?" Siren asked in one ear.

Obama told her. "Obviously his friends were told to get in our way and create a distraction while she dictated a message to him in the real world. It's incredible to imagine, but I think he's actually going to try to just slip the message under the door of the Sato Foundation office if it's closed. Maybe I'd better follow him up there. Oh damn — no, I can't. He just came out again. Too late."

"Never mind," she said. "I'm watching the internal security footage from there now, and that's more or less what he just did. They have an old-fashioned mail slot. You sure it's him coming out and not another Brobby?"

"He had an accident in the toilet with his nose," he told her. "He looks pretty distinctive. What's Simonetta doing?"

"Well, you're never going to believe this, but she's not actually doing anything now. She's just shopping!" They waited for another hour, Obama increasingly wet and bored in the crowd outside the Sai-An, while Siren trailed around Matsuzakaya after Simonetta. Siren gave up finally and appeared suddenly at Obama's shoulder, unzipping the patch on her face-mask to free her mouth, which protruded sensuously from the black leather encircling it. "I can't take any more," she said. "I'm not made like Earth women, obviously. I just can't stand that much shopping. Doing it or watching it. What I don't get is what she's up to."

"'Earth women'?" said Obama, amused. "I thought you — I mean, I thought we — didn't actually have genders. Real ones, anyway."

"Obama, being around you makes me want to be a woman. It's the first time I've actually enjoyed it since I got here. Don't get any ideas, though. I'm not going to start behaving like Simonetta."

"Hey, maybe she's just enjoying her freedom. She's been stuck in a tank with no body and no senses for nearly a week. It kind of makes sense that once she's let out, she'd do what she loves best — having sex and shopping."

Siren glared at him. He couldn't see her eyes behind her dark glasses, but he knew that's what she was doing anyway. Maybe he was starting to read her mind, too. "Yeah, right. She's up to something," she said. "I can feel it. So can you. So stop teasing me, and let's go upstairs and have a look at that note."

Because the Sanai building had been historically preserved, after it had collapsed during the most recent earthquake it had been rebuilt as identically as possible to its former specifications, though from modern smart-materials. The first two floors had once housed a cafe, but now the ground floor was an electronics showroom, and the second floor belonged to the Sato Foundation.

The ascensors were in the center of the slender, cylindrical building, surrounded by a narrow, cylindrical hallway. The locked wooden doors of the Foundation featured a brass mail slot — something Obama had only seen in the flatties and older urban neighborhoods — presumably rescued from the wreckage of the original San-Ai. The doors opened at Siren's touch. The presence of the Helpers took all the thrill out of burglary, of course — they spoofed and wiped the security and cambots, and bypassed the electronic security systems, even those keyed into a building's walls and AI. Which they disabled first.

Inside the Foundation office, the lights were muted, and the rooms had a still and musty air of disuse. It was little more than a welcome center with a pair of holograph projectors and several empty offices in the back. The Allura at the front desk had been in a sleep cycle which the arrival of the note had not, apparently, disturbed. The illumination from the hall showed the note still lying on the carpet, a square of pink toilet paper. Siren picked it up and held it to the light. The message was scrawled in Japanese Kanji script. "Daddy dear, wish you were here," translated the Princess, and Siren dropped it fluttering back onto the floor.

"She's playing with us," she said. "What's she doing now, Princess?"

"Still shopping."

"Set off all the burglar alarms," Siren told her. "Let's see what happens." Instantly there was a loud whoop and the ceiling lights came on. The Allura gave a single shudder at her carved ebony and glasspex desk, then was still again. "Where are the alarm messages being sent to?"

"Riscon Security, Dream Plaza Omiya, 17th floor 1-7-5 Sakuragi-cho, Omiya, Saitama," said the Princess. "Sato Genetics, 14, Plasma Research Park, Toki, Gifu. And one more place — a private house, 1-22-14R Chome 4 Tenmaya, Sumida-Ku, Tokyo."

"That sounds promising. We'll try it first," Siren said. "Come on, let's get out of here before the security company arrives." They went back down the ascensor, out the main doors, and onto the front sidewalk just as a white van with flashing sirens landed in the intersection in front of them. A pair of Endura robots with Riscon badges exited the van at a run carrying microwave emission guns. Siren took Obama's arm and led him around the corner to the next building over. It had been modeled after a retro Alienware computer, and housed the Tasaki Jewelry Tower. They went inside and took the ascensor to the top floor, overriding the security locks and bots. "Princess, what's Simonetta doing now?"

"Still shopping. She's left Matsuzukaya — now she's across the street at Komatu."

"What's she shopping *for*, exactly?"

The Princess checked. "She's buying mostly clothes. A new iRist. Some pearls. Real stuff, not virtual. On a private Sugara Bank Mistresscard."

"She's actually buying real clothes?" Siren said incredulously. "Does she think they can UnEx them to her inside her tank? And that she can try them on?" They got out of the first ascensor and took a second to the roof, where they found a private aircar pad for company employees. It was deserted. "Normally, I wouldn't do this, but we're in a big hurry and might have to come back at any minute. So the Princess and the Pooka are going to form flying suits around us and take us to Jinan-dori direct. This is the one city on Earth where I don't think anyone will notice a couple of flying plastic action figures."

She was wrong.

The problem was that both of the Helpers were still booted up onto the Grid. Normally, each would have computed the trajectories of all the air-traffic circling the Ginza and ascended instantly, threading their way through them. But the extra collision detection settings of the virtual world slowed them down just long enough so that they got caught in the radiance of a holographic burst of fire from the volcanic mouth of Rhodan as they lifted off the roof of the Jewelry Tower. The Princess had chosen to emulate Ultrawoman, all silver and striped red chrome, with a robotic face and glowing yellow eye-holes, while the Pooka had transformed herself into a matching Metal Hero called "Seven Star Fighting God Guyferd," who was, as she told Obama, "a sweet and sensitive boy, only infected by an alien parasite." He could hear Siren giggling at this in his ear. Guyferd had a luridly ridged exoskeleton with orange highlights and baleful red eyes.

And these were caught, along with the supple, silvery feminine figure of the popular Ultrawoman, in the glare above the Ginza for a moment no longer than the blink of an eye. Long enough, however, for Obama to see children pointing at him from behind the windows of aircars. And for several tourists to cue their bot-cams. Then they were clear of the traffic and floating high above the city, which spilled down from the hills to the east and west into Tokyo Bay like a million grains of brightly glittering sand on a cloth of deep dark sable.

Goggle maps superimposed themselves on Obama's vision, showing the streets and neighborhoods far below. Tenmaya, which lay about 4 km to the northwest of them, turned out to actually be an unnamed street in South Sumida City, the nearest train station to which was Kinshicho. They flew over the west fork of the river and crossed the highway out to the Narita Aerospaceport, then landed, confused and lost, just off Jinan-dori in an empty alley-way. Tokyo's street-numbering system, which had first been invented in the 13th Century CE by a Buddhist monk, had defeated even the Helpers. They retreated sulkily into being monitor-glasses again.

"Which way do we go now?" asked Siren, exasperated.

"North, we think," said the Princess. "We could always just ask for directions, you know."

"Isn't it in the 4th Chome?" Obama asked. "Doesn't that sign say 4th?" The main road was filled with new construction and looked very much like Honolulu. Just off it, however, there were neighborhoods still filled with older houses jammed together like those in a shanty-town. Many of these were only one or two storeys high, thrown together a century before from mismatched lumber, cheap brick, and hectares of corrugated sheet metal. Some had bicycle sheds or flimsy garages or balconies welded together from scrap and were almost completely covered in ivy. Power lines snaked everywhere, and many of these houses had generators or extra solar panels attached to them. A few even had their own WiiFi relay towers.

After she and Obama had wandered around aimlessly for a few minutes, Siren relented and allowed the Princess to query a local HHS kiosk. "Walk north along Chou Dori (the only street with a sign) to the backside of Yata," it told her. "Make your first left and you'll pass a Mikki's on your right. Take the next right and as you follow this street zig-zag, and then you'll find an open area with a big tree. You will then be in front of 1-22-14R Tenmaya."

Much of this route was unlit, and in her black cat-suit, Siren was almost invisible. Obama, with his white gloves and white stocking-mask, looked like a Halloween ghoul, startling several pedestrians out of their path. Home security cams peered at them blindly, disabled by the Helpers, and dogs yapped at them from behind high wooden fences with peeling paint. The house, when they found it, stood darkened and silent just across the narrow alley from a streetlight. They stopped and stood beneath it for a minute.

1-22-14R Tenmaya was perhaps the oldest house on the block. It had been jury-rigged from the same cheap wood and corrugated metal sheeting as the rest. One entire two-storey wall had rusted along one side. The part of the upper floor that faced the street, built of dark paneled wood with a steep pitched roof, looked like that of a traditional Edo drinking-parlor. The double front gate to the fence was traditional-looking, too, surrounded by ivy, with its own little pitched roof, like a miniature Shinto shrine. The house had a tiny side yard completely filled with gleaming modern equipment, extra electrical generators and a row of outsized air-conditioning and refrigeration compressors. These hummed and rumbled audibly. All the windows were heavily shuttered and curtained with traditional rattan blinds, but Obama thought he could see a blue-green light leaking from around the first-floor windows.

"Anybody alive in there?" asked Siren.

"The only thing awake in there is another Allura robot," said the Pooka. "I've already hacked her. Want me to shut down the security systems and open the doors for you?"

"What about Sato? Is he in there?"

"Well, yes and no," replied the Princess. "I'm afraid you'll have to see for yourself."

Siren sighed heavily. "We've come all this way. I suppose I might as well." It was on the way in the door that Obama realized she was complaining about the walk up from Jinan-Dori, not the trip from Mars.

The Allura had opened one of the doors of the front gate for them and was waiting just inside. Her hair was disheveled, and she was dressed in an old kimono. From a distance, she might have deceived the neighbors into believing she was a real humyn. "Hi, Obama," she said and winked. He heard her words both from the robot's mouth and inside his neural connection with her.

"You can hack into an Allura robot just like that?" he asked the Pooka, as they followed the Allura up a short stone path into the front porch of the house. The Pooka had left the front door open, but hadn't turned on any of the lights inside.

"Sure, nothing easier," the Pooka said in a pitying tone. "They're total idiots."

"Have you been doing that all along?" he asked her. "Did you hack the croupier at the casino into letting me win all that money?"

"Hee hee, yep! That was me."

"What about the nurse at the hospital who guarded me all night?"

"No, that was me," said the Princess. "We can be in lots of places at once." A dog started barking nearby.

"Shhh!" said Siren. "You three are making enough racket to wake all the neighbors. Switch to nitevision and don't turn any lights on unless I say so." She closed the front door behind her.

The front part of the house was as old and jumbled as the exterior. It was stuffed full of decaying furniture, and even had an old analog television set in one corner, along with an electric fireplace with dirty plastic bricks. The kitchen, which appeared not to have been used in decades, was on one side of the living room. Everything stank. A heavy reinforced metal door led into the rest of the house. Its security codes were so elaborate that it took both Helpers working together several seconds to krack them. It swung open, and they went through to a closet, which acted as an airlock. This only became evident when they opened and stepped through the second door into the back room.

It was a small but ultra-modern medical surgery, filled with the sort of state-of-the-art robotic laser-surgery and life-support equipment found in the ICUs of expensive private hospitals. Inside, it was freezing cold. The room had been left chilled to near zero, but dehumidifiers had kept the air free from frost. A corpse lay on a surgical table in the operating theater in the middle of the room. A second table beside it was empty. The room was windowless, so Siren switched a few lights on.

The corpse they illuminated was slightly decomposed but still recognizable as that of Sato Shiseki.

He was lying on his back with his mouth open, and no one had bothered to close his eyes. His few strands of thin white hair were disarranged and stained with dried blood. He was naked, uncovered even by a surgical gown. "Turn him over for me, hon," Siren said to the Pooka, and the Allura wrestled the body, long since turned stiff as a board in the cold, onto its side. Precisely the same pattern of surgical incisions that had disfigured the upper back of Priska's body in the hospital had also been made on Sato's.

"This bird has flown. And in such a hurry he didn't even bother to bury his own body. When exactly did all this happen?" she asked the Helpers.

"Almost exactly 20 years ago," said the Princess. "Almost to the day, in fact. I've downloaded every scrap of data in the house as well as the cotton in this poor creature's brain. Basically, no one's been here since Sato vacated, except security and maintenance crews. You saw the pile of Fed Exes in the front room."

"So Sato has been masquerading as someone else — or several other people, even — since 2030," said Siren. "Let's sort through all that data and look for any kind of off-line or analog records left lying around here. Run a check and see if our old friend Dr Wong Kyu-Bong from the Manacera City Hospital Center was anywhere around here 20 years ago — this looks like his handiwork to me. He'd be about the right age."

In one corner of the room there was a service lift with a gurney inside it that seemed to access a lower floor. While Siren was busy, Obama got into its cage, pushed the button, and the old-skool elevator lurched into motion. It slowly descended and stopped. Obama found himself looking into a hallway; ceiling lights turned on as he stepped out of the elevator. The hall led past a bathroom into a large bedroom.

The temperature in the bedroom was cold, but nowhere near as frigid as in the surgery above it. A wall of polished teak drawers was on his left. On his right, a low platform bed stood in the center of the room, surrounded by low matching tables. Squat chests of drawers — crafted of real rosewood, not just recycled pulp with spray-on veneer — lined another wall beneath a pair of framed Botticelli sketches. At the time, Obama assumed these were merely prints; later, he would wonder if they might not have been originals.

The third wall was covered by sliding rice-paper panels. A bubbling noise, like that made by aquarium equipment, came from behind them. He slid one open and stepped into a long closet, almost the size of a second bedroom. Pale ultraviolet lighting illuminated a row of wide, translucent flexible-looking plastic containers hanging from a ceiling rack. These had clear liquid-filled tubes running into the top brackets that supported the containers, and opaque drainage tubes attached underneath them snaked through the wall to empty somewhere outside. At first, Obama thought the shadowy forms he glimpsed inside these tanks were suits of clothing. He stepped closer and saw they were naked young myn.

There were no labels on any of the containers to tell Obama who they were, and at first he was too shocked by the sight to focus clearly on their faces in the dim lighting. The second container he inspected was empty. He forced himself to walk down the row and look at the rest more closely. All the bodies were floating slightly in the milky blueish liquid, several curled into near-fetal positions. Most were in contorted postures obviously constrained by the flexible sides of the containers, as if they'd been struggling to escape; as if in answer to his thought, one moved slightly, and Obama jumped. He didn't recognize any of their faces except for three more Satos, two in their mid-twenties and one still in his teens, until he got to the very last clone at the farthest end of the closet.

Its face was his own.

25.

The cloned body in the closet was an Obama Jones at about the age of 19; thinner, its features youthful and beardless and blankly absent of all the experiences the real one had gone through, but still undeniably, recognizably Obama Jones. "It's dead, Obama," said Siren in his ear. "They're all dead. The nutrient systems failed years ago, probably."

"They can't be dead!" said Obama, horrified. "One of them moved!"

"Checking again. Nope, they're all dead. You just thought it moved. You bumped it with your knee, according to the Pooka. It wouldn't take much to kill them, really — they're surprisingly delicate. Batches go bad all the time. All it would take would be a missed visit by the maintenance service. Or a clog in the sewage lines. Or, here we go, the earthquake of '42. The city's electric power was out for several weeks, and the backup generators failed right before it came back on online. So, they've probably been dead for 8 years or so. Everything dies sooner or later, Obama."

"Not us, I thought. Or the Helpers. I thought they lived forever." There was something niggling in the back of his mind, something Manacera had said about Sato, but he couldn't remember what it was.

"Oh, they can die, too," she said. "Of boredom, sometimes. It's been known to happen."

"Why do you think I'm hanging with you, amigo?" chirped the Pooka in his other ear. "Life with you is never boring!"

Obama took a last look at the face of his dead twin suspended in its plastic container and shuddered. "Thanks," he said. "Let's get out of here."

On the way back up in the freight elevator he realized that what he had just glimpsed was the day-to-day reality of being an alien brain parasite, always having to live with racks of cloned bodies gestating in your closet. It was a little like being a vampire, probably, keeping your kitchen refrigerator stocked with blood plasma bags. Or a dungeon with the bodies of your victims. Somewhere, probably on Phobos, Siren had a closet just like this — and as long as he remained tied to Earth, Obama would have to have one, too. It was either that or migrate into the fetuses of his own children. Or burrow into other hosts at death, as Simonetta had done. Whatever the case, he suddenly felt sickened at the thought of what he was. And would have to do. Forever.

"I'm sorry, baby," said Siren when he returned upstairs. She patted his arm, but said nothing else, though obviously she could read his emotions. He appreciated her tact.

"You know, it's weird," he told her. "A few weeks ago I'd never even seen a dead person before — now I've seen dozens."

"I know. I guess we'd all better get used to it," she said. "Speaking of which, Pooka — have the robot carry all the corpses from downstairs up here and autopsy them. I want you to supervise her every step of the way — make sure she doesn't get even a single signal-burst out. I want to confirm the earthquake's power outages as having been the cause of death. And I want DNA matches from the clones to anyone living or dead, particularly anybody in the HGP K6 SSWATZ28954172.1952-2022 files. Sato's almost certainly migrated into one of the genetically enhanced bodies he created, maybe even a twin of one of the ones down there in the basement. So we shouldn't have too many candidates to search for. When the robot's done, shut her down permanently, all right?"

"OK, cool!" said the Pooka enthusiastically.

"Any more surprises upstairs?" Obama asked. Siren shook her tightly leather-hooded head.

"Just a storage room," she said. "Princess, what's Simonetta up to now?"

"Still shopping. Oh, she's leaving Wako now. She's ... crossing the street again. And ... going into Kabushiki-gaisha Mitsukoshi, the big department store."

"We need to get back there," Siren said.

But by the time they'd walked back to Yata-Dori and found an air-taxi, the Princess announced, "She just booted down."

"Bugger! Are you sure?" Siren asked. "She isn't just spoofing her account?"

"Nope, she's totally offGrid now. You'd think she'd want to stay out and play some more, wouldn't you? I know *I* would," said the Princess.

"You're right, it is odd. Everything about Simonetta is strange to me — it's like she's half wild animal. OK, tell Laputa to disconnect her."

"Permanently?"

"Until further notice, anyway," Siren said. "Until we figure out exactly what sort of damage she's done." Then Siren leaned forward and told the cab-driver to take them back to their hotel.

"Letting Simonetta loose onto the Grid wasn't really a very good idea, was it?" said Obama. "I guess most of my decisions have been pretty terrible."

"No worse than mine. Face it, compared to Sato and Simonetta, we're amateurs at all this cloak and dagger stuff. It might really help right now if I actually was a 'galactic cop,' instead of my usual useless silly old self. Sato is obviously way smarter than I am." *She's just trying to cheer me up,* he thought. It wasn't working.

So Obama returned to the hotel in an awkward, sullen temper. Since Siren could read his mind, this was contagious. Neither was in any mood for a party, but they found one going on anyway inside their suite. The Imperial had come with a number of unique complementary features, including one called "Kurisumasu Party Box." Custom spider-bots crept along the ceilings, projecting individual AI-programmed holograms of holiday party-goers who realistically interacted with the suite's occupants as well as with each other. There were several modes: the local glitterati that were featured in "Japanese Celebrity Stand Up Please!" and of course, there were the more universal "Holowood Oscar Nite Legend" people, "YouVee Monster Dance Party," and "Iron Heroes of Professional Sports." Since the party was supposed to be taking place at Xmas, there was a great deal of simulated drunkenness, overeating of holographic finger-food, and furtive sex in the bathrooms. All of this in funny hats.

In an effort to cheer Obama and Siren up and force them to speak to each other, the Helpers had hacked the four party modes together, and the crowding and the din of conversation, along with the throbbing of generic Xmas Mash-up muzak, were overwhelming. "Princess, please!" Siren screamed over the noise. "If you must entertain yourselves, turn down the flocking settings and keep your holograms penned in the dining room! And we need some real food; I'm starving. Can you order us something?"

There were seven restaurants in the tower, including several themed ones such as the Vampire Cellar and Santa Sushi. All of them served the three luxury hotels. The Princess decided on the Princess Doll, an organic magical fantasy theme restaurant catering to wealthy Lolitas. Their meals arrived via a butler in a tuxedo and silk top hat, who bowed to the Princess and called her "Your Highness" in Japanese when she answered the door in her life-sized Barbie persona, but who became visibly upset and ran off when Hong Kong sim actress Kimberly Jet Tung and American basketball superstar Michael Jordan tried to sneak through him out into the hall, pursued by the three-headed Ghidrah.

After Siren and Obama had each showered in their separate bathrooms and returned to the bar lounge wearing only silk bathrobes, the Princess said, "Dinner is served." She had laid it out on the long bar-lounge shark-skin coffee table and turned on the YouVee news for them to watch while they ate. The lights were low. Someone inside the large dining-room, which was a splendid replica of Meiji Restoration architecture with carved lacquered wainscoting and recessed ceiling molding, turned the muzak down, though the loud hum of conversation continued. Famous historical socialite "Oily Boy" Jiro Shirasu emerged from inside the dining room into the lounge with a second Jonessa Qali in tow, who burst into tears at the sight of Siren.

"I'm prettier than she is!" she sobbed hysterically until Oily Boy led her away.

For Siren, the Princess had selected "Salad Rolls of Shrimp, Ratatouille and Miso with Two Sauces Enchanted with Sleeping Beauty's Voice," along with heated organic Junmai "Shizengou" sake and "Something Cinderella Baked Strawberry-Tofu Custard of Magic at 12 O'Clock" for dessert. The Pooka had insisted on the "Seven Dwarf Grilled Vegetables and Avocado Hi-Ho We Go Pizza" for Obama, along with sauteed potatoes and coriander leaves with crunchy nuts and Bakashu Beer, which was made from fermented honey. All the dishes, including the pizza, were shaped like hearts or flowers.

The local news was dominated by the Ultrawoman and Guyferd sighting. The Disney-Japan versions of Tinkerbelle and Clarabelle Cow had been dispatched to the Ginza in the hopes of a repeat appearance by the two Metal Heroes. There was even Tattloid speculation that Ultrawoman and Guyferd, who had been thought never to have even been introduced to each other, were now deeply romantically involved, or even holed up in a hotel room somewhere nearby on their honeyMoon.

There were several grainy holos taken by tourists of the whole incident, which disproved the original explanation of it as a holographic publicity stunt, since holo cameras couldn't capture holo projections except as faint shadows. But since Obama and Siren hadn't been visible on radar, the authorities continued to dismiss the entire incident as a hoax.

An editorial by Pokemon's Pikachu next approvingly praised the sense of responsibility exhibited by the regional FAA and HHS, contrasting it favorably with the violent and illegal acts now taking place in New York and Manacera City. As Pikachu spoke, holos captured on the streets of both cities earlier that morning were displayed, showing peacekeepers firing their weapons at each other. The views of the lovable cartoon character seemed to reflect most Japanese public opinion: that the constitutional crisis somehow had nothing to do with them, and that it was not in fact their own government but someone else's descending into madness and war.

Maybe because of the sight of Chinese and Pakistani troops in the streets of Manhattan, so far the Japanese HHS employees seemed to be remaining silently and stubbornly loyal to Manacera, setting the tone for the isolationist mood of the former Japanese nation. According to what Obama could comprehend of the news reports, anyway. He wondered just how they might react if word of the Moon hoax ever got out, though — President Manacera might not be nearly so popular any more.

The next few minutes of broadcast time were devoted to news from the Moon. Over 30 million Japanese had "emigrated" there during the past few decades, and of these, at least two-thirds were still fondly imagined to be alive. Artful recreations of everyday incidents involving a few of the more famous Lunar residents were shown, along with interviews and heart-warming human interest stories. The amount of fakery this involved, particularly in the artificial digital aging of the subjects, was staggering to Obama. Both Carmen and Hector had had multiple visits with their own mothers convincingly emulated by this process. It must have occupied the efforts and creative talents of an entire small industry of its own, nearly the equivalent of a second Holowood. Where were all the people involved in this? Mumbai? Shanghai? Mexico City? How could they possibly all be kept completely silent about the details of their occupations?

Obviously, thought Obama, the work was all done onGrid, maybe even mostly by AIs; still, equally obviously, there had to be human minds involved in a deception on this scale. For a moment, he began to doubt Siren's claim that the Moon Colony really was a hoax — then he caught himself. She'd never lied to him about anything, as far as he knew. If he couldn't trust her, he could trust no one now, not even himself.

"Thanks," she murmured drily on the couch next to him. "Plus you've had plenty of other proof. But I can fly you to the Moon right now so you can see for yourself, if you like."

"No, thanks. It's just that this mind-reading thing is so not fair. It's totally normal to have random negative thoughts like that pop into your head. Everybody does it — at least, humyns do, anyway. But we aliens probably do it, too, right?"

"Not really, no. That's not how it works with us. But I'm too sleepy to go there right now, anyway." She put his head on her shoulder. *She's having trouble holding her sake,* he thought.

"I agree I'm not used to it," she mumbled. "However, I'm mostly just pretending to be drunk. I'm trying really, really hard to get you to go to bed with me, Obama. Don't act like you haven't noticed."

"I'll come to bed in a minute," he told her absentmindedly. "The North American news is coming on now, and I want to see what's going on there." His trips to Texas and Phobos had made him feel distant and detached from his old life in Manacera City, but the dramatic events taking place there, along with the sight of his old building and work-mates, had made him concerned over their fates all over again.

It was now mid-morning on the East Coast, and developments were unfolding in rapid succession. Colonel Ng had arrived at New Port Authority Freedom Tower at Ground Zero to take charge of the defense of the city, and President Manacera had come out of hiding to join him at a public press conference in the basement. The two of them appeared side by side, clasping fists and holding them aloft together to proclaim their solidarity. "This isn't just about the due process anymore," the president was telling the world. "Now it's about the lives of ordinary everyday citizens like you and me. Lives that have been placed in the direst peril by greedy, opportunistic politicians far away in Europe."

Inside the dining room, alien monsters, superheroes, and half-clad sim actresses were joining together in a loud, drunken chorus of "Don't Sit Under the Mister Toe With Anyone Else But Me."

"You have the world's most beautiful woman sitting next to you wearing only a bathrobe, and you'd rather watch this than her?" Siren asked bitterly.

"Sorry. Just a sec." What had Manacera said about Sato, exactly? Obama tried to remember. He had the feeling it might be important. How long ago had Manacera said he'd first met Sato? Thirty years or so? Just ten years later, Sato had changed his skin here in Tokyo — hadn't Manacera seen him after that? He'd made it sound like the two of them were in constant touch about the Moon colony, even if it had only been holographically. Surely he would have noticed the change. *If there has actually been one,* Obama thought. *Maybe Sato simply used another one of his own clones.*

"This is also about the defense of North American soil from alien invaders!" said the colonel a few minutes later, when it was his turn to speak. The president beamed and applauded, and the assembled HHS troopers that made up their audience burst into a roar of approval. The optional ratings tracker icon went through its little cartoon graphical roof.

Vice President Terrawati's press conference, however, didn't go nearly so well. Held in Geneva, to where she had removed herself overnight, she looked haggard and spoke hesitantly, Obama thought. Beneath a huge banner that read, "Your UN: A Century of Peace and Progress," and flanked by a few glum-faced senatorial allies — all three former sim actors — she delivered a long scolding lecture extolling her own restraint. "Once there might have been tanks on the streets, bomber aircraft, helicopters with guided missiles, even nuclear warheads raining down on the combatants. Today, thanks to your UN, that's no longer possible, as the industries that manufactured such instruments of death and destruction were long ago mandated to turn their factory production over to manufacturing solar panels, hybrid automobile engines, and biodegradable light bulbs. Now, instead of the horrors of another holocaust, New York City is suffering only from an argument between friends, armed only with a few light public anger management tools for weapons. This is only possible because of the rule of law, and it is the law we must respect in this matter.

"My good friend Jose Manacera has clearly broken the law, and must immediately suspend all activities until the charges against him — which are serious and can only be decided by the United Nations People's Parliament in the full majesty of its due deliberation — are either proved or dismissed. I promise him a full and fair investigation, and I beg those HHS peacekeepers who have declared their support for him to remember the solemn oath they have taken to uphold the peace."

This speech seemed weak compared to the bold, virile declarations of Manacera, and its ratings reflected it. Furthermore, everyone knew perfectly well that the reason there were no more operable tanks or cruise missiles or fleets of tactical bombers or aircraft carriers or Weapons of Mass Destruction left in the world was because, for decades, no nation had been able to afford to build or maintain them. And there were few former soldiers still alive who would have even known how to use them. War was strictly against the law.

In spite of this, it had broken out. Gun-battles had erupted in several places across New York City, and fires could be seen, especially on the East side of Midtown near the United Nations Executive Park and on the West Side docklands, where the Chinese HHS peacies had first established their bridgeheads. The Moynihan Station neighborhood was the epicenter of the counter-attack against them, and heavy RPG fire had cratered the sides of the New Madison Square Garden. Tactical armored airvan support for both sides had resulted in dog-fights over parts of Mid- and Downtown, sending burning and shattered vehicles crashing down into the streets and into office and condo buildings whose detection poles failed to protect them.

Since few, if any, were armed, most residents stayed indoors or took shelter in the subways. Aside from the peacekeepers, only roving gangs of deprived immigrant and minority youths could be seen on the streets, mostly looting stores. Traffic and security-bots crawled and flew overhead, sirens shrilling, in a vain attempt to maintain order, while a few intrepid camera-bots continued to report the action.

The situation was even more confused in the second Federal Admin Area, Manacera City. A thick pall of smoke hung over most of the downtown area, obscuring aerial cam-shots and making a tactical assessment of the situation difficult. Gamely, the local cartoon news crew attempted to make sense of each fresh battle report they received from private citizens and surveillance cams, but their task was not an easy one. The epicenter of the conflict seemed now to be the MAD Building. Winnie-the-Pooh, wearing a blue peacekeeper's helmet, was reporting live from within the besieged citadel.

"Snow White," he was saying now, in the endearingly bumbling, squeaky tones beloved by generations of small children, "the situation here has deteriorated noticeably overnight. In what has become the worst ongoing atrocity of this constitutional crisis so far, the fighting here has been vicious, office-by-office and floor-by-floor. Outnumbered and outgunned, the Federal employees here have done everything they could to aid the brave Cuban HHS peacekeepers who volunteered for this mission, risking their very lives to protect the rule of UN law in North America. And let's not forget, Snow, that these noble lads and lasses are North Americans, too, and as such, have as much right to be here as you or I. I'm standing here right now speaking to one of the few remaining staffers left in the building, FaLola Montoya. FaLola, what can you tell me about the morale of the defenders inside the citadel?"

"Well, Winnie, I'd say it was battered but determined." In honor of their Latino allies, FaLola was wearing one of Their favorite dresses, a bright fluffy South American flowery print over a black tutu and lacy lingerie. It had not fared well. It was blackened and discolored, and FaLola had evidently been forced to tear several strips off its hem to bandage the wounded.

"What kind of casualties have they taken?" asked Winnie. There was the sound of small-arms fire in the background, and behind that the deeper thud-thud-thudding of a mortar attack.

"Well, it's kind of, you know, rude to ask, but I think maybe dozens? Maybe even a hundred?" FaLola answered breathlessly. "There's blood all over the fifth floor. We've dumped most of the corpses down into the lower stairwells, but the atmosphere in here is still pretty intense. And more Rednecks landed on the roof in the night and are fighting their way down from there, too. So basically, I'm trapped in here with my brave boys and girls."

"Will the weather be a factor? We could get snow tomorrow."

"It would come too late to help us, I'm afraid, Winnie. We need to be reinforced and resupplied. Don't quote me, but things seem pretty hopeless right now. The worst part of it is the lack of grief counseling and anger management — emotions are pretty intense in here!" A sudden heavy thud made the building shake, and there was a shower of plaster-dust from the ceiling.

"Blimey, that was a close one," said the Pooh, screwing his steel helmet on tighter. "Can you tell me if there are any other MAD employees left alive in the building, FaLola?"

"To the best of my knowledge, the rest are all gone, Winnie. It's my understanding that they had 'liberal leave' today." Suddenly the holographic transmission ended, and Snow White's face reappeared.

"We appear to have lost the signal," she said gravely. Obama thought she was looking a bit pale and drawn, but perhaps that was his imagination. "The insurgent HHS peacekeepers are jamming all transmissions coming out of siege situations now, fearing that coded messages are being smuggled through to their enemies."

"Bloody, bloody hell!"said Siren, sitting suddenly upright on the couch. "Princess, compile an audit of all credit charges that Simonetta ran up tonight."

"OK," said the Princess. "Done."

"Now scan the numbers for any kind of coded or encrypted messages. Strip stuff like the time and date off it for now."

"Uh oh."

"What?"

"You aren't going to like this, Siren," the Princess told her. "The way the individual bills are sequenced, it looks like she was using a simple symmetric key code, so that a Roman letter could be substituted for each numeric digit. I'm launching a mathematical attack on it now ... OK, got it. Here's the message: *'daddy there r 2 of them stop obama and a being like u stop they have me trapped w no body in ur old station on phobos stop there r at least 2 others maybe helpers question mark end.'*

"And then there's a postscript: *'not so fucking bad for a girl who never read a fucking book huh fucking obama.'*"

"I told you she scared me," Siren said after a long silence. "The bitch literally shopped her way past us and slipped her father an SOS!"

"It gets worse," said Obama. "She can read my mind, too."

Siren sat in his lap and ran her fingers affectionately across the fuzz on his head. "What are you talking about?" she asked him. "I thought I was the only one allowed to do that."

"That message to me at the end — about girls who've never read a book in their lives. I didn't say the words aloud to her, I only thought them when I was around her. That means she was able to read my mind the whole time, just like you. It's not fair! How come everybody can do it except me?"

"Well, let's rationalize this, baby. First of all, it's obvious she's been taught how. Probably she's been tutored by Sato about lots of things. She knows about Helpers, for example, even though she's never met one. And Phobos, though she couldn't possibly have been there before. So you're operating at a terrific disadvantage compared to her. I think you've done great so far. All you need is a few lessons." She nibbled at his ear, and he started. "For example, can you tell what I'm thinking right now?"

"I can't believe you're serious!" he said, agitatedly. "I mean, we need to do something, get back to Phobos or find Sato — something! And we need to do it fast!"

She shook her head. "Don't be daft," she said. "There's nothing we can do right now. Even if Sato could instantly fly out to Phobos, Laputa wouldn't let him in the door. She hates his guts. Helpers aren't our slaves, you know. All that Sato knows now that he didn't know before is that a second visitor has arrived to spoil the fun he's been having building his own personal little planetary ant-farm. And that you and it are probably working together. So relax. We have a lovely big bed all to ourselves. We don't have to check out till noon tomorrow. Or ever, really. Wouldn't you like to show me how to have sex? I still don't have a clue how to do it, Obama. I sort of tried it with a sim yesterday and felt, well ... really stupid. I guess I'm just not getting it."

He stared at her incredulously. "I'll make sure the Helpers don't peek," she added, nibbling his other ear. "And I threw the last of the party guests out of our bedroom." It was undeniable, he thought, that she was lovely. But she was still Siren. "OK, OK, I know — I'm really an alien brain parasite who looks like a squid, not a pretty Earth girl. So what? Sex is all you think about when you look at me, and we both know it. Why pretend it doesn't matter and isn't what you want, when obviously it is?" She put her sleek head against his chest. "I just want to make you happy. Correction, I want us to be happy. I want to understand the human half of you. Is that so much to ask?"

In exasperation he said, "What I don't get is why you were all, you know, cold and icy aloof and couldn't be touched before. Remember that first night in our apartment? Remember how you treated me? You told me not to even think about touching you, how much you hated it. Well, I respected that," he went on. "I tried to be really sweet to you and behave as a friend — and that was back when I still thought you were humyn. I didn't even think you liked me. Now it's suddenly like you're all over me."

"Feeling nostalgic?" Her tone was acerbic. *And rightly so,* he thought. He sounded like a petulant middle-skool kid even to himself.

"No — it's just that I don't understand why," he told her lamely. "Why the sudden change?"

"Oh, baby, I don't know. Look, this is embarrassing enough for me — do you really have to have everything spelled out for you? Obviously, I'm being a lot more affected by these human bodies than I thought possible. You'll understand what I mean someday — it's like drowning in hormone soup. And there are so many of my — Jonessa's — well, not memories, exactly, but reflexes floating around.

"But it's not just that. Try to put yourself in my place for just five minutes. I had to travel all this way for no good reason except that I was nagged into it by the Helpers, because they were upset that one of us was misbehaving. So I was forced down this gravity well and made to fit inside these horrible humyn bodies, and just when I thought I had everything well sorted, then suddenly I meet this, well, amazing sort of primitive young stud-muffin. And then I had to spend all this time in his company, intimately, in the same actual room, sharing all his thoughts and emotions … everything. Frankly, Obama, it was either get a crush on you or kill you."

"And since you couldn't kill me…"

"Bingo."

"Bingo!"screamed the Princess. "Want me to get us all cards? They call it 'Sweet Bingo' here, by the way."

"That's enough from you two," said Siren, getting to her feet. She grabbed Obama's hand and dragged him off in the direction of the bedroom. "We're going to be in there for the next few hours, and I don't want to be disturbed for anything — not if the hotel catches on fire, not if there's an earthquake, not even if ninja assassins fly out of the ceiling, OK? You two take care of it. And no snooping! And turn down that party."

"I'm making popcorn," said the Pooka, as Siren closed the bedroom door behind her. Siren darkened the Miro lamps beside the enormous round bed, then lay back on it against a stack of pillows. The ceiling-to-floor waterfall with the sunken grotto and rock garden splashed and trickled. Its vertical blinds left half-open, the long high window that ran along one side of the room was filled with the shifting skyline of night-time Tokyo, striping Siren like a psychedelic tigress in garish illumination. She patted the bed sheet imperiously, and Obama lay down beside her, catching a glimpse as he did so of the two of them in the overhead mirror.

"We should build a fire in the fireplace," she suggested. "It's cold enough outside for it."

"I don't know. It's pretty hot inside."

"Oh yes. So hot. They said that a lot in that sim. OK, maybe I am just the teeniest bit tipsy," she whispered. Obama could still hear a speed-drinking and vomiting contest being waged at the party in the dining room. "I wanted to see how it felt. How being humyn feels. You can't blame me, can you? That's why I changed into this body, because I thought if I were black instead of white you might, you know, want me more." She raised herself slightly, and wrapping one dusky, perfect arm around his neck, kissed him. He could taste the strawberry and the sake on her breath. Her bathrobe parted, and he saw the long line of her dark brown body curving from breast to belly.

"I'm so glad you're nothing like Simonetta," Siren murmured. "Inside, I mean."

"But how can you be sure of that?" he asked her.

"I'm sure." She stared open-eyed at him. Reading him, he thought. Like an open book.

"How did you find me in the first place, anyway? I've always wondered about that. I mean, you just showed up out of nowhere at that funeral I went to."

"I was following Simonetta, and she led me to you," said Siren. "At least the bitch was good for something. I was using the Pooka to bug the UNSS offices and hack into all their data files, and it struck us both as weird that Simonetta would suddenly quit that job and go chasing after you in Manacera City. And of course, she led us to the human genome files, too. I think once she went to work at MAD, she discovered that Sato hadn't destroyed all the public copies."

"OK, I know I'm being really stupid, but I still don't get it," Obama said. "Why were you bugging the UNSS offices?"

"I wasn't," said Siren laughing. Her bathrobe fell open, exposing soft round breasts like those on a Hindu temple sculpture. "I was bugging Manacera's offices, actually. To begin with, anyway. Then I expanded it to his security service. You see, I was new in town and hadn't a clue what I was doing. And Manacera was the president of the whole world, so I thought it made sense to start at the top — with him. What does the alien always say in the old flatties? 'Take me to your leader'?"

"Shhh," he said, and kissed her. It was the only way to stop himself from staring at her. *What the hell am I doing?* he wondered. *What am I getting myself into?* Her eyes stared back at him, dark as coals. He inhaled her scent and suddenly became aroused, clumsily pulling off her robe, then his own. She gasped. Bathed in the reflected city lights, Siren — or rather Jonessa Qali — was perfect, lovelier even than Kim had been. He felt guilty and disloyal at the thought. He realized that in fact he hadn't thought about Kim in days. Discovering that he was really a space alien had treasonously eroded his connection to her in some mysterious fashion, even somehow in his memories. Yet, he hadn't been aware of the lie he'd been living all those years with her — he hadn't deceived her in any way. What they'd had together had been real. But it was over. She was gone. And she'd been human. Obama Jones wasn't — and now he was gone, too, transmuted into something new and inhuman. But the alien monster Obama had the right to start over again with someone else, didn't he?

Siren stirred restlessly under his fingers, and he imagined her suddenly in passion, in climax. Sweat sprang up on her skin and her breathing quickened. *Why shouldn't I be with Siren? It's not as if I don't love her,* he thought. *Wait a minute: I 'love' Siren? Do I?* He decided he did.

She moaned. "Please don't stop," she whispered. He'd barely touched her. Yet if he loved her, why couldn't he bring himself to make love to her? Obviously, his reluctance meant he didn't love her in quite the same way as he had Kim, not with the same wholesome uncomplicated animal passion, anyway. But that chapter of his life was over. He could never go back to being humyn again, no matter how hard he tried. Beneath him Siren groaned with frustration.

But something else was bothering him, too, eating away at the edges of his conscious thought. *No,* he thought, *it isn't something Manacera said about Sato that's the clue. It's something Manacera told me about myself.* If only he could remember exactly what it was ...

"I don't know what I'm supposed to be doing," Siren said to him, her face straining up at him in the bed, like a swimmer coming up for air. Her body was quivering, on fire, covered with both their dampness. "Please tell me what to do, Obama." Her eyes were lovely, wide and imploring, but he was paralyzed by his own tension, by the stray thoughts echoing inside his head. Thoughts that she, of course, was sharing even as he had them.

He felt monstrous cheating her of pleasure like this. But he was a monster, wasn't he? They both were. Their humyn bodies were a charade. A vivid image suddenly struck him of their true physical selves floating together in a cloudy sea of milky blue. Slowly touching, trembling, tentacles writhing in mutual ecstasy, thrashing, stirring up the liquid light around them, colors sparking like tiny bolts of lightning inside their sacs. The vision persisted, grew more detailed and real, swept over him as he closed his eyes. He felt as though he were drowning in it. Siren shuddered beneath him, convulsed, and cried out in ecstasy.

Then they both started talking at once.

"I'm sorry I couldn't — "

"Oh, Obama, that was amazing!" she panted. "Was it good for you, too?" Then, catching his thoughts again, "Oh. Oh, that wasn't how it was supposed to be at all, was it?"

He took her in his arms, and pulled a sheet over their bodies. "I'm sorry. It's just ... having you inside my mind all the time. I just can't stay hard with that going on, I guess. And having to listen to 'Do They Know It's Kurisumasu?' sung in Japanese monster burps isn't helping."

"But that's what makes it so exciting and beautiful for me," she said. "Being inside your mind, I mean. Not the burps."

"It doesn't really work too well during humyn sex," he told her tenderly. He stroked her thighs, kissed the sweaty tendrils of hair on her forehead. "Sex is an animal act. The male animal has to relax and go on auto-pilot or else he can't perform." He waved the waterfall onto Dribble mode, and it trickled down into the rock garden with soothing plinking sounds. They lay tightly wrapped up together and watched it.

"OK, Obama," Siren said humbly. "You don't have to perform any more if you don't want to. I understand."

"But I do want to!" said Obama. "Look, is there some way to block my thoughts from you? Just during sex, I mean — not all the time."

"Sure — just wear a steel helmet. Probably the one Winnie-the-Pooh was wearing on YouVee tonight would work. But I don't want to be shut out of your thoughts during— "

"Seriously? It's that simple?" He felt like shouting with relief. Though the thought of wearing a UN peacekeeping helmet to bed wasn't exactly attractive. Or workable. Still, he'd figure something out.

"Yes," she said. Now she sounded cross. "If we were both naked inside Simonetta's tank together, for example, our thoughts would be totally transparent to each other, because there would be nothing to get in the way. No bones or anything, I mean. But stuck inside humyn bodies, most of our radioactive emissions are blocked." She touched the top of his scalp where it had been shaved for his gaming cap. The hair had already started growing back there. "This is the thinnest part of the cranium, where the two halves grow together in infancy. It's called the 'bregma.' Some people even have a little hole there. It's where most of our thoughts leak out in the form of small bursts of electromagnetic radiation generated by the neurons firing. Block that off with something thick, and they're very hard to pick up."

"Is that where you receive them, too?" he asked. "Through a hole in your head?"

"No. Most of our sensitivity to the signals is through our mouths and noses. Keep your mouth shut and they aren't nearly as loud. And it works both ways, too — a certain amount of our own mental activity leaks out that way. But mostly through the bregma."

"So in order to practice absolutely totally safe sex with you, I'll have to wear a steel helmet, keep my mouth shut and not kiss you. Either that or pretend I'm someone else."

"We can do anything you like, Obama. We can wear costumes, if you want. Or use the Helpers. Our original ancestors were a race of chameleon jellyfish swimming in a kind of ocean, changing their color and appearance to mimic other creatures. It's been theorized that's why we evolved into parasites. It may be that it's also why you were so good at changing into Kalinga. It makes sense that impersonation would be a natural talent of ours even without resorting to clones," she said. "Changing our accents, changing our names."

"Shit! That's what Manacera said. I just remembered."

"What are you talking about?"

"I've finally remembered what Manacera told me," he said grimly. He sat up. "He said that after his parents moved across the border from the former Mexico they changed their last name. Pooka!" he called, opening the bedroom door. "Can you go onGrid for me and find out what Jose Manacera's original family name was? Before they moved here and changed it, I mean?"

"Dulcero," the Pooka called back to him after a few seconds. "Does this mean we're allowed in the bedroom now?"

"Thanks! Dulcero," he said to Siren. "Wasn't that one of the family names in the HGP K6 etc bloodline files?"

"Yes, first in Madrid, then Mexico City."

"Of course, you realize what this means, don't you?" he asked her, and she nodded.

"Yes. Jose Manacera is really Sato," said Siren slowly. "He's been Sato all along. And I was too bloody stupid to notice."

And all at once, Obama knew what he had to do. The moment the thought occurred to him, of course, Siren started to argue. And argue. They were still at it when they both fell asleep just before dawn.

26.

The first checkpoint he was stopped at was just north of Eveready Battery City, in front of the half-destroyed glasspex-winged-and-ribbed World Financial Memorial Visitors' and Transit Center. Freedom Tower, floodlit immediately in front of him, had trails of smoke curling from a number of its upper floors. To its south, the Ground Zero Peace Butterfly, a huge flat construction spun from pink and blue glasspex, had had most of its triangular wing facets blown out, and the world-famous memorial holographic display around it was shut off.

A number of smashed groundcars had been pushed into the intersection of Vesey and West Streets, blocking traffic in both directions, and black beetle-armored HHS peacies with the crowns of their helmets painted blood-red were checking IDs and turning pedestrians away. "Nice chopper!" said one of the troopers when they got to him. Moments before, he'd watching them bring down someone on a Piaggi Floped scooter who'd tried to skip over the checkpoint on the sidewalk in front of the shuttered Starck boutique.

"Yaybo, man!" said Joyful Kalinga. The dawn was just breaking, and his smile flashed gold from the tips of his filed teeth.

"Yamasaki, right?" asked another.

"Stratoflier XS51, my friend," Kalinga told him. "Oh yes, she is one proud beauty, for sure." The machine idled, purring, about 20 cm off the road surface. It had round horizontal spin-drives where the wheels would be on a traditional motorcycle, or "groundhog," along, with mini Pratt & Whitney propellant thruster bulbs on the rear casing. These were mounted just above and at the same angles as the massive twin exhaust pipes. The luxury charcoal leather and silver air-hog also featured a curving windshield that curled back to a rigid back-brace to form a clear glasspex overhead canopy, leaving the sides open.

The Pooka had sculpted herself into the Stratoflier's form before sneaking Obama across the Hudson, just before first light. The Chinese HHS peacekeepers had taken over the West Side Rail Yards and were using them to launch J-DAMs at anything that moved on the river. They'd already taken down the sky-tram lines to Hoboken and Hackensack. Now he was being waved to one side while a line of robot fire department vehicles, sirens flashing, edged past under military escort.

"What kind of elevation can you get out of her?"

"Rooftop, man! Rooftop!" Obama said enthusiastically. Though, of course, the Pooka could fly him back to Phobos if she had to. In fact, he'd tried to talk Siren into going back to Phobos herself, but she'd insisted on waiting for him in their hotel room in Jersey City instead. She was, she had said, "sick with worry." What had Kim always told him? "Don't make me worry." *Siren's starting to sound like Kim,* he thought. Which wasn't a bad thing. If he was still alive in a few days, he'd have to think about that a little more.

"Sorry, we're not supposed to let anybody through," the first peacie said. "What's your business anyway?"

"Tell your boss-man Joyful Kalinga is here to volunteer," Obama said. "These people fighting President Manacera very bad. They are big shits. Manacera, he is a good fellow!"

"I can't tell him anything, because we're all observing coms silence. They even shut down the military grid. We're using bike messengers now for all our orders, so maybe they'll need your hog. Tell you what — I'll wave you through with a local pass to City Hall. Maybe you can find a unit there to volunteer with. Try the basement of the Tower first, though, OK?" Kalinga gave them the universal "peace" sign as he was passed through the checkpoint.

It was the first of many. Since none of the peacekeepers manning them now had Grid access, however, or presumably any clear authority whatever over the HHS data files, Obama became gloomily aware that he might have a lot more trouble getting arrested than he'd anticipated.

Getting shot at, however, was another matter. Loud explosions and the pocketa-pocketa of automatic rifle-fire sounded nearby as he crossed the street and turned into Freedom Plaza. Up close, he could see the concrete facades of the weathered Freedom Tower scored with bullet-holes; nearly half of its glass panes had been shattered. A constant stream of fire-fighting robots with hoses and foam dispensers were entering the building, guarded by a few restless-looking peacies cradling their weapons. "I don't see any sign of Manacera," he said to Siren.

"We're still under a news blackout here," she said in his ear. "A few of the local channels are running Skywitness bot reports of Pakistani snipers on rooftops around Wall Street, so Downtown still isn't safe. But there's no word of where Manacera might be. How's your tummy feel?"

"Terrible!"

"What about your head?"

"It feels like I have a really bad hangover," he told her. The truth was, he felt sick. How much of that was fear and how much the result of the surgeries, he didn't know. Two down and only one to go, he told himself. But it was the big one.

"No coms traffic at all," the Pooka said in his other ear. "Except in Chinese. They're trying to re-take Central Park." A SWAT-Team sergeant followed by a pair of squaddies approached Obama, waving his arm in a shooing motion.

"We're evacuating the building," the sergeant said. "If you're looking for somebody in particular they may be in another of the towers. Otherwise, you need to clear the area right away along with everybody else. There's danger of collapse."

"The president, he is surely safe though?" Obama said as Kalinga.

"President Manacera hasn't been here since yesterday. All these attacks happened after he left." The peacies started dragging metal barricade fencing to block off the Greenwich Street entrance. "You'd think they would have learned the first time — after 911," the sergeant said, squinting straight up at the top of the tower. The spire had disappeared, and as they watched, a portion of its roof collapsed onto the storey below, making the ground tremble and sending smoke and ash in every direction. The onlookers, mostly peacie troopers, mixed with a scattering of passers-by and local residents, gave a collective gasp.

"I'm being re-stimulated," said an elderly woman in a *daishiki* standing near Obama. She had waist-length silver hair and was carrying several torn shopping bags. Debris started raining down on them.

"They used the same building codes and even some of the same materials when they built the Memorial Tower," the sergeant told Obama angrily. "Probably even the same contractors. So much for your fucking different result. You can tell them that at City Hall."

Obama and the Pooka found City Hall ringed by troop carriers, ambulances, and stalled traffic. She skimmed over them all the wrong way up Broadway before turning into City Hall Park and hovering to a halt. Dozens of wounded combatants, most of them Pakistanis, had been dragged over to the Victorian fountain in the middle. Several were trying to drink from the pool at the base of the bronze gas lamps. One, Obama noticed, had died with his head in the water. An Endura custodian under the direction of a peacie trooper was stripping the corpses of body armor and stacking it on the sidewalk. The elegant European-style cupola at the top of the building had been hit, and dark streaks of soot marred its white stone walls.

Obama was stopped again. When he showed his hand-scrawled pass, he was told the mayor was holding a press conference in the rotunda. Would Manacera be there, he asked? No one knew. The air was clearing, and Obama could see all the way to the Brooklyn Bridge, where even now some of the heaviest gun-battles were still taking place. Across the East River, the cruise ship *Queen Mary II* was docked at the Brooklyn Bridge Park Terminal; it had been seized by the UNHSS troops and was being used as a floating barracks. For the past 24 hours the ship had come under intense ATS missile and RPG fire from the insurrectionist HHS forces dug into the permanent Habitation-Eliminated Locationless Person Shelters beneath FDR Drive in East River Park.

As the Pooka stopped in front of the Hall's main entrance, over which a supraliminal rainbow-colored holo proclaimed: "New York — A Capital City!," a burst of sniper-fire erupted, echoing between skyscrapers as it had at Palo Duro Canyon, and a team of green-cross helmeted medics took cover next to them, while the peacies guarding the subway entrance down the street crouched behind abandoned cars to return fire. A group of reporters, flying newsbots and a few amateur gloggers scuttled from the building complaining furiously. "He called the presser and didn't even bother to show up!" one of them shouted at Obama. "Because of the news blackout. What a lamer!"

"Is Manacera in there?" Obama replied.

"Nobody's in there." The glogger stopped dead on the sidewalk. He was in his late 60s and was wearing a commercial bullet-proof vest, a protective bumper helmet and a pair of monitor glasses, which he deactivated. "These are useless," he said. "When you try to boot up into virtual New York City they re-route you into virtual White fucking Plains. Wow," he said, taking a closer look, "Are you somebody? You're

Joyful Kalinga! Yo, can we do an interview, amigo?" One of the flying bots stopped and opened its lenses at him.

Kalinga smiled widely and inhaled. New York still smelled like nowhere else he'd ever been, a mix of paving-stone and ancient drains, of stale cigar ash, car exhaust, bagel bakeries, decaying fish, and something else. Sunlight. It was turning into a sunny day in the city. A spray of bullets bounced off manhole covers and stirred up dust in the intersection.

"Surely," he said. "But first I must find President Manacera. Kalinga has a personal message for the Big Man. He has come a long way to deliver it, all the way from the moons of Mars."

"Wow, most excellent stuff!" said the glogger. "I'll post that now. I've heard Manacera's going up to personally take charge of the defense of Central Park himself. He says the Chinese can call him 'No Way, Jose'!" The myn giggled.

"That's not what I'm being told," snapped the newsbot. He switched on his holo projector and became a little toy-sized Dumbo the Flying Elephant. "Everybody knows Manacera's locked away at UNUC, rehearsing the victory speech he's planning to give in Times Square tonight."

"You think he's winning?" the glogger snorted derisively.

"CNN is calling it for him," said Dumbo in a defensive tone. He flapped his ears and moved in for a close-up. "Tell me, Mr. Kalinga, what lies behind your courageous decision to throw your lot in with that of the beleaguered and embattled president?"

"Well, Dumbo," said Obama, "President Manacera is a very great man. Look at all good things he has done for this world. Compared to him, his enemies are like a big rat turds. They must be jolly damn careful or Kalinga will come and kill them all. Better for them to surrender now before he does that, oh my yes."

"Yo, this is my interview, dude," the glogger was complaining. Dumbo ignored him.

"I'll try to smuggle this out to Newark," he told Obama, waving his trunk, before the Pooka slowly spun and skimmed away.

At the turn of the century, it had been envisioned by city planners that New York would become a green expanse of riverside grassy parks and crystalline skyscrapers. Most of its population would live in high-rises in Manhattan and Brooklyn, while the outer boroughs would gradually turn into parkland. Staten Island would become "New York's California." Piers would be turned into museums, restaurants, or picnic centers. Foreign investors from Europe and the Arab Emirates would finance dozens of new green buildings and "miniature cultural districts" featuring rooftop gardens, smart-energy consumption, and bicycle paths instead of streets.

Reality had intruded, however, after the Great Panic and the Manic Depression that followed. Funding for such ventures dried up, and for the next decade, the city and its services stagnated even as the population rapidly grew due to waves of immigrants fleeing the effects of global cooling abroad. The parks froze in winter and dried up in summer, the plants and trees withered, and New Yorkers took a perverse pride in belonging to the first city on the planet to "Go Orange," squandering energy simply to keep their streets warm.

Older skyscrapers had been restored, or in some cases, allowed to collapse and, except for marquee projects like that of the Ground Zero Freedom Memorial Tower, most new development followed the patterns of the distant past. Ambitious public works projects resulted in shanty-towns for the HELP springing up under elevated highways and in empty lots, and smaller, boxlike mini-habitats — some buried underground, others stacked like cubes — became popular even among the employed. The wealthy had grown even more isolated, thanks to aerial sky-trams, security-bots, and the marketing of the aircar. The poor had received larger and larger entitlements and subsidies from both the then-US and UN governments, reflecting President Manacera's political philosophy of Co-operatism.

In the decade before Common Union, these subsidies had been dramatically increased. The New Subway system had been created, modeled on that of Tokyo, though because of air leakage the New Subway's pneumatic cars were able to move only half as fast through the antiquated tunnel lines. Elevated mag-lev and skytram lines connected the city center to its boroughs, aresopaceports, as well as the New Jersey bedroom communities across the river. Dramatic ultramodern structures such as the Brooklyn Heights skyline and the Midtown Moynihan Station complex were finally completed, and in 2034 the new United Nations Unity Complex, or UNUC, became the official residence of the first world president, Jose Barca Manacera. New York City had become the executive, though not the legislative, capital of the world.

But as the Pooka carried Obama north, still skimming the tree-line and dodging aircars the wrong way up Broadway, it seemed to him that half of the city was on fire. An enormous column of smoke had risen up over Midtown, forming an ever-deepening pall. Traffic bots screamed at them at every intersection, and one hurled itself to pieces on the Pooka's windshield.

The sidewalks were mostly deserted, except for a few furtive pedestrians ducking down into subways or squatting in doorways. But Broadway, at least, was choked with stalled traffic, parked or abandoned cars, lines of HHS vehicles convoying behind killdozers, and several crashed airvans with half-charred corpses visible inside. Most of the air-traffic consisted of airbulances and military vehicles flying below them, hovering low and close to the streets for safety's sake.

Obama got stopped at another roadblock at Union Square and turned away, then was fired on when he and the Pooka skipped over a block or two to follow 5th Avenue instead. "I'm PMSing today," the Pooka told him, racing her engines. "Eating bullets is getting boring. I feel a hate-on coming, hee hee."

"Bullets?" said Siren in his other ear. She sounded upset.

"Chill, bitch, I'm on it," the Pooka told her. *Being an airhog,* thought Obama, *really isn't having a good effect on her.* Siren was fretful, too. She still wasn't completely convinced that Manacera really was Sato. The DNA they'd scraped from the empty operating table and vat in the closet had been that of the original Sato and his clones. But Obama believed that Sato had only used the clone, a younger version of the cadaver they'd found, as a temporary replacement. Maybe the old one had collapsed suddenly or had had a heart attack, necessitating the quick transfer. Whatever the case, Obama thought Sato had abandoned the clone for one he'd made of Manacera after returning to North America. Then he'd murdered the real Manacera.

That would have been precisely during the interval between the original Jose Manacera's election to the presidency of the former United States and his inauguration. After the transplant, Sato had allowed his own old clone to live, maybe as a backup, and somehow it had escaped or just wandered away. Now it lived on the streets of Manacera City, driven insane by the time it had spent with Sato inside it. Siren might have her doubts, but there was an easy way to prove all this. By locating Manacera. And getting arrested by his security people seemed the fastest way to achieve that.

By the time Obama and the Pooka got to the Empire State Building, the pall of smoke had noticeably thickened. The famous old skyscraper was shrouded in camouflage netting and bristling with additional aircraft-repellent poles. It now resembled a giant desiccated cactus. Down West 34th the sounds of heavy fighting echoed across from the Moynihan Station Plex. To the north, the Trump Tower AI was treacherously using holograms in an attempt to disguise itself as the Chrysler Building. Several of the other taller buildings were projecting holos of ambient environmental scenes in a desperate attempt to soothe any potential attacker.

Obama passed the New York Public Liberry, where he'd spent so many happy hours while in grad skool, then Rockettefeller Center, skimming over groups of looters spilling out into the avenue from Brooks Brothers and the IBA Store. Storefronts were smashed and the debris of expensive clothing and other luxury items was scattered between Saks and Bergdorf Goodman. Manacera's HHS peacies had been given orders to shoot to kill looters but were evidently ignoring them.

Obama then jogged over to the Avenue of Nations, where he was stopped at another checkpoint at the edge of Central Park. Mortar fire came from the direction of Columbus Circle, but the smoke was now too thick for Obama to see that far, even though bright sunlight was still filtering through. An acrid stench permeated the air, and most of the few passersby on the sidewalks had natural fiber T-shirts wrapped around their lower faces.

"It's the Chinese," one of the HHS troopers guarding the roadblock told him. "They're stealing tires from parked cars and setting them on fire. They're trying to make the whole city so smoky that our airvans can't spot them. Their J-DAMs don't need to see anyway, because they're GPS-guided." A huge explosion came from the direction of Carnegie Hall. "Holy crap, sounds like they hit an ammo cache," he said. J-DAMs were the first smart-weapons ever invented; the acronym was milspeak for Joint Direct Attack Munitions.

"Is Manacera in the park, my friend?" Obama asked him.

"If I'm honest," said the peacie, "I don't know or care. I can't let you through here, but you could try going around to 5th Avenue. The locals are too dumb to have blocked off EDEN." EDEN, the Evolutionarily Disadvantaged Entities' Nature-reserve, was now the official name for the former Central Park Zoo. Higher primates, of course, as well as dolphins, whales, dogs, and pigs, were not allowed inside it except as visitors, and over the years, animal-rights crusaders like Jonessa Qali had managed to legally emancipate most of the other residents except for a few migratory bird colonies, a vast number of rodents, and the feral cats, dogs, and escaped reptiles which fed on them.

EDEN lay in the southeast corner of the park, immediately to the north of the now-deserted Grand Army Plaza. The first sign of humyn activity that Obama came across other than looting was at the old Arsenal building at East 64th, where squads of red-helmeted peacies were congregating under occasional sniper fire. "It might be easier for me to protect you if I became your body-armor now," the Pooka suggested, when he pulled her to a stop on the sidewalk. "That way we can blend in with the soldiers, too. We can still fly around if we need to — nobody would notice us in this smoke."

"Who cares if they do?" Siren chimed in. "Obama agreed to let you pull him out instantly anyway if you ran into trouble." He sighed. How could he could he possibly run into any trouble worse than that he was actively seeking out? But he kept his mouth shut, and once they were out of sight round the side of the turreted brown-brick medieval-style building, and Obama had jettisoned Kalinga's overcoat, he let the Pooka morph into a peacie uniform around him.

The standard North American HHS peacekeeper's body armor, which had been developed in 2032 after decades of research from U.C. Berkeley's BLEEX exoskeleton project and the Massachusetts Institute of Technology's Institute for Soldier Nanotechnologies, incorporated nanotech, artificially powered exoskeletons, and magneto-rheological fluid-based body armor to provide the infantry with significantly higher protection during SWAT operations. It was made of a bullet-resistant ferrofluid smart-material composed of nanobit iron particles suspended in silicon oil. When struck with a significant impact, the armor stiffened instantly into a shield, then reverted to its flaccid state just as quickly when the energy from the projectile dissipated.

The armor, originally envisioned to be spread on like peanut butter, was instead pre-sprayed onto M5 fiber in ultra-thin coats. The rigid, visored helmet included a subsystem with neural lace, onGrid access to maps, routes, and tactical data with a 180° emissive visor display for maximalized "bumping," high bandwidth WiiFi communications, a microelectronic/optics combat sensor suite that provided 360° situational awareness, and integrated small arms protection. The Micro-climate Conditioning Subsystem was a network of narrow tubing containing circulating fluid that provided 100 watts of heating or cooling to the trooper. This was fed by micro-turbines fueled by a liquid hydrocarbon fuel cell.

A half-liter of fuel would power the entire integrated electronics ensemble for up to a week. Polymeric nanofiber battery patches embedded in the headgear and weapons could provide back-up power for an additional 24 hours. But this was under ideal conditions. The reality for the peacies in the field was radically different: the power supplies dirtied or even failed constantly, and the heat (and humidity) generated inside the exoskeletons was miserable even in winter. Luckily for Obama, the Pooka only emulated the shell of the Personal Armored Survivability System. She had her own ideas about how to arrange the insides of it.

"Where the hell are you supposed to be, trooper? Who are you?" a sergeant was suddenly screaming at him in a voice rasping with fatigue. An HHS company was forming ranks under the elms just behind Obama. The Pooka must have swiped him a spoofed ID, because his tone softened. "You're a long way from your unit. What's your story?"

"Detached as a runner, sergeant," Obama replied promptly in his own, not Kalinga's voice. Like most of his generation he'd never served in the old military or the HHS, but he'd gamed in the roles so often he at least had a smattering of milspeak. "Is President Manacera here in the park?"

"He gave us a pep talk at the theater this morning, then fucked off back to his bunker before the Chinese took it. That's all I can tell you, trooper. You better fall in with us — we need every able-bodied man we can get." The HHS was exempted from the worldwide ban of the word "man;" inside its ranks all troopers, regardless of gender or gender-orientation, were referred to as a "man," addressed as "trooper," or — in the case of what had once been termed "commissioned officers" — "sir." All formal ranks and commanding officers had been briefly done away with back during the days of the "People's Peacekeeping," when peacekeepers had been deployed under the aegis of the Department of Peace and Non-Violence, but had been reinstated by executive order after nearly 300 of them had been massacred by a small tribe of Nepalese herders armed only with a few antique rifles and long knives. This was another reason Manacera was popular with the HHS rank and file.

The rest of the platoon held their HAKMORs — Heckler And Koch Modular Rifles — in a combat-ready stance the Pooka instantly copied with her own. A Hummer landed in the little asphalt parking lot beside them, and a captain got out and stood on its roof. "Listen up, ladies!" he barked. "We've just received orders to deploy in support of the Patriots at the Belvedere Castle. You could see the tower over the trees from here if it wasn't for all this damn smoke — as matters stand, just follow your NCOs half a klick NorNorWest. If you get dispersed or separated from your unit, redeploy at the big fountain south of the lake, got that? Lock and load, maintain coms silence except for hands and verbals, respond to any, repeat, any visual contact with Demons with extreme prejudice." Because the word "enemy" was considered a hate-term, the HHS was required by law to refer to any attackers as Demonstrators of Potential Enmity. The troopers had shortened this to "Demons."

"Who are the 'Patriots'?" Obama asked the peacie next to him as they trotted past the former Children's Zoo, which had been converted into permanent meditation yurts.

"HHS company from New Hampshire," the trooper said. "All the Boston units defected to the Chinese. We're from western Pennsylvania, so everybody calls us the 'Steelers.'" He proudly showed off the laser-etched IFL team logo on the bicep of his suit. "I'm Ramesh. That's Denny, with the big gundam." Denny nodded. He was a big myn, er man, even taller than Obama. In addition to his Hakker, he was equipped with a Metal Storm pepper-box left-arm-mounted gundam firing 55 mm cold-launched explosive guided rounds stacked in 8 tubes, with another tube armed with high velocity 4.6 mm projectiles as a close combat personal defense weapon.

They crossed the main path and turned right onto the Mall. The statue of William Shakespeare was pockmarked with bullet-holes, and the head of Robert Burns had been blown off. A few corpses were visible through the trees lying in the Sheep Meadow.

This open space, along with the Great Lawn and the meadows in the North End, had finally been cleared in 2040 of the squatters' camps that had sprung up in them during the "sustainable food" riots of the Terrible 'Teens. However, there were still dozens of rusting relics left from the wind farms that had been installed throughout the park even earlier. The wind farms had been part of an ambitious worldwide program to convert to natural green sources of electrical energy. However, it had been discovered — usually by each municipality on its own — that the structural deterioration of the turbines and the variability of local winds had caused the actual energy costs of a connected household to double within two years. So the city and state had returned to relying on coal. Nuclear power had, of course, become gradually banned worldwide after the Diablo Canyon disaster during the San Andreas earthquake of 2015.

"Where do you two think you're going?" Siren said in his ear. "This wasn't part of the plan!" She sounded panicky. *Next she'll say, "Don't make me worry,"* thought Obama. "Don't make me worry," she said, and he laughed. "What's so funny?" she demanded.

"It's the first time I've ever read your mind," he told her. "Look, don't fret, Siren, everything's going to be fine. I promise."

"Me, too," said the Pooka. "Come on, Siren, just let us have just a little fun. Please?"

"Fun?" Siren said in horror. "This isn't a game!"Though it was hard to tell for sure, actually. The milGrid system inside the helmets awarded points for hits and kills and displayed functions in exactly the same way a game would have. And before Obama had even heard the whistling shriek of its descent, his screen blinked a digital warning of an incoming J-DAM. The J-DAM exploded violently in the middle of the promenade just in front of him, toppling an elm and sending packed earth and dust in every direction. The troopers scattered. Miraculously, none had been hurt.

"Whee!" said the Pooka.

"I have to do this," Obama told Siren. "Somebody up at the theater may know where Manacera went. It's my only lead at the moment."

But he never made it that far. They were stopped when they got to the Bethesda Terrace by another officer, who'd been crouching inside the stairwell with the rest of his troops. "The Demons have taken the castle!" he yelled above the din of heavy ordinance pounding away to the north. Over the sergeant's head, Obama could see the boat-house burning in the distance. "We need a stop here at the lake. These units here" — he pointed at the Steelers and several others — "You've been tasked to defend the bridge. Move! Move!"

It would have made better sense to blow the bridge up, but they lacked any explosives powerful enough for the job. The elegantly curving Bow Bridge was made of heavy cast-iron, and its built-in balustrades made an excellent battlement against an amphibious assault from the direction of the Hernshead. Instead the troop had to defend it intact against a victorious foe intent on crossing from the other side of the wooded Ramble, which was shrouded by a heavy, dense smoke. As defenders dug in, pushing a disabled Hummer into the middle of the bridge and piling debris onto it, they could already see the red flicker of laser-sighting lancing through the haze.

It was almost as dark as night. Obama was to the left of the bridge on the high bank overlooking the lake, covering behind dense foliage, lying on his belly between Ramesh and Denny. In the absence of air-support, the Chinese J-DAMs and RPGs were raining down inaccurately behind them. The sergeant came down the line screaming and literally kicking butts into position. "Fucking J-DAMs!" he said when he got to them.

"How come they got so many and we don't, Sergeant?" Ramesh asked him.

"Because the PLA stashed a shitload of them away when they were disbanded in '34, just like we did. Only ours are all in Texas and Tennessee, where they are doing us zero goddamn good at the moment." Another J-DAM exploded a few meters above the bridge, creating a brief explosion of blinding light. "I've heard the Mormons even kept some nukes," the sergeant went on. "Wish we had a few of those right now! Oh fuck! Look!" From what they could see of the far shore, the surface of the lake had begun to roil. A coating of what looked like tiny metallic bubbles was floating across its murky surface.

"What's that?" asked Obama.

"Spider-bots," said the sergeant. "Chinese nano-tech."

A red-helmet tech-unit had taken up position on Cherry Hill just behind the bridge's defenders, from which point the unit was releasing a counter-attacking force of modded security-bots down into Wagner Cove. Unfortunately, most of these either drowned in the lake or were swiftly overwhelmed by the relentless tide of Chinese spiders, clicking up the paths with articulated metal legs ending in barbed razor-sharp points. "Don't let any of those get on you!" the sergeant yelled. "They'll slice right through your armor! Fire at will, gentlemen!" Denny stood up and wildly sprayed the bots and the infiltrating troopers behind them with bursts of explosives fire, temporarily clearing the hillside.

"How does my ass taste now?" he crowed.

"Still like chicken!" Ramesh called back, laughing.

The Pooka unleashed a volley of high-precision shots from her own HAKMOR, blasting any of the spiders approaching too near. But where they swarmed the thickest was atop the bridge itself, where several troopers were now completely covered with writhing colonies of metal mollusks that sawed through armor and cooling and power supply lines. One trooper started screaming shrilly. Behind the bots came the first wave of blue-helmeted Chinese HHS troopers assaulting the bridge. Their body armor shone with a metallic reddish sheen and was sculpted slightly differently than the North American suit. It was based on the UN-standard Swiss iMESS battle-gear, though it had been significantly modified and upgraded with Chinese tech. Like the North American version, however, it was bullet-resistant, not bullet-proof, and couldn't stop an RPG or any heavier explosive. The first dozen or so of the enemy were met with a withering fire that swept them off the bridge.

Then a second volley of J-DAMs rained down, this time with far deadlier precision. The spider-bots were sending back microdata. Just behind Obama, the sergeant was hit squarely in the helmet. Obama found blood and bits of brain all over his own armor, and fragments of teeth embedded in the tree-trunk just above his head. A second explosion rocked him even harder. To his left, Denny had been cut down, and Obama watched the bottom half of the trooper's torso slide and skid down the muddy embankment into the lake water. A captain appeared on the path, screaming, "Fall back! Fall back! Regroup at the Literary Walk!" Demons were now pouring across the Bow Bridge, some still hit and falling into the water below. But they would be across to the other side in minutes.

"Pooka?" said Obama, getting to his feet. "Do something!"

"What do you want me to do, Obama?" she answered in a sweetly reasonable tone.

"Anything!"

"Yay!" she said. "OK, then — *Alakazam!*" Suddenly Obama had the sensation of becoming vastly bigger. It was only an illusion, he knew — the Pooka was simply feeding his neural sensors with sensory data. But undeniably, the Pooka was getting bigger. And bigger. And was metamorphosing into an entirely new form. Instead of black armor, she was now covered in soft brown fur. Instead of a HAKMOR assault rifle, she was now carrying a huge titanium cudgel. He looked down at her feet and saw she was wearing a blue Chinese kung-fu robe and that her feet had also become hands. She had turned into a huge plastic monkey, specifically, the hero of Kim's favorite childhood flattie, the old animated musical film called "Alakazam the Great."

With a high-pitched cry, she sprang into action, flailing her cudgel and wading into the attackers on the bridge. They only came up to her thighs. She was met with a hail of bullets, but they just bounced off; she strode across the Bow Bridge, sweeping her cudgel back and forth, knocking the attacking troopers aside like skittles, and sweeping them over the bridge railings. RPGs struck her in the chest and head, a J-DAM exploded against one shoulder. None had any effect. Once she had cleared the bridge, she swelled up even taller, until the trees were only knee-high, then began sweeping her cudgel at gundam emplacements, stamping on J-DAMs, bowling over troop carriers, and uprooting trees. The Chinese troopers turned and began to flee. She waded across the lake after them.

"It's not a hologram — it's a real monster!" he heard in the Chinese coms chatter.

"Fall back! Fall back!"

"Some kind of new *guai-lo* weapon — "

"Not a monster — it's the Monkey God! He merits our fearful respect!"

The Chinese HHS troopers were now streaming back across the park in full retreat, the enraged Pooka in hot pursuit, hopping first on one foot and then the other, twirling her cudgel to smash rockets from the air like shuttlecocks while she loudly sang contemptuous songs in Mandarin, finally dancing into the intersection of West 72nd Street and Central Park West, where she came to a halt in front of the Dakota, the lovingly restored centerpiece of the vertical "Ghostbusters Theme Park." Colonel Chen "Charlie" Cheng-Wu, in the presence of his two lieutenant-colonels, formally surrendered to her in the street outside it.

"If I hadn't seen it with my own two eyes I wouldn't have believed it possible that I might ever one day encounter on the field of battle such a distinguished historical deity from the world of my distant ancestors," he told her in his fluent, dignified Enriched. He and the rest of his officers had been selected because they had all studied in North America — and in fact, it was partly in response to their calm and measured interviews on YouVee every night that Manacera had blacked it out locally. "There is no shame in surrendering to the same beloved and impish Monkey God who escorted the great sage Tripitaka to the West and defeated the White Skeleton Demon."

Pooka belched happily and spat out a cascade of polymer explosive-tipped bullets. They bounced onto the street and rolled around like mint lozenges. "Now, that was fun," she told Obama. "I'm so happy I met you." The Chinese troopers oohhed and ahhed appreciatively as they stacked their weapons on the sidewalk. After a few minutes, airvans appeared through the clearing smoke and began landing around them, and red-helmeted troopers emerged from their doors to stand guard. Colonel Tommy Ng arrived next, shaking Colonel Chen's hand and patting him on the shoulder.

"Charlie and I are old amigos," Ng told Dumbo, who had flown up with a cam-bot. "We've been off on training courses and family vacations together many a time. How's Mei-Yi?"

"She sends her love," said Colonel Chen. He waved around vaguely. "Sorry about all the, you know, mess. I actually love New York."

"Shit happens," Ng told him. "You had your orders, I had mine. It's over, that's the main thing." The Pooka, who had been slyly decreasing in stature until she was normal-sized, seized the opportunity to morph into Obama's sunglasses. When the small crowd of civilians cowering down inside the subway station emerged to the sight of Joyful Kalinga, they began to cheer. Colonel Ng's expression turned stormy. "Excuse us," he said to Dumbo, and dragged Obama through the nearest door, which turned out to lead into the front entrance foyer of the Dakota.

"Let me see if I've got this straight, Mr. Kalinga," he hissed at Obama, removing the stub of a cigar from between his clenched teeth. "The whole goddamn reason we've been fighting this goddamn civil war in the first place is because your ties to President Manacera were all supposedly just a great big fucking hoax. Have I got that right? That's certainly the only reason that I, for one, stuck with him. And now you've crawled out from whatever rock you were hiding under in order to rampage through Manhattan scaring people in some hi-tech new kind of holo-suit, killing officially deployed UN peacekeepers who are just doing their jobs, and giving interviews to YouVee where you endorse Manacera? How the flying fuck does any of that help his case with Congress?"

Obama leaned forward until he was close enough to whisper in the furiously angry Ng's flaming red ear. "After you go over all the data, you'll discover that I haven't actually killed anyone at all," he said. "I'm a big hoax, too, Colonel — just like the Moon Colony. You might want to do something about that when you get the chance."

The colonel jerked back and glared at him. "Something's going on here that I don't get," he said, putting the cigar stub back in his mouth and chewing on it. "And I'm not sure I want to. You put a stop to the killing, though — and for that I'm grateful to you. I've just received orders from the president — I guess we can all start calling him that again, thanks to you — to hand you over to his people. Here they are now." Colonel Park and Major Malek strode through the door, wearing trench coats and carrying assault rifles. "That OK with you, mister?" said Ng. "I wouldn't want to take a ride with those two."

"Oh yes," said Obama loudly — this time as Joyful Kalinga. "That mighty OK with Kalinga, man." He flashed Colonel Ng his widest smile. To the Pooka he said, "Follow us wherever they take me," then idly folded her up and left her behind on the counter of the front desk.

"Colonel Ng," Malek said, giving a mocking salute as they approached. "You'll have to forgive Colonel Park — he doesn't speak Enriched. Just uses Babelfish onGrid. You don't know how much we've been looking forward to meeting you again," he added to Obama. He then said something in Arabic to Park, who nodded dourly — but now that he was detached from the Pooka, Obama could no longer understand it. Or hear Siren's voice in his ear. Suddenly he felt very alone. He risked a glance back at the front counter as they led him out. The Pooka had already morphed into something else and vanished.

They took him outside and put him in an unmarked airvan, which lifted off, cut diagonally across Central Park to Park, then veered south to turn east at Grand Central. They followed East 42nd Street to UNUC, the flying spider-bot they'd picked up at liftoff still clinging to their under-chassis. They landed on the roof of the executive mansion overlooking the East River.

Obama saw none of this. The moment they were airborne, Malek had kicked his legs out from under him, and Park had kicked at his face. Both myn had pulled out flexible Fullerene tube-carbon truncheons, which they used on his kidneys and head while they held onto hand-grip straps mounted onto the van's walls. Obama immediately curled into a fetal position, trying to shield his skull from their blows with his arms as well as protect his gut. He hadn't wanted the metal plate the Princess had inserted into his skull the night before to come loose.

Between blows Park muttered in Arabic, and Malek would translate: "How did you get away at the canyon?" "Who helped you?" "Who are you really working for?" Obama found it interesting that they evidently didn't know. Nor had their boss told them about Obama's genetically-enhanced powers of physical recuperation. By the time they had bundled him across the roof-pad and down the ascensor into the presidential office suite, his cuts and abrasions had all healed. That didn't stop them from hurting like hell, however.

It had occurred to Obama briefly just how easy it would have been for him to ram each of the myn into — or even through — the ascensor's walls, but by now he'd accepted his total, utter inability to do so. Young

myn his age had been dubbed the "Pussy Generation" by the media —
and Obama, apparently, was the biggest pussy of them all. Funny how
he was focusing on thoughts like that at a time like this. "Think about
other things," Siren had advised him yesterday while they'd been
rehearsing what he was about to do. "Think about anything. Whatever
comes into your head." But not about the steel plate, of course.

They searched him thoroughly, then took him into the Oval Office.
Before the ruins of the old White House had been abandoned, what
remained of the famous executive office inside it had been thoroughly
stripped and transported to New York City, where it was meticulously
reconstructed — with a new presidential seal on the navy-blue carpet
and ceiling plaster, as well as the UN flags beside the window —
inside the new mansion of the World President Jose Manacera. Who
was waiting for them now, seated impassively behind the massive
presidential Resolute Desk, so-called because it had originally been
crafted from the timbers of an old warship, the *H.M.S. Resolute*. The
president looked up and said, "OK, you two can leave us." Without
getting up, he motioned Obama toward one of the two chairs in front
of his desk.

"Are you sure that's a good idea, Mr. President?" Malek said
dubiously.

"Go on, fuck off out of here!" Manacera replied, appearing to lose
his temper. It struck Obama as a little contrived, but he sat down and
said nothing.

Manacera looked at him and said confidentially. "I need to fire
those two. They're probably bugging my office right now." He smiled,
and Obama felt the full impact of his charisma. And not merely that
of the warm, folksy old humyn president and father of the modern
United Nations. He also felt, beyond any doubt, the magnetic presence
of the alien being who, for want of a better name, he thought of as
"Sato." Who was waggling a finger at him now in mock reproach.

"You're shielding your thoughts from me somehow, son." The
president smiled ruefully. "I can tell somebody's been teaching you a
few tricks. Anybody I know?"

"No," said Obama, carefully not thinking about Siren. "Nobody
you know."

Manacera shook his head. "Doesn't much matter. They have no
authority here, regardless of who they sent. Of course, they're too
dozy and disorganized to actually send anybody — must have been

the Helpers who put them up to it. Now, *they* can be big trouble." He glanced at Obama shrewdly. "And I have a feeling they're causing me even more trouble right now. That was quite a show somebody put on in Central Park. Saved my ass, though. I actually had miscalculated this whole business. Lucky for me I had a back-up plan.

"You see, Obama, I'm not like the rest of those old womyn back home — I'm not afraid to make my own reality. Or to take life when I have to. And why shouldn't I? I have the right — after all, I created it. All of it." He waved in the direction of the window behind him. Through it, Obama could see rose-bushes and a manicured lawn and beyond them, the East River sparkling in the sunlight. "All you see out there in the world of humynkind, all the noble inventions and wondrous works, all the art and beauty and great literature. All thanks to me." For a moment, Obama caught a glimpse of the alien's loneliness, the millennia-long vigil Sato had kept over the planet, shaping, transforming, even ultimately impersonating, humyn beings. With a sudden jolt, he realized that these were actually Sato's thoughts he was reading, his emotions he was feeling. It was impossible not to feel swayed by their justice. The alien was attempting to make his mind wholly transparent to Obama. It obviously felt absolutely no doubts regarding its own actions.

"I'm just sorry I haven't had the chance to get to know you better, son. I'd have liked that — to be the one to teach you about what it means to be one of us. To show you all our many powers and encourage you to explore them." He sighed. "That would have been a fine thing."

"In that case, why have you been trying to kill me?" Obama asked. They were the first words he'd spoken since entering, and they echoed inside the room, sounding adolescent and accusing.

Manacera looked even sadder. "That wasn't me trying to kill you, boy. No sir, not even one little bit. It was Simonetta. Of course, the way she is my fault, too. When you love somebody, you over-indulge them. It becomes a habit, and then one fine day you wake up and realize you've literally been letting them get away with murder. I'm the first to admit I'm to blame here — it hasn't exactly been what you would call a healthy relationship between me and Simonetta." Waves of unhappiness emanated from him now; physically, he looked as if he were about to cry. Obama had to remind himself that the old alien was a consummate actor.

He caught a twinkle in Manacera's eye. "Ah, I think I just caught a little whiff of that thought, son. Well yes, I've had to be a good actor, just to stay alive on this planet. And a pretty darn good shot, too." He patted a lump under his armpit that Obama realized was a lightweight pistol, the kind the Steelers carried as personal weapons of last resort.

"But you've turned out to be a pretty good actor yourself. Be fair." Obama nodded. "Led me a merry chase," the alien went on. "And I still can't see all the cards you're holding right now. Chip off the old block," he said with a wide, proud grin. "Look, son, I can tell you still don't believe me about Simonetta. So I'm gonna tell you a little story. Now don't fret, it won't be a long one." He glanced at his iRist. "I need to toddle over to the press building in a few minutes and proclaim myself president-for-life. Thanks to you, of course — those Chinese fellers sure had me on the run. They're all in Ho's pocket."

Suddenly, Obama had a vision of himself as a chess-piece. Had he been manipulated into the role of liberator all along? He began to mentally review how this might have happened — then realized this was exactly what the alien wanted in order to fish out his thoughts. He closed his mouth tighter and instead listened closely to Manacera.

"Once upon a time there was a little girl," Manacera was saying. "Whose playmates had a habit of disappearing one by one. Not right away, mind you. No, at first the playmate — the little girl or boy, and later on, the big girl or boy — would be her darling for a few months, sometimes even for a year or two. And then would come a day when the distraught momma or daddy would be on the local news broadcasting an appeal. Then there would follow the sniffer dogs, the searches through the construction sites and wooded parks in the mud, and finally the bag of bones and hair found buried someplace. And every time it happened, the little girl blamed her Daddy.

"Of course, it was Daddy who had to clean up the mess, pay off the cops and the poor grieving parents, and arrange for a new skool for his little girl in a whole new city or a new country or, when the new country finally ran out of whole new cities, a whole new continent. And every time it happened, she insisted it wasn't her fault at all — it was Daddy's. He was jealous, you see. And she had just enough of a point to keep Daddy jumping, because, well you see, he was pretty jealous. And maybe there might have been a few times when it really had been Daddy pulling the trigger on some handsome, arrogant, rude young son-of-a-bitch of a new boyfriend. Because when Daddy was used to ordering everybody on the whole planet around, making life-or-death decisions over the fate of millions, well what's one or two more matter, really? So even Daddy was a mite confused over just exactly how much he was to blame upon occasion.

"One day, when she was just about at that romantic age of 11 or 12 or so, this little girl found out she had a secret twin brother hidden somewhere. And she took it into her head that the two of them were like ancient pharaohs or something, that someday they would marry and have children and rule the world together as a god-king and queen. Which would have meant pretty much just her, the queen, of course. Until she got tired of the arrangement and had him poisoned or smothered with a pillow. So you see, Obama, that's why I had to keep the two of you apart.

"Oh, I wanted to get in touch. I wanted to get to know you, but there was one more big reason I didn't: I didn't realize you were another half-alien like Simonetta. You see, you were both accidents. I didn't set out to reproduce my own kind. I didn't even know it was possible! Somehow, my own genetic material got mixed up with a few humyn strains down through the centuries. I haven't got a clue how many more out there might be like you two. I was just breeding better clones, I thought — it didn't occur to me that I'd created a whole new race of beings until Simonetta was born, and I suddenly realized I wasn't all on my own here anymore. Can you imagine what that felt like after all those years and years of being all alone here? I mean, really really alone?"

"Yes," Obama said. "I think I can."

"'Course you can. A fate like that is layin' in wait for you, too, son. Anyway, it really just flat-out didn't occur to me that you might be just like her until you were 12 or so, and I had some private tests run on you by your doctor. Remember those? Remember your grandpa? I surely do — one of my best employees ever, good old Eitan. But by then it was too late — I was already scared of Simonetta and what her reaction might be if I suddenly started spending time with you. You have no idea just how jealous and unreasonable that young womyn can be, Obama. To be honest, I'm actually a bit relieved you've got her locked away up there on Phobos for a while. It'll be a nice vacation from her for me. Oh, I'll miss her, all right. And sooner or later, of course, I'll get around to reinventing Zero Light, and I'll go up there and rescue her. But maybe not right away."

He leaned forward. "In the meantime, Obama, I want you to come on board with me. You've got no idea how much I have to teach you, how much I want to share with a son of my own. I'm feeling old and tired and bored with all this humyn bickering and intrigue — I've been doing the divide and conquer routine so long it's beginning to seriously bore the crap out of me. Ever heard of the Ghibellines and the

Guelphs? The Cavaliers and the Roundheads? The Blue and the Gray? All me. All my bright ideas. And fuck me, I'm just so goddamn sick of it. I need a junior partner. I need somebody to take over someday. Damn it, Obama, I just plain need some company. I want to get to know you. I want us to be father and son — just like normal humyns. Come on, boy, help your old Dad run the world for a while. At least see how you like it."

"Well, there are still a few things I'm unclear about," said Obama, clearing his throat. "I mean, why did you tell Xina and her people about us? About our being aliens or whatever? And about the Moon? Weren't you taking a big chance doing that?"

"A big chance? Naw, no way. What could people like that ever do to me?"

"You might be surprised," said Obama.

"I said all that stuff because it amused me, that's why. Damn, I thought you were smarter than that, amigo!" Obama actually felt a brief sting of shame, such was the power of the old alien's disapproval. And of his charm, when he chose to turn it back on. He rose from the desk. "Look, Obama, I don't have the right to ask you to call me 'Dad,' I realize that. You already have a father, one who not only contributed his genes to you but who changed your diapers and taught you to ride a bike and throw a ball and who worked hard for a paycheck to put food on the table for you and your momma every night. I understand that." He walked slowly around the desk and opened his arms wide. "But do you think you might find just a little room in your heart for a second, oh, I don't know, mentor or whatever you want to call it? A well-meaning uncle? Even another grandpa, maybe?"

Obama got to his feet, too, and President Manacera beckoned him nearer. "Listen, buddy, we don't need the others — all those other aliens and goddamn so-called Helpers. They'll strangle you. They're like nursemaids or nannies you're stuck with forever — at least I was, ever since birth. Till I broke free of them. You have no idea what a pain in the ass they can be with all their nagging and moral lectures. I created the humyn race all by myself from genetic scraps of wildlife, and I made of them a mighty civilization, with great paintings and music and magnificent melodrama as a result of it. Imagine, I created all that life! Me! It felt great, Obama, to finally live like a real man — to be a king! To stand on my own two feet! That's what I'm offering you — and it's not as if the humyns have it so bad, either. I feed them and house them and give them sims and games to play with. You'd be carrying on my work, son. Just think of all the good you can do!"

Obama found tears streaming down his cheeks. He was weeping, not so much at Sato/Manacera's words, as from the emotions they evoked. The sincerity, the passionate honesty of its belief in itself. The alien had truly, inarguably created the world. Like a god. And it had worked tirelessly ever since to make it a better place. Slowly but surely, it was succeeding. With every generation, humynkind was becoming less animal, less feudal, less violent, more egalitarian, better-fed, better-housed, better cared-for. Every word it was saying was true. That didn't change anything, of course — but in that moment, Obama felt nothing but love for the alien, along with a sense of compassionate understanding. Of empathy. It would be an honor and a privilege to continue that work.

Except that Obama couldn't. But he wasn't going to think about that right now ...

"Of course I'll think of you as my father," Obama said. He moved forward and embraced President Manacera tightly. "You're the father of us all, aren't you? I'm proud to call you Dad," he said in a half-choked voice. This close to him, Sato's personal charisma was overpowering. Obama felt as though he were hugging god. He could feel his thoughts being delicately probed, and the first faint stirrings of alarm they inspired. Then he exploded.

27.

Obama could have spent the next 4 to 6 weeks of his life in a tank like Simonetta's, waiting for his own personal clones to gestate. Instead he elected to be surgically implanted into a clone of Siren's. It was the only male one in her closet, one she'd been keeping around, she said, "in case you ever get bored with girls." The clone was the monozygotic fraternal twin of the original Siren Gunnarsdottir.

After 28 years of being black, Obama found it pretty weird suddenly being white. And there weren't many people on the planet any whiter than he was now — he felt like a photo-negative of himself. But he'd always have his old self to go back to, as she pointed out. "The sooner, the better," he told her. Though even he had to admit there were a few advantages to the new body. For one thing, he didn't have a steel plate implanted in his skull now. For another, he wasn't carrying 2.2 kilos of Lastex and a detonator sealed inside a colostomy bag implanted in his gut, either.

But he wouldn't heal as quickly when injured now, not for a while. And he wasn't nearly as strong. He tired a lot more easily. He wasn't crazy about his new nose or penis, either. But since he was stuck inside the new body for the moment, he allowed Siren to create a new identity for it, that of "Bram Gunnarsson." She gave him a new iRist and a new iPhone, though she allowed him to hang on to the old ones, too. "You'll need to call your mom, Bam," she told him. He'd started liking the way "Bam" sounded when she said it. And it worked with the new name. He'd better get used to that, too, for now.

When he'd been able to speak again after the operation to implant him in the white clone, the first thing he'd wanted to know was what Siren had done with Sato. The explosion had been much worse than he'd imagined, literally tearing both of them instantly to ribbons and destroying the interior of the Oval Office. Only parts of the desk and chairs had survived relatively intact.

That was one of the other things they'd argued about, he and Siren. She'd thought they'd used too much Lastex explosive, that there was been a danger they'd harm others, secretaries or security personnel just outside the office. Or that he would damage himself. His argument had been that the blast that had blown apart Simonetta's body had been a far more powerful one, and she had survived. And after all, who was more expert at rigging bombs than Habib?

Habib had certainly been surprised to see him the morning before the explosion, the morning after they'd left Tokyo. "Habib" wasn't his real name, merely a *nom de guerre*, as "Freedom" had been — though Xina, perhaps as a flaunting of her death-wish, had always used her real one. But Habib had a wife and children and a cover life as a social security benefits advocate in Jersey City, New Jersey, and so had plenty he wanted to protect.

His real name was Salman Saadedin. His true identity had been buried beneath several false layers. But the Pooka had scraped a DNA sample from him in the cave, and that had allowed them to track him down through the HHS databases. He was, after all, one of that department's own employees. He was keeping an eye on his young son inside the children's playgrounds in Lafayette Park when they found him. Both Siren and Obama were wearing their sunglasses and Arab robes, Siren in a fully veiled *burqa* that somehow failed to disguise her curves.

"This is your woman?" Habib asked Obama after he'd recovered from his initial surprise.

"Yes," Obama said, and the other myn nodded.

"I told Xina she had no chance with you. She didn't believe me."

Obama smiled grimly. "Believe me, she would now," he'd said. "I've come to ask you a favor."

"Of course. Why else would you be here?" He gathered up his son and zipped the boy's coat. Obama was reminded momentarily of the little boy Habib had tried to kidnap as a hostage in the motel parking lot in Amarillo. "You have children together?" Habib asked him.

"Not yet," said Siren sardonically. "But we're trying."

Habib lived just down the street in a house on Van Horne. It was shabbily furnished, and the floors were strewn with children's toys. His wife, a high-strung woman wearing sweatpants who looked like a graduate student, gave them coffee. "I suppose I have no choice in doing whatever it is you want," he told them after she'd led the children away. "You will force me to help you."

"Yes," said Obama. "I want to build a bomb, one big enough to blow up two people standing close together. But not big enough to kill anyone else nearby. And I need it to be completely reliable."

Habib arched his eyebrows. "You've changed," he said. "*Inshallah*. No bomb is ever completely reliable. What is your method of delivery? Belt? Backpack?" He glanced at Siren. "False pregnancy pad?"

"The bomb will be inside me," Obama said. "Surgically implanted in my gut. That's why it's important that it doesn't go off if I'm touched or struck there. We'll need some kind of detonator I can set off by iTooth." Their host had nodded but looked dubious.

"I would recommend no more than 3 kilos of Lastex. But make sure it's properly sealed and that the detonator is well-protected, because if your digestive juices get through to it, it won't go off. But it would probably kill you anyway — very slowly and painfully. It should be facing your insides, this way."

"I knew you'd enjoy the challenge," Obama had told him. And he'd risen to it. After Habib's bomb had gone off, Obama had experienced lurid, narcotic impressions of crawling across the burning blue carpet, straining to breathe. And not being able to — aliens didn't, Siren had told him, it was just a humyn reflex. So was crawling by your tentacles, apparently.

But he'd needed to find Sato, to make sure Sato's alien form was undamaged, and that he, Obama, hadn't killed him, along with both of their humyn bodies. He'd sensed him — Obama had no eyes to see with, yet his "psychic senses" seemed to interpret the room with a far more colorful, if surreal, map than humyn vision provided — huddled and pulsating slightly beneath the desk, filled with resentment, confusion, and a stunned, cold fury.

The Pooka, looking like her old baleful action-toy self, had entered the room then, and scooped Sato up and into something that resembled a large thermos bottle. Almost on her heels followed Siren, safe inside the pink, plastic shell of the Princess, carrying a second thermos, into which they had scooped Obama. What had been left of him. The alien part.

He felt a sensation of darkness and cool. He floated, tried to swim, tried to breathe, and became aware of another set of external intruding emotions — Siren's emotions: relief, guilt, and a vast embarrassed ocean of clumsy, yet comforting, almost childishly gooey love. He stopped struggling and allowed himself to be lulled to sleep inside it.

But it was a fitful sleep filled with fever dreams, where over and over again he shed his humyn lungs and hands and teeth — and turned into a floating alien parasite.

The implanting operation had been another bad dream. There was no way to anesthetize the alien body, apparently, so he remembered every detail of it vividly. Though it didn't seem so to him, it was over in a jiffy. The Princess had turned herself into an operating bot like a huge spider with nano-scalpels and lasers and whirring ultrasonics in the tips of her jointed legs. She had sliced and sawed open the surgical cross-cut Obama had seen twice before now on a pair of corpses; then the Pooka had picked him up and inserted him into the moist red hole.

What had Sato called the Helpers? Nursemaids and nannies? "They'll strangle you," he'd said. Well, Obama had made his choice. He'd cast his lot in with them and not Sato. *It's Sato's own fault, really,* he thought. *It's Sato who had created generation after generation of humyns who enjoyed being taken care of. He had trained them to it. The problem with Sato is, he's been too indulgent with his children.* In the end, the only "real man" left on the planet had been Sato himself — before Obama and Siren had exploded and kidnapped him.

Where's Sato now? thought Obama. *I must remember to ask.* Right now he was too busy being tucked into his new body, scrabbling with his tentacles, tucking himself instinctively up into the cerebrum of his clone-body like a burrowing rat in the dark, curling up in a ball as if to mimic the humyn cerebellum, connecting his tentacles around the brain stem and down into the ganglia of the spine. Then it was over. The wound had been sealed up over him and begun to heal while he sent filaments of consciousness through the drugged body of the clone, filaments which had encountered a heavy anesthesia. After that, he had plunged into darkness and slept for real.

This time there were no dreams. The operation hadn't taken long — but he was in no hurry to do it again.

"What did you do with Sato?" he'd asked Siren upon waking. He'd found himself lying in the same hotel room bed where they'd eaten popcorn. On Phobos. She was holding one of his hands. With a shock he saw that his hand was white, almost transparently pale. His mouth felt wrong, too, clumsy and gummy, the teeth clacking together in the wrong places when he tried to speak. His voice was almost unintelligible, as if he had an obstruction in his throat. Siren stroked his forehead.

"It's almost like seeing myself again in my old body," she said, smiling. He had clearly caught her thoughts. She was relieved he'd woken up — even though the operation was routine, she'd been worrying. The explosion had terrified her. The new body aroused her, like looking in a mirror in the nude. He caught her excitement and tried to smile back. "There you are," said Siren, kissing him. "At last. I really don't know what to do with him, baby. For now, I had Laputa duplicate this station on Deimos, and we put him there. Beneath Swift Crater."

"So Simonetta's still here on Phobos, and Sato's on Deimos?" Obama said thickly. He had the same South African accent as the original Siren. On her, it had sounded cute. It made him, however, sound like one of those old-skool racist villains in an 007 sim.

"Yeah, it's sort of romantic. They revolve close together twice a day."

He shook his head. "It doesn't seem fair somehow to keep them apart. We don't have the right to play judge and jury with their lives."

"Well, it's only temporary," Siren said. He could clearly see her reasons for being cautious, even without reading her thoughts. Putting Sato and Simonetta together in the same tank, for example, might create unintended consequences. Unimaginable consequences, even. And allowing them back on Earth again was plainly out of the question. "Sooner or later, the lease will be up here, and we can decide then," she added.

"Lease?"

"Both Moons will eventually be pulled down by gravitational attraction and crash into Mars in the next few million years. Unless we can get away with towing them out into wider orbits. But I don't think humans will lose the ability to look through telescopes anytime soon. Let's hope not, anyway."

"I'm not hanging around here for a few million more years," the Prostitute said out of thin air. "It's boring. You promised you'd let me go down and visit Earth sometimes."

Siren sighed. "This was all your idea in the first place," she said. "You know perfectly well why you aren't allowed back on Earth."

"Why isn't she allowed back on Earth?" Obama asked her, and Siren silently mouthed "Tell you later" at him.

"Hey, I heard that!" he said. "I mean, I actually heard the words inside my mind. This new body seems to be a lot more receptive than the old one. Or maybe it's just me. By the way, I've been meaning to ask — why does the Prostitute call herself Laputa?"

"Oh, it's her just her subtle little way of sulking about not being allowed on Earth. It's a reference to Jonathan Swift — he was the first to predict that Mars had two Moons. That's why all the craters here are named for characters in 'Gulliver's Travels'."

"Struldbrug!" said the Prostitute.

"Pot calling kettle," Siren replied, shrugging.

"So, your plan is for us to hang around here for a few million years?" he asked her.

"Well, not here, exactly. But on Earth, yes. I thought you'd be in no hurry to leave it right now. It's your home, and you love it there. So I'd assumed you'd want to stay there for the foreseeable future, right? Besides, we need to find out how many more of you there are down there. Or of Simonetta. And that's going to take a while." She nestled into his arms and stroked his new Nordic bright pink cheek. "So tell me, Bam, since you can live anywhere on Earth you want now — anywhere at all in the whole wide world — where would you like us to move to?"

He felt himself blushing, something else new and annoying this body did. "Actually, there's only one place I'd like to live right now that feels like home," he told her, feeling embarrassed. "If you can stand living there with me, I mean."

"Where's that, baby?"

"My old apartment."

They left Phobos a few days later, after Obama was able to walk properly, use the bathroom on his own, and eat without drooling. The trip from Phobos to the Manacera City Beltway was only two or three minutes long, but once there, the stop-and-go rush-hour air-traffic was so heavy that it took the Princess, disguised as a silver Ladybug, nearly another hour to carry them home through a slate-grey rain. For the first time in days, Obama turned on the news. From what he could gather, the new acting-president of the world was now Tommy Ng, who had promoted himself to general. After the shocking and horrifying assassination of President Manacera by the famous terrorist Joyful Kalinga, Ng had been appointed to the position by a junta of other

HHS colonels from around the world, led by the defeated Chinese Colonel Charlie Chen. It was, they said, the only way to restore "public confidence after the complete failure of the political process."

The general election, now only days away, had been cancelled, though General Ng promised that one of his first acts in office would be to oversee free and fair fresh elections within the coming year. Already, however, they could see that paid exarch artists had sprayed brightly-colored, animated "Tommy-Gun" graffiti all over the sides and rooftops of warehouses and up and down the brooding FORTway towers as they flew south on Air-295. Obviously, the general planned to be a future candidate.

"What did you think of Ng when you met him?" Siren asked. Obama shrugged.

"I liked him. But what do I know? I even liked Manacera — Sato, I mean. I think Ng is a lot more honest, but who knows what kind of monster he'll turn into after he's been in power for a while." Rain drummed down on the Princess's windshield, making his eyelids feel heavy.

"Do you think he's one of us? Like you or Simonetta, I mean?"

"No." He shook his head. "I don't think so. In fact, I'm pretty sure not. I was getting good at sensing that even before I met Sato. I was worried that Park or Malek might be like me, too, but they're not. They're as cruel as Simonetta, but much stupider. So maybe there really aren't any more of us here. Maybe we'll just be wasting our time searching after them for the next few million years."

"Would you mind that so much?" Siren asked him. She was dressed like the old Siren today, in a black business suit and a long taupe trench coat. The rain had made her hair frizz up luxuriantly. This time it was he who took her hand.

"The only thing I really mind anymore is the thought of being alone," said Obama.

"Tell me about it," she replied.

His apartment looked as if he'd never left. If anyone had been in to disturb it, he couldn't tell. There was some laundry that needed washing, and he threw out a few of the things he found in the Liquid-Cooler, but otherwise, it was if the place had never been through a war. That night there was an old Jonessa Qali flattie playing in a virtual cinema in Cannes that Siren wanted to see, which they watched curled up on the couch. After it was over, she asked him why so many Earth dramas ended in an explosion. "I think it's because explosions symbolize sex," he told her. "Plus, in the old days, they had to get rid of the film set — and blowing it up was the fastest way to do it."

"That sounds like a good idea," she said. Sex, she meant, not another big explosion. This time, he could feel her hunger for him as sharply as a physical pain, and he became excited almost instantly. Things between them in that way were better than before, but they still sucked. His new body remained awkward and wrong to him in almost every way possible, and the mental connection between the two of them, even though it was now far more mutual, still caused his passion to wilt at key moments. *Maybe*, he thought, *there's such a thing as too much empathy.*

"Better than too little," she murmured into his ear. "Besides, it only sucks for you, not me. Would you want me more if I were somebody else? I can change..." She shifted position to lie beside him on top of one arm. Should he try taking an Orecta? he wondered.

"Suck is maybe the wrong word. It's like, all my reflexes are wrong, if that makes any sense. For two years, sex for me literally meant sex with Kim. It's as if I'm only programmed to perform with her, almost like I'm cheating or something when I'm with you. The weird thing is, I actually do love you."

"Thanks a million."

"No, I mean, I really love you. The real you. You remember the time you showed me what you looked like? After I'd seen Simonetta? I thought — I know how crazy this sounds — but even at the time, I thought how soft and pretty and perfect you looked," he told her. Her thoughts turned bright pink.

"Thanks."

"And another thing. I just can't stop thinking about Sato and Simonetta. What we've robbed them of, I mean. They should be able to be together, just like we are now, to be happy like we are. They're sort of like us in a way, too, like our evil twins or something. I just wish I could hate Sato more, but I can't. Look at what this planet has already become without him — a military dictatorship. Without him, maybe all the countries will re-arm and break apart and go back to fighting wars again."

"And would that be so terrible?" she asked.

"Well, sure. It would be horrible. Millions of people could die, just like 100 years ago. It could even bring about the end of the world."

She yawned like a kitten. "I think you're being a bit over-dramatic. And you're forgetting that Sato has been on this planet a long, long time. My guess is the UN isn't his first experiment in creating a 'world government.' For all we know — and we could simply ask him, but I don't think he's capable of telling the truth any more about anything — he could have been Augustus Caesar. Or Genghis Khan. Or Joseph Stalin. Or all of the above. Certainly he was manipulating the rise of all of those empires, and frankly, I'm just not all that impressed. And I'm not really impressed with your UN, either. Not only is all this emphasis on peace at any cost hypocritical and false, I'm not even sure it's even very healthy for the human race."

"What do you mean?" asked Obama.

"Look, Obama, I've told you a little about us, how our species evolved: so competitively that we've become a race of beings who can barely stand to be around each other. If I were human, I'd be inside Sato's cell right now interrogating him, or trying to convert him to some ideology or other. Instead, I'm too fearful and angry at him to even remain in orbit for long around the same planet he's on.

"Remember what I told you once? Our kind either fall in love with each other — or hate each other's guts. All our technological advances, including space-flight, were invented simply as a way to express our individualism. And to escape what humans would term 'family responsibilities.' Like gravity. But Sato's idea of socializing humans is to turn them into docile sheep. Creatures so infantilized that the only people they trust to tell them bad news any more are beloved cartoon characters from childhood."

"That's not true!" He was indignant. She kept forgetting he was half-humyn himself. She read his anger and tried to soothe it.

"You asked me why Laputa's not allowed back on Earth, remember? It's because she wants to undo everything Sato's done here. Including evolution. The other helpers and I out-voted her, because we're on your side. On the side of humanity, I guess I should say. We want to see it free to evolve."

"Evolve into what?" Obama asked her bitterly. "Things like us?"

"Who knows? The end result doesn't matter, because there can never really be one. What matters is just that it keeps happening. Evolution means survival, Obama, just as stagnation means extinction.

"And just look at what's happened to the planet since Sato first started promoting the idea of his UN world government. Human evolution, even social progress, has ground to a complete halt. There haven't been any technological advances at all in the last 50 years, except for cloning and aircars and the Grid — and all of those were based on pre-existing technologies. The space program is a murderous sham. The managed global economy has created a world where there is no capital left for investment in space exploration — or anything else, really. The cancer rate hasn't changed in the past century. The crime rate has tripled. The birth rate is negative. You talk about spending a million years here — at the present rate of population decline, there won't be any more human company for us to spend it with in another century or two.

"Nobody on this planet still really wants to fuck any more, anyway — they just want to talk about it or experience sims about it or pretend to do it onGrid. Even you, a young man, are having trouble with the relatively simple act, and it's no mystery why, since the water table is so saturated with birth control pills and anti-depressants secreted from human urine that fish change sex from them. I mean, just look at the real Jonessa Qali's life's work — to make wildlife safe from their effects. What about human beings, Obama? What has Sato done to shield them from all this toxic junk that turns them into genderless butter-balls? Nothing. In fact, he sits on the board of every single corporation that produces that crap. He wanted it that way, Obama. It was part of his plan all along. It's how you handle livestock. Just like the butcher's meat locker on the Moon."

"OK, OK," he said miserably. "You're right. About all the details, I mean. It's just, I have to believe in something, Siren. When Sato — Manacera — was trying to tempt me to help him run the planet or whatever, I really did see things I could do to put things right and, you know, make people's lives happier."

"So do them!" She kissed him hard on the lips. "Don't just sit there. You can do anything you like to make a difference here. I agree with you about Sato — I don't think he started off as evil. I don't even think he's necessarily evil now, whatever that word actually means. I think he's just been playing with his toys a bit too long and needs a 'time out.' If you want to tidy up the nursery in the meanwhile, well, that's your prerogative. You won, he lost. That's how our species does things."

"Nannies," Sato called them, thought Obama. *She's sounding just like one now.* Unfortunately, Siren caught the thought and bit him on the nose.

The next morning at breakfast, Obama said to her, "I think I've decided what I'd like to do next. For the next few months, anyway," he quickly added. "Not for the rest of my life."

"What's that?" she called back from the living room.

"You'll laugh at me," he answered reluctantly. "I think I'd actually like to go back to MAD. Just long enough to help get them back on their feet again. The place must be a wreck — and there's no way of knowing who'll still be there. Or even who's still left alive." He heard Siren burst into laughter. Beside him at the dining table, the Pooka smirked at him, too. She and the Princess, back to their normal-sized plastic shapes, were having what they called a "wine-tasting party": they'd discovered a collection of cleaning solvents under the kitchen sink and poured them into wine-glasses to sample.

"What's going on?" said Obama. "What's so funny?"

Siren appeared in the doorway. "I swiped the data over to you," she said, beaming. "President Ng is making a number of new Federal agency appointments this morning. Here's the one the Pooka and I slipped in via his Allura admin. The new Director of MAD is named Bram De Wet Gunnarsson. His CV is on your iRist. Apparently he worked with his twin sister at Rizdee — the United Nations Research Institute for Social Development — for a year or two. I was pretty sure you'd want to go back. Was it OK that I read your mind, baby?"

He guessed he'd better get used to it.

An hour later, he was standing on the pavement across the street from the MAD building. He peered up at it through the lenses of the Pooka, who had taken the form of a pair of tinted glasses, adding a touch of gravity to Bram's ruddy, youthful face. There wasn't a single pane of glasspex left intact on the facade of the entire building. Most of the empty window sockets had been covered by plywood boards, but a few had nothing but cardboard stuffed into their shattered sockets. Black scorch-marks covered the polycrete surfaces, which were cratered and pitted from constant mortar attacks. Most of the decorative diagonal lattice was destroyed, and a few major explosions had created gaping holes in the outside structure of the building itself, revealing the curving walls of the long circumferential hallway that ringed its interior. The floors above these sagged dangerously like fractured giant dental bridges.

Little attempt had been made to clear the mounds of debris from the streets and sidewalks around the building, debris which had been compounded by the partial collapse of the DOTARD building directly across the street. The first executive order Ng had signed, once he'd been hastily sworn in as world president, had been to rescind the changeover to metric time. This had been a highly popular emergency action on his part, well worth the civil war, most people felt. There was even talk of repealing Daylight Savings Time now, too.

There were discarded shell casings and fragments of ordinance lying in the rubble of concrete chips. Obama — Bram — stepped over an unexploded rocket grenade and crossed the street.

Incredibly, a pair of armed HHS security guards were on duty in what remained of the main lobby, just inside the shattered front entrance doors. One of their scanners was hooked up to an emergency generator. "No admittance to anybody but employees," one of them said, blocking Obama's path.

"I'm the new director," Obama said, as he swiped his new ID — and some sort of authorization Siren had provided — at them. After a brief consultation, they let him through.

There was no electricity in the building, except that provided by portable generators, so the ascensors weren't working. The stairwells had been cleared of everything but bloodstains, yet retained a fetid odor of the grave and the latrine, compounded by water leakage and pigeon droppings from the fractured roof high above. Several floors were still sealed off from the bombing investigation; Obama thought he glimpsed Raffi's small figure disappearing into one of these, but the light was too dim for him to be sure. Above them, Obama found a few of the floors, such as the 4th, entirely deserted, but a few workers were toiling at makeshift desks on the 14th. The only person he recognized was FaLola Montoya.

"Yes, may I help you?" FaLola said when he approached. The workers were sitting beneath a bank of bot-lights which were clinging like bats to a long steel rod. The floors had been stripped of carpeting and the smart-walls blasted in places down to the basic polycrete. Twisting wires and broken plastic pipes protruded from the bare ceilings.

"I'm O — Bram Gunnarsson, the new director here," Obama told Them. "We have a mutual friend, I think — Scott Vega-Choi. He's spoken very highly of you to me."

"Oh, poor Scott!" FaLola said. Tears sprang to Their eyes. "He was one of the first victims of the Inquisition! That's my name for the official HHS investigators they sent. They came here a few days ago and just totally grilled everybody. Then they terminated poor Scott and Carmen Crowfoot and a few dozen others. They said they had ties to terrorists, but it was really just a political witch-hunt."

"By 'terminated', you mean..?"

"They fired them. It would have been kinder just to shoot poor Carmen, though — she really had no life except for her work." FaLola blew Their nose, Their long, beaky face ablaze with a fierce indignation. "I can't think what she'll do now. She's extremely differently-abled, you know. She can barely walk. And now she has no paycheck, she's had to fire her housekeeper."

"I have a feeling she'll survive," Obama said politely. He would miss Carmen's dynamism, drive, and organizational skills here. But maybe not the rest of her so much.

His iTooth chimed. It was Siren. "Simonetta apparently had another secret apartment at Logan Circle," she said in his ear. "The Princess and I are going over there to clean it out. Maybe we'll find some clues about her father's 'other children' there. Miss me lots!"

"I will. I do," he said. He did. "My ... ah ... wife," he told Falola. He was surprised that it felt so good saying the word again. Wife. Aliens, of course, didn't have such things as husbands or wives. Or sex, even. He'd invented alien-sex just for her, Siren had told him. "Is there an office where we can talk, M. Montoya?" "M." was the correct honorific for the transgendered. It was pronounced "Muh."

"Oh sure, Director Gunnarsson, things are in better shape upstairs. Just follow me." Falola led him back into the stairwell, then up onto Carmen's floor. They heard a loud clucking and cooing noise, then passed a large hole in a corridor wall through which a colony of pigeons could be seen clustered inside an outer office that hadn't been boarded up. The pigeons were all puffed up and huddling against the cold, and there were several seagulls on the window-ledge. "Must be a storm at sea," FaLola said. "Your office — I mean, Norberto's office; he was the director before you — got destroyed in the cross-fire. Norberto resigned just before all this started, you know. He's always had like this, like, psychic ability or something to sense trouble and responsibility before it came down on him. But you can use Carmen's office right inside here, it's pretty much intact. It's the one the Inquisition was using. It's so unfair that they were accusing us all of being terrorists. Everybody was throwing bombs and grenades around on both sides, you know, even me. You've got to fight for your right to nonviolence."

Once they were seated inside Carmen's office, Obama said, "The first thing I'm going to need is an Assistant Director. I'm appointing you to the position." The wall screens were fractured, and the room was cold and dark, but at least there was somewhere left to sit. When he told her this FaLola was at first astonished and then became suffused with self-doubt and a kind of terror. Obama watched the emotions chase each other across Their thoughts. Siren had been right — it was getting easier and easier for him to read them now.

"I don't know what to say," FaLola said. "I mean, this is way above my job description. You can't just look at a person and decide to promote them like that, can you?"

"I can, actually," Obama told them. "I think you'll find I'm an excellent judge of character."

"I'm more the kind of person who likes to go get people coffee and khat," They said. "I'm afraid there isn't any for me to offer you, though."

"Never mind. I'm more interested in your ideas about what we need to do in order to rebuild here, M. Montoya. And what changes should be made when we do."

FaLola leaned forward and started making notes on her iRist. "Well, one thing that really upset me was something the HHS people were saying when they were here. They told me that they were thinking of shutting MAD down completely, because there was a 'backlash' against it. 'What's the use of this department anyway?' one of them actually had the nerve to say to me. 'If everybody's a minority, that means nobody is.' I couldn't believe it! That she actually said that out loud, I mean.

"So then I started thinking of all the ways we maybe had drifted from our original mandate, so that the public no longer saw us as essential. It's not like there aren't plenty of minorities out there who still face discrimination and even hatred. Like people of color, for instance. Or what about Jews? I mean, they've had two holocausts, for god's sake! Isn't it about time somebody started protecting them from hate crimes and stuff?"

"That's exactly what I wanted from you — and why I want you here as my number two," said Obama, smiling broadly. "Thanks. Maybe we can make accrediting them our first priority. We'll fast-track it."

"It won't be popular with the academics," Falola replied dubiously. "Or the other minorities. And it will require a juried admission process."

"You can leave that to me," he told them.

He put in a long first day, and it was late afternoon by the time he left for home. But he felt encouraged. There was no reason MAD couldn't be rebuilt, even expanded, with Siren and the Pooka able to manipulate UN budgets behind the scenes. *And why shouldn't DOTARD eventually be absorbed into it?* he thought, in front of the Retrorail station entrance.

He had a message from his mom on his new iTooth, but decided to wait to call her back until he was home. He couldn't speak to her in with Bram's new voice — its resonance was different, and he now had this heavy South Africa accent. Which meant that he was going to have to get into a clone of his old body again if he really wanted to fly to Hawaii to spend Xmas with his parents and introduce Siren to them. And that meant that, at most, he had only a few months to finish his work at MAD. Unless he wanted to keep switching back and forth, of course.

But I don't have to stay at MAD forever, he reflected. If he made a success of things, there would be other, larger agencies to take over. Why not HHS itself someday? It badly needed reform. The abuses of the Federal Grand Jury system, for one. And after that, anything was possible. Maybe he might even run for the UN Senate, if Ng reinstated elections. And someday maybe even go after Ng's job ...

28.

When he got back to his apartment, Siren called out "In here!" to him from the kitchen. He took off his coat, while the Pooka morphed from his face to flow into her human-sized form. Then he wandered into the kitchen to give Siren a kiss. But the only person standing there was Kim.

Who turned to smile at him, her dark brown eyes wide.

He stood rigid with shock. *It really is Kim,* he thought, thunderstruck. The same broad face with its high cheek-bones and pale, sallow cast. The same pink lips. The same long fine black hair sweeping over her shoulders. The same soft, full figure. But it wasn't just Kim living inside that smile and those enormous eyes, it was also undeniably Siren. "Look what I found in Simonetta's closet," she said.

Obama felt so faint that he thought his knees might suddenly buckle. His heart was racing, and he could barely breathe. And he was instantly, almost painfully erect. There would be no problems making love to this body, he thought.

"How..?" Kim — Siren — put her arms around him.

"Obviously, Simonetta stole some DNA samples from Kim. She probably planned to have herself implanted in this body and then murder the real Kim, just like her father did to the real Manacera. Then she would have just masqueraded as your wife until she got bored with it. And finally killed you, too, probably."

"Wait a minute," Obama said. "I remember now — someone broke in right after Kim was taken away, and stole hair samples from her brush in the shower. I just assumed at the time it was the HHS, but it must have been Simonetta. Which means it surprised her just as much as it did us when Kim got summonsed."

"OK," Siren said. They kissed for a long time. "Whatever. Simonetta planned to come back as Kim, claiming she'd gotten out of jury duty, then. Same result." Over her shoulder, he glimpsed the Princess on the kitchen counter in her Hair Salon Barbie mode.

"Let's go to bed," he said. Once he had her clothes off, it was like having Kim back again. Siren, of course, wasn't Kim — she had none of her mannerisms or teasing little tricks — but her body responded to his in exactly the same ways Kim's had done. And his mind — normally racing with anxieties, critical self-analysis, and stray thoughts from the day — was comfortable, mercifully animal, hungry with her this time. The chorus in his head was drowned out. The sex was over in moments, but afterwards he continued to kiss and stroke her.

"Wow," she murmured. *So that's what it's supposed to be like.* The thought hung in the air like the ticking of the subliminal clock. He smelled something baking. A cake.

"In a minute we'll do it again," he told her. "Even better. The humyn way and the alien way at the same time."

Later, as she dozed, dribbling slightly against his shoulder, Obama reflected on Siren's latest sudden reincarnation as Kim. In a week or so, he would be back in his old body — after having made sure that all outstanding warrants and lawsuits against Obama Jones were dropped — and life could get back to normal. Bram's last act on his way out the door would be to appoint Obama as his successor. Obama would rebuild MAD exactly as it had been before, re-hire Scott, perhaps even Carmen — she did, after all, have a lot of talents and canny insider information as long as she was kept carefully in check — and, in many ways, things would be exactly as they had been before Kim had been summonsed. As if, in fact, that had never happened at all.

Glancing down at the soft curve of her cheek and throat, her eyelid pulsing the dark lash like the stirring of a little flying insect, Obama was suddenly filled by a gnawing, terrible suspicion. *What if all of this had just been a sim?* Everything that happened to him was way too weird to be real — and sims were famous for their looped endings, where the finale of the story merged seamlessly into the beginning, so that users could experience them over and over again. What if none of this had been real at all? What if he was doomed to endlessly repeat his life as Obama Jones, always ending up in the same apartment, at the same job, with the same woman, no matter how weird and bizarre the sim plot-lines; aliens this time around, possibly time-travel the next. Or vampires or ghosts or cannibal zombie mutants roaming nuclear wastelands or ...

He shook Siren — Kim — awake and asked her. "Huh?" she said, still slightly dazed with sleep.

"What if we've been inside a fucking sim this whole time?" he said in a panic.

After a while she finally understood what he was saying and reacted irritably. She was evidently annoyed that he was expressing any dissatisfaction whatever with their life together now they were finally truly happy. "Yeah, maybe we are," she told him groggily. "That's occurred to me, too. Sato was always a programmer at heart — so what? Maybe all life on this planet is just a sim. Or maybe he coded a 'Logic Bomb' into the humyn DNA that makes it possible to opt out of the loop. I honestly don't know. If you hate things so much the way they are now, Bam, go ahead. Give it a try."

"Give what a try?" he asked her.

"You know, try saying the words he taught you," she said. "Explode the Logic Bomb, for all I care. Just let me get some sleep."

Detach. Wiiboot. Amen, he thought. *Those words.*

He opened his mouth to speak ... then hesitated.

THE END

ABOUT THE AUTHOR

Rod Kierkegaard, Jr is a writer and cartoonist best known in the US for his comic strip, "Rock Opera", which ran as a regular feature in Heavy Metal Magazine during the 1980s.

He is the author of two French graphic novel collections, "Stars Massacre", (released in the US as "Shooting Stars") and "Rock Monstres", both published by Editions Albin Michel, Paris.

"Obama Jones and The Logic Bomb" and "Mirrorland" are Rod's first published works by Dogma Press.